James Hall

**Legends of the West**

Sketches illustrative of the habits, occupations, privations, adventures, and sport of

the pioneers of the West

James Hall

**Legends of the West**
*Sketches illustrative of the habits, occupations, privations, adventures, and sport of the pioneers of the West*

ISBN/EAN: 9783337096755

Printed in Europe, USA, Canada, Australia, Japan

Cover: Foto ©Andreas Hilbeck / pixelio.de

More available books at **www.hansebooks.com**

# Legends of the West:

## SKETCHES

*Illustrative of the Habits, Occupations, Privations, Adventures and Sport*

OF THE

## PIONEERS OF THE WEST.

BY

### JAMES HALL,

*Author of "Romance of Western History," "Tales of the Border," etc.*

CINCINNATI:
ROBERT CLARKE & CO.,
1869.

# PART FIRST.

# PREFACE TO THE FIRST EDITION.

THE sole intention of the tales comprised in the following pages is to convey accurate descriptions of the scenery and population of the country in which the author resides. The only merit he claims for them is fidelity. It will be for others to decide whether this claim is well supported.

The legends now presented to the public are entirely fictitious; but they are founded upon incidents which have been witnessed by the author during a long residence in the Western States, or upon traditions preserved by the people, and have received but little artificial embellishment. They are given to the American reader with great diffidence, and with a disposition to submit cheerfully to any verdict which public opinion may award.

of the Kickapoos and Pottowattamies lingered about the sources of the Wabash and the branches of the Illinois; the Winnebagoes roamed over the wide plains to the North-west; and the Saukies and Foxes were the sole possessors of the beautiful and romantic grounds about Rock Island. The noted Black Hawk and the princely Keokuk dwelt there, at their native village, as yet undisturbed by white men.

The settled parts of the State were organized into counties, but the institutions, the manners and customs of the people, were those of the frontier. The country was thinly inhabited; between the settlements were vast districts of wilderness, over which the traveller might ride whole days without meeting with a human habitation. The panther and the wolf still lurked in the forests, the marshes and pools were alive with water-fowl, and the broad plains, covered with unbroken carpets of verdure and wild-flowers, were tenanted by myriads of prairie fowl.

The inhabitants came from Kentucky, Tennessee, and North Carolina, and were still living in the rude log-cabins in which they had first found shelter. They were the pioneers, and the immediate offspring of the pioneers, who had crossed the mountains, and fighting their way through an incredible series of hardships, privations, and dangers, had subdued the beautiful valley of the Ohio to the dominion of the white man. Among the older men were some who had slept by the camp-fire of Daniel Boone, and had followed the daring footsteps of Clarke, Shelby, and Logan, in long marches and hard-fought battles. The greater number were the offspring of the pioneers, accustomed in childhood to the alarms and vicissitudes of border warfare, reared in the log-hut, familiar only with sylvan occupations and sports, and whose eyes were just opened to the dawn of civilization. They were all farmers, but their character was rather pastoral than agricultural;

commerce had scarcely reached them—there was no market for the products of the soil; they raised a little grain and vegetables for food, but depended chiefly on herds of cattle and hogs that roamed at large in the common pasturage afforded by the boundless wilderness. They were all hunters, expert in the use of the rifle, skilled in woodcraft, and familiar with the haunts and habits of every wild creature, from the bear and the wolf down to the tiny honey-bee. The record of their accomplishments may be briefly made up: they were daring and skilful riders, loved horses, and had a gentlemanly propensity for racing and horse-swapping; such of them as sought office developed an innate aptitude for stump-oratory, an art which was greatly admired and cultivated; and at their public assemblages, at courts, elections, vendues, and the like occasions, they betted freely, drank hard, and uttered compound oaths, with extraordinary copiousness of language and vehemence of elocution. Ordinarily they were a frugal and abstemious people, living quiet, unambitious lives, varied chiefly by the vicissitudes of the seasons, and occasionally diversified by the episode of a *spree*. Honest and simple were they in their ways, brave and hospitable in their deeds.

Among such a people the author commenced the practice of the legal profession, at an early age, with about the usual stock of dreamy reminiscences of Coke and Blackstone, Kent and Chitty, but with a somewhat richer store than ordinary of history, poetry, and romance. It was the search of adventure, rather than of actions at law, that enticed him to the wilderness. The legends of the West, scattered in fragments over the land, were more alluring than imaginary clients or prospective fees. In the event, he became a laborious practitioner; while the constant and unavoidable contact with the people, enabled him to glean the field of traditionary lore, without any interference with professional duty

The backwoodsmen were not the only inhabitants of Illinois, at that time. There were the French, at Kaskaskia, Cahokia, and Prairie du Rocher, who had been settled here for several generations, without losing their national characteristics. They were a very primitive people, whose character and legends afforded much curious matter for reflection. There was an English colony recently settled near the Wabash; and there were some other inconsiderable settlements, which might form exceptions from the general and very brief sketch we have given of the mass of the people.

The lawyers not only rode large circuits, embracing nine or ten counties each, but those circuits were so arranged to follow each other in succession, that the bar could pass from one to another through several of them, and an industrious practitioner passed half of his time on horseback. The counties were extensive, and the county seats being widely separated, the journeys were long and toilsome. There were no hotels, few roads, and fewer bridges. The traveller often passed from county to county by mere bridle-paths, leading from one settlement to another, crossed streams where "ford there was none," and when the channels were filled by heavy rains, found both difficulty and danger in getting over. Sometimes the close of the day found him far from the shelter of a human habitation, and then, like the hunter, he must light his fire, and encamp under a spreading tree, the want of an *inn* obliging him to camp *out*. The more usual resting-place was at the log-house of a farmer, where a cordial welcome, and a board spread bountifully with the products of the field and the forest, awaited him.

The seats of justice were small villages, mostly mere hamlets, composed of a few log-houses, into which the judge and bar were crowded, with the grand and petit jurors, litigants, witnesses, and, in short, the whole body of the county—for

in new counties every body goes to court. Here was no respect to persons; they ate together, slept together, congre-
gated together in the crowded court-house, and assembled
together around the stump to hear the bursts of patriotic
eloquence from the candidates for office.

Such were the scenes, and such the population among
which the author spent twelve years in the exercise of a profession, which, above all others, opens to its members familiar
views of the whole organization of society, and of much of
all that passes in the business and bosoms of men. Travelling
continually on horseback, over broad and beautiful prairies,
and through forests shaded and tangled with all the luxuriance and majesty of their primitive state—encountering the
hunter in his solitary ramble, or sitting with him by his fireside, breaking his bread and partaking of his convivial cup—
living with them, in short, from day to day, and from week
to week, as their fellow-citizen, their counsellor, and their
guest—his opportunities for becoming well acquainted with
the haunts and homes of the backwoodsmen were quite as
favourable as could be well imagined.

How well, or how imperfectly, those opportunities were
improved, is another question. They were enjoyed with exquisite relish, and left impressions which have remained vividly
engraved upon the memory. The backwoodsman is a social
person, whose heart yearns to the heart of his fellow-creature.
Without wealth, but little acquainted with traffic, gaining an
abundant subsistence with but little exertion, and spending
long intervals in repose or recreation, he knows nothing of
the influence of the magic term *business*, which sways and
excites the mind and the energy of the great mass of our
nation. He is the only American who is never in a hurry—
never too busy to enjoy the sweets of sleep and the refreshment of social intercourse. Brave and hardy, he does not

shrink from any privation or danger. For days, and even weeks together, he will live in the woods, hunting all day, sleeping on the ground, eating game only, and drinking from the running stream, enduring exposure to all extremes of weather, and practising abstinence with the patience of the Indian. At his own board he feeds well and entertains freely, for although the fare is simple, it is spread out in prodigal abundance, and pressed upon the guest with lavish hospitality. Though usually taciturn in the presence of strangers, he is communicative to his friend or his guest, has often strong colloquial powers, with quaint, singular, figurative, and even eloquent forms of expression. His language, which is commonly brief, sententious, and abrupt, becomes, when excited by the interest of the subject or by passion, highly expletive, and redundant with exaggerated forms and figures of comparison. When he swears—and he is probably not more given to this exceedingly vulgar vice than other men—but when he does swear in earnest, his philology becomes concentrated, and explodes with an appalling energy, which would have astonished even the celebrated army in Flanders.

In the conversations of this people there is much to interest and entertain the stranger. To wile away the tedium of a dull day's ride, or a long winter evening, they recite their adventures, or communicate their observations on subjects familiar to them, but strange and curious to others. Scraps of history, reminiscences of noted men, incidents of the chase and of border violence, the deeds of their fathers in battle, the traditions of the wilderness and the war-path, form the staple of these discussions; and it was from such sources that the writer derived the lore which he has presented to the public in the several volumes he has published.

Since these Legends were written, great changes have

taken place in the West. The pioneers and Indian-fighters have passed away. Their children have been scattered and driven off by an overwhelming deluge of immigration. In Kentucky and Tennessee, where there is a homogeneous population, protected by certain institutions, the Western character remains unchanged, except so far as it has been modified by the natural, though rapid, increase of population and wealth, of comfort and luxury—by the change from border states to peaceful and flourishing civil communities, surrounded by sister states, equally flourishing and peaceful. But the genuine backwoodsman has vanished from the valley of the Ohio; the crack of his rifle and the baying of his dog are heard no more; his cabin must be sought on the great plains far to the west. The river boatmen, of whom Mike Fink was the representative, with their fleets of keel-boats and barges, no longer float on the bosom of "the beautiful river;" the boat-song which broke the sweet silence of the wilderness at sunrise, and the blast of the horn which came winding on the evening breeze, as the boat glided into sight from behind the island of willows, are heard no more. The log-cabin has ceased to be the only structure, and is fast disappearing from the shore; the gracefully rounded hills are shorn of their forests; and now the farm-house and the cottage-ornée, the meadow, the orchard, and the vineyard, crown the river hills, while towns, villages, and steamboats give evidence that art and commerce have taken possession of the land. Troops of laborious Germans and light-hearted Irish are scattered broadcast over the land; and the universal Yankee nation is here, teaching school and driving bargains, making railroads, running steamboats, and going ahead generally in every path where industry and perseverance may find emolument, however novel the enterprise or difficult the achievement. That peculiar phraseology which marked the conversation of the Western people thirty years ago, is seldom heard. For some of it the schoolmaster has substituted a purer, though not a more significant language; while the mongrel vulgarisms of various tongues and people have flowed in and corrupted the whole mass. The tourists who have pretended to describe the colloquial peculiaries of the West, have in some instances indulged freely their own inventive powers, and in others have been misled into the grossest absurdities, so that, to use the figure of an old writer, one would suppose they had been at a feast of languages, and carried away the scraps.

# PREFACE TO HARPE'S HEAD.

THE reader of the following pages, should they be so fortunate as to find any, will naturally wish to know whether any of the incidents introduced are founded upon fact, or whether the whole narrative is a fabrication of the author's own brain. Perhaps it would be good policy to evade this question, leaving him to exercise his own judgment upon the probability of the events and the reality of the characters, and by thus awakening curiosity, excite more interest than our unadorned tale will be likely to produce by its own merits. But holding, as we do, that in all cases honesty is the best policy, we have determined to acknowledge candidly our obligations to history, and to avow, in the face of the world, our paternal relation to so much of the work as is the offspring of invention.

Two of the characters introduced are historical. Their deeds are still freshly remembered by many of the early settlers of Kentucky, and their names will be instantly recognised by all who are conversant with the traditions of that State. The real incidents of the lives of those persons have been very sparingly alluded

to, as most of them were of a character too atrocious
for recital in a work of this description, and because
they could not be used without the introduction of
other names, which the writer does not consider himself
at liberty to place before the public in this manner.
The individuals alluded to have therefore been merely
introduced into a tale wholly fictitious, placed in
situations similar to those in which they really appeared,
and made to act in conformity with their well-known
characters.

It has been the intention of the writer in this,
as in the other fictions published under his name, to
draw from nature. He has invented but little; but
professes simply to connect together the traditions of a
region in which he has long resided, and to the
population of which he is attached, as well by a sincere
admiration for them and their institutions, as by many
endearing ties.

# HARPE'S HEAD.

## CHAPTER I.

AT the close of a pleasant day, in the spring of the year 17—, a solitary horseman might have been seen slowly winding his way along a narrow road, in that part of Virginia which is now called the Valley. It was nearly forty years ago, and the district lying between the Blue Ridge and the Allegheny mountains was but thinly populated, while the country lying to the west, embracing an immense Alpine region, was a savage wilderness, which extended to the new and distant settlements of Kentucky. Our traveller's route led along the foot of the mountains, sometimes crossing the *spurs*, or lateral ridges, which push out their huge promontories from the great chain, and at others winding through deep ravines, or skirting along broad valleys. The Ancient Dominion was never celebrated for the goodness of its highways, and the one he was now endeavouring to unravel was among the worst, being a mere path worn by the feet of horses, and marked by faint traces of wheels, which showed that the experiment of driving a carriage over its uneven surface had been successfully tried, but not generally practised.

The country was fertile, though wild and broken. The season was that in which the foliage is most luxuriant and splendid to the eye, the leaves being fully expanded, while the rich blossoms decked the scene with a variety of brilliant hues; and our traveller, as he passed ridge after ridge, paused in delight on their elevated summits, to gaze at the beautiful glens that lay between them, and the gorgeous vegetation that climbed even to the tops of the steepest acclivities. The day, however, which had been unusually sultry for the season, was drawing to a close, and both horse and rider began to feel the effects of hunger and fatigue; the former, though strong and spirited, drooped his head, and the latter became wearied with these lonesome though picturesque scenes. During the whole day he had not seen the dwelling of a human being; the clattering of his horse's hoofs upon the rock, the singing of the birds, so numerous in this region, the roaring of the mountain stream, or the crash of timber occasioned by the fall of some great tree, were the only sounds that had met his ear. He was glad, therefore, to find his path descending, at last, into a broad valley, interspersed with farms. He seemed to have surmounted the last hill, and before him was a rich continuous forest, resembling, as he overlooked it from the high ground, a solid plane of verdure. The transition from rocky steeps and precipices to the smooth soil and sloping surface of the valley was refreshing; and not less so were the coolness and fragrance of the air, and the deep and varied hues of the forest, occasioned by the rank luxuriance of its vegetation.

It might be proper, as it certainly is customary, before proceeding to narrate the adventures of our hero, to introduce him to the particular acquaintance of the reader by a full description of his person, character, and lineage; but this manner of narration, supported as it is by respectable precedent, we must be permitted to decline. As we have no record before us showing that the gentleman in question ever

passed under a regimental standard, we are not aware that
his exact height could now be ascertained; and as he was
neither a deserter from the service of his country, nor a fugitive from the protection of his guardian, we cannot think it
necessary to set forth the colour of his hair and eyes, or to describe what clothes " he had on when he went away." To
enlist the sympathies of our fair readers, whose approbation
we would fain propitiate, it is enough to say that he was a
young and handsome bachelor, leaving each of them to fancy
him the exact image of her favourite admirer; but as we do
not admire the practice of peeping into gentlemen's hearts or
pocket-books without any other warrant than the bare license
of authorship, we cannot tell what precious billet-doux may
have filled the one, or what treasured image might have
occupied the other. These are questions which may be
incidentally touched hereafter; and the curious reader will
find ample materials in the following pages, for the gratification of a laudable thirst for knowledge on these interesting
points.

The sun was about to set, and our traveller, having completely left all the mountain passes behind him, could have
enjoyed the serenity of the calm hour and the bland landscape,
had not other thoughts harassed him. He needed rest and
refreshment, and knew not where to find the one or the other.
While considering this matter, he reached a spot where two
roads crossed, at the same instant when two other persons,
advancing from a different direction, arrived at the same
point. They were an elderly gentleman and a young lady,
both of prepossessing appearance. The former was a portly
man, hale and ruddy, with a gay eye and a profusion of gray
locks, as if the frost of age had prematurely touched his head
without penetrating so deep as to chill the fountains of life.
His dress was that of a country gentleman; it was not expensive, nor yet well assorted, but rather evinced the carelessness of one who, living secluded from the fashionable

world, felt independent of its forms, or who adopted with
reluctance the changes which seemed every year to depart
further and further from certain standards of gracefulness to
which he had been accustomed in his youth, as well as from
the peculiar notions of comfort that fasten upon the mind
with the approaches of old age.   He was mounted upon a
fine high-bred horse, rather oddly caparisoned; for the
bridle, though silver-mounted, was broken in several places,
and the fractures had been remedied, at one part by a hard
knot, at another by a coarse seam, and at a third by a thong
of buckskin; while a Spanish saddle, which might once have
done honour to the best cavalier at a bull-fight, having lost the
stirrup-leather on the near side, was supplied with an accom-
modation-ladder of rope, and the girth was patched with
leather and linsey, until the original material was hardly discoverable.   The worthy gentleman wore one spur, either
because he was too indolent to put on the other, or from a
conviction, founded on a well-established philosophical principle, that the effect produced on one side of his animal must
be followed by a corresponding result on the other, and that
consequently one armed heel is as effective as a pair.   Indeed,
that gentlemanly weapon seemed to be worn more from habit
than necessity, for the free-spirited steed needed no prompter;
and the rider, who sat with the ease and grace of an experienced horseman, would have esteemed it a breach of the
dignity becoming his age and station to have proceeded at
any pace faster than a walk.   He was evidently a wealthy
planter, accustomed to good living and good society, who had
arrived at a standing in life which placed him above any
merely outward forms that interfered with his comfort, and
who felt privileged to think as he pleased and do as he liked;
while the frankness and benevolence of his countenance at
once assured the stranger that his heart was alive to the best
feelings of kindness and hospitality.   His companion was a
lovely girl of eighteen, richly and tastefully habited.   Care-

less as were the apparel and furniture of the elder rider, that of the lady was studiously neat and appropriate. Her palfrey had the fine limbs, the delicate form, and the bright eye of the deer, with a gentleness that seemed to savour more of reason than of instinct. His hair was smooth and glossy as silk, his harness elegantly and neatly fitted; and as the rider sat gracefully erect in her saddle, the proud animal arched his neck as if conscious of the beauty of his burden.

As the parties met at the junction of the roads, each of the gentlemen reined up his horse to allow the other to pass; the elder bowed and touched his hat, and the other returned the salutation with equal courtesy. There was a momentary embarrassment, as neither rider seemed disposed to take precedence of the other; which was relieved by the young lady, who, slackening her rein as she touched the neck of her steed with a hazel switch, rode forward, leaving the gentlemen to settle the point of etiquette between them, which they did by silently falling in abreast, the road being just wide enough to admit the passage of two riders in that manner.

In our country there is none of that churlish policy or that repulsive pride which in other regions forbids strangers who thus meet from accosting each other; on the contrary, our hearty old Virginian, on meeting a young, well-mounted, handsome stranger, with the appearance and manners of a gentleman, felt bound to do the honours of the country. He accordingly opened a conversation, and was so well pleased with the stranger's frankness and intelligence, that he determined to take him home, and entertain him, at least for the night, and perhaps for a week or two; and the worthy old man felt no small inward gratification in the idea, that while he was discharging his duty as a true son of the Ancient Dominion, he should secure a companion, and enlarge for a time his own little circle of enjoyments. But the stranger anticipated his invitation by observing,

"I have business with Major Heyward, who resides somewhere in this neighbourhood, and am glad that I have fallen
in with you, sir, as you can probably direct me to a tavern
near his house, where I may lodge for the night."

"That I cannot; but I will with great pleasure show you
to the house itself," replied the other, who was the identical
Major Heyward; "I am going directly there, and will conduct you to the very door."

The stranger civilly declined this offer, under the plea that
he was totally unacquainted with the gentleman alluded to,
and that his visit was solely on business. He wished, therefore, to lodge for the night at a public house, and to despatch
his business in the morning as early as might be.

"I suspect," replied his companion, "that you will not do
the one nor the other. Public house there is none; you are
now in Virginia, sir, where hospitality is not an article of
trade; therefore you must of necessity lodge with a private
gentleman. And you are under a mistake, if you think to
despatch your business to-morrow, or the next day, or under
a week at least."

"Why so?"

"Simply because, in this country, we do not turn people
out of our houses, nor treat a guest as if he were a sheriff's
officer. There is to be a *barbecue* to-morrow, to which you
will be invited; then you must hunt one day, and fish another, and after that——but see, there is the house."

The stranger halted: "I really cannot intrude——"

"Intrude, my dear sir! Why, young gentleman, you
were certainly not *raised* in Virginia, or you would have
learned that one gentleman can never be considered as an intruder in the house of another, especially one who brings so
good a letter of introduction as yourself."

"Pardon me, sir, I have no such credentials."

"Oh yes, you have—yes, you have," returned the planter,
laughing at his own wit, and bowing to his companion; "as

a late writer hath it, a good appearance is the best letter of introduction; and your modesty, young sir, is an endorsement which gives it double value. Come along, I'll be answerable for your welcome."

"But I am a total stranger."

"True, and so you will remain until you are introduced; then you will be so no longer."

"But it is so awkward to go to a gentleman's house just at nightfall, as if begging for a night's lodging."

"The very best hour in the world, for then you are sure to catch the gentleman at home, and at leisure to entertain you. Virginia, my dear," continued he, calling to the young lady, who rode a few paces before them, "will you not join me in a guarantee that this young gentleman shall be welcome at Walnut Hill?"

"With great pleasure, if it were necessary," replied the lady, "but your introduction, my dear uncle, will be all-sufficient."

The stranger, who began to suspect the truth, and saw that he could not, without rudeness, decline the proffered kindness of his hospitable guide, now submitted, and the party entered a long lane which led to the mansion. On either side were large fields of corn and tobacco, lately planted, and exhibiting the distinctive characteristics of Virginia agriculture. The scale was extensive, but the manner of cultivation rude. The spacious domain, spreading for more than a mile on either hand, was covered with flourishing crops, which attested the fertility of the soil; and the immense worm-fences surrounding the enclosures, and dividing them into accurate parallelograms, were as substantial as they were unsightly. The corners and skirts of the fields, and every vacant spot, were grown up with weeds and briers. Stumps of trees blackened with fire, and immense tall trunks, from which the bark and smaller limbs had fallen, showed that not many years had elapsed since the ground had been cleared; but those sylvan remains became fewer and more decayed towards the mansion of the owner, which was in the centre of the opening, as if the occupant, after fixing his dwelling, had been gradually clearing away the forest from around it in every direction. An apple orchard had been planted so recently as to be now ready for bearing its first crop, and peach-trees were seen scattered in every direction; wherever a kernel had fallen by accident, and the young shoot had escaped the plough, or outlived the nipping of the cattle, was a flourishing tree, promising a luxuriant harvest of this delightful fruit.

The mansion stood on a rising ground, overlooking the whole plantation, and was composed of a cluster of buildings rather inartificially connected. A stone house with two rooms had been first erected; then a framed building was added; and year after year, as the family increased in wealth or numbers, subsequent additions had been made, consisting of single apartments, all on the ground-floor, except the original building, which contained an upper story—the whole connected by piazzas, and being, in fact, a number of separate, though contiguous houses, inconveniently adapted for the residence of a single family. The offices were scattered about in the rear of the main edifice—the kitchen, the ice-house, the smoke-house, being each a separate building. Still further back were the negro-cabins, and beyond them the stables; so that, altogether, the place had more the appearance of a village than of the residence of a single family. The aspect of the whole was pleasing and respectable. Had it been surrounded by a wall and a ditch, it would have borne no small resemblance to some of the earliest of those old castles in which the barons resided with their followers in patriarchal simplicity. The out-buildings were so disposed as not to intercept the view from the front of the mansion; and the latter, being painted white, looked well in spite of its structure. A beautiful lawn surrounded it, set with fine forest trees, the venerable and gigantic aboriginals of the soil; and on one side was a garden, laid out with taste, and highly embellished with flowers and ornamental plants.

As soon as the party entered the lane, droves of young negroes ran out to gaze at them, hiding behind the trees and fences, or peeping through the bushes; and the worthy host began to exercise his lungs, in speaking alternately to the negro children, to the blacks who were returning in troops from labour, and to his guest.

"Get away, you young rogues! what are you peeping at? There's fine corn, sir. Here, you Cato, tell Cæsar to come to me.—That corn has just been planted six weeks.—Pompey, come and take these horses.—There's the best tobacco in this county.—Luke, where's Peter and John? Primus, tell Adam to get some fresh water, and you go, Finis, and help him. Virgil, you dog, come out of that peach-tree. I'll take you and Milton, and knock your heads together.—These plagues destroy all my fruit, sir, before it is ripe.—Open that gate, Moses—help him, Aaron. Come here, Cupid, and hold your young mistress' horse. Run, some of you, and tell Venus to get supper.—Come, sir, alight; you are welcome to my house."

The stranger, who throughout this singular colloquy had found no opportunity to address his host, had placed himself beside the young lady, to whom he addressed his conversation during the few minutes that preceded their arrival at the house, where he assisted her to dismount; and the whole party were soon seated in one of Major Heyward's spacious piazzas.

Walnut Hill was the seat of plenty and hospitality; and in a few minutes servants were despatched in different directions in pursuit of refreshments. The worthy proprietor himself, in respect of his age, and certain habits of reverence to which his whole household had been long accustomed, received the first attention. His niece placed his great arm-chair, a little negro fetched his pipe, another brought tobacco,

2

a third fire, a fourth a glass of water, a fifth slippers; and in a few minutes he was comfortably seated, enjoying his accustomed luxuries; while his guest retired to arrange his dress.

On the return of the latter, he found his host in the same position in which he had left him; and approaching him, said,

"I have perhaps been to blame in delaying so long to announce my name and business."

Your name, my young friend, I shall be glad to hear, whenever you please; as for your business, we will talk of that when we get tired of every other subject."

"I am well aware of your hospitality, and that towards either a friend or a stranger it would be cheerfully exercised; but neither of these characters can be claimed by *Lyttleton Fennimore.*"

The old man started as he heard this name; a cloud passed over his features, and his frame seemed agitated with painful recollections. These feelings he endeavoured to suppress, as he replied,

"I had rather you had borne another name; but that is not your fault."

He then rose, extended his hand to his guest, and emphatically added, "Mr. Fennimore, pardon an old man for not being able to forget in a moment that which has been a subject of bitter reflection for years. The antipathies of parents should not be entailed on their children. You are cordially welcome to my house—make it your home, and consider me as your friend."

Tea was soon announced; and Major Heyward, as he introduced his guest to his niece, Miss Pendleton, resumed his usual courtesy of manner, but his gaiety had entirely forsaken him, and immediately after this meal he retired to his apartment, leaving the young couple to entertain each other. We need hardly add, that, predisposed as the latter were to be pleased with each other, the evening passed agreeably ; and that when Mr. Fennimore retired, he could not but acknowledge, that whatever might be the character of the uncle, the niece was one of the most agreeable women that he had ever seen.

# CHAPTER II.

ON the following morning, Fennimore rose early, and sallied forth, but found that he had been preceded by Major Heyward, who was bustling about, without his hat or coat, in the sharp morning air, giving orders to his servants. The cloud of the last evening had passed from his brow; the reflections of his pillow had been salutary; and he now met his guest, with his usual cheerfulness of countenance and kindness of manner. "Mr. Fennimore," said he, "I did not receive you, perhaps, as I ought, and I ask your pardon. I must be frank with you, for I cannot be otherwise. Things have passed between our families which I have not been able to forget. But the ways of Providence are always wise; it was necessary for my peace that you should come here. I am too old to cherish an unsettled feud. Let the past be buried. We are friends."

"I know so little of the particulars of the affair to which you allude," replied Fennimore, "that I can say nothing, except that I desire to stand in no other relation to Major Heyward than that of a friend. I had not thought of introducing that subject. My business relates to a pecuniary transaction——"

"Well, we'll talk of that another time. Any time will do for business. We can settle that in five minutes. There is to be a *barbecue* to-day, Mr. Fennimore; we are all going—you must go with us."

In vain did Fennimore plead that his engagements required his attention elsewhere—that he had no time for parties of pleasure—that he had no taste for such amusements, &c.

"No taste for a barbecue!" exclaimed Major Heyward. "You surprise me, Mr. Fennimore; no taste for a barbecue! Well, that shows you were not raised in Virginia. Time you should see a little of the world, sir; there's nothing in life equal to a barbecue, properly managed—a good old Virginia barbecue. Sir, I would not have you to miss it for the best horse on my plantation!"

"Talking of horses," continued the cheerful old man, "reminds me that I can show you a sight worth seeing;" and without waiting for a reply, he led his guest to his stables, where the grooms were feeding and rubbing down a number of beautiful blooded animals. These were successively paraded, and the proud owner descanted upon the merits of each, with a volubility that excluded every other subject, until breakfast was announced.

"Has Mr. Fennimore consented to join our party to-day?" inquired Miss Pendleton, after they were seated at the breakfast-table.

"Certainly, my dear," replied the Major; "Mr. Fennimore would be doing injustice to us, and to himself, if he did not improve such an opportunity of witnessing a festivity peculiar to our State. I am sure he would not be deprived of it upon any consideration."

"I cannot resist the temptation," said Fennimore, with a bow which Miss Pendleton took to herself, while her uncle received it as a tribute to his favourite amusement; and after a hasty meal, the parties separated to prepare for the excursion.

The horses were soon at the door, and the party proceeded, attended by several servants, to the place of meeting. It was a gay and beautiful morning. They passed over a high mountainous ridge, by a winding and rugged path, which at

some places seemed impracticable; but the horses, accustomed
to these acclivities, stepped cautiously from rock to rock, or
nimbly leaped the narrow ravines that crossed the road, while
the riders scarcely suffered any inconvenience from the irregu-
larities of the surface.   Sometimes the path led along the
edge of a precipice, and they paused to look down upon the
broad-spread valleys that lay extended in beautiful landscape
before them.  The song of the mocking-bird arrested their attention, as he sat among the branches of a tall tree, pouring
forth his miscellaneous and voluble notes, imitating successfully all the songsters of the grove, and displaying a fulness,
strength, and richness of voice, which often astonishes even
those who are accustomed to his melody.  Upon reaching the
highest elevation of the ridge, they wound along its level surface, by a path well beaten and beautifully smooth, but so
seldom travelled as to be covered with a growth of short
grass.   Its width was sufficient only to admit the passage of
a single horseman, and its course so winding that the foremost
rider was often concealed from the view of the last of the
train.   Dense thickets grew on either hand, and the branches
of the trees interlocking above the riders' heads formed a
thick canopy, giving to this romantic path the appearance of
a narrow, serpentine archway, carved with art out of the
tangled forest.  Virginia, when she reached this elevated plain,
seemed to feel as if in fairy land, and, loosening her rein,
bounded away with the lightness of a bird, gracefully bending as she passed under the low boughs, gliding round the
short angles, and leaping her beautiful steed over the logs that
sometimes lay in the way.  Fennimore galloped after, admiring her skill, and equally elated by the inspiring scene;
while Major Heyward, who thought it undignified to ride out
of a walk, at any time except when following the hounds,
followed at his leisure, wondering at the levity of the young
people, which made them forget their gentility and ride like
dragoons or hired messengers.

Suddenly the path seemed to end at the brink of a tall cliff, and far below them they beheld the majestic Potomac, meandering through its deep valleys, and apparently forcing its way among piles of mountains. The charms of mountain scenery were enhanced by the endless variety of the rich and gorgeous, the placid and beautiful, the grand and terrific, that were here embraced in one view. At one place the tall naked rock rose in perpendicular cliffs to an immense height, terminating in bare spiral peaks; at another, the rounded elevations were covered with pines, cedars, and laurel, always indicating a sterile soil and a cold exposure. The mountain-sides were clothed with verdure, in all the intervals between the parapets of rock; and the clear streams of water that fell from ledge to ledge, enlivened the prospect. Far below, the rich valley spread out its broad bosom, studded with the noblest trees of the forest, the majestic tulip-tree, the elegant locust, the gum, the sugar-maple, the broad spreading oak, and the hickory. The numberless flowering trees were in full bloom, and their odours filled the air with a rich perfume. The river, with its clear blue waters, was full of attraction, sometimes dashing round rocky points of the mountain, and sometimes flowing calmly through the valley; at one point placidly reposing in a wide basin, at another, rushing over a rocky ledge whitened with foam.

"How beautiful!" exclaimed Virginia, as she reined up her horse and gazed, with a delighted eye, over the wide-spread landscape.

"How exquisitely beautiful!" re-echoed Fennimore, as his admiring glance rested on the form of his lovely companion. Her deer-like animal, smoking with heat, and just sufficiently excited by exercise to bring every muscle into full action, to expand his nostrils and swell his veins—his fine neck arched, his head raised, his delicate ear thrown forward, and his clear eye sparkling, stood on the very edge of the cliff. The light figure of Virginia was rendered more graceful by an elegant

riding-dress, closely fitted to her person, and extending below
her feet.  She sat with the ease of a practised rider.  But her
chief attraction, at this moment, was the animated expression
of her features.   Her bonnet was pushed back from her fine
forehead, her eye lighted up with pleasure, her cheek flushed
and dimpled, her lips unclosed ; and as she extended her whip
in the direction indicated by her glance, Fennimore realized
the most exquisite dreams that his fancy had ever formed
of female loveliness.

   She turned towards her companion, as his expression of
admiration met her ear, blushed deeply when she discovered
that his impassioned glance was directed towards herself, and
then, with a little dash of modest coquetry, which is quite
natural in a pretty woman of eighteen, laughed, and resumed
her descriptions.   But her tones softened, and her conversation, without losing its sprightliness, assumed the richness and
vividness of poetry, from an involuntary consciousness that
all the young and joyous feelings of her heart were responded
in kindred emotions from that of her companion.

   In a few minutes they were joined by Major Heyward, and
the whole  party  descended  the mountain by a  precipitous
path, which led to a part of the valley bordering on the Potomac.

   Arrived at the place of rendezvous, a novel and enchanting
scene was presented to the eye of our stranger.   A level spot
on the shore of the river had  been divested of all its bushes
and trees, except a few large poplars, which were left for
shade, whose huge trunks had risen to a majestic height, while
their spreading branches interlocked, so as to form a canopy
impervious to the sunbeams.  Having been the scene of these
festivities for many years, the ground was trodden hard, and
covered with a thick sward of short grass.   On three sides
the forest was seen in its native wildness, tangled and luxuriant as it came from the hand of nature ; on the other flowed
the river.  At the back part of the area was a fountain of

limpid water—the Virginians always congregate around a cool spring—issuing from the rock, and filling a large basin, which served as a wine-cooler, and in which a few trout, kept with great care, sported their graceful forms.

The company began to assemble at an early hour; a gay and miscellaneous assemblage, somewhat aristocratic, but by no means exclusive. It was all of the class of freeholders, but included every variety of that class. Some were members of ancient families, well educated, polished, and wealthy, proud of their birth and of their estates, simple and hospitable, though somewhat stately, in their manners. Some were decayed gentry, a little prouder than the nature of the case seemed to require, in consequence of their poverty; and others were plain farmers and their families, stout built, well fed, well clad,—an intelligent and independent race, who lived on their own farms, and justly considered themselves the peers of the best in the land. In the whole circle there was much of the sturdiness and simplicity of an agricultural people, together with a degree of polish not often found among mere farmers, and resulting here from the hospitable customs of the country, which induced a continual round of social intercourse, and from the fact that the land proprietors, being the owners of servants, had leisure to cultivate their minds, and visit their neighbours. Among them were many gentlemen of liberal education, some professional men of high attainments, and men in public life, or of large fortunes, who, spending a portion of every year in large cities, had acquired all the elegance of manners and cultivation of intellect which is found in the best circles. One peculiarity which usually marks a fashionable, or, more properly speaking, an exclusive society, was wanting here, namely, that uniformity in dress, in manners, in thought, and in phraseology, which results from a servile obedience to the canons of fashion—that dismal monotony of taste which forces every gentleman to furnish his house after a prescribed model, and a whole community to dress as much

2*

alike as a body of soldiers in regimentals; reminding one of
Pope's description of a garden, where

> "No pleasing intricacies intervene,
> No artful wildness to perplex the scene,
> Grove nods at grove, each alley has a brother,
> And half the platform just reflects the other."

This neighbourhood being secluded, and distant from the sea-
board, fashions, coming with a tardy step and from different
quarters, were partially adopted, and never generally acqui-
esced in, nor carried to excess.    Manufactures of every kind
were at that time at a low ebb, and mechanics were not to be
found in country neighbourhoods.    The Southern people, too,
are habitually indolent, and while they often exhibit on the
one hand great fondness for show, as often betray on the other
the most absolute carelessness for appearances; an apparent
contradiction, which arises from the fact that though lavish in
the expenditure of money, they will not endure any personal
labour or discomfort in the purchase of luxury.    If a splendid
dress, vehicle, or article of furniture, can be readily procured,
it is eagerly bought, without regard to the price; but if it
cannot be had, the nearest substitute is cheerfully adopted;
and they are too independent, either to value each other on
such adventitious possessions, or to mar their own happiness
by repining at the want of them.    From these various causes
it arose, that while one lady was rolled to the fête in an elegant coach, with four fat horses, and plated harness, another
of equal wealth came in a sorry vehicle, which might have
been very superb in the days of her grandmother, but was
now faded and crazy, drawn by a pair of blooded nags, hitched
to it with tackle marvellously resembling plough-gear.    An
ancient spinster, whose last will and testament was a matter of
interest with all kinsfolk, and of curiosity with the rest of her
acquaintance, rode in a sorry affair, which had once been a
creditable chaise, but was now transformed by repeated mend-
ings into something resembling a hangman's cart; having un-

dergone the same mutilations to which our ships of war are subjected, in which timber after timber is supplied, until none of the original material is left; the only difference being, that in the case of the carriage no care had been taken to preserve the model, or to adapt the last repair to the one which had preceded it. The horses were generally elegant—but such a heterogeneous assortment of equipments! How could it be otherwise? There was not a saddler within fifty miles, and a gentleman who had the misfortune to break a rein, or carry away a buckle, not being able to procure a new article, must necessarily submit the old one to a negro cobbler, or leave it to the ingenuity of his own groom. The most usual plan was to supply the rent with the nearest string. Thus it happened that many of the animals were nobly caparisoned; elegant saddles, dashing saddle-cloths, martingales, and double-reined bridles, were abundant; but when one of these spruce affairs had chanced to be broken, a knot or a splice, with a thong of deer skin, not unfrequently united the several parts, while a rope or strap of leather was sometimes substituted for a girth. Some gentlemen rode saddles without girths, and some rode with blind-bridles; for among this equestrian order any thing that could be ridden with, or ridden upon, was better than walking, and any thing at all was far better than staying away from the barbecue!

However odd all this might seem at first sight to a stranger, there was something in it that was remarkably pleasant—a something which showed that the most detestable of all pride, that which estimates an individual by his external appearance, was totally wanting. There was a cordiality, a confidence in being kindly received for one's own sake, which was cheering to the heart. The girls, too, looked charmingly; and it was marvellous to see them coming in pairs, two on a horse, or mounted behind their fathers and brothers, laughing and chatting, and just as happy as if they had ridden in coaches. And then the greetings! one would have thought that a single clan

had peopled the whole neighbourhood; the stately old gentlemen as they shook hands saluted each other as cousin Jones,
cousin Lee, and cousin Thompson, with here and there an occasional Mr. or Sir; but the girls were all cousins, and the
old ladies were aunts to all the world—that is, to all that part
of the world which paraded at the *barbecue.*

It was a gay scene; the horses hitched to the surrounding
trees, the ladies sitting in groups or parading about, and the
gentlemen preparing for the diversions of the day. Some
dispersed into the woods with their fowling-pieces, some dis-
tributed themselves along the rocks that overhung the river,
and threw out their fishing-lines, and others launched their
canoes in the stream, and sought the finny tribes in the eddies
of the rapid current. A few of the ladies participated in the
amusement of angling, whether to show their skill in throwing
out a bait, or to prove that they possessed the virtue of patience, is not known; but it is certain that they broke quite
as many rods and lines as hearts.

# CHAPTER III.

IMMEDIATELY opposite the spot at which our party was assembled, the river rushed over a series of rocky ledges, intersected by numberless fissures, affording channels to the water, which at the same time foamed and dashed over the rocks. A number of the youth were amusing themselves in navigating these ripples with canoes. By keeping the channels, they could pass in safety down the rapids, but it required the greatest skill to avoid the rocks, and to steer the boat along the serpentine and sometimes angular passes, by which alone it could be brought in safety through the ripples. Sometimes a canoe, missing its course, shot off into a pool or eddy, where the still water afforded a secure harbour; but if it happened to touch a rock, in the rapid descent, inevitable shipwreck was the consequence. The competitors in this adventurous entertainment soon became numerous; several of the young ladies, who loved sport too well, or feared the water too little, to be deterred by the danger of a wetting, engaged in it; so that some of the canoes were seen to contain, besides the steersman, a single female, for these frail vessels were only intended for two persons.

They first pushed their canoes up the stream with poles, keeping close to the shore, where the current flowed with little rapidity, until they reached the head of the ripple; then taking their paddles they shot out into the stream, guided their boats into the channels, darting down with the velocity

of an arrow, sometimes concealed among the rocks, and sometimes hidden by the foam, and in a few minutes were seen
gliding out over the smooth water below, having passed for
nearly a mile through this dangerous navigation. Sometimes
they purposely forsook the channel, and showed their skill by
turning suddenly into the eddies on either side, where they
would wait until the next boat passed, and dart after it in
eager chase. Dangerous as this amusement appeared, there
was in fact little to be apprehended; for the upsetting of a
canoe, which seldom occurred, would throw the passengers
into shallow water, or lodge them against a rock, with no
other injury than a wetting, or perhaps a slight bruise.

Fennimore, who had walked with Miss Pendleton to the
shore, and watched the canoes for some time, proposed to her
to join the party.

"Can you manage a canoe?" inquired she, hesitating.

"Try me," said he, gaily. "I would surely not venture
to take so precious a charge without some confidence in my
skill. I have been a western ranger for several years, and
am quite familiar with the use of the paddle."

Virginia stepped into the canoe, and having seated herself
in the prow, while Fennimore took possession of the stern,
exclaimed,

"A ranger! I am surprised, Mr. Fennimore; why, you
do not look like a ranger!"

"Am I at liberty to consider that doubt as a compliment?"

"Oh no—I do not pay compliments. But I always thought
that a ranger was a great rough man, with a blanket round
his shoulders, a tomahawk at his belt, and a rifle in his
hand."

"Such indeed is a part of the equipment of the backwoods
soldier; and believe me, Miss Pendleton, many of the most
gallant men of this day have earned their laurels in such a
dress."

"Oh, terrible! you will destroy some of my finest associations. I never think of a hero without fancying him a tall elegant man in dashing regimentals, with a rich sword-knot, and a pair of remarkably handsome epaulettes."

"Add to your picture a powdered head, a long queue, a stiff form, and measured tread, and you have the beau-ideal of a soldier of the school of Baron Steuben."

"Say not a word against that school, Mr. Fennimore; it has produced a noble race of heroes. What would have become of our country had it not been for those fine old generals, who trained our soldiers to war in the late revolution, and who were models of that neatness and military etiquette, which I am afraid you undervalue. We have a dear old gentleman here, whom you will see at dinner, and who is an excellent specimen of by-gone times."

"Who is he?"

"General Armour, one of our revolutionary veterans, a most excellent man, but who seems to think that the highest degree of human excellence consists in looking and acting like a soldier. He continues to wear his three-cornered hat, his buff waistcoat, and his blue regimental coat turned up with red, and would rather part with his estate than with his black cockade."

"I honour such men," said Fennimore; "but see, here we are at the head of the rapids."

Fennimore paddled his light canoe over the smooth water above the rapids, advancing towards the reefs and then retiring, describing circles with his little vessel, as if to try his skill before he ventured among the breakers. He was evidently quite familiar with this exercise; and Virginia, as she beheld with admiration the strength and dexterity with which he handled the paddle, felt no longer the slightest timidity, but enjoyed the exciting sport.

"Let me now acknowledge freely," said Fennimore, as he cast his eye over the ripple, "that I am unwilling to attempt a dangerous navigation, which is new to me, with so valuable a charge."

Virginia smiled. " I have often passed these rocks," said she, " and feel no fear ; but if you have the slightest desire to return, let us do so."

The stranger hesitated ; his prudence restraining him, while the natural ambition which a young man feels in the presence of a lady urged him on, until Miss Pendleton relieved him by saying, " Let us run no risks, Mr. Fennimore. I should not relish a wetting ; and I am in fault for not telling you sooner, that it would be difficult, if not impossible, for you to pass through the rapids without knowing the channel."

At this moment a canoe darted past them, containing a young lady and a gentleman. Both were laughing ; and the young man, proud of his skill, in attempting to flourish his paddle round his head, as a kind of salute to Miss Pendleton, unluckily threw it from his hand. An exclamation of affright arose from both parties ; for the canoe was rapidly approaching the breakers, while the steersman had no means of directing its course.

" Shall I follow ?" cried Fennimore.

" By all means," exclaimed his companion ; and in a moment he was rapidly pursuing the drifting canoe. The latter kept its course for a little while, then swinging round, floated with the broadside to the current, rising and sinking with an unsteady motion; now striking one end against a rock, and whirling round, and now the other, and sometimes darting head-foremost through the spray. Fennimore pressed on with admirable skill, urging his canoe forward with all his strength to overtake them, and guiding it with unerring sagacity. He had nearly reached the object of his pursuit, when it struck a rock, and upset, throwing the lady and gentleman into the deepest part of the channel.

" Keep your seat, Mr. Fennimore ! Guide the canoe !" exclaimed Virginia rapidly, as with admirable presence of mind she rose from her seat, kneeled in the boat, and leaning forward caught the floating lady by the arm, while Fennimore at the same instant, by a powerful exertion, threw the canoe into an eddy where the waters were still. The whole was the work of an instant; but it was witnessed from the shore, and a burst of applause excited by the presence of mind shown by Fennimore and Miss Pendleton. The dripping lady was drawn into the boat; the drooping gentleman, who had crawled on a rock, was taken in as a passenger; and, when they reached the shore, it would have been difficult to guess that any of the laughing party had met with a disaster. They were greeted with a hundred merry voices as they ascended the bank, and Mr. Fennimore forgot, in the lively scene, that he was a stranger.

It was now nearly noon, when the arrival of a hunting-party that had gone out at daybreak, attracted universal attention. At its head rode an elderly man of large frame, whose face was browned by many a summer's sun. He wore a suit of plain homespun, a handkerchief was bound closely round his head instead of a hat, and his legs from a little above the knee downward were wrapped in buckskin, to protect them from the briers, in riding rapidly through the forest. Under one arm hung a large powder-horn, on the other side was suspended a square pouch; and a broad leathern belt, buckled closely round him, kept his dress and accoutrements confined to his body. A large buck, the noblest trophy of the morning's chase, was thrown across the horse, behind the saddle, and bound to the rider's back, with the head and feet dangling on either side against the flanks of the steed. After him came a dozen hunters, mostly young men, variously equipped, some in gay hunting-shirts, with elegant rifles, and others in the plainer garb of ordinary woodsmen. Among them, they brought several deer of a smaller size, and a variety of wild turkeys, and smaller game.

"What a fine buck!" exclaimed several voices. "Ah, Colonel Antler, you always carry the day!"

"And so he should," said General Armour, "the veterans should set good examples to the new recruits. I congratulate you, my old friend."

"True enough," replied the hunter, "we ought to lead the young fellows; but to tell the truth, I have trained these lads until some of them know almost as much as myself."

A loud laugh from the hunters followed this speech.

"Come," said General Armour, "do us the favour to make your report; tell us how the buck was taken, before you alight."

"Hard duty, that," replied the leading hunter, "for I am as dry as a powder-horn. But the story is very short. We had agreed to *drive*. I had seen large tracks about the Cold Spring, up in the North Hollow, lately, for several mornings in succession, and I knew that a big buck *haunted* about there. We determined to surround him, and accordingly stationed ourselves at different points. I placed myself behind a large tree on a path leading across the hollow. A driver was sent in to start the game, and presently I saw this fine fellow stealing along at an easy gallop, treading as gently as a cat, and leaping over the logs so lightly as hardly to crush a leaf. There was a light breeze from the south, and some of the young men had gone up in that direction, expecting that he would run with his nose to the wind—and so he did, until he scented them, when he suddenly turned towards the place where I stood. I knew exactly where he would stop, and remained perfectly still. On he came at an easy *lope*, until he reached the top of a little knoll about sixty yards from me. There he halted, wheeled round, and stood perfectly still, with one fore-foot raised, the ear thrown forward, and his eye flashing—listening and snuffing the breeze. I fired, and down he fell. In a moment he rose and dashed off; but I knew I had *saved* him, dropped the butt of my rifle, and began to load.

A hunter, General, should never quit the spot from which he fires, until he loads up again."

"That's right, Colonel, on military principles."

"I know it to be right, on hunting principles." .

"It is mathematically and morally right," replied the veteran; "military rules are all founded on the immutable basis of truth—but I beg pardon; proceed, sir."

"The company all knew the crack of my rifle, and came galloping up, the dogs took the trail of the blood, and away they all went in chase, as hard as their horses could carry them. I mounted, rode quietly over the hill, and fell in ahead of them, just as the buck had turned to bay. Up came the young gentlemen and slipped in between me and the game, but without seeing me. Charles Cleaveland had raised his gun to his face, and my nephew Will, the rogue, was taking aim, when I said, 'Boys!' They both looked round, and at the same moment my bullet whistled between them and knocked over the buck."

"Bravo!" cried several voices.

"That was not fair, uncle," cried Miss Pendleton; "you outwitted the other gentlemen by your superior knowledge of the woods."

"Hey? Cousin Virginia; not fair! Why, what's the use of an old hunter's experience but to outwit the bucks—the old bucks of the woods, and the young bucks of the settlements."

"I have done, uncle," replied Virginia, laughing.

"Well, here's one who has nothing to complain of—George Lee; he found a fat yearling doe on the pine ridge, and brought her off. Henry Mountfort has another, and the rest of them have shot small game."

The party now alighted, and the servants were soon employed in preparing the game for dinner.

A long table was now spread under the trees, and loaded with an abundant and not inelegant repast. Venison, poultry,

hams, and rounds of beef, cooked on the ground, sent up their
savoury vapours, while numberless huge baskets of cold viands,
consisting of pullets, tongues, bread, cakes, and pastry, supplied that variety and profusion of eatables, which are supposed to have characterized the hospitality of our worthy
grandmothers.  The company took their seats with great decorum and no small parade of etiquette ; and the preparations
for a general onset, like the breaking ground of a besieging army, advanced with system and with a due attention
to all the little details customarily observed on such solemn
occasions.  But as the scene became more lively, good things
were said and eaten with a rapidity that would have defied
the skill of even a modern reporter ; and amidst the Babel
of voices, a few only of the most prominent speakers could be
occasionally heard.

"I'll trouble you, General Armour, for a slice of that venison,—take it rare, if you please,—pardon me for interrupt-
ing you——"

"I was about to remark, that when General Washington
determined to cut off the supply of provisions from Philadelphia——"

"Bad business that—cutting off provisions," remarked the
venison-eater.

"General, a morsel of the fat, if you please."

"—When General Washington in '77 determined——"

"Allow me to recommend this fish, General."

"I am very well helped——determined to cut off——"

"Did you say fish, madam ?  With great pleasure.  Let
me add some of this butter, and a glass of wine.  My father,
madam, who was a very facetious old gentleman——"

"He detached six hundred militia over the Schuylkill, under General Potter——"

"Quite a wit ; I knew him well."

"He intercepted their foraging parties, as directed by the
commander-in-chief——"

"—Was very fond of fish, madam."

" Who, General Washington?"

" No, sir, my late father. He used to say that fish should swim three times——"

" On the roads leading to Chester, Lancaster, and——"

"Three times, madam; first in the water, then in butter, and then in wine."

" General Washington remarking that——"

" —Dancing was a popular amusement——"

" —Gave strict orders——"

" The fiddlers should be kept sober."

" What did you say about the tender passion, madam?"

" General Knox——"

" —Who played the first fiddle——"

" —Wrote the Essay on Man——"

" —Between sunset and roll-call——"

" —So the leather affairs were sent to General Lee——"

" —A very pathetic story——"

" —Told in Hume's England."

" —For my father, you know, ma'am, was a witty man."

Buzz! buzz! buzz! all became a confused clatter, which continued until the cloth was removed and the ladies retired. A separation of the three estates now took place ;—the elder gentlemen remained at the table, the matronly portion of the females betook themselves to the surrounding seats, and the youthful part of the assembly arranged themselves in sets for dancing. Mr. Fennimore had already discovered that Miss Pendleton was emphatically *the Belle ;* and her title to this distinction became more evident when the younger part of the company, relieved from the presence of their seniors, were enabled to act out their own characters more freely. The young ladies evidently yielded to her the precedence, and the gentlemen were emulous in paying her attention. As the acknowledged heiress of Major Heyward, her expectations, in point of fortune, were of the brightest character, and in beauty

she had no superior; while her vigorous understanding, the
decision of her mind, and the playfulness of her conversation,
threw an air of freshness and originality around her, as rare as
it was captivating.    Among her constant admirers, the most
devoted was George Lee, a young gentleman, whose fine person was only equalled by the utter imbecility of his mind.
He was tall, stout, well built, and easy in his deportment.
.His features, taken singly, were manly and handsome; but
his face, as a whole, had not the slightest expression of any
thing but good-nature.    Amiable, kind, generous to prodigal-
ity, and simple as a child, there never lived a more artless, a
better tempered, or a weaker man.   His fine appearance and
gentlemanly deportment never failed to earn him respect on
a first acquaintance, and the goodness of his heart rendered
him a general favourite among those who had known him long.

"Will you dance with me, cousin Virginia?" said he, as
soon as he could plant himself at her side.

"I have almost promised not to dance to-day."

"But with *me:* I know you will dance with *me.*  I have
been trying all day to get to speak to you."

"I am glad you were so much better employed."

"No, that was not the reason; but you are always so sur
rounded.   You know that I would rather talk to you than do
any thing else in the world."

"Do not talk so, cousin George."

"Why not?  You know I think so.   I am not ashamed of
it.   You know that I have always told you so.   But you do
not know the half that I feel——"

"I will dance with you, Mr. Lee," said Miss Pendleton,
willing to interrupt his silly courtship.

"Thank you, but don't call me *Mr. Lee*—you know I can't
bear that;" and away they tripped.

The company separated at an early hour; and Mr. Fennimore was not displeased at having shared the festivities of this
agreeable day, or at being destined to pass another night under the hospitable roof of Major Heyward.

# CHAPTER IV.

A S Mr. George Lee will come occasionally under the notice of the reader, during the progress of this history, we think it advisable to devote a few pages to some special details relating to his parentage and character. This interesting young gentleman, the descendant of an ancient family, was the only son of a respectable planter who lived and died upon his own estate, adjoining that of Major Heyward, to whom he was distantly related. The elder Mr. Lee was only distinguished among his neighbours as an industrious man, who superintended his labourers faithfully during the day and smoked his pipe contentedly at night. He pursued this life so evenly for many years, that the only vicissitudes which marked his days were those produced by the revolutions of the seasons or the changes of the atmosphere—except, indeed, that he was occasionally induced to join a hunting expedition in the mountains, or allured to the lowlands to participate in a feast of oysters. Having been reared on the borders of the Blue Ridge, he had been early instructed in the use of the gun ; and long before he reached the age of manhood, could track the timorous deer through all the labyrinths of the forest. He had even ventured upon more dangerous enterprises, and on more than one occasion had joined the gallant volunteers of his native state in repelling the incursions of the savage tribe. When he married, he hung up his rifle and laid aside his moccasins, but still cherished them as old acquaintances, and could be prevailed upon at any time, by slight entreaty, to resume them both.   He had many acquaintances among the lowland gentry, who loved his society because he had a good appetite and a hard head, was fond of oysters and apple-toddy, and was an excellent listener; and, what was perhaps not the least of his good qualities, he seldom made them a visit without carrying with him a fat mountain-deer, as a present.   He was, therefore, an occasional, and always a welcome visitor, at those glorious fish-feasts at which the gentlemen of Virginia display such consummate skill, in catching, cooking, and consuming the inhabitants of the deep.   He was so well pleased upon such occasions, that he might have become a punctual participant in these festivities, had it not been for the frequent admonitions of Mrs. Lee, who observed that her husband, though rigidly temperate at home, never returned from such merry-meetings without exhibiting a certain unnatural exhilaration of spirits, not exactly conforming with this good lady's notions of propriety.   She therefore more than once hinted that oysters and toddy did not agree with Mr. Lee; and that gentleman, who had implicit faith in the penetration of his helpmate, as readily promised to eat fewer oysters and more trout, and to substitute brandy-and-water for toddy.   But as this arrangement neither produced the desired effect, nor satisfied the lady, he at last compounded matters, like a good husband, by agreeing to go to the lowlands but twice a year. Under this convention, which was kept inviolate, matters went on like clock-work; the plough and the loom were plied incessantly; the fields grew wider, and the tobacco crops more abundant; the negroes were fat and well clad; and Mr. Lee, as he ripened in years, increased in substance.  The lady who was the moving cause of this prosperity may be sketched off in a few words.   Like her husband, she came of an aristocratic stock; but, unlike him, she was shrewd, sensible, active, and gifted with an uncommon knack for managing every thing and every body around her.   She managed the plantation, the dairy, the poultry, the household, the negroes; she managed her husband; and, what was better than all, she regulated her own temper and conduct with great decorum, and managed to be the most popular woman in the neighbourhood. Of book-learning she had not much, for ladies, in that dark age, were not taught the sciences, did not visit lyceums, and had no souvenirs. But then Mrs. Lee had a mind of her own; her sensibilities were acute and her ambition great; and as she carefully improved every opportunity for gaining information, she became as intelligent as a lady could well be without the interesting aids above mentioned.

Such had been the prosperous condition of this family for several years, when the oppressions of Great Britain began to awaken her colonies to a sense of their rights. Mr. Lee for a long time turned a deaf ear to the murmurs which surrounded him. Having been in the habit of waiting on all occasions for Mrs. Lee to go foremost, it never occurred to him to be discontented while she seemed to be satisfied. He was as happy as a clam. His horses thrived, and his corn yielded famously; and when his neighbours indignantly repeated their long catalogue of grievances, he quietly responded that King George had never done *him* any harm. But no sooner did that good lady take the patriot side, and incautiously drop a rebellious expression in his hearing, than he began to examine the case with different eyes. By degrees, as the wrongs of his country were more clearly developed, a radical change was operated in his feelings and habits. He became a frequent attendant at public meetings, employed an overseer to conduct his business, and took to reading the newspapers; he lighted his pipe more frequently than usual, and walked to and fro for hours on the lawn before his door, with the air of a person in great perplexity. His wife observed all this with silent anxiety, for she was not in the habit of crossing his humours, but rather of directing them skilfully to the accomplishment of her own purposes; and after some

3

days she ventured to ask her husband what engaged his
thoughts so busily. Mr. Lee, like a boy who is about to
ask a boon which he expects will not be granted, had not
courage to face the question when thus suddenly presented;
and hastily replying that he hardly knew what he was thinking about, put on his hat and sallied forth to his accustomed
promenade. After marching about for several hours with
unusual agility, he returned with the air of a man who has
made up his mind, and sitting down by his good lady, said,
"I'll tell you, Mrs. Lee, what I have been considering about.
I think that King George is neither an honest man nor a gentleman; and if he sends any more of his soldiers to murder
their fellow-subjects in these colonies, I'll be the first man to
shoulder a musket against them." To his surprise, his excellent better half not only applauded this spirited resolution,
but complimented his patriotism in the most flattering terms.

As we design to write the history of the father only as in-
troductory to that of the son, we shall not ask the reader to
accompany the former through all his campaigns. Suffice it
to say, that he was a brave though not an active officer, and
that after serving his country faithfully during the whole war,
and attaining the rank of captain, he retired, when the struggle
was over, to his beloved retreat among the Blue Mountains.
Besides some honourable scars, he brought back with him several new propensities. He rose at daybreak, and, having
swallowed a mint-julep, sallied forth bare-headed, in his
slippers, and without his coat; and having cooled himself in
the open air, repaired to his station in the chimney-corner.
This, which he called "turning out at reveillè," he practised
at all seasons. He had, moreover, learned several military
and political maxims, which, as a soldier and a revolutionary
patriot, he felt bound to live up to. One of these was, that a
captain should command his own company, a proposition
which he failed not to repeat to Mrs. Lee, whenever he suspected her of intruding upon his authority; and another

referred to the "indefeasible" right of *pursuing happiness*, as laid down in the Declaration of Independence, which guaranteed to him, as he supposed, the privilege of entertaining as much company as he pleased, and of eating as many oysters and drinking as much brandy as he found pleasant and palatable. His pipe became his inseparable companion, and the management of all his affairs devolved on his wife. He was a diligent reader of the newspapers, and pored incessantly over the numerous political tracts which issued from the presses of that day. He became a great talker, and described the various scenes of the war in which he had been engaged with a minuteness which nothing but their intense interest could have rendered tolerable. Of his own personal adventures he spoke sparingly and with great modesty, though his merits had been great. Once or twice only he informed a confidential friend, that he deserved to have been made a general for his exploits, and would undoubtedly have attained that rank, had it not been for his want of talents and education; but he ventured such remarks with great caution, and never until after dinner.

It will be readily imagined that Mr. George Lee, junior, was an apt pupil in the school of so meritorious a parent. The heir of a large estate, he early learned that he lived only to enjoy it, and to spend it like a gentleman. The descendant of a revolutionary hero, he felt it incumbent on him to support the dignity of his family. Accustomed to see his father's table loaded with a profusion of the bounties of nature, and surrounded by crowds of welcome guests, hospitality became, in his eyes, the chief of the cardinal virtues. His father, doating upon the beautiful boy, who was said to be the exact image of himself, carried him with him, not only in his daily walks and rides around his own plantation, but to the numerous parties and carousals upon which he was now a regular attendant. Before he was twelve years old, this precious youth could follow the hounds at full speed through the

woods, with the dexterity of a practised fox-hunter; at fourteen, he was a member of a fishing-club and an excellent
judge of cookery and Madeira; and at sixteen, when his
worthy progenitor was gathered to his fathers, the accomplished heir took his place in society, qualified in all respects
to fill the void occasioned by this melancholy event.

To be brief—George Lee was a good fellow, a thorough
sportsman, and a most hospitable man. His purse, his
horses, and his wine, were always at the service of his friends.
Too good-humoured to make an enemy, too generous to envy
others, and too feeble of intellect to lay any plan beyond the
enjoyment of the present moment, he had no desires which
extended farther than the next meal, nor any anxieties which
a bumper of Madeira could not dispel. His mother had long
since abandoned the hopeless task of training his mind to any
serious pursuit or any solid excellence, because it was impossible to cultivate that which did not exist. But he had affections which were easily moulded, and through these she
obtained all that in such a case was practicable : the entire
management of his estate, and the accomplishment of any
temporary purpose on which she had set her heart.

It was in consequence of a plan early matured by this
politic lady, that George Lee attached himself to Virginia
Pendleton. The latter was an orphan, the niece, not of Major
Heyward, but of his wife. She was adopted by them in her
infancy, and, as they had no children of their own, became the
idol of their hearts and the acknowledged heiress of Major
Heyward's fortune. When Mrs. Heyward died, Virginia
was quite young, and Mrs. Lee supplied, to some extent, the
place of a mother to the orphan girl, by giving her advice
from time to time, and directing her inquisitive mind to
proper studies and correct sources of information ; and often
did she wish that she had found in her son a pupil of equal do-
cility and intelligence. It therefore very naturally occurred
to her, that if George was deficient in intellect, it was the

more necessary that he should have a highly-gifted wife, who could manage his affairs, and by her talents and personal charms acquire a decided influence over himself. For this office Virginia was eminently qualified, and to this important station Mrs. Lee had the kindness to devote her, even in her childhood. They were thrown together continually; the affectionate appellation of *cousin* was used between them, and their intercourse was that of brother and sister. Virginia, grateful for the kindness of Mrs. Lee, the full value of whose friendship she had the discernment to see and the sensibility to feel, became sincerely attached to George—but with an affection precisely similar to that which she felt for his mother and Major Heyward. They stood to her in the place of relatives. And such also were the feelings of George Lee, until he was nearly grown to manhood, when the judicious hints of his mother, pointing out the eminent attractions of Virginia, the suitableness of their ages, tastes, and tempers, and the contiguity of their estates, opened his eyes to a new idea, which, once indulged, remained for ever implanted in his heart. Not that he for a moment entered into the spirit of his mother's calculating policy; he was too careless of wealth, too improvident, and too generous to form a sordid wish; but when the possibility of a marriage with Virginia was suggested to his fancy, her own matchless charms warmed in his heart a love as fervent as it was disinterested.

Virginia discovered this passion, in the altered manner of her young friend, with unaffected regret, and with a determination to discourage it by every means in her power. She continued to treat him with the same kindness and confidence which had always characterized their intercourse; while she endeavoured to withdraw herself from his society as much as was practicable, without exciting observation. With Mrs. Lee she was more explicit; and when that lady, at first to feel her way, and afterwards to advance a project which seemed feasible, threw out repeated hints which at length became so broad as not to be misunderstood, she replied to them with a frankness, an earnestness, and a spirit which convinced the female politician that she understood, deplored, and disrelished the whole plan.

But Mr. Lee was not so easily repulsed. He was not sufficiently keen-sighted to discover the bearing of a gentle hint, nor were his sensibilities delicate enough to be wounded by a slight repulse. He remained true to his first love, following the idol of his affections into every company, besieging her at home, and urging his suit with pressing importunity whenever a favourable opportunity—or an unfavourable one, for he was not very particular—occurred. More than once was his suit kindly and respectfully, but decidedly, rejected. After a repulse, George betook himself to his horses, his dogs, his gun, and his wine, with unwonted assiduity. No one discovered any evidence of despair in his voice or look; his laugh was as loud as ever and his song as joyous; but the number of foxes that he took, and the bottles that he cracked after each refusal, was marvellous. A few weeks, or at most a few months, brought him back to Virginia's feet. Such was the state of affairs at the period which we have chosen for the commencement of this history.

# CHAPTER V.

IT was sunset when Major Heyward and his party reached home. Never had Fennimore passed so delightful a day. The hospitality and politeness of his entertainment had taught him to forget that he was a stranger. Their free and joyous hilarity had excited his feelings and given a fresh impulse to his heart. His conversational powers were naturally fine, and were rendered peculiarly agreeable by a simplicity and frankness peculiar to himself. But, under the influence of a high flow of spirits, his manner acquired a more than ordinary vivacity, his language became copious and brilliant, and the rich stores of his mind began to exhibit their exuberance. Two hours passed rapidly away; the parties, pleased with each other, conversed with that freedom which is the result of perfect confidence, and with a degree of wit and animation which showed how highly they all enjoyed the intellectual repast. It was one of those happy moments which seldom occur, when persons, pleased with each other and surrounded by propitious circumstances, are happy without effort and agreeable without design.

Major Heyward was in the habit of retiring early to bed, and when his servant appeared to attend him to his chamber, Mr. Fennimore desired an audience of a few minutes, with so much earnestness, that he was invited to accompany the worthy old man to his sleeping apartment. Here they remained some time engaged in business, and then all the parties separated for the night.

Mr. Fennimore, finding that it was still early, sat down to write a letter to his friend Charles Wallace, a young attorney in Philadelphia, in which the events of the day were alluded to and certain characters described in language which the reader may well suppose was quite as sentimental as the occasion required. We shall not copy this epistle, but will content ourselves with treating the reader to one or two of the concluding paragraphs.

"—— So much for Virginia Pendleton, the belle of the Blue Mountains, the fairest and the brightest vision that has ever warmed my fancy! How faint until now were all my conceptions of female loveliness! How little did I dream of that concentration of attractions, that intensity of excellence, that combination of charms, which I have now witnessed! How many excellent qualities have I this day seen combined in the character of this extraordinary female—exquisite beauty, superior intelligence, elegant wit, and the utmost sweetness of disposition! Of the other attributes of her mind and heart I am ignorant; but with respect to those that I have enumerated, I cannot be mistaken."

If the reader will pardon us for the interruption, we suggest that the last averment savours of what the lawyers call *surplusage*. It is certainly an unnecessary averment, for how *could* a young gentleman be mistaken in such plain matters? We admire the argument of a love-letter, or of any letter treating of the mysteries of this all-pervading passion. Let us proceed :

"You will no doubt, now, take it into your wise head that I am in love, or at least that I am rapidly imbibing the delightful, the dangerous poison. Let me assure you seriously that nothing is further from my intentions. I have already wooed a mistress, under whose banner I am enlisted. Plighted to the service of my country, with the path of fame bright before me, I may not linger in the bowers of pleasure. Even Miss Pendleton has no charms when weighed in the balance against my duty. But why should I speak of her? I a penniless man, unknown to fame—a needy soldier, depending on my sword, with an aged mother to support? And she, the 'observed of all observers,' the darling of her friends, the heiress of a noble fortune! It is painful to reflect on the disparity between us, yet dangerous to think of her in any other light.   \*    \*    \*    \*    \*    \*    \*

"To-morrow morning I must bid adieu to Walnut Hill, to Miss Pendleton, and to the generous-hearted Major Heyward. When I left Philadelphia, to rejoin the army now encamped in the wilderness bordering on the Ohio, I was intrusted with despatches for General Wayne. At my earnest request I was permitted to take this place in my route, and to halt one day, to attend to my own personal affairs, but was admonished at the same time, that as the letters committed to my care were important, any further delay would not be allowed. I have, therefore, no choice; and perhaps it is well for me that I have none. Virginia Pendleton is not a common woman, and it would be madness for me to remain within the magic circle of her attractions."

At the very moment that Mr. Fennimore was inditing these amorous and heroic sentiments, Miss Pendleton was seated at her writing-desk, penning a note to her bosom friend, Mrs. Mountford, a young lady recently married. The ideas of the fair writer ran off in the following strain:

"I am sorry, my dear Caroline, that you were not with us to-day; we had such a delightful party! You cannot think how much I regretted your absence, nor how much you lost by it. The weather was very agreeable, and the scenery of the river-shore and the mountains was never more beautiful than at this moment. The arrangements were charming. I think I never saw a barbecue pass off so happily. There was no shower, nor any disastrous accident, excepting the upsetting of a canoe, by which nobody was hurt. Mrs. Lee superintended the preparation of the dinner with her usual

3\*

taste; General Armour had a new story for the occasion; the
Peytons had new bonnets; and we had a new beau. The
latter made quite a sensation among the girls, and I have no
doubt I shall have a dozen morning visitors to-morrow, for
he is staying with us. Can you guess who it is? If you cannot, you must remain in the dark, for I can give you little
assistance. He is a young officer, just dropped into our
neighbourhood from the moon, or from the frontier, or from
some other parts unknown. He is at our house, so that I
have the honour of entertaining him. He is not at all handsome, though I think him clever.

"I shall not be able, dear Caroline, to spend to-morrow
evening with you, as I proposed, for my uncle cannot accompany me, and you know I am unwilling to leave him alone.
Mr. Fennimore, our guest, will remain, I suppose, some days
with us, and although his visit is entirely to my uncle, and on
business, I must, as in duty bound, make my appearance as
lady of the mansion, and do the honours to the best of my
poor ability. Mr. Fennimore has travelled a good deal,
and is quite intelligent; I think you would be pleased with
him.

"Do come and dine with me to-morrow—you and Mr.
M——. If you are still determined on taking that dreadful
journey over the mountains, it may be useful to you to see
Mr. Fennimore, who is just from that country, and can tell
you all about it. He is remarkably agreeable in conversation; I am very sure you will like him."

Having sealed this note, Virginia retired to repose, and
was soon wrapped in that calm forgetfulness which attends
the slumbers of the young and innocent. About midnight
she was awakened by the terrific cry of "fire!" Springing
to the floor, she hastily threw a cloak around her, and rushed
to the chamber-door, but as she opened it, a thick volume of
smoke burst in, and she beheld with affright a sheet of flame
enveloping the whole staircase; retreat in that direction was

impossible. She had the presence of mind to close the door, and recollecting that the roof of a piazza extended under her window, she determined to make her escape that way. But here an object met her view, more terrible than the devouring element: the shoulders and head of a man of most hideous appearance occupied the window to which she was approaching. The face was larger than common, and, to her excited imagination, seemed of superhuman dimensions. The complexion was sanguine, and its redness heightened by the glare of the fire; the features were harsh and savage; a beard of several weeks' growth covered the lower part of the face; while the uncovered head displayed an immense mass of tangled, coarse red hair. The malignant eye that scowled upon her was full of savage ferocity, and a demoniac laugh which distended the mouth of this human monster, conveyed to the affrighted girl a sensation of horror, such as she had never before experienced. A single glance told her that the apparition was not imaginary, that the form was that of a stranger, and that the purpose of his visit was sinister. But Virginia was of an heroic mould—she neither screamed nor fainted, but summoning all her resolution, turned towards a window in the opposite direction, and was retreating, when Fennimore entered the chamber, having clambered up the blazing staircase at the risk of his life.

"Fly, fly! Miss Pendleton!" he exclaimed, as he caught her hands, and drew her towards the same window at which she had seen the object of her terror.

"Oh, not there! not there!" she cried; "stop, for mercy's sake, we shall all be murdered!"

Fennimore, attributing her incoherent expressions to an excess of terror caused by the fire, delayed not; but catching her up in his arms, proceeded towards the window.

Virginia uttered a piercing shriek, and struggled to release herself.

"Pardon me," said Fennimore; "excuse my rudeness,"

as he threw up the window, and passed through it with his
lovely burthen.  In a moment he stood on the roof of the
piazza.

"See there !" screamed Virginia, as her eye caught a
glimpse of the figure of a man stealing behind a distant
chimney.  " Oh fly, Mr. Fennimore ! hasten from this dreadful spot."

Fennimore involuntarily turned his head in the direction
indicated, and saw a man leaning against the chimney.  He
looked again and the figure had disappeared.

The servants, who were filled with consternation, and
crowded round the blazing pile, running to and fro without
order or definite purpose, now beheld them and hastened to
their assistance.  One of the stoutest negroes mounting on a
table under the eaves of the low roof was enabled to receive
his young mistress in her arms, while Fennimore leaped
nimbly to the ground.

No sooner was Virginia in safety than she looked round
for her uncle, and not perceiving him in the crowd that
pressed round to congratulate her on her escape, eagerly inquired for him.  The negroes, habitually indolent, timid, and
thoughtless, stood gazing in terror on the conflagration without thinking on the possibility of extinguishing the flames or
of rescuing either life or property.  But they loved their
master, and when his name was mentioned made a general
movement towards his apartment.  In a moment the voice of
Fennimore was heard like that of one accustomed to command, leading and directing them.  The passive blacks, used
to implicit obedience, followed him with alacrity ; but it was
all in vain.  The fire seemed to have originated in Major
Heyward's chamber, and the flames were bursting from every
window.  Fennimore burst open a door and rushed in, but
was speedily driven out by a volume of smoke and flame.
"Follow me !" he exclaimed impatiently to the blacks;
"rush in and save your master !" and again he entered the

apartment with some of the most intrepid of the negroes. Their efforts were herculean. Several times they had nearly reached the bed, and as often were driven back by the flames; and the negroes at last returned, dragging out Mr. Fennimore, who was struck down by a falling rafter. Exposure to the cool air revived him instantly, and he returned with desperate courage to the room, exclaiming, " Follow me! in there! in, my brave boys!" It was a forlorn hope, but the effort was gigantic. The negroes, attached to their master and excited by the heroic bearing of their young leader, now worked as if in their native element. The side of the house, which was of frame, was torn away, and in a few minutes the lifeless body of Major Heyward was dragged out of the ruins.

By this time the whole pile was in flames. There was no longer any occasion for exertions, except in removing the furniture from some of the apartments. The neighbours, who began to arrive, and the domestics, stood round in silence. Virginia hung in mute agony over the body of Major Heyward, who had been to her more than a father. Nor was she alone in her sorrow. Though none of those around her were possessed of sensibilities as keen as her own, or had the same personal cause for grief, yet the respect and affection entertained by all for the worthy old man, and the awful manner of his death, caused universal sorrow. At length the flames began to sink; Virginia was torn almost by force from the spot, and carried to the house of her friend Mrs. Mountford; the neighbours dispersed; darkness and silence settled over the spot, and a heap of smoking ruins occupied the place which was so lately the seat of hospitality and cheerfulness.

# CHAPTER VI.

THE whole neighbourhood assembled at the funeral of Major Heyward, and it was a melancholy sight to behold the same individuals, who but two days before had mingled together on a festive occasion, now collected to pay the last sad duties to one of the most conspicuous of the number. The feelings excited by this reflection were rendered the more vivid by the awful nature of the catastrophe which had occurred; and as the sad procession moved silently away to the family burial-place, an uninterrupted silence pervaded the company. The deceased had been universally loved and respected. His age, his wealth, and his standing in society, had given him an influence over those around him, which had been honestly and kindly exercised, and although he held no official station, it was felt that his decease was a public loss. Another must inherit his wealth and sway its influence; but would his conciliatory spirit descend to his heir, and his virtues be practised by the inheritor of his estate? Such were the mingled sensations of those who followed the remains of this most excellent man to their last earthly receptacle.

But that intensity of feeling which, on the occurrence of an unexpected and strikingly melancholy event, absorbs for a while all other subjects, and employs every faculty of the mind, is of brief continuance. The practice observed at military funerals, of marching to the grave with solemn

music, and returning from it with cheerful, inspiring notes, is
natural, and beautifully expressive of human character; for
it is thus that the heart of man throws off the burthen of
sorrow, and though bowed low for the moment, regains its
cheerfulness, as the flower, weighed down by the morning
dew, erects itself as the sun exhales the incumbent moisture.
As the mourners retired from the grave, the silence which had
prevailed among them began to be broken, and curiosity,
which had heretofore been suppressed by grief and astonishment, became audible. A thousand surmises and reports,
touching the fatal accident, were repeated and canvassed.
Every one had his own version of the catastrophe, and its
attendant circumstances.

"Have you heard the particulars?" inquired an old lady,
in a tremulous tone, and conveying the remainder of the
inquiry by a mysterious shake of the head.

The person addressed applied her handkerchief to her
eyes, and only ejaculated the words, "Too shocking!"

"One hardly knows what to believe, there are so many
stories," said an old maid.

"I am told," said a gentleman, "that our lamented friend
has lately been in the habit of reading in bed, and it is supposed, that, having received some letters, which he had not
had time to examine sooner, he had caused a light to be
placed by his bed-side——"

"All a mistake," cried Colonel Antler, "no man of sense
ever went to bed to read letters; my worthy friend rose at
daybreak, and retired early to his pillow for repose."

"He was a man of plethoric habit," said a consumptive
gentleman, who now intruded his ghostly form between the
last two speakers, "very plethoric—and you know, gentlemen, that such persons hold their lives by a very uncertain
tenure. Your full-fed, lusty, corpulent men are short-lived
at best, and subject to very sudden attacks. There is very
little doubt that this was a case of apoplexy, and that, in his

struggles, a candle, that happened to be within reach, was thrown over——"

"That is all surmise," said another speaker.

"Mere surmise," rejoined yet another; "the truth seems to be, that when Major Heyward was last seen by his servants, he was sitting at a table covered with papers, in his arm-chair, with his spectacles on——"

"I am sure that you must be misinformed," cried a lady, "for Mrs. Lee, who is very intimate with the family, assured me that he had gone to bed fully two hours before the alarm took place."

"I spoke to the Major's body-servant, this morning," said Colonel Antler.

"Oh! did you?"

"Then you know all about it!"

"Major Heyward and Mr. Fennimore, the young gentleman who was on a visit there, had some private business, and retired to the Major's chamber after tea——"

"There!" cried a lady, "that is just what I heard. The business was of a very mysterious character, was it not, Colonel?"

"I cannot say as to that."

"But did you not hear that both the gentlemen became very much irritated, and got to such high words that Virginia Pendleton, becoming very much alarmed, rushed into the room just as Major Heyward ordered the young man to leave his house instantly?"

"No, madam, I did not hear that; and I am very certain that Major Heyward never ordered a stranger to leave his house in the night."

"But, my dear sir, if he suspected the stranger of a design to rob and murder him?"

"That, indeed, would alter the case."

"Well, I assure you, sir, I had it from a lady who heard it from a particular friend of the Walnut-Hill family, and that when this Mr. Fennimore arrived, Major Heyward received him with great coldness, and was very unwilling to permit him to stay all night."

"Yet he introduced him to us the next day as his friend."

"*That* was very singular," said the old maid.

"An act of wonderful imprudence in our benevolent friend who is gone," said the consumptive gentleman.

"It is quite mysterious, I declare," continued the lady, "but I am sure I cannot be mistaken—Major Heyward and Miss Pendleton was sitting at tea, in the front piazza, when the stranger rode up: 'Is your name Heyward?' said he. 'That is my name,' said the Major. 'I have some business with you,' said the stranger. 'We will talk of business when I have nothing else to do—you must call again,'—replied the Major."

"I heard it a little differently," interrupted another lady—"Major Heyward was walking on the lawn, and Miss Pendleton was sitting in the piazza, talking with George Lee, (you know they are to be married soon,) when the stranger rode up, and inquired where Major Heyward lived; the old gentleman replied, 'That is the house, and I am the man;' on which the stranger remarked, 'Not a bad-looking house, and quite a pleasant landlord ;—I believe I'll stay all night.'"

"The impudent rascal !" exclaimed the consumptive gentleman.

"He has a forward look," responded the old maid.

"I am sure *you* are mistaken," said one of the former speakers; "for Mr. Lee does not go there now ; there is quite a serious coolness between the families."

"Dear me, cousin ! I'm sure you are altogether wrong there—if you had seen them at the barbecue, you would not have said *that*. Virginia refused to dance with any one else; she refused several others, but danced with him as soon as he asked her."

"Straws show how the wind blows."

"I believe you are right there; there has always been a strong attachment between them."

"Say rather a powerful attraction between Walnut Hill and Locust Grove. The estates are large, and we all know what an excellent manager Mrs. Lee is."

"Did you not hear it surmised that Major Heyward has latterly entertained different views for Virginia, and that Mr. Fennimore is the son of a wealthy merchant in Philadelphia, and came by express invitation to see Miss Pendleton?"

"La! no!"

"Yes, indeed, it is more than suspected."

"Well, who would have thought it?"

"Then it was to marry Miss Pendleton, and not to murder and rob the family, that this young gentleman came?" said Colonel Antler.

"Oh—I had forgotten that. I am sure that this Fennimore is nothing more nor less than an incendiary—for I am told that Virginia, who was in a high fever, and delirious all the next day, continually exclaimed, 'Take away that dreadful man! protect me from that horrid wretch! He has murdered my uncle—he would destroy us all!' and similar expressions."

"Very strange, that! she certainly must know something."

"The evidence of a young lady in a state of delirium is quite conclusive," remarked Colonel Antler, drily.

"It is certainly a curious fact," said one of the gentlemen, "that this Mr. Fennimore has entirely disappeared since the fire, and that no one can give any account of him."

Colonel Antler seemed puzzled, while the rest of the company united in considering this circumstance as one of a most suspicious character.

"The young man is a stranger to me," said the Ccolonel; "he may be a terrible fellow, for any thing I know—but at the same time, I don't believe a word of it. He looks like a gentleman, and no one ever heard of a gentleman committing arson."

"Then you do not believe that he fired the house purposely?"

"Believe it! no: why should I believe it? what object could the young man have?"

"His purpose was undoubtedly to run off with Virginia. Incendiaries often set fire to houses in order to plunder them during the confusion. They say that as soon as the alarm was given he rushed into Virginia's apartment, caught her in his arms, and although she screamed dreadfully, attempted to carry her off."

"And what prevented him?"

"They say he forced her through a window, and succeeded in reaching the roof of the piazza, where one of his confederates was waiting to assist him in his villainous design, when the screams of Virginia drew the negroes to her relief. and they rescued her."

"Poor Virginia screaming bloody murder all the while," continued the consumptive gentleman.

"Poor Virginia!" echoed all the ladies.

"I am told, Colonel Antler, that no will can be found."

"All exertions to discover any trace of a will, have, unhappily, been fruitless. Every gentleman who has been on such terms of intimacy with Major Heyward, as to render it likely that a document of that kind might have been deposited with him, has been applied to in vain. Mr. R., who has been his legal adviser for many years, declares that a will was executed long since, which he is sure remained in the possession of our lamented friend, but declines giving any information as to the contents."

"Then Miss Pendleton will not be a great fortune, after all."

"Oh dear, what a pity!"

"Such a belle as she was!" exclaimed one of the old maids; "I wonder if she will be as much admired now."

" Poor cousin Virginia !"

" Dear Virginia! how I feel for her! But you know, Colonel, she had no right to expect any thing else. She is not related to the Heywards, and there are a number of heirs-at-law."

" She *had* a right, madam !" replied Colonel Antler, warmly ; " if not related to Major Heyward, she is niece to the late Mrs. Heyward, and their adopted daughter. Major Heyward's intention of leaving his whole fortune to her has been declared so frequently, and is so well understood, that no man of honour will dispute her claim."

" There will be claimants, I suppose, nevertheless."

" Then they ought all to be——"

" Speak lower, Colonel: there are some of them within hearing."

" I care not who hears me. The girl was raised under Heyward's roof, and is entitled to the estate ; and no true son of the Old Dominion would take it from her."

The conversation was here interrupted by the approach of Mrs. Lee's carriage, containing that lady and the unhappy Virginia. As the beautiful mourner passed slowly along, a common feeling of sympathy for the sudden and melancholy stroke of fortune, which had in a single moment blighted her brilliant prospects and reduced her to sorrow and dependence, pervaded the whole party ; and dropping off, one by one, they repaired silently to their respective dwellings.

# CHAPTER VII.

ON the following morning, at an early hour, Mrs. Lee visited the distressed Virginia, who was now more composed; and the worthy lady successfully exerted her talents in endeavouring to calm the mind and fortify the courage of her young friend. Although artful and politic, she was really a benevolent woman, in all cases where the interests of others did not interfere with her own; and being sincerely attached to Virginia, she now devoted herself assiduously to the task of administering comfort to the mourner. Her common sense, her practical business habits, and that delicate perception of propriety in matters of feeling, which all women possess in a greater or less degree, enabled her to do this with much effect; and, after leading Miss Pendleton into the garden, where they could converse without interruption, she began to speak in a kind and rational manner of that young lady's prospects, and, carefully avoiding those topics which would be merely calculated to awaken sensibility, soon engaged her in earnest consultation. Virginia acknowledged that Major Heyward had more than once assured her, that, on his death, she would inherit his estate, but he had never mentioned his will in her presence, nor did she know whether he had ever executed such an instrument.

"On that subject," said Mrs. Lee, "my own information is more accurate. Knowing the determination of my excellent friend to make you the sole heiress of his property, I repeatedly hinted to him the necessity of making a will, and the propriety of performing this duty without delay, and in the most careful manner. He afterwards informed me that it was duly executed. I have no doubt, my dear Virginia, that my evidence, with that of the gentleman who wrote the will, and of the witnesses to its execution, will restore you to your rights."

" Do not speak of that," replied Virginia firmly ; " owing every thing, as I do, to the benevolence of my uncle, I should be most ungrateful to appear in a court of justice, engaged in a contest with his legal heirs."

" My dear Virginia, how often have I reminded you, that feeling is a deceitful guide in the serious concerns of life! You are no longer a young girl, protected by a fond guardian, and sporting in the beams of affluence, without any other care than that of imparting to others a share of the happiness which you enjoyed yourself. You are now a woman, your own mistress, having duties to perform and rights to assert ; and you cannot, my dear, testify your respect for the memory of Major Heyward more suitably than by insisting upon the exact execution of his own views in relation to his estate. Besides, are you aware who your opponents would be ?"

" Indeed, I do not know exactly—my uncle had no very near relations."

" He had not, but a great many who are very distant ; and the embers will hardly be cold on his ruined hearthstone, before a number of claimants will be fiercely engaged in litigation for this noble estate."

Virginia melted to tears. Contending emotions of pride and affection for the dead swelled her heart. A number of affecting associations arose in her memory, and the thought that the spot which had so long been the abode of peace, happiness, and hospitality, was about to become the scene of bitter contention, filled her mind with sorrow. " Dear Mrs.

Lee!" she exclaimed, "I shall never be a party to so disgraceful a contest. Oh, no! never, never!"

"I venerate your affection for the memory of Major Heyward," replied her friend, calmly: "it is natural, and perfectly right. But, my dear, what obligations do you owe to his relations?"

"None, particularly. They have always treated me with respect and cordiality."

"Except in a few instances," urged the politic Mrs. Lee, in an insinuating manner. "Openly they could not do otherwise, for the very stones would have cried out at the slightest incivility to the dear girl that we all loved and admired so much. Besides, you were the presumptive heiress of a fine estate, and, as mistress of your uncle's mansion, dispensed its hospitalities. But you forget that you have sometimes been charged with holding your head higher than became you, and with having used some address in procuring the execution of this very will. Even I have been accused of interested motives in my exertions on your behalf."

Virginia turned pale with emotion, and that spirit, which on some occasions animated her heart, and gave a surprising degree of decision and vigour to the conceptions of her mind, flashed for a moment in her eye. But the sensibility of a delicate mind overcame all other feelings. Unconscious of a sordid motive, she shrunk with indescribable repugnance from the thought of encountering a suspicion of that description, and begged Mrs. Lee to change the subject.

"You have now," said she, "given the strongest reason why I should not set up any claim to this property. The bare idea of having ever been suspected of entertaining the interested views at which you hint, is too shocking. Not for worlds would I do an act, or give the sanction of my name to any proceeding, which might bring the disinterestedness of my conduct into question, or throw the slightest shade upon the purity of my affection for my dear uncle. Let his relatives take the estate. It will be happiness enough for me to be grateful for his goodness and to love and cherish his memory."

Mrs. Lee knew well the decision of her young friend's character, and, aware of her inflexibility on points which involved principle or touched her feelings of delicacy, determined, like an able politician, to change her mode of attack, and to resort to arguments which she had before resolved studiously to conceal. And the manner in which she opened her batteries anew was after the following fashion:

"There are two claimants to this property, of whose pretensions you are probably not aware, and it is right that you should be informed in relation to them. The first of these is my son George."

"Indeed! I heartily wish my cousin George success."

"Your wishes, my dear, are not his own. He has not the slightest disposition or the most remote intention to set up any claim, unless it may become necessary for your interest. With the exception of one person, whom I will presently name, my son is undoubtedly the nearest relative of our deceased friend. There are several others, however, who claim to stand in the same degree of consanguinity. Now, what I would suggest is, that as my son has never for a moment thought of placing his claim in competition with yours, you might, should your own right to the property be thought doubtful, or should you persist in refusing to assert it, avail yourself of his. Understand me, my dear—do not get impatient—all that I propose is the use of his name, agency, and friendship, to procure that which is undoubtedly your own; and when the intimacy between our families is considered—when you recollect that from infancy you have shared my affection with him, there can be no impropriety in his assuming towards you the place of a brother. I have surely some claim, my dear Virginia, to the privilege of discharging towards you the duties of a mother; and if George can never call you by a dearer title, you may, you ought, to give him the confidence and affection of a sister. Confide to us the management of your affairs, and rest assured that your name shall never be used in a manner that shall implicate your delicacy."

Virginia was affected and embarrassed. There was a mixture of policy and of genuine affection in the whole conversation of her friend, so characteristic of the woman, that it touched while it perplexed her. But she remained firm to her purpose, and decidedly, though with delicacy and feeling, declined the proposal. Mrs. Lee was puzzled, but not defeated. She now artfully alluded to the magnitude of the estate, and to the almost unbounded influence which the possession of great wealth would give to a young lady who was so eminently endowed with beauty, intellect, and accomplishments, as her young friend. Failing in all her appeals to the affections and the ambition of our heroine, she now determined to awaken, if possible, her resentment.

"The other name, which I have withheld out of respect for your feelings, is that of this Mr. Fennimore."

Virginia turned upon her friend a mingled look of surprise and curiosity, but made no reply.

"He is more nearly related to the late Major Heyward than either of the other would-be heirs; supposing it to be possible for him to establish his identity with the person whose name he bears, which I suspect is rather doubtful."

"Can you suppose it possible that Mr. Fennimore would be guilty of an imposture?"

"I suppose nothing, my dear; the law will require him to prove that he is really the person he pretends to be; and this, I imagine, will not be in his power. It is hinted, moreover, that being aware of the disposition which your uncle had made of his property, the object of his visit at Walnut Hill was to induce Major Heyward to revoke his will, and that, failing in this, he has possessed himself of that instru-

4

ment, by means of which we have all witnessed the dreadful
effects."

Miss Pendleton became dreadfully pale on hearing this
insinuation. The allusion to the melancholy event which
had deprived her of a home and a protector was in itself
sufficiently distressing, but the foul accusation against the
handsome stranger, whose image was associated in her mind
with the recollection of a few of the most happy hours of her
life, shocked and sickened her heart. Determined to listen
no longer to what she could not consider as any thing but
slander, unwilling to offend one whose schemes in relation to
herself had been mingled with a long series of valuable kind-
nesses, and dispirited by the afflicting troubles which seemed
to thicken in her path, and to add new embarrassments to her
situation, she now enjoined her friend to change the subject,
in tones of such pathetic supplication as left no room for
denial. They returned to the house, and Mrs. Lee soon after
took her leave.

To prevent further importunity on the subject which had
so greatly distressed her feelings, Miss Pendleton addressed
a note to Mrs. Lee on the following morning, informing that
lady of her intention to accompany her friends, the Mountfords, in their proposed journey to Kentucky, to which country
they were about to remove, and where Virginia had an uncle,
who had more than once invited her to accept a home under
his roof.

# CHAPTER VIII.

A FEW weeks subsequent to the transactions narrated in
the last chapter, a heavy travelling-carriage was seen
slowly winding its way among the mountains of the Allegheny
chain, drawn by a pair of tall horses, whose fine eyes and
muscular limbs bore testimony, to an experienced observer,
of excellent blood and gentle breeding, but who now tottered
along galled, raw-boned, and dispirited, from the effects of a
long journey. The heavily laden vehicle bore also incon-
testable marks of rough usage, and resembled in its appearance
a noble ship, which, having been dismantled in a storm, is
brought with difficulty into port. It had once been both
strong and costly, and was in truth one of the most elegant
of those cumbrous machines which were used by such of our
ancestors as were sufficiently wealthy to indulge in such luxuries, bearing a coat of arms upon its panels and being amply
decorated in the patrician taste of that day.

A journey over the Allegheny mountains, then inhabited
only at distant intervals, and whose best roads were mere
bridle-paths, beaten by the feet of pack-horses and occasionally
travelled with difficulty by wagons carrying merchandise,
had left to the shattered coach but few vestiges of its former
splendour. The tongue, which had been broken, was replaced
by the green stem of a young tree, hastily hewed out of the
forest for the purpose; a dislocation of one of the springs had
been remedied by passing a long stout pole underneath the
body of the carriage; and a shattered axletree, which had

been spliced repeatedly, bent and creaked under its load, as if every revolution of the wheels would be the last. In matters of less moment the havoc had been even greater. The curtains, by frequent and rather violent collision with the overhanging branches of the forest, had been rent and perforated in many places, and the straps within which they were usually furled, having been torn away, they now floated in the breeze in tattered fragments or flapped against the sides of the carriage like the sails of a vessel in a calm; while a bough had occasionally penetrated so far as to tear away the velvet lining and its gaudy fringe.

Two ladies, both of whom were young, and a female negro servant, occupied this weatherbeaten conveyance; accompanied, as every experienced reader will readily imagine, by a voluminous store of trunks, bandboxes, baskets, bags, and bundles. The husband of one of these ladies, a plain gentlemanly-looking man of five-and-twenty years of age, rode in advance of the cavalcade on horseback, encumbered with no other appendage than a brace of large pistols suspended across his saddle in a pair of holsters.

Then came a train of wagons, some drawn by horses and others by oxen, carrying household furniture, farming implements, and provisions. Behind these a drove of horses and cattle stretched along the mountain path, strolled lazily forward, halting frequently to drink at the clear rivulets which crossed the road, or straying off to graze wherever an inviting spot of green offered a few refreshing mouthfuls of herbage to the wearied animals. Mingled with the cavalcade or lagging in the rear, was a large company of negro servants, men, women, and children of every age, from helpless infancy to hoary decrepitude, whistling and singing and laughing as they went, inhaling with joy the mountain air, and luxuriating in the happy exchange of daily labour for the lighter toils of the road.

Such were the retinue and appearance of a wealthy planter

from Virginia, who was emigrating with all his family and
moveable property to the newly settled wilds of Kentucky,
and who bore no small resemblance to some ancient patriarch, travelling at the head of his dependants and herds, in
search of wider plains and fresher pastures than were afforded
in the land of his fathers. Mr. and Mrs. Mountford and the
unfortunate Miss Pendleton were the principal persons of the
party which we have attempted to describe, and whose adventures will occupy the remainder of this chapter.

They had passed nearly all the ridges of those formidable
mountains, and were now looking eagerly forward towards
the land of promise, and imagining every cliff that rose before
them to be the last. The day was drawing to a close when
they reached the summit of one of those numerous ridges
which compose the Allegheny chain, and halted for a few
moments to rest the animals who were panting and wearied
with the toilsome ascent. Looking forward, they beheld before them a deep valley, bounded on the opposite side by a
range of mountains as steep and as high as the one on whose
crest they were now reposing. Its sides were composed of a
series of perpendicular precipices of solid rock, clothed with
stinted pines, laurel, and other evergreens, and which at this
distance seemed to oppose an impassable barrier to the
further advance of the travellers. On more minute examination, parts of the road could be seen winding along the edge
of the cliffs, and surmounting the ascent by a variety of sharp
angles. A troop of pack-horses, with their large panniers,
were seen descending by this path, at a distance so great as
to render it barely possible to distinguish their forms and ascertain their character—sometimes stretched in an extended
line along the summits of the elevated parapets of rock, then
disappearing behind a projecting cliff or a copse of evergreen,
and again turning an abrupt angle, as if countermarching to
retrace their footsteps. The sun was now sinking behind the
western hills, and though still visible to our travellers, no

longer shone upon the eastern exposure of the mountain which they were contemplating, a circumstance which gave a still more shadowy appearance to the descending troop, whose regular array of slow-moving figures impressed upon the perpendicular sides of the cliffs, resembled the airy creations of a magic lantern, rather than the forms of living beings. Now they were seen traversing the extreme verge of some bold promontory, where the sunbeams flashed from the shining harness, and afforded a momentary disclosure of a variety of different colours, which again were blended into one dark mass as the cavalcade passed on into the deeper shades of the mountain glens. As they gazed, the silence was agreeably broken by the inspiring notes of the bugle, with which the .drivers cheered their lonesome way, and whose sprightly sounds echoed from hill to hill, sometimes faintly heard and sometimes bursting on the ear in full chorus, gave a tinge of wild romance to the scene.

From the contemplation of this prospect, their attention was drawn to the western side of the mountain on whose summit they stood, and whose declivities they were about to descend. Looking downward, they saw from their dizzy height a series of precipices, with bald sides and turreted and spiral crests, terminating in a dark valley, which seemed to be almost directly below their feet, although the distance was so great as to render it impossible to distinguish objects in the deep abyss. Here, as on the opposite side of the valley, the path wound from cliff to cliff, and from one natural terrace to another, like the angles of a winding staircase; but little of it was visible from the spot occupied by our travellers. In this direction the sound of voices was heard ascending and approaching nearer and nearer; and presently a large drove of cattle, conducted by several men, was seen winding along the base of the precipice on which the party stood, at a short distance from them, and where the terrace traversed by the road widened into a plain surface containing several acres. Here a sudden terror seized the cattle. The foremost of the animals halted and began to smell the ground with manifestations of violent agitation, and then uttered a low terrific yell. At this signal the whole herd, which had been loitering drowsily along, urged slowly forward by the voices of the drovers, rushed madly towards the spot, bellowing with every appearance of rage and affright. In vain the drivers attempted to force them onward. The largest and fiercest of the herd surrounded the place where the first had halted, roaring, pawing the ground, and driving their horns into the earth, while the others approached and retreated, bellowing in concert as if suddenly possessed by a legion of demons. Foaming at the mouth, their eyes gleaming with fury, and all their muscles strained into action, they seemed a different race from the quiet, inoffensive animals who but a few minutes before had been seen lazily toiling up the mountain-path. Those who were intimately acquainted with their habits at once pronounced that blood had recently been spilt in the road. With the assistance of Mr. Mountford's negroes, the alarmed herd was at length driven forward, but not until one of the drovers, in leaping his horse over a log, at some distance from the road, discovered the corpse of a man concealed behind it, and partly covered with leaves. An exclamation of surprise and horror announced this discovery, and drew the other drovers to the spot, where Mr. Mountford soon joined them. The body, which was that of a young gentleman, was marked with several wounds, which left little doubt that a murder had been committed.

However men may have been accustomed to danger or to scenes of violence, there is something in the crime of murder which never fails to alarm and shock them. Even where the injured party is a stranger, and no particular circumstances occur to awaken special sympathy for him or for those who may survive to mourn his fate, the dreadful act itself, stripped of all adventitious horrors, strikes a chill into the heart.

When such a scene is presented in the solitary wild, where the gloom of the forest and the silence of the desert are all around, and the quick breathing of the terrified spectator is whispered back by the woodland echo, a deeper shade of solemnity is thrown about the melancholy catastrophe. The busy crowds, the cares and levities of life, are not there, to call away the heart from the indulgence of natural emotions; it has leisure to contemplate undisturbed the cold image of death, and to reflect on the atrocities of man. Fancy spreads her wings and looks abroad in search of the perpetrator and the motive of the crime, and the absence of every trace which might lead to discovery or explanation involves the dark transaction in the shadows of mystery. The deceased seems to have been struck by some invisible hand, and a similar blow may be impending over the spectator, on whom the eye of the homicide may even now rest, as he meditates some new violence in the concealment of an adjacent thicket or the gloom of a neighbouring cavern.

Such were the meditations of some of the party who were collected around the body of the murdered stranger. A consultation was immediately held as to the course which ought to be pursued, when it was arranged that a party should remain with the corpse, while an express was sent to the nearest settlement to apprize the legal authorities of the outrage. Both of these duties were cheerfully undertaken by the drovers, with the assistance of Mr. Mountford's servants. The latter gentleman resumed his journey, and on reaching the bosom of the valley, and learning that his road still lay through an uninhabited wilderness for many miles, determined to encamp here for the night.

It was an inviting spot. Though surrounded by mountains as savage and sterile as the imagination can well conceive, the glen in which the party rested was beautiful and fertile. The rich soil was covered with a luxuriant growth of forest trees and shrubbery. The sunbeams, which during the

day had been reflected from the bare rocks and silicious sands
of the mountain, afflicting the eyesight of the travellers by
their intense brilliancy or overcoming them with excessive
heat, were now intercepted by the tall summits of the ridges
lying towards the west. The foliage was fresh and green, and
a delightful coolness pervaded the atmosphere. A wide, clear
rivulet, meandering through the valley, imparted an agreeable
moisture to the air, and invited the thirsty herds to its brink,
while it afforded more than one luxury and convenience to
the travellers. By the margin of the stream, on a spot trodden hard by the feet of successive travellers, who had been
accustomed to encamp here, and covered with a short green
sward, the cavalcade of carriers had halted and were unlading
their pack-horses; and Mr. Mountford, passing on, chose a
similar place on the farther side of the rivulet. The arrangements for encamping were soon made. Two large tents were
taken from the wagons and pitched for the accommodation of
Miss Pendleton and her friends, on a plain of table-land near
the brink of the water-course. In the rear of these, smaller
tents, composed of coarser materials, were arranged for the
sable troop of dependants. A large fire was kindled upon
the ground, and the servants began to prepare a substantial
meal for the hungry party.

4*

# CHAPTER IX.

HAVING seen the tents pitched, the horses and cattle turned out to graze, and every necessary arrangement made for spending the night in as much comfort as circumstances would admit, Mr. Mountford, invited by the refreshing coolness of the evening and the beauty of the scenery, proposed to the ladies a stroll upon the bank of the stream. They wandered slowly along, following its meanders for a short time, until its serpentine course brought them nearly opposite to the point from which they had set out; and they found themselves on a projecting point which overlooked the pack-horse camp, and placed them within a few yards of its noisy inmates, from whom they were concealed by a clump of underbrush. The horses had been unharnessed and were now grazing at large; the packs of merchandise which formed their lading were piled up together and covered with canvass. The men had thrown themselves lazily on the grass, except two or three, who were wrestling and playing with a degree of hilarity which showed how little they were affected by the toils of the journey.

At this moment the party was joined by a horseman, who addressed them with the frankness of an acquaintance, though he was obviously a stranger to them all. He was a young man, dressed in a hunting-shirt, carrying a rifle on his shoulder, and having all the equipments of a western hunter. His limbs were as stout and his face as sunburnt as those of the rough men around him, but neither his appearance nor carriage indicated a person accustomed to coarse labour. He had the plainness of speech and manner which showed that his breeding had not been in the polished circle, mingled with the freedom and ease of one accustomed to hunting and martial exercises. He threw himself from his horse, leaving the bridle dangling on the neck of the animal, who quietly awaited his pleasure, and seated himself among the carriers with the air of one who felt that he was welcome, or who cared but little whether he was welcome or not. His dress, though coarse and soiled, was neatly fitted, and adapted to show off his person to the best advantage, and all his appendages were those of a young man who had some pride in his appearance. His features, though not handsome, were lively and intelligent; indicating a cheerful disposition, a good opinion of his fellow-men, and an equally good opinion of himself, arising, no doubt, out of his republican principles, which would not allow him to place himself below the level of others. There was a boldness in his eye, a fluency of speech, and a forwardness in his whole deportment, which, without approaching to impudence, gave a dashing air to his conduct, and a freshness to his conversation. His horse seemed much fatigued, and from his saddle hung the hinder quarter of a deer recently killed.

"Gentlemen, good evening," said he, as he dismounted, "this has been a powerful hot day."

"Very sultry," replied one of the carriers.

"No two ways about that," said the hunter; "there's as good a piece of horse-flesh, to his size, as ever crooked a pastern, and as fast a nag as can be started, for any distance from a quarter up to four miles; but this day has pretty nearly used him up."

"You seem to have been hunting."

"Why, yes; I have been taking a little tower among the mountains here. I have just killed a fine deer, and as I felt sort o' lonesome, I turned into the big road, in hopes of meeting with a traveller to help me eat it."

This offer was, of course, well received; the venison was sent to the fire, and the stranger prepared to encamp with his new acquaintance.

The quick eye of the hunter was now attracted to two of the youngest of the company, who were engaged in a *tussle*, an exercise common among our western youth, and far superior to wrestling or boxing, as it requires greater skill and activity, and is far less savage than either of those ancient games. The object of each party is to throw his adversary to the ground, and to retain his advantage by holding him down until the victory shall be decided; and as there are no rules to regulate the game, each exerts his strength and skill in any manner which his judgment may dictate, using force or artifice according to circumstances. The two persons who now approached each other seemed each to be intent on grappling with his adversary in such a manner as to gain an advantage at the outset. At first, each eluded the grasp of the other, advancing, retreating, seizing, or shaking each other off, and each using every artifice in his power to secure an advantage in the manner of grappling with his opponent. Then they grasped at arm's-length, and tried each other's strength by pushing, pulling, and whirling round, testing the muscular powers of the arm and the nimbleness of the foot to the utmost. Finally they became closely interlocked, their bodies in contact, and their limbs twined, wrestling with all their powers, and after an arduous struggle came together to the ground, amidst the shouts and laughter of the spectators. But the struggle was not over; for now a fierce contest ensued, in which each endeavoured to get uppermost, or to hold his antagonist to the ground. Their muscular strength and flexibility of limb seemed now almost miraculous. Sometimes the person who was undermost fairly rolled over and over his adversary, and sometimes he

raised himself by main strength, with his opponent still
clinging to him, and renewed the struggle on foot; and often
their bodies were twisted together and their limbs interlocked until every muscle and sinew were strained, and it
was difficult to tell which was uppermost. At last their
breathing grew short, the violence of the exercise produced
exhaustion, and one of the parties relaxing his efforts, enabled
the other to claim the victory. The tired parties, dripping
with perspiration, ceased the contest in perfect good-humour.

"You must not tussle with me no more, Bill," said the
victor; "you see you ain't no part of a priming to me."

"That's very well," cried the other, eyeing his comrade
with perfect complacency; "I like to see you have a good
opinion of yourself. If I didn't let you win once in a while
to encourage you, I could never get a chance to have no fun
out of you."

It was now perceived that while the attention of the company was fixed upon the sport, another stranger had joined
them. He cautiously pushed aside the thick brushwood
behind the merry circle, threw a quick jealous glance upon
the party, and then advancing with circumspection, halted in
the rear, and remained for a while unnoticed. When the
contest which we have described was over, the eyes of the
whole party fell on the intruder. His appearance was too
striking not to rivet attention. In size he towered above the
ordinary stature, his frame was bony and muscular, his breast
broad, his limbs gigantic. His clothing was uncouth and
shabby, his exterior weatherbeaten and dirty, indicating continual exposure to the elements, and pointing out this singular
person as one who dwelt far from the habitations of men, and
who mingled not in the courtesies of civilized life. He was
completely armed, with the exception of a rifle, which seemed
to have only been laid aside for a moment, for he carried the
usual powder-horn and pouch of the backwoodsman. A
broad leathern belt, drawn closely round his waist, supported

a large and a smaller knife and a tomahawk.   But that
which attracted the gaze of all the company into which he
had intruded, was the bold and ferocious countenance of the
new comer, and its strongly marked oppression of villainy.
His face, which was larger than ordinary, exhibited the lines
of ungovernable passion, but the complexion announced that
the ordinary feelings of the human breast were extinguished,
and instead of the healthy hue which indicates the social
emotions, there was a livid, unnatural redness, resembling
that of a dried and lifeless skin.   The eye was fearless and
steady, but it was also artful and audacious, glaring upon the
beholder with an unpleasant fixedness and brilliancy, like that
of a ravenous animal gloating upon its prey, and concen-
trating all its malignity into one fearful glance.   He wore no
covering on his head, and the natural protection of thick
coarse hair, of a fiery redness, uncombed and matted, gave
evidence of long exposure to the rudest visitations of the
sunbeam and the tempest.   He seemed some desperate outlaw, an unnatural enemy of his species, destitute of the nobler
sympathies of human nature, and prepared at all points for
assault or defence, who in some freak of daring insolence had
intruded himself into the society of men, to brave their
resentment or to try the effect which his presence might
occasion.

Although there was something peculiarly suspicious and
disagreeable in the appearance of this stranger, there was
nothing to excite alarm or to call for the expression of any
disapprobation.   He was armed like other men of that frontier region, and the road was a public highway, frequented by
people of various character and condition.   Still there was a
shrinking and a silent interchange of glances among the
carriers on discovering his silent and almost mysterious
intrusion ; one whispered, "What does that fellow want ?"
and another muttered, "Keep a red eye out, boys—that chap
is not too good to steal."   The young hunter who had just

joined them was not of the kind of mettle to sit still on such an occasion. He jumped up, and addressing their visitor in a blithe, frank tone, said, " Good evening, stranger."

The person addressed turned his eye deliberately towards the speaker, and returned his salutation with a nod, without opening his lips.

" Travelling, stranger?"

" Yes," replied the other. The sound of his voice, even in uttering this monosyllable, was cold and repulsive, and any other than a resolute inquirer would have pursued the dialogue no further. But the young Kentuckian was not so easily repulsed.

" Which way? if it's a fair question," continued he.

" West," was the laconic reply.

" That fellow's mouth goes off like a gun with a rusty lock," said the hunter aside; then addressing him again, " To Kentucky, eh? well, that's right—there's plenty of room there—game enough, and a powerful chance of good living. No two ways about that. Come from old Virginia, I suppose?"

The stranger, instead of answering this question, turned his head in another direction, as if he had not heard it, stepped a few paces off, as if about to retire, and then again halted and faced the party.

" No, I'll be d'rot if ever that chap came out of old Virginny," muttered the young man aside, " they don't raise such humans in the Old Dominion, no how. I'll see what he is made of, however."

Then winking at his companions he approached the stranger, and taking a penknife from his pocket presented it to him with a civil bow. The stranger was not to be taken by surprise. He received the knife, looked at it and at the donor inquiringly, as if he would have said, " What means this?" and then coolly put it in his pocket without saying a word. His tormentor did not leave him in doubt.

"It is a rule in our country," said he, "when a man is remarkably ugly, to make him a present of a knife. Keep that, if you please, stranger, till you meet with a homelier human than yourself, and then give it to him."

This practical joke would, in some countries, have been considered as a quiz; in Kentucky it was a kind of challenge, which the receiver might have honourably avoided by joining in the laugh, or which, on the other hand, gave him ample cause to crack his heels together, and assert that he was not only the handsomest, but the *best man* in company; which assertion, if concluded, as the lawyers say, with a versification, would have been tantamount to calling for "pistols for two." The stranger did neither, but pocketed the knife and the affront, and quietly turned to walk away

To a brave man nothing causes more painful regret than to have given an unprovoked affront to one who is unable or unwilling to resent it. Had the stranger shown the slightest inclination to take up the gauntlet which had been thrown to him, the young Kentuckian, who viewed him with intuitive dislike, would probably have challenged him to instant combat, and have engaged him with the ferocity of a hungry brute; but no sooner did the latter discover that the person he addressed neither relished his joke nor was disposed to resent it, than his generous nature prompted him to make instant atonement.

"Look here, stranger," he exclaimed, drawing a flask of spirits from his pocket, and offering it; "you are a droll sort of a white man; you won't talk, nor laugh, nor quarrel—will you drink? Take a drop, and let us be friends."

This appeal was not in vain. The uncouth man of the woods took the flask, raised it silently to his lips, and drained the whole of its contents, amounting to nearly a pint, without stopping to breathe; then placing one hand on the shoulder of the young man, and leaning towards him, he said, in a low voice, "We shall meet again," at the same time grasping the handle of his long knife and casting a look of defiance at the whole party. Whether he intended to strike is doubtful, for the young man, stepping back, stood on his guard, looking at his adversary with an undaunted eye, while the carriers started to their feet, prepared to defend him. In another moment the stranger had turned, and dashing into the thicket, disappeared.

"Well, if that ain't a droll chicken, I'm mistaken," exclaimed the Kentuckian. "I say, gentlemen, the way that fellow takes his brandy is curious. He is not of the right breed of dogs, no how. There's no two ways about that."

Before any further remark could be made, the attention of the party was arrested by an exclamation of terror from a female voice ; the cause of which shall be explained in the next chapter.

## CHAPTER X.

MISS PENDLETON had left the place of her nativity under a melancholy depression of spirits. Reared in affluence, the favourite and only object of affection of a kind guardian, surrounded by friends, followed by a train of admirers, and accustomed to every indulgence, the sudden reverse of her fortunes afflicted her heart with keen anguish. She was too high-minded to mourn with unavailing regret over the blight of those advantages which merely elevated her above her companions. The truly generous mind estimates the gifts of fortune at something like their real value. But the loss of the dearly loved guardian of her youth, and the dreadful catastrophe which produced that melancholy bereavement, deeply touched her heart, and awakened all her sensibilities.

The measure of her grief seemed to be full; but when she came to the resolution of quitting the scenes of her childhood and parting with her early friends, she found that her heart had still room for other afflictions, and she left her native land sorrowing and bowed down in spirit. Possessed, however, of a strong intellect and a buoyant temper, the exercise of travelling, the change of scene, and the kindness of her companions, if they did not diminish her sorrows, rendered them supportable. By degrees her mind began to assume its natural tone, and she reflected more calmly on the scenes through which she had lately passed. In these reveries the

image of Fennimore continually presented itself. His visit
seemed to be intimately yet strangely connected with the
death of her uncle. She had heard enough of the circumstances which we have detailed to know that it had relation
to a pecuniary claim against the estate of Major Heyward,
but knew nothing of its justice, extent, or character. Mrs.
Lee had spoken of it as a demand which would absorb the
whole of her venerable relative's vast fortune, and which placed
the claimant in the position of a competitor with herself, and
had thrown out imputations against his integrity of the dark-
est import. On the other hand, she remembered that he had
been received not only with the hospitality extended to all
visitors at Walnut Hill, but with affectionate cordiality. Her
uncle, who was a man of excellent discernment, had treated
him with the confidence of friendship, and she was slow to
believe either that he was deceived in the character of his
guest, or that he had professed a show of kindness which he
did not feel. Mr. Fennimore's appearance and manners were
highly prepossessing; there was especially about him a
frankness and manly dignity which could hardly be deceptive.
She passed in review the agreeable hours of his short visit,
and a flush of maiden pride mantled her cheek as she recollected his earnest yet respectful attentions, and confessed that
of all the homage which she had received in the triumph of
beauty, none had ever been so acceptable as that of this
handsome and gallant soldier. We have little faith in the
romantic doctrine of love at first sight, but on the other hand
we cannot think it strange that an intelligent and susceptible
woman should readily draw a distinction between the com-
monplace civilities of ordinary men, or the silly gallantries
of mere witless beaux, and the enlightened preference of a
gentleman of taste and judgment, nor that she should feel
flattered by an appearance of partiality from such a source.
She was at an age when the heart is feelingly alive to the
tender sensations, and it would have been singular if she had

not become interested in a modest and highly-gifted man, so
nearly of her own years and condition, who had been her
companion for several days; nor would it have been natural
for one so accustomed as herself to the attentions of the other
sex, to mistake the effect which her own attractions had produced on the mind of the agreeable stranger.  Then the
ready gallantry with which he risked his own life to rescue
her from the flames, and his courageous efforts to save her
uncle—these, though she never spoke of them, awakened a
sentiment of gratitude which she felt could never be effaced.
Again, when she recalled the circumstances under which he
left the neighbourhood of Walnut Hill, without any explanation to the friends of Major Heyward of the object of his
visit, and without leaving any message for herself, his conduct
seemed incomprehensible, and strangely at variance with
what she supposed to be his character.  But these mysterious
circumstances, although they excited momentary doubts, and
sometimes awakened a slight glow of resentment, only served
in the end to render Mr. Fennimore more interesting to Miss
Pendleton; for without inferring, as some ill-natured persons
would do, that the mind of woman is made up of contra-
dictions, it is enough to say that she exercised her ingenuity
in imagining a variety of *possible* explanations, by which his
conduct might be placed in a favourable light and his character exalted, until she persuaded herself that such develop-
ments *would* undoubtedly be made in due time.

Mrs. Mountford, although she had never seen Mr. Fennimore, had made up her mind that he was an impostor; a
mere fortune-hunter, who had visited Walnut Hill in the
prosecution of some desperate scheme against the person and
fortune of her fair friend.  Without having any definite ideas
of that plan, or being able to trace its connection with subsequent events, she was charitable enough to attribute the
catastrophe which had marred the fortunes of Virginia to this
source, and spoke of Fennimore as little less than an incen-

diary. Perhaps there might have been policy in this; for discovering that Virginia always defended her uncle's visitor with some spirit, she often introduced the subject for the sole purpose of disturbing her reveries, and awakening her mind from the apathy into which it seemed to be sinking. In these discussions Miss Pendleton, with her usual frankness, recapitulated all the evidence in favour of Mr. Fennimore, with some of the arguments which her own ingenuity had suggested, and thus became accustomed to defend his character. After all, there was but one argument which had any weight with the pertinacious Mrs. Mountford; it was the same which had appealed so forcibly to the genuine Virginian feeling of Colonel Antler, namely, "that a gentleman would not commit arson." "If he is really a gentleman, my dear," was Mrs. Mountford's usual conclusion, "that settles the question; but how few of those do we find north of the Potomac? and this Mr. Fennimore, you know, did not pretend to have been born in the Old Dominion."

The unexpected discovery of a murdered body in the road had deeply affected our heroine, and had led her thoughts back to the most melancholy events in her own history. She was this evening unusually depressed, and it was in the hope of diverting her reflections into some other channel that her friends, though much fatigued, had proposed the walk which led them to the vicinity of the pack-horse camp, and had been induced to linger, the concealed witnesses of the rude scene which was there enacted.

The events which we have described arrested her attention. It had so happened, however, that she stood in such a position as not to see the face of the person whose appearance caused so much curiosity, until the moment of his drawing his knife, when a movement of his body brought him full before her, and to her utter dismay she recognised the same savage countenance which she had discovered at her window on the night of the conflagration! Her alarm and agitation may be easily conceived. An involuntary expression of horror burst from her lips, which drew the attention not only of her own friends, but of the party on the opposite side of the stream. With some exertion she resumed her self-command, and returned immediately to the camp. She had heretofore described to Mr. Mountford the apparition which had so greatly terrified her on the occasion above alluded to, and that gentleman as well as others had supposed that she had been deceived by her imagination. But now, on her repeating that incident, the description which she gave of the supposed incendiary corresponded so completely with that of the remarkable person they had seen, as to leave little doubt of the identity of the one with the other; and he hastened to the encampment of the carriers to acquaint them with his suspicions and procure assistance to arrest the stranger. Their services were offered with alacrity, and all the adjacent coverts were carefully examined, but night coming on, any extensive search was impracticable.

Virginia spent a miserable night. In addition to the afflicting recollections that had previously depressed her mind, the events of the day had suggested a new and dreadful train of thought. Might not the unfortunate person whose remains had been found concealed by the mountain-path have been one in whom she felt an interest which she could not conceal from herself? She had not seen the body, and the friend for whose safety she now trembled was unknown to Mr. Mountford. She knew that Mr. Fennimore was on his way to the western frontier when he called at Walnut Hill—his presence there on the night of the conflagration had probably defeated to some extent the designs of the incendiary—and now a young gentleman, whose description answered too well with his, was found murdered in the very path that he had taken. She had seen the murderer of her lamented uncle; and circumstances had occurred to render it not unlikely that the same terrible assassin had waylaid Mr. Fennimore and was now tracking her own footsteps! A dreadful mystery seemed to hang over her fate. In vain did she endeavour to find some clue to these dark transactions. Major Heyward had been the most inoffensive of men; she herself had no enemy, and why should she, now an unprotected and penniless orphan, be thus persecuted? These thoughts tormented her already agitated mind and drove sleep from her pillow.

Miss Pendleton occupied a tent containing her own bed and that of a negro maid-servant. Mr. Mountford's negro train were accustomed to spend their evenings in those festivities to which the whole of that careless race are so much addicted. They had now collected a great pile of logs, whose blaze illuminated the camping ground, and threw a brilliant glare for some distance into the surrounding forest. A gray-haired fiddler, whose musical abilities had contributed to the amusement of several successive generations of the Mountfords—white and black—sat on a log scraping his merry violin, while his sable comrades danced on the green. Happy in the absence of all care, and under the protection of an indulgent master who had grown up from childhood among them, and was endeared to them by the ties of long association and the interchange of kindness known only to those who are acquainted with the relation of master and servant, these thoughtless beings gave themselves up entirely to merriment. They had no property to care for, no want to supply, no peril in anticipation to excite their fears, no speculation in their eye to poison the enjoyment of the present moment; and although undergoing the fatigue of a toilsome march, their eyeballs glistened, their sable cheeks shone, and their snow-white teeth became visible at the first note of the fiddle. Seated in a circle round the blazing log-heap, they ate their rations, told merry tales of "Old Virginny," and then joining in the dance capered with as much vigour and agility as if their whole bodies were made upon springs and muscles, while streams of perspiration rolled from their shin ing visages. At length that part of the accompaniment, to which, not being a musician, I am unable to give a scientific Italian name, but which consists in certain drowsy nods and comfortable naps, on the part of the artist, interpolate between the tunes, and spreading off like the shading of a picture, so as to mingle insensibly with the brighter and gayer parts of the performance, began to preponderate; the heavy eyelids of the musician were raised less frequently and with a duller motion, the elbow lost its elasticity, the sable belles crawled away one by one to their pallets, and the hilarity of the night died away into a profound silence.

Our heroine, however, did not share the contagious drowsiness. She remained in a feverish state of excitement, sometimes wrapped for a few moments in abstracted thought, as ruminating on the past, and sometimes endeavouring to banish reflection, by listening with an ear acutely alive to the slightest sound. As the vociferous notes of merriment died away, other tones more congenial with her frame of mind invaded the silence of the night. The atmosphere was clear and chill; not a breath shook the trees or disturbed the repose of the valley. The murmuring of the rivulet, scarcely perceptible during the day, now fell distinctly and pleasantly on the ear. An occasional and distant tinkling was heard at intervals, by the bells attached to the cattle and carriers' horses. "The wolf's long howl," reverberating from cliff to cliff, was answered by the bark of the travellers' dogs; but even these sounds ceased when the faithful animals sought repose by their masters' sides. The owl hooted from her solitary den; and once, when every other voice was hushed, and nature seemed to repose in death-like stillness, a huge tree, probably a majestic pine, which had braved the mountain storm for ages, fell on the ground with a terrific crash, which re-echoed from rock to rock, and from one cavern to another, rolling along the valley like the prolonged reiterations of thunder or a continuous discharge of artillery. The scared owl shouted in alarm, the dogs rushed howling from their beds, the wolf renewed his savage complaint, and again all was silent.

Miss Pendleton, exhausted by a variety of contending emotions, at last sunk into a feverish slumber, from which she was awakened by a slight noise. She raised her head, and the strong light still brightly reflected from the expiring fires upon the white canvass, enabled her to see distinctly the figure of a man at the entrance of the tent; his head—that dreadful head, so strongly pictured upon her memory—already protruded within the opening, and one hand, which grasped a knife, was employed in cutting a number of strong cords by which the entrance was closed. She uttered a loud scream, but the villain, nothing daunted, continued his efforts, cutting and tearing the slight obstacles, with a violence which showed a determination to accomplish his dreadful purpose at all hazards. Accident, aided perhaps by the confusion of guilt, delayed him for a moment; his feet became entangled in some harness carelessly thrown before the tent: the screams of Virginia roused the watch-dogs; Mr. Mountford seized his pistols and hastened to her relief, while the foiled assassin hastily retreated, leaping nimbly over every obstacle, pushing aside the bushes with gigantic strength, and disappearing in the gloom of the forest.

5

# CHAPTER XI.

TWO days after the occurrence of the events detailed in the last chapter, the inhabitants of the little village of Stanford, in Lincoln county, Kentucky, were surprised by the appearance in their streets of a singular group of travellers. Although emigrants of various descriptions were continually passing through this place to the newer settlements, lying still farther to the west, there was something about this party which attracted universal attention. The leader of the cavalcade was the ferocious individual who has already been more than once brought under the notice of the reader. He was, as before, bare-headed, and carried on his shoulder a long rifle, while his belt supported two knives, a pistol, and a tomahawk. Without turning to the right or left, and scarcely appearing to notice objects around him, he moved forward along the middle of the street with a firm and rapid step and an air of audacious defiance. Yet a close observer might have noticed, that although he neither turned his head, nor seemed to regard those who passed near him, his fierce eye rolled rapidly from side to side with suspicious watchfulness. Behind him followed three women, two of whom were sun-burnt, coarse, and wretchedly attired, and the other somewhat more delicate and better dressed. The females led two horses, almost broken down with fatigue, on whose backs were packed a few cooking utensils, an axe, several guns, some blankets, and a small quantity of provisions. Three or four half-naked children, wild, sallow, and hungry-looking, with small fierce eyes, glancing timidly about, followed next; and lastly came a man, smaller in size than him who led the party, but similarly armed, having the same suspicious exterior, and a countenance equally fierce and sinister. The deportment of all the individuals of this company was that of persons who considered themselves in a hostile or an alien country, and who, accustomed to the apprehension of danger, stood ready to evade by flight, or resist even to death, any assault which might be made on them. Even their dog, a thievish-looking cur, resembling a wolf in looks and action, stole along with a stealthy tread, his tail drooped, and his malignant eye scowling watchfully around. Their determination seemed to be to proceed rapidly on without halting; but when they had passed the most populous part of the village, and had nearly reached its farther limit, they stopped, apparently for the purpose of procuring some article of which they stood in need. The leader proceeded to a small shop, while the rest of the party stood in the middle of the road, exposed to the burning rays of the sun, and showing no inclination either to seek shelter or to hold intercourse with the inhabitants.

At this moment a different scene was presented in the other end of the village. A horseman, mounted on a foaming steed, covered with dust, came spurring in at full speed, and dismounted at the house of one of the principal inhabitants, who was also a magistrate. He had brought tidings of the murder committed in the mountains, and had traced the supposed perpetrators to this place. Without disclosing his business to any other person, he sought a private interview with the magistrate; and in a few minutes a plan was prepared for the arrest of the suspected persons. Intelligence was secretly and rapidly passed from house to house, and the hardy villagers, accustomed to arm hastily for war, sallied forth with their rifles and tomahawks, and dividing themselves into small parties, came so suddenly upon the supposed mur-

derers, that it was equally impossible for them to resist or
escape.  They expressed neither surprise nor fear, neither the
shame of guilt nor the courage of conscious innocence, but
submitted to their captors in sullen insolence.  Some articles
were found in their possession, and a variety of facts proved,
which rendered their guilt so probable as to justify their com-
mitment for further examination.

At that early period in the history of our country, jails
were neither abundant nor particularly well adapted for the
safe keeping of prisoners.  There was none at Stanford, and
it became necessary to send the culprits to Danville, where a
wholesome institution of this kind had been provided.  The
men were therefore placed under the charge of a party of
armed citizens and marched off, while the women and children, who were left at liberty, followed at their leisure.  The
escort rested that night at the house of a farmer, a comfortable log cabin, in one apartment of which the prisoners,
securely tied, were placed, under the charge of two sentinels,
while the rest of the guard threw themselves down to repose
on the floor of the same room.  Here I must introduce a new
character, who came on the scene at this place.

Hercules Short, or, as he was more frequently called,
Hark Short, was the only son of a poor widow, whose miserable cottage stood on the borders of an extensive swamp in
North Carolina.  It was a wretched abode, consisting of a
single apartment, plentifully supplied with crevices, which
admitted the light of heaven, and gave free access to the
balmy airs of spring as well as the rude blasts of winter.
On three sides it was surrounded by a range of barren ridges
covered with a stinted growth of evergreens.  In front was
a dismal swamp filled with huge trees, whose great trunks
supported a dense canopy of foliage, which excluded the rays
of the sun from the gloomy mass of turbid waters that covered the earth.  An undergrowth of tall weeds and rank
grass, nourished by the fertilizing ooze, but deprived of the

light and warmth of the sunbeam, shot up into a sickly and dropsical luxuriance. Here the moccasin-snake might be seen gliding over the roots of the melancholy cypress, or exposing his loathsome form on the decaying trunk of a fallen tree. Here the tuneful frogs held nightly concerts, astonishing the hearer by the loudness and variety, if not by the melody, of their voices. This, too, was the favourite haunt of that musical and valiant insect, the musquito, whose thirst for human blood is so distressing to all persons of tender feelings. The bear, too, loved to wander and repose in these solitudes, wading with delight among the flags and rushes of the ponds, in search of tender buds, or snoring securely in the hollow of a tree, where the sound of a human footstep never disturbed his pleasant slumbers. His neighbour, the owl, sometimes kept bad hours, screeching her untimely song at mid-day, when all discreet brutes should be sleeping; but this he had learned to consider as a pleasant serenade.

Other innocent and playful animals tenanted these shades, but the spectator who should have visited them at an hour while the sun was above the horizon, would scarcely have believed that any living thing existed here. All around him would be motionless and silent. Even the humid atmosphere seemed here to have lost its elasticity and power of circulation. One animated being alone might occasionally be seen winding his way through the morass, with the stealthy tread of the midnight prowler. It was a youth, whose slender and emaciated form of dwarfish height seemed a living personification of hunger. His diminutive skeleton was covered with a skin sallowed by the humid damps, and imbrowned by exposure. His gait was slow, from caution as well as from indolence. His features were stolid, and the muscles of his face as immovable as if nature had denied them the power of expressing passion or emotion. A small gray eye alone, moving warily in its socket, and continually glancing from side to side, with the watchfulness of apprehension, indicated the existence of feelings common to the human animal. He was bare-headed and bare-footed; his tangled hair seemed never to have known the discipline of a comb; while his coarse and torn garments, which certainly performed no useful or agreeable office in relation to the comfort of his body, might have been worn in deference to the customs of his species; and this was probably the only instance in which he complied so far with the prejudices of society as to identify himself as a member of the human family.

This promising young gentleman was Mr. Hark Short, the boy of the swamp, and the heir of the pleasant cabin described above. His father had, from necessity or choice, found it convenient to select a retired country residence; and after his demise the widow, whose love of solitude seemed congenial with that of her lord, continued to inhabit the family mansion. The earliest employment of our hero was to gather for his mother the pine-knots, which not only constitute the fuel of that country, but are the most fashionable substitutes for spermaceti candles; his first amusement in life was to spear frogs and rob birds' nests. His ambition, however, soon rose above these humble pursuits, and before he was twelve years old he took to killing snakes, hunting opossums, catching fish, and finding wild pigs in the woods. His practice in relation to pigs was a little remarkable. The farmers in that country suffer their hogs to run at large in the woods, paying them little attention except that of marking the ears of each generation of pigs while in their infancy, so that each owner may be able to distinguish his property. Our friend Hark, well aware of this practice, and of the care with which the farmers performed it, whenever an increase in their swinish families rendered it expedient, reasoned plausibly enough that every pig which was not marked must be common property, or, as he expressed it, *a wild varment*, subject to be converted to the individual use of any one who should first appropriate it to himself. Whether he inferred this doctrine from the principles of natural law, or practised it as an instinct, is not important, and could not now be precisely ascertained. We deal only in facts, and the truth is, that although Hark never acquired a pig either by descent or purchase, he made it a rule to place his own mark in the ear of every juvenile animal of this species which he found unmarked in the woods. Whenever the maternal care of a female swine, wilder or more cunning than usual, induced her to hide her litter in some unfrequented covert of the woods, or in some solitary islet of the swamp, inaccessible to the owner's search, or when any unfortunate orphan strayed from the herd and escaped the owner's eye, Hark was sure to find them. His dexterity in accomplishing this feat was remarkable. He would lie at the root of a tree watching a herd for hours; but no sooner were the grunters nestled in their beds of leaves than Hawk commenced operations, crawling towards them with a noiseless and almost imperceptible motion, until he could place his remorseless hand upon an innocent pig, who never dreamt of being marked until the knife was at his ear, while the left hand of the dexterous Hark grasped the snout with such skill as to stifle the cries of the affrighted animal. A whole litter would thus pass through his hands in the course of a short time.

If any should be so squeamish as to object to the propriety of this mode of gaining a livelihood, we must urge in its extenuation the same apology which is considered as sufficient in most of the ordinary transactions of life, and especially in reference to its pecuniary concerns,—that of necessity. Hark had been raised a gentleman, that is to say, he had never been taught to work; he had no fancy for agricultural pursuits, and the barren sands around his mother's cabin were ill suited to that employment. He therefore necessarily resorted to the woods for a support, where he sometimes shot a deer; but although he handled a rifle well, he disliked its use; the labour of carrying the weapon was

irksome to one of his gentlemanly nature, and the noise of its
report particularly uncongenial with his habits of privacy
and meditative turn of mind. Besides, gunpowder and lead
cost money, which is not to be picked up every day in the
swamps of North Carolina. And why should not marking a
pig be considered as respectable as gambling, or as honest as
overreaching a neighbour in a bargain? Hark could see no
difference. He knew little, of course, of morality; but an
intuitive greatness of mind induced him, early in life, to
adopt the magnanimous rule of the Spartan, which attached
no shame to any act, except that of doing it so awkwardly as
to be detected. Hark had no ambition to make a noise in
the world, but on the contrary shrunk habitually from observation and courted the society of his own thoughts. Like
many great men, he seemed to have discovered that ingenuity
is a nobler quality than brute force and that discretion
is the better part of valour. His mother's table, therefore,
was tolerably well supplied with game, consisting entirely of
the flesh of animals that might be taken without labour or
insnared by art. In the spring he caught fish, in the autumn
he shook the stupid opossum from the persimmon trees and
pawpaw bushes, and during the rest of the year he took—
whatever chance threw in his way. Sometimes the weather
was inclement, and nothing stirred in the woods but the
creaking bough or the trembling leaf, and sometimes Hark,
who like other persons of genius had his dark days of despondency and lassitude, was disinclined to hunt, and he and
Dame Short were reduced to short allowance; but they were
used to this, and it was marvellous to see with what resignation they could starve. They polished the bones which they
had picked before, and when this resource was exhausted,
passed whole days without eating, the goodwife croaking over
the fire with a short black pipe in her mouth, and Hark
nestling in his pallet, like some hybernating animal who sleeps
away the long months of winter.

Solitary as was the life of Hark, it was not passed without amusement. Every intelligent mind is apt to become addicted to some pursuit, which soon grows into a master passion of the soul; and although we can hardly conceive that the practice of cruelty could ever afford enjoyment, yet, strange as it may seem, it is no less true, that *destructiveness* has been strongly developed in men of the most magnanimous souls. From Nimrod, the "mighty hunter," down to Black Hawk, the Sac warrior, the magnates of the earth have ever taken great delight in killing animals and cutting the throats of their fellow-men. Setting down this remarkable thirst for blood as one of the undoubted attributes of high ambition, we see no reason why Hark should not be ranked with "Macedonia's madman and the Swede."

The bent of his genius lay particularly towards the killing of reptiles. With a slight spear, formed of a pointed stick or slender cane, he would sit for hours by a pond, transfixing every frog which showed its head above the surface of the water, or with a great switch in his hand, lie in wait for lizards by the decaying trunk of some great fallen tree. But his soul panted for higher exploits than these. He entertained a special antipathy for snakes, and like Hannibal vowed eternal enmity against the whole race. Nothing delighted him so much as to encounter a serpent, no matter to what variety it belonged, the intrepid rattlesnake, the lurking copper-head, the insidious viper, or the harmless black snake; he no sooner beheld his enemy than he prepared for battle with the eagerness of an amateur and the skill of an experienced gladiator. A martial hatred flashed from his eye, and his swarthy visage, flushed with a chivalrous intrepidity, assumed an unwonted animation. His mode of proceeding on such occasions was perhaps a little singular, for, either to show his contempt for the reptile, or his indifference to danger, or because he thought it the most scriptural plan of bruising his adversary's head, he invariably jumped upon the crawling animal with both his feet, and trampled it to death.

The world went quietly along with Hark until he approached his eighteenth year, when several untoward events occurred to mar his felicity. In childhood he had been an honest boy, with a character perfectly unblemished except by certain little improprieties, such as sucking eggs or milking the neighbours' cows when he found them grazing in the swamps; and it was thought that the undue severity of the farmers in flogging him for these little frailties of his nature caused him to grow up with the shy and misanthropic habits for which he was so remarkable. But as he became older his large herd of swine began to attract attention; the farmers, who believed in the adage of the civil law, *partus sequitur*, &c., which means in plain English that the offspring belong to the owner of the mother, began to complain that the descendants of their hogs were passing frequently into the possession of Hark the snake-killer and threatened him with the visitation of Lynch's law; indeed, it is rumoured that he was actually arraigned before a tribunal exercising this impartial jurisdiction, but as there is no report of the case we suppose the allegation to be slanderous. Dangers, however, were thickening around him; he now spent all of his days in the deepest recesses of the swamp, and grew so wild that whenever he heard the tramp of a horse or the crack of a rifle, he crept into some hollow tree or bounded away with the caution of a startled fox. The fear of Lynch's law was continually before his eyes, and he would rather have crawled into a den of rattlesnakes than have shown his face in the neighbouring settlement.

But the longest lane will have a turning, and the time was arrived when the destiny of Hark was to be materially changed. One night on returning home he found his mother expiring. He would have gone in search of a physician, but she knew that the hand of death was upon her, and charged him not to leave her bedside. He lighted some pine-knots, and as the blaze illumined the cheerless cabin, gazed in stupefied wonder at the pale and distorted features of her who had been his sole companion through life. She was the only human being who had ever treated him with kindness. He had not been taught obedience by precept or example, but had served and supported her from that kind of instinct which induces animals to consort together for mutual protection, or to follow the hand that feeds them. Blunted as his feelings were by his habits of life, he discovered for the first time an emotion of tenderness swelling at his heart. He watched for hours in silence the expiring taper of existence. Unable to render any assistance, and unskilled in those tender assiduities which soothe the pillow of disease, he felt how helpless and how hopeless is the sorrow of him who watches alone in the chamber of death, awaiting the departure of the soul of a beloved object, whose flight he cannot arrest nor retard. At length, when her breathing became indistinct, he leaned over the ghastly form and sobbed in broken accents, "Mother, don't—don't die!" The dying woman recognised the voice of her son; she turned her eyes towards him; a gleam of maternal tenderness passed over her face, and in the next moment her spirit passed from life to eternity.

Hark, who was naturally superstitious, would now have fled from the house of death, but a decent sense of propriety restrained him, and renewing the blaze upon his now solitary hearth, he sat with his face buried in his hands, giving unrestrained vent to his sorrow. These were new feelings, and, like all sudden impulses, they were evanescent. Grief soon exhausted itself, and when day dawned and the beams of the sun began to dissipate the mist that hung over his dwelling, his wonted habits resumed their empire. The events of that day need not be told. The following night the moon shone brightly. A hunter who had strayed far from home in search of game, returning at a late hour, discovered

the diminutive form of Hark, perched on the summit of a
small knoll not far from the cabin of the late widow. He
sat motionless, with his head resting on his hand, unconscious
of the hunter's approach. The latter, who knew the wary
habits of the boy, was surprised at his remaining thus motionless, and supposing he was hurt or had fallen asleep, drew
near with a friendly intent to awaken or assist him. But the
sound of his approaching footsteps soon broke the reverie of
Hark, who no sooner became aware of being observed than
he started up, and after a cautious glance around instantly
fled in terror from the spot. The astonished hunter, on
examining, found that the boy had been sitting by a newly-
made grave, over which the moist earth had just been closed.
The spade lay there with the fresh soil still clinging to the
blade. Alone, and by moonlight, this singular being had performed the melancholy rite of sepulture. On the following
morning some of the neighbours visited the cabin by the swamp,
but found it deserted; nor was Hark ever seen again in that
vicinity. Sometimes the hunter, when engaged in the mazes
of that wild morass, fancied he heard a sound like that of a
man striking his feet rapidly on the ground, and it was
said that the form of Hark the snake-killer was seen gliding
quietly over the turbid pools. But his fate remained unknown;
whether in his solitary wanderings he had been stung to death
by some venomous reptile or sunk in a quagmire, or whether
the Evil One, who seemed to have long since marked him for
his prey, had carried him off, none could conjecture. It is
said that a variety of noxious animals took possession of the
deserted cabin, as if in triumph over their persecutor; and
when it was visited long afterwards, it was surrounded by a
rank growth of weeds, and the entrance choked with thorns
and briers; a she-wolf had hidden her litter under the ruins of
the chimney; a numerous colony of rattlesnakes coiled their
loathsome forms beneath the dilapidated floor, and the roof

afforded a congenial solitude to the bat; from the hollow of a blasted tree hard by, the owl shouted a savage note of exultation, and a thousand voices arising out of the green and stagnant pools, proclaimed that the tenants of the swamp had increased in number and security.

# CHAPTER XII.

CONTRARY to all the conjectures which had been formed respecting him, Hark Short, the snake-killer, was still in the land of the living. Some months after his disappearance from the place of his nativity, he presented himself nearly naked and almost starved at the house of a farmer in Kentucky, where he was received in conformity with the hospitable usages of that country, without suspicion or question. It was enough that he was destitute and a stranger. He was fed and clothed and continued to linger about the house, wandering off in the daytime to the woods to hunt or kill snakes, and creeping quietly into the cabin at night, where he nestled in a blanket upon the hearth, with his feet to the fire. When called upon to assist in any of the labours of the farm, he complied with the most evident distaste. He could not handle any farming implement but the hoe and axe, and these but awkwardly; and evinced a thorough dislike against all domestic animals. If sent to ride a horse to water, or lead him to the stable, he was sure to pinch or prick the creature with a thorn, until those which were most sagacious and spirited learned to show their antipathy for the unlucky boy by laying back their ears whenever he approached. In short, he could do nothing useful except to hunt raccoons and opossums or to assist the farmer in catching his half-wild hogs, which, as in all new countries, ran at large in the woods. On occasions like the latter, his exploits were the subjects of wonder and merriment. It seemed to afford him an honest pride to exhibit a genius superior to that of the swinish multitude. He was an overmatch for the fiercest and most bulky of these animals, evincing clearly in his triumphs the vast disparity between intellect and instinct. Having selected the object on which to exercise his dexterity, he would lie for hours coiled upon a log, until his victim approached, or would drag his body along the ground towards it so slowly that the motion was imperceptible, and at last springing upon its back, seized the bristles with his left hand, and press his heels into its flanks, clinging with so firm a grasp, that the enraged animal could neither assail nor dislodge him, until he brought his prey to the ground by passing his knife into its throat. If he failed to alight on its back, or if his position was unfavourable for this exploit, he seized one of the hinder limbs, and when the animal happened to be large and strong, it would dart away on three legs, dragging the light form of Hark rapidly over the dried leaves and fallen timber. But it was impossible to shake him off; in vain did the enraged swine dash through the closed thickets or plunge into the miry swamps; Hark retained his hold until the dogs and men came to his relief.

These feats gained him applause, and rendered his society tolerable to those who would otherwise have been disgusted with his unsocial temper and unamiable habits. The only brute that he could endure was the dog; even these he at first viewed with manifest symptoms of repugnance; but after witnessing their good qualities in catching hogs, and hunting, he admitted that if dogs would not bark, they might be made very useful. There was one redeeming quality in the conduct of this singular being, which was fondness for children. He had never until now associated with any of the human race but his mother; of men he had an instinctive dread, and seemed to hate the whole brute creation; towards children alone did he evince a show of kindness. It was a kindness which displayed itself in mute and almost negative actions, like that of the faithful dog, who watches the playing infant with a complacent eye, and suffers it to sport with his paws and teeth, to pull his ears, and even to torment him, without the least show of resentment.

It was to the house of the farmer with whom Hark had found a temporary home, that the prisoners taken at Stanford were brought, on the evening succeeding their arrest. On their approach, the boy, who sat in a corner, in his accustomed moody silence, was the first to hear the tramp of horses. Without speaking to any body, he rose, stole cautiously out, and under the shade of an out-house watched the dismounting horsemen. With his usual stealthy habits, he continued to linger about, listening to all the conversation he could catch, without making his appearance. At last, as if satisfied that no immediate danger threatened his own safety, he entered the room in which the prisoners had been lodged, veiling his constitutional fear of strangers under an assumed apathy of countenance, or only betraying it by an occasional wild and timid glance, like that of the wolf, who, crouching in his den, listens to the distant bayings of the hunters' dogs.

After a little while, the men who guarded the prisoners left the apartment, some to take care of their horses and others sauntering around the house, so as still to be near enough to prevent the possibility of their prisoners' escape. The latter sat upon a bench, with their feet bound together, and their arms strongly pinioned behind them, while Hark continued immovable in his corner, until one of the men, in a coarse tone, asked him for a drink of water. The boy arose, and, as if determined to profit by the opportunity which thus presented itself of indulging his curiosity without hazard, presented a gourd of water with one hand, while he held a candle with the other. The person to whose lips he held the cooling draught, who was the larger of the two

felons, looked sternly at him ; their eyes met, the boy seemed
to recoil, but the features of both their countenances retained
their imperturbable apathy.

"Hark," said the man, in a low, harsh voice, "do you
know me?"

The boy hesitated, as if afraid to reply.

"Put down the light," continued the man, "and sit near
me."

Hark obeyed, replaced the candle on a table, and threw
himself on the floor as if disposed to sleep, yet so near the
man as to hear him speak in a low tone.

"Do you know me?" was again repeated.

"Nobody ever saw Big Harpe, and not know him again,"
replied the killer of snakes.

"Is that all you know of me?"

"Well—I can't say—in peticklar,"—replied the boy in evident embarrassment; "I have *heern* tell that your given
name was Micajah."

"Did you never hear your mother speak of me?"

"Not—in peticklar—as I know of."

"Where is she?"

"Mammy's dead."

Here a pause ensued.

"Will you do me a service?" resumed Micajah.

"Did *you* ever do any good to any body?" asked Hark.

"None of your business!" replied the man fiercely, but
still in the same under-tone; "how dare you speak to me
that way, you stupid wretch?"

Hark edged a little further off, and gazed at the man with
intense curiosity and fear, while his limbs shook with trepi-
dation.

The felon seemed to think it necessary to change his ground,
and try the effect of conciliation.

"And so your mother's dead—I'm sorry—you say she
never spoke about me?"

" Not, in peticklar——"

" But she said something; I'd like to know what it was."

" Mammy didn't know as you'd ever hear it."

" Then it was something bad ?"

" Not in peticklar."

" Then you might as well tell me what it was."

" It would make you mad."

" No, it wouldn't—I don't mind what women say, no how."

" Well, she said, if any body was to rake hell with a fine-comb, they could not find sich a——"

Here he hesitated.

" Out with it, boy."

" Sich a tarnal villain."

" Was that all ?" inquired the man coolly, and as if disappointed in not getting out some fact which he was endeavouring to draw from his stupid companion—" did she say nothing more ?"

" Well—I don't know as she ever said any thing else, in peticklar."

" Give me some more water," said Harpe; and as the boy held the gourd to his lips, instead of drinking, he whispered something, in a hurried, authoritative tone.  Hark stepped back in surprise and retreated across the room, much agitated.  He then resumed his former position in the corner most distant from the prisoners, coiled himself up upon the floor, and appeared to sleep; and when the men composing the guard returned, every thing seemed quiet.

As the night wore away, these hardy backwoodsmen continued to sit to a late hour around the fire; for although it was early in the autumn, the night was cool, and a cheerful blaze glowed on the hearth.  They amused themselves in conversing of their early homes from which they had emigrated, of the incidents connected with their journeys, and of their adventures in hunting and war.  These subjects are so

interesting as always to awaken attention, and they became
particularly so when discussed by a race of men who are eloquent by nature, and speak with a freedom of sentiment and
fluency of language which are not found in any other people
who use our dialect.

At last, one of the hunters, wrapping a blanket about his
brawny frame, threw himself on the floor, and soon slumbered
with a soundness which the bed of down does not always
afford; another, and another, followed his example, until two
only, who were appointed for the purpose, were left to keep
watch over the prisoners, for whom a pallet had been made
upon the floor. In the mean while, Hark had been lying in
the corner unnoticed, and apparently fast asleep; his eyes
were closed, and those who might have looked towards him,
would not have been able to discover, by the uncertain light,
that one eyelid was partially raised, and that, while seem-
ingly asleep, he was attentively watching all that passed. He
had changed his position too, unobserved, and the prisoners
having been placed near the middle of the small apartment,
he was now lying near them.

At length, one of the guards left the room, and the other
was sitting with his back towards the prisoners, intently engaged in cleaning the lock of his rifle. Hark now drew himself silently along the floor, until he placed himself in contact
with the pallet of the captives, then passing his hand rapidly
under the blanket which covered them both, cut the thongs
which bound their arms, placed the knife in the hand of the
one nearest him, and hastily resumed his former place in the
corner. All this was the work of one minute; and in another, the Harpes were on their feet rushing towards the
door, and the sentinels started up only in time to witness
their escape. The whole company was instantly alarmed;
men and dogs dashed into the surrounding thickets in eager
pursuit, but the murderers eluded their skilful search, and the
party returned dispirited and angry with each other. An

animated debate occurred as to the cause of the disaster, but its real author was not suspected until it was found that Hark was missing. In the confusion of the first alarm he had slipped away, and was seen no more in that neighbourhood.

# CHAPTER XIII.

SOME of our readers are perhaps disposed to throw this volume aside, in disappointment at not finding in it any of those touching love-scenes which constitute the charm of most novels. It will, perhaps, be said that the hero is the most insignificant character in the book, and the heroine not half so interesting as some of the other personages. This objection has been urged against some of the most delightful pictures in our language, but has not been found sufficient to prevent the circulation or diminish the celebrity of those admirable works. It has been said of Scott that he has made his heroes secondary characters, while the highest powers of his mighty genius have been employed upon those who play subordinate parts. We may admit the fact as stated, without, by any means, conceding that it forms a valid ground of objection. We can see no reason for the assumption, that the young gentleman, the story of whose love is interwoven with our tale, should, as a matter of course, be intruded upon the reader at every turning, or that all the writer's best powers should be exhausted in embellishing him, who being already so attractive as to have made a deep impression on the heart of the heroine, ought to be, in all conscience, attractive enough for the rest of the world. Besides, we wish to be permitted to tell our story in our own way, and to pass our hero in silence until we find him achieving some adventure worthy of being told. As for love matters, we have little taste for them, and are content to leave them to be imagined by our tasteful and sentimental readers.

If there be any who are disposed to listen to a dry detail of events, which are necessary to explain and connect the circumstances which have been hinted at in this history, we shall introduce them into a small Dutch tavern on the frontiers of the settled part of Pennsylvania.   It was a stone house, built with an attention to solidity which showed that the proprietor entertained the hope of transmitting it to his descendants.   On the sign-board, which hung conspicuously before the door, was painted the bust of a woman with arms extended and with a great suit of long hair streaming like a birch broom down her back, grasping a looking-glass in one hand and a comb in the other, while the lower extremity of the figure tapered off into something resembling the tail of a sea-serpent.   Over this singular representation was written " THE MARE MADE," and underneath, " By Jacob Shultzhoover."   The front door opened into a bar-room, in the centre of which was placed a large tin-plate stove, around whose heated sides was collected a circle of teamsters, smoking their pipes, and conversing with all convenient deliberation in the harmonious accents of the Dutch language.   In a back room, similarly warmed, was a table from which a traveller had lately risen, and over whose ample surface was scattered in gigantic ruin the remains of a great dish of sour-kraut and pork, the relic of a capacious apple-pie, and a rye loaf, flanked by pitchers of cider and milk. Several bouncing girls, with faces "round as my shield," rotund forms, and fleshy sun-burnt arms bare to the elbow, were clearing away the wreck of the evening meal with a marvellous activity, simpering and smiling all the while, as they covertly peeped at the handsome young gentleman who sat picking his teeth by the stove, so deeply plunged in meditation as not to notice what was passing around him.   I am not aware whether picking the teeth is altogether heroic, but a fit of abstraction is the very thing—it looks so lover-like and

interesting. This meditative gentleman was our friend Mr.
Fennimore, who was hastening to join the army on the frontier. Shortly after supper he retired to his chamber, took a
set of writing materials from his valise, and spent the evening
in composing a long letter, from which we shall take the liberty
of making some extracts :

*Lieut. Lyttleton Fennimore, to C. Wallace, Esq.*

"My father was a native of England, who came to Virginia
when he was quite a young man. He was of a good family,
and well educated; if my mother be considered a competent
witness in such a case, he was even more,—highly accomplished and remarkably interesting in person and manners.
He brought letters of introduction and was well received; and
as soon as it was understood that his extreme indigence was
such as to render it necessary that he should embark in some
employment to earn a support, he was readily received as
private tutor in the family of a gentleman residing not far
from Mr. Heyward, the father of the late Major Heyward,
whose melancholy death I have described to you. Mr. Heyward also employed him to give lessons in drawing and the
French language to his only daughter, then a girl of about
seventeen. A mutual attachment ensued between my father
and this young lady, which was carefully concealed, because
the Heywards, though generous and hospitable, were proud
and aspiring.

"I do not know how it was that my father became unpop-
ular among the young gentlemen of the neighbourhood. His
manners might not have been sufficiently conciliating, or his
spirit might have been above his station, and have prompted
him to exact attentions which were not thought due to a private tutor. Perhaps his attentions to Miss Heyward were
suspected, and regarded as presumptuous. Whatever might
have been the cause, the result was that he was coolly received
in society and subjected to many petty indignities. The

younger Mr. Heyward, who had at first treated him with kindness, no sooner suspected him of paying attentions to his sister, to whom he was tenderly attached, than he became his
violent enemy, and insisted on his immediate discharge.   The
elder Mr. Heyward, too magnanimous to do a deliberate act
of injustice, took time for reflection.   During this interval an
event occurred which brought matters to a crisis.

"Although the American colonies were at that time loyal
to the British king, and no plan of revolution had been
matured, yet extensive discontents prevailed, and language of
the strongest reprehension against the ministry was currently
used.   My father had, in writing to England, drawn a vivid
picture of the state of public sentiment in Virginia, and the
letter having been shown to a cabinet minister, he was so well
pleased with the spirit displayed in it, as well as with the
talents of the writer, that he intimated a wish that the
correspondence should be kept up.   This led to a series of
letters, written by my father, expressly for the eye of the
minister.   He was a Briton by birth and allegiance, and did
nothing dishonourable in acting thus, as an agent of the government; and as he adhered strictly to truth, and depicted the
motives of the colonists even in favourable colours, he could not
be justly considered as violating hospitality.   This correspond
ence, however, was discovered; its author was represented as
a spy, and loaded with all the opprobrium which the indignation of an enraged community could suggest.   Nothing but
sudden flight could have saved his life.   Miss Heyward was
the first to warn him of his danger.   Having already given
him her affections, and being prepared to share his fortunes,
she proved her sincerity and her devotion by nobly consenting
to elope with him and become the companion of his poverty
and misfortune.   They commenced their flight at the dawn of
day, and before its close had indissolubly united their fates by
the marriage bond.

"They retired for a while from notice, hoping that my

mother's friends would become reconciled; but this expectation proved deceptive. Major Heyward, though of a generous disposition, was a man of aristocratic feelings; he loved his sister tenderly, and had, perhaps, indulged some views in relation to her settlement in life which were blasted by her marriage with my father. He had also a great antipathy to foreigners, and considered his family degraded by the marriage of one of its members with a person who, however estimable, was an alien to our country. For even at that early period, many of the oldest families among the colonists felt a pride in their native land, and gloried in the name of American, though it was then but a name. He refused to be reconciled to my mother on any terms, and spoke of my father in language which forbade any subsequent advance on their part. They settled in Philadelphia, where they lived in the most retired manner, supported by the scanty pittance earned by my father as a merchant's clerk. Of that unfortunate parent I have no recollection, for he died while I was an infant. My mother, left penniless in a strange city, was reduced to a state of extreme necessity, but her pride would not permit her to return to her father's house, where she would now undoubtedly have been received with open arms. You have seen my excellent mother, and you know that she is a woman of uncommon talents and remarkable fortitude. When thus thrown upon her own resources, she resolved to make the best of her unfortunate situation. She took a secluded lodging, and applied herself with unwearied industry to her needle; and being patronized by several fashionable ladies, maintained herself creditably, though with extreme frugality, by fabricating the most elegant and expensive articles of female dress. Her taste and skill in these delicate manufactures were unrivalled. I cannot express the feelings of anguish which I experienced, while a mere child, in witnessing the silent, the incessant toils of my mother, which were secretly undermining her health, and the devotion with

6

which all her affections were concentrated in myself, the only
earthly object of her regard. And I can remember, too, the
fervour with which I mentally vowed to devote my whole life
to her service. The death of a relative of my father in England placed us in possession of a small annuity, which relieved my excellent mother from the necessity of labouring
for a support, and enabled her to educate me in a manner
suitable to her wishes; though we were still poor, and obliged,
as you are aware, to live in the most frugal manner.

"At the decease of my grandfather, Mr. Heyward, we
learned that a considerable sum of money would fall to my
mother, under the provisions of a settlement made at the
marriage of her parents. But again her pride and her
wounded feelings induced her to prefer obscure indigence
rather than make her situation known in any manner to her
family; nor until I became old enough to take the management of my affairs into my own hands, would she consent to
have her claim investigated. This was the purpose of my
visit to Virginia. I have detailed to you most of the events
attending that visit: it is enough to add, that my uncle
satisfied me that we had been misinformed. No marriage
settlement had ever existed, his father died intestate, and he,
under the rule of primogeniture, which then prevailed in Virginia, was the sole heir. Thus a hope long cherished in secret
by my mother was in a moment blasted."

## CHAPTER XIV.

AT the close of a fine autumn day, a solitary traveller found himself bewildered among the labyrinths of the forest, near the shores of the Ohio. He had taken his departure early in the morning from the cabin of a hunter, to whose hospitality he had been indebted for his last night's lodging and supper—if that deserves the name of hospitality which consisted of little more than a permission to spread his blanket and eat his provisions by the woodman's fire. We call it so because it was granted in a spirit of kindness. When he parted from his host in the morning, he learned that the settlement to which he was destined was fifty miles distant, and he spurred onward in the confident hope of reaching his journey's end ere the setting in of night. Before the day was half spent, he began to suspect that he had taken the wrong path; but unwilling to retrace his steps, he still pushed on in the expectation of meeting with some human habitation from which he could take a new departure.

It was, as we have before remarked, forty years ago, and this country was still a wilderness; the Indian tribes had been driven to the opposite shore of the Ohio, but continued to revisit their ancient hunting-grounds, sometimes in peace, but oftener impelled to war by their insatiable appetite for plunder and revenge. Small colonies were thinly scattered throughout the whole of this region, maintaining themselves by constant watchfulness and courage, and every here and there a *station*—a rude block-house surrounded with palisades —afforded shelter to the traveller, and refuge in time of danger to all within its reach. Between these settlements, extensive tracts remained uninhabited and pathless, blooming in all the native luxuriance and savage grace which had captivated the heart of their earliest admirer among the whites, the fearless and enterprising Boon.

On the same evening, Mr. Timothy Jenkins, the sole proprietor, occupant, and commander of "Jenkins' Station," might be seen alternately plying his axe, with a skill and vigour of which a backwoodsman alone is master, and shouldering huge logs of wood, under the burthen of which any other sinews than such as were accustomed to the labour would have been rent asunder. It was evident that Captain Jenkins was preparing for a vigorous defence of his garrison against an enemy of no mean importance, and was determined to guard against the inroads of a hard frost, by building a log neap in his fire-place. That the latter was of no ordinary dimensions might have been readily inferred from the quantity of fuel required to fill it; for Timothy, like a true Kentuckian, never considered his fire made until the hearth was stowed full of the largest logs which his herculean limbs enabled him to carry. An unpractised observer might have supposed that he was laying in a supply of fuel for the winter, when the hospitable landlord was only performing a daily labour. And here it is necessary to inform those who have not enjoyed the luxury of reposing in a cabin, that the fireplace is generally about eight feet in width, and four or five in depth, so as to contain conveniently about a quarter of a cord of wood, which quantity produces a cheerful warmth, the more necessary as the doors are left standing open.

Having performed this duty, Captain Jenkins threw down his axe with the air of one greatly relieved by having gotten fairly through a disagreeable job, and relaxing into the ordinary indolence of manner, from which the momentary stimulus

of necessary exertion had aroused him, sauntered round his
enclosure with one of his hard bony hands stuffed in either
pocket. Perceiving that an aperture had been made in the
outworks by the removal of one or two of his pickets, which
had rotted off and fallen to the ground, he proceeded to close
the breach.

"They are of no use, no how," said the Captain; "the
Indians have not paid me a visit these eighteen months, and
may never come back. It seems right hard to be at the trouble of barricading them out when they don't try to get in;
but, howsever," he continued, as he raised the prostrate tim-
bers and propped them in their places, "I'll put the *wooden
sogers* on post again, if it's only for a show—they keep the
hogs and wild *varments* out, and if an *inemy* should come, it
will *sort o'* puzzle 'em to find out the weak place." Having
thus compromised with his indolence, he stopped the breach
in such a manner as to have deceived the eye of a hasty
observer, and returned to the house, hastened by the sound
of loud talking and mirth which proceeded from his
guests.

The fortress popularly known as " Jenkins' Station," consisted simply of a circular enclosure, formed by a picketing
composed of long sticks of timber planted firmly in the
ground, and was intended to protect the domicil of honest
Timothy against a sudden onset of the Indians. At that
period every farmer who ventured to pitch his tent in advance
of the settlements, fortified his house in this manner; others
who followed settled around him, and sought shelter in the
*station* upon any sudden emergency. Thus these places,
although private property, partook of the nature of public
defences, and became widely known: the travellers made
their way from one station to another, so that they also
became houses of entertainment, and those of the owners of
them who would accept pay from wayfaring persons, were, in
a manner, forced into the business of tavern-keepers. The pro-

prietor, moreover, became a *captain*, by common consent, because as the people gathered here in time of danger, and it was natural that he should command in his own house, that office fell to him during a siege, and of course pertained to him through life. And such is the love of military titles among a people who are mostly descended from warlike ancestors, that however the individual thus honoured may be afterwards distinguished, though he may become a legislator, or even a magistrate, his military designation is seldom merged in any other.

The dwelling of Captain Jenkins was composed of two log houses, covered under the same roof so as to leave a wide passage between them, after the most approved fashion of a Kentucky log cabin. Round the fire-place, which occupied nearly the whole gable-end of the house, sat five or six men recently dismounted from their horses, who were compensating themselves for the fatigue and abstinence of a day's travel, from the contents of a bottle which was circulating rapidly among them.

" Come on, Tim Jenkins," said one of them to the land-lord, as he entered, " step *forrard*, and touch the blue bottle to your lips. Your whiskey is as good as your fire ; and that is saying a great deal, for you are the *severest old beaver* to *tote* wood that I've seen for many a long day."

" I like to warm my friends inside as well as out, when they call on me," rejoined Jenkins, " the nights are getting powerful cold, and they say it's not good for a man to lie down to sleep with a chill in his blood."

" I say so too," said the other : " I don't know what cold is good for, except to give a man an appetite for his liquor——"

" Or long nights," continued the host, " but to get sober in —so here's good luck to you, Mr. Patterson, and to you gen-tlemen, all."

At this moment the attention of the company was arrested

by a loud "hallo!" uttered without, and Mr. Jenkins hastened to receive a new guest. He soon returned, introducing a young gentleman of a very prepossessing appearance, whose dress and manners announced him as an inhabitant of a more polished country than that in which he found himself. It was our friend Mr. George Lee, who having been lost in the forest, as we have seen, had continued to grope his way in great perplexity, until he chanced to fall into a path which led to the "Station." Bowing cheerfully to the rough sons of the forest, as they greeted him with the usual "How d'ye do, stranger?" he seated himself and began to throw off his spurs, leggins, gloves, and other travelling accoutrements, while Patterson and his companions, after a passing glance, resumed their bottle and their mirth.

Tired and cold, Mr. Lee drew his chair towards the fire, and remained for a time in the enjoyment of its comfortable warmth. Patterson sat by the table replenishing his glass and pressing his companions to drink, talking all the while in a loud and overbearing tone, and growing more and more boisterous, until the annoyance awakened Mr. Lee from a kind of stupour that was creeping over him. He raised his head, and discovered the eyes of one of the party fixed upon him, with a gaze so eager and so malignant as to attract his own instant attention. The man, whose countenance displayed nothing remarkable, except a ferocity unmingled with the least touch of human feeling, no sooner caught the eye of the young traveller than he drew back, as if to avoid observation.

Mr. George Lee was a young gentleman by no means remarkable for penetration; but he was bold and manly, had mixed with the world more than most persons of his years, and had a tolerable faculty of knowing men by their looks—a faculty which by no means evinces a high degree of intellect, but more frequently is found in ordinary minds. He looked round upon the company into which he had been accidentally

thrown, and for the first time his eye rested upon the savage
features of Patterson. The latter was a large stout man, evidently endued with more than common strength. There was
a considerable degree of sagacity in his countenance, and his
strong peculiar language seemed to be that of one accustomed
to think and speak without constraint. His blood-shot eye
and bloated skin betokened habitual intemperance ; the fierce
and remorseless expression of his face was rendered more terrific by a large scar on his forehead and another on his cheek,
while the whole appearance of the man was bold, impudent,
and abandoned. He possessed, or what was more likely,
affected, joviality and humour, continually pressing his companions to drink, and giving to every remark a strangely extravagant and original turn, which always created laughter.
Another peculiarity was the loudness of his coarse voice—
partly from habit, partly out of an assumed frankness and an
affectation of not caring who heard him, and partly to produce an impression of his superiority upon those around him ;
he always spoke as loud even in a small room as another person would in haranguing a multitude. But when intoxicated,
this peculiarity became very striking ; then he bellowed and
roared—uttering his sentiments with an astonishing energy of
language and a horrible profusion of the most terrific ðaths,
in a voice naturally loud, and now pitched to its highest and
harshest note, and with a wonderful vehemence of gesture.
This characteristic had gained for him the nickname of " Roaring Bob," by which he was as well known as by his proper
christian and surnames.

Our friend George Lee, who had never before seen a man
whose presence excited so much disgust, turned from him and
looked round upon his associates. They were a villainous and
ruffian set, who seemed fit instruments to perpetrate any crime
however base or bloody. There was one person present, however, whose countenance drew his regard the more forcibly,
from the contrast it presented with those around. It was that

of a young man whose placid features and neat though coarse dress indicated an acquaintance with the decencies of social life. There was a fine expression of ingenuousness in his face, and his clear blue eye sparkled with vivacity and intelligence. He seemed to be under some constraint, for although addressed by the party as an acquaintance, his answers were brief, and while he treated them with civility, he appeared to be not disposed to join their conversation or share their mirth. At an early hour a plentiful supper was spread, to which the whole of this ill-assorted party sat down; and immediately after, Mr. Lee, pleading fatigue, retired to repose.

A weary traveller needs no poppies strewn upon his pillow "to medicine him to that sweet sleep" which is the reward of toil; and on this occasion, although the imagination of our friend George, never very active, was considerably excited by the novel scenes he had just witnessed, his reflections were soon drowned in forgetfulness. He had not slept long when his slumber was suddenly broken by a cold hand which grasped him by the shoulder. He started up in alarm, and was about to speak, but was prevented by a voice addressing him in a firm but hurried tone, so low as to be barely audible: "Do not speak—you are in danger—rise and follow me—be quick and silent!" The first impulse of the traveller's mind was distrust towards his mysterious visitor, for whose secret warning he could not readily perceive any rational ground; but as he proceeded mechanically to obey the mandate, his generous nature, not easily awakened to suspicion, repelled the hasty suggestion of doubt, and induced him to follow his guide with confidence. The latter, again cautioning him to silence, led the way to the open air, and proceeding under the shadow of the house to an aperture in the stockade, passed out of the enclosure and hastily penetrated into the forest.

Mr. Lee pursued the rapid but noiseless footsteps of his conductor, amazed at the suddenness of the adventure, and perplexed with his own endeavours to guess its probable cause

6*

or issue. It will be readily imagined that his conjectures could lead to no satisfactory conclusion, and that his situation —decoyed into the solitude and darkness of the forest, by a stranger—perhaps one of those whose felon glances had attracted his attention—was such as to have created alarm in the stoutest heart. Yet there is something in every young and chivalric bosom which welcomes danger when it assumes an air of romance; and George Lee, while internally blaming his own imprudence, which seemed to be leading him from a fancied to a real danger, could not resist the curiosity which he felt to develop the mystery, nor resolve to abandon an adventure which promised at least novelty. His uncertainty was of short duration; for his guide after a few minutes' rapid walking emerged into an open clearing and halted; and as he stood exposed in the clear moonlight, Mr. Lee had no difficulty in recognising the young forester whose prepossessing appearance he had remarked as affording so strong a contrast to the suspicious looks and brutal manners of his associates.

Pointing to a ruined cabin near which they stood, "It is fortunate for you, sir," said the guide, "that our landlord's stable within the stockade was filled before you arrived, and that your good nag was sent to this sorry roof for shelter."

"I shall be better able to appreciate my good fortune," said Lee, endeavouring to imitate the composure with which the other had spoken, "when I learn in what manner I am to be benefited by the bad lodging of my horse."

"By the badness of his lodging nothing," said the other, "by its privacy, much—to be brief, you must fly."

"Fly! when—how?"

"Now; upon your horse, unless you prefer some other mode of travelling."

"Fly!" repeated Mr. Lee incredulously, "from what?"

"From danger—pressing and immediate danger."

The young traveller stood for a moment irresolute, gazing at the placid features of the backwoodsman, as if endeavouring to dive into his thoughts. His embarrassed air and suspicious glance did not escape the forester, who inquired,

" Are you satisfied ?—will you confide in me ?"

" I cannot choose but trust you—and there is that in your countenance which tells me my confidence will not be misplaced ; I only hesitated under the suspicion that I was to be made the subject of some idle jest."

" I have been too familiar with danger," said the other, " to consider it a fit subject for pleasantry. Had you looked death in the face as often as I have done, you would have learned to recognise the warning voice of a friend who tells you of its approach."

" Enough," replied Lee, " pardon my hasty suspicion—and let me know what has excited your apprehensions for my safety."

" First let us saddle your horse,—we delay here too long." So saying, the young woodsman hastened into the cabin and with Mr. Lee's assistance equipped the gallant steed, whom they found sounding his nostrils over a full trough, with a vigour which announced as well the keenness of his appetite as the excellence of his food.

" Your nag has a good stomach for his corn," said the backwoodsman, leading him out into the moonlight, " and if he does not belie his looks, he travels as well as he feeds;" and without waiting for a reply he threw the bridle over the animal's neck, and returning into the cabin, produced the baggage, great-coat, and other equipments of Lee, who now more than ever astonished at the conduct of his companion prepared in silence for his journey.

" Are you ready ?" said the forester.

" I am ready."

" Then mount, and follow me."

" The guide struck into the woods, and proceeding with the same noiseless steps which Lee had before remarked, strode forward with a rapidity to which neither the darkness of the forest nor the thick undergrowth of tangled bushes seemed to present any obstacle.   They proceeded in silence, the horse following instinctively the footsteps of the forester, until the latter striking into a hard foot-path halted, and advancing to the horseman's side, placed his hand on the pummel of the saddle.

"With common prudence you are now safe," said he—and after a moment's hesitation he continued in a low rapid tone: "those scoundrels in the house have laid a plan to rob and murder you."

"Is it possible?   Can they be such base——"

"It is true—I have not alarmed you on bare suspicion.   I overheard their plan—and knowing the men, I was satisfied that you could save your life only by flight."

"But our landlord—surely he is not privy to their design."

"He is not."

"Why then should I fly?   If he and yourself will stand by me, I could defy a regiment of such fellows."

"You do not know your danger—to return would be madness—Jenkins, though an honest, is a timid man ; as for myself, I would cheerfully aid you, but circumstances forbid that I should embroil myself with those men at present.   Besides, you cannot remain at the Station always, and your departure can never be effected with such safety as now, before the enemy is on the alert.   Farewell—keep that path, and you are safe."   So saying he disappeared, and our traveller, with a heavy heart, resumed his journey.

If Mr. Lee had found his situation perplexing on the preceding day, while wandering in uncertainty through the forest, it was certainly more so now, when surrounded by the gloom of night.   Unable to see the way, he was obliged to trust entirely to the instinct of his horse, who kept the path with surprising sagacity.   Sometimes he found himself descending into a ravine, sometimes the splashing of water announced

that he was crossing a rivulet, and sometimes a bough overhanging the path would nearly sweep him from his seat; but
he continued to move cautiously along, satisfied that he could
encounter no danger more pressing than that from which he
had escaped. He was aware that the outlaw is often found
on the extreme frontier of our country, perpetrating deeds of
violence and fraud, beyond the reach of the civil authority.
In those distant settlements, and at the early period of which
we write, the inhabitants, thinly scattered, were fully occupied
in providing for their own defence and sustenance, and the
wholesome restraints of law, if they existed, were but feebly
enforced. At such points, gangs of ruffians would sometimes
collect, and for a time elude or openly defy the arm of justice. Carefully avoiding to give offence to their own immediate neighbours, and striking only at a distance, they for a
time escaped detection. The honest settler, simple and primitive in all his habits, unwilling to meddle with laws which he
little understood, endured the evil so long as the peace of his
own community remained undisturbed; until roused at last
by some daring act of violence, he hunted down the felon, as
he would have chased the panther. That Patterson and his
associates belonged to that class of marauders, Mr. Lee had
little doubt; and he judged correctly, that if they had really
marked him out as their prey, he could only be protected by
a force superior to their own.

Occupied with such reflections, he continued to grope his
way, until he supposed the night must be nearly exhausted.
The moon, whose beams had occasionally reached him through
the shadows of the forest, had gone down, and the darkness
was quite impenetrable. He stopped often, turning his eyes
in every direction, to discover the first beam of the morning.
Never did night appear so long—he counted hour after hour
in his imagination—until his impatience became insupport-
able. The silence of the forest, so long continued and so
death-like, became painfully distressing; but when it was sud-

denly broken by the savage howl of the wolf, or the fearful
screaming of the owl, the traveller involuntarily started, and
was not ashamed to acknowledge a thrilling sense of danger.
Even now the panther might be silently crawling along his
track, watching for a favourable opportunity to spring upon
his prey ; the hungry wolf might be scenting his approach, or
the Indian crouching in his path.   Wearied with conjecture, a
feverish excitement took possession of his frame, and he
thought he could cheerfully encounter any peril rather than
be thus tortured with darkness and suspense.   Bodily fatigue
was added to his sufferings, and at length he dismounted to
seek a momentary relief by a change of posture, and threw
himself on the ground at the root of a tree, holding his bridle
in his hand ; and the vividness of his sensations subsiding with
the inaction of his frame, he was unconsciously overcome by
sleep.

When George Lee awoke, the morning was far advanced.
The bridle had fallen from his hand, and his horse was grazing
quietly near him.   Stiff and aching with cold, he remounted
and pursued his journey.   The road, if such it could be called,
was no other than a narrow path, winding through the forest,
of sufficient width to admit the passage only of a single horseman.   Pursuing the course of a natural ridge, the traveller
passed through a hilly region, clothed with oak and hickory
trees, and thickly set with an undergrowth of hazel-bushes
and grape-vines ; often halting to seek the path which was
concealed by the intertwining brush or covered with fallen
leaves, and sometimes delaying to gather the nuts and fruit
which offered their luxuries in abundance.   Thence descending into the rich alluvion flats, his way led through groves of
cotton-trees and sycamore, whose gigantic trunks ascending to
an immense height were surmounted with long branches so
closely interwoven as almost to exclude the light of heaven.
Sometimes the graceful cane skirted his path, and he waded
heavily through the tangled brake, embarrassed by the nume-

rous tracks beaten by the wild grazing animals, who resort to such spots, or alarmed by the appearance of beasts of prey, who lurk in these gloomy coverts. Alternately delighted with the beauties of nature, or chilled by the dreary solitude of the wilderness, our traveller passed rapidly on, sometimes enjoying those absorbing reveries in which young minds are apt to revel, and sometimes indulging the apprehensions which his situation was calculated to excite. For the bear, the wolf, and the panther, still lurked in these solitudes, and the more dangerous Indian yet claimed them as his heritage.

The sun was sinking towards the western horizon when he reached the broken country bordering on the Ohio. His heart, which had been saddened by the monotonous gloom of interminable flats and the intricacy of miry brakes, was cheered as the hills rose upon his view, and his faithful horse moved with renewed vigour when his hoof struck the firm soil. Still the apprehension of approaching night was not without its terror. The backwoodsman alone, accustomed to such scenes, inured to the toils of the chase, and versed in the stratagems of border warfare, can contemplate with indifference the prospect of a solitary encampment in the forest; and our traveller began to look impatiently for the signs of human habitation. He listened with intense interest to every sound. In vain; the deer still galloped across his path, stopping to gaze at the harmless stranger, then throwing back their horns and leaping leisurely away with graceful bounds. The owl hooted in the dark valleys, sending forth yells so long, so loud, and so dismal, as to mislead the traveller into the momentary belief that it was the mournful wail of human misery; while the long shadows falling across the deep ravines, and seen through myriads of yellow leaves which floated on the breeze, assumed fantastic shapes to the now heated fancy of the tired wayfarer.

## CHAPTER XV.

MR. GEORGE LEE had been accustomed from his youth
to active sports and severe bodily exercises; he was
perfectly at home in the saddle, and loved to wander about
the woods, better than to do any thing else except to drink
wine. There were, therefore, some pleasures mixed with the
perplexities of his present situation. He bore the fatigues
into which he was so unexpectedly thrown, like an experienced
hunter, accustomed to long and weary excursions; his native
courage rendered him careless of the dangers of the way, and
his taste for forest sports was frequently gratified by the sight
of animals which were new to him, and of places charmingly
suited to the amusements in which he delighted. The only
thing that distressed him was hunger. Although he was in
love, and had travelled all the way from Virginia, in pursuit
of Miss Pendleton, whose hand he considered indispensable
to his happiness, yet he was so unsentimental as to be actually
hungry—and well he might be, for the poor young man had
now been riding twenty-four hours without food.

When suffering a privation of this kind, we are apt to torment ourselves with the recollection of the good things that
we have eaten in happier days. And who had been more
fortunate in this respect than our friend George, who had not
only

"—— Sate at good men's feasts"

all his life, but kept expert cooks, and gave famous dinners himself? He looked back with pleasurable and mournful reminiscence, similar to that of the man who is suddenly reduced from opulence to poverty. He, too, was reduced in his circumstances, for he was denied the luxury of eating, which is the most important circumstance of life; and the visions of departed saddles of venison, turkeys, hams, roast pigs, oysters, and various other dainty dishes, which the Virginians have in great perfection, and dispense with prodigal hospitality to their friends, rose before his mind's eye in mournful yet delicious profusion.

These reveries he dwelt upon until their sameness wearied his mind. He began to grow faint and tired; excessive hunger produced drowsiness, accompanied with such callousness of feeling, that a propensity was creeping over him to throw himself on the ground and sleep away his senses arfd existence. He tried to recollect some text of scripture which might comfort him, but for his life, he could think of nothing but " eat, drink, and be merry," or something that had eating and drinking in it. He attempted to sing, but his songs were all bacchanalian, and only served to provoke thirst. He would have repeated some stanzas of poetry to keep him awake, if he had known any; but he had never cultivated the muses, and not a line could he recollect but

> Little Jackey Horner, sitting in a corner,
> Eating a Christmas pie;

and the dreadful conviction fastened itself at last upon his alarmed fancy, that if he should escape a miserable death by starvation in the wilderness, he would surely meet a wretched end by surfeit whenever he should come in contact with food. Never did George Lee commune so long with his own thoughts or reflect so seriously.

All at once his tired horse, who was moving slowly along the hardly perceptible path, with the bridle hanging on his neck, suddenly stopped as the path turned almost at right angles round a dense thicket.  A few paces before him, and until this instant concealed by the thick brush, stood a miserable squalid boy, intently engaged in watching some object not far from him.  A small, gaunt, wolf-looking, starved dog crouched near him, equally intent on the same game, so that even his quick ear did not catch the tread of the horse's feet as they rustled among the dry leaves, until the parties were in close contact.  The dog then, without moving, uttered a low growl, which the ear of his master no sooner caught than he looked round, and seeing Mr. Lee, started up and was about to fly.  But George exclaimed, " My little man, I've lost my way," and the lad stopped, eyed the traveller timidly, and then looked earnestly towards the spot to which his glance had been before directed.

" I have missed my way," continued Lee, " and am almost starved."

" Can't you wait a minute till I kill that *ar* snake," replied Hark—for it was he.

The traveller looked in the direction indicated by the boy's finger, and saw an immense rattlesnake coiled, with its head reared in the centre, his mouth unclosed, his fierce eyes gleaming vindictively, and all his motions indicating a watchful and enraged enemy.  Hark gazed at the reptile with an eager and malignant satisfaction.  His features, usually stupid, were now animated with hatred and triumph.  The scene was precisely suited to interest the sportsmanlike propensities of Mr. George Lee, if he had not happened to be too hungry to enjoy any thing which might delay him any longer in the wilderness.

" Kill the snake, boy," said he, impatiently, " and then show me the way to some house."

Hark motioned with his finger, as if enjoining silence, and replied laconically, " It ain't ready yet."

The rattlesnake now raised his tail and shook his rattles, as if in defiance ; and then, as if satisfied with this show of valour, and finding that his enemies made no advance, but stood motionless, slowly uncoiled himself, and began to glide away. Hark left his position, and, with noiseless steps, alertly made a small circuit, so as to place him in front of the enemy. The snake raised his head, darted out his tongue, and then turned to retreat in another direction; but no sooner had he presented his side to Hark, than the intrepid snake-killer bounded forward and alighted with both his feet on the neck of the reptile, striking rapidly first with one foot, and then the other, but skilfully keeping his victim pinned to the ground so as to prevent the use of its fangs. The snake, in great agony, now twisted the whole of its long body round Hark's leg; and the boy, delighted to witness the writhings of his foe, stood for a while grinning in triumph. Then carefully seizing the reptile by the neck, which he held firmly under his foot, he deliberately untwisted it from his leg, and threw it on the ground at some distance from him, and seemed to be preparing to renew the contest.

"You stupid boy," cried Mr. Lee, " why don't you take a stick and kill the snake?"

"That ain't the right way," replied Hark; and as the venomous creature, disabled and sadly bruised, essayed to stretch its length on the ground to retreat, the snake-killer again jumped on it, and in a few minutes crushed it to death with his feet. Then taking it up in his hands, he surveyed it with his peculiar grin of joy, counting the rattles as he separated them from the body, with an air of triumph as great as that of the hunter when he numbers the antlers of a noble buck.

Mr. Lee gazed at this scene with unfeigned astonishment. Though no mean adept himself in the art of destroying animal life, he had never before witnessed such an exhibition. The diminutive size of the youth, his meagre and famished appearance, his wretched apparel, together with the skill and intrepidity displayed in this nondescript warfare, with a creature scarcely his inferior in any respect, strongly excited his curiosity.

"Well, you've beaten your enemy," said he in an encouraging tone.

"Yes, I reckon I've *saved* him."

"But why did you not take a club to it?"

"It ain't the right way. I never go snakin' with a pole."

"What is your name?"

"Do you live about here, stranger?"

"No, I am a traveller from Virginia, and was going to Hendrickson's settlement, when I lost my way."

"People's mighty apt to get lost when they don't know the range," replied Hark familiarly, encouraged by the stranger's affability.

"Where do you live?" inquired Mr. Lee, endeavouring to conciliate the half-savage being whose friendship was now important to him.

"I don't live nowhere, in peticklar."

"But you seem acquainted with these woods."

"Yes, I *use* about here some."

"How do you employ yourself?"

"I hunt some, and snake a little; and when I *haint nothen* else to do, I go a *lizardin.*"

"Lizardin! what in the name of sense is that?"

"Killen lizards," replied the boy, rather consequentially. "I use up all the varments I come across."

"Then you must *frog it some*," said Mr. Lee, laughing.

"Oh yes—and there's a powerful chance of the biggest bull-frogs you ever see down in the slash yander. It would do you good to go there in the night and hear 'em sing. I reckon there's more frogs and water-snakes there than they is in all Virginny."

"I have no curiosity to see them. And now, my lad, if you will guide me to the settlement I will satisfy you generously for your trouble."

Hark made objections—it was too far—he could not tell the distance—but it was farther than he could walk in a day. Mr. Lee then begged to be conducted to the nearest house ; but the snake-killer shook his head.

"Surely you lodge somewhere," exclaimed the Virginian, growing impatient; "take me to your camp, and give me something to eat. I am starving."

Hark seemed irresolute, and continued to eye the traveller with a childish curiosity, mingled with suspicion; then, as if a new idea occurred to him, he inquired, " Where's your gun, mister ?"

"I have none."

For the first time the melancholy visage of Hark distended into a broad grin, as he exclaimed, " Well, I never see a man before that hadn't a gun. If it ain't no offence, stranger, what do you follow for a living ?"

".Why, nothing at all, you dunce," said George ; "I am a gentleman."

Hark was as much puzzled as ever. " In North Carolina," said he, "where I was raised, the people's all gentlemen, except the women, and they've all got guns."

"All this is nothing to the purpose—will you not show the way to your camp ?"

"Well—I reckon,"—replied Hark, withdrawing a few steps, "I sort o' reckon it wouldn't be best."

"What objection can you possibly have ?"

"I am afeard."

"You need not fear me; I can do you no harm, if I felt so disposed ; and I have no disposition to injure you."

"Won't you beat me ?"

"Certainly not."

"Nor take my skins from me ?"

"No, no. I would not harm you upon any consideration."

"Well, then, I reckon I'll take you to my camp."

So saying, Hark marched off through the woods, followed by Mr. George Lee.

# CHAPTER XVI.

THE snake-killer urged his way through the forest with a rapid but noiseless step, followed by our friend George, whose weary horse was scarcely able to keep pace with the hardy boy. After travelling a short distance, they arrived at the top of a hill, whence the river Ohio could be seen at a distance, gliding placidly, and reflecting the sunbeams from the broad mirror of its clear and beautiful surface. Here Mr. Lee was requested to dismount and leave his horse; an arrangement with which he was by no means disposed to comply, for he was too good a horseman not to love the generous animal which had borne him safely through the fatigues of so long a journey. But the cautious policy of Hark was not to be overthrown by any argument; and after some discussion, the saddle and bridle were stripped of and hung upon a tree, and the horse turned out to graze, with his legs secured in such a manner as to prevent him from wandering far from the spot. They then descended the hill until they reached an extensive plain of flat alluvion land, covered with a thick forest of tall trees, skirting the shores of " *the beautiful stream*," and forming what is called in this country, the river bottom. Here, concealed in a tangled thicket of brushwood, matted with grape-vines, was a small lodge, constructed of slender poles, covered with bark. Hark paused, and cast furtive glances of apprehension around, before he disclosed the entrance to this primitive and wretched abode, examining

with his eye the neighbouring coverts, and then looking timidly towards his companion, as if still balancing in his mind
between prudence and hospitality; while the dog, imitating
his master's caution, crept silently round the spot, snuffing
the air. At last, Hark, as if satisfied, pushed aside the leafy
branches which concealed his place of retreat, and entering
hastily with his guest, carefully replaced the bushes behind
him.

If Mr. Lee had been astonished before, at all he had seen
of the mysterious being into whose company he had been so
strangely thrown, his wonder was not decreased on finding
himself introduced into "a lodge in some vast wilderness,"
which seemed a more fit habitation for a wild beast than a
human creature. The lodge was square, and not more than
eight feet in diameter, while its height was barely sufficient
to allow the dwarfish proprietor to stand upright in the
centre. It was dry and tight. The floor was formed by logs
imbedded in the ground, and covered with dried grass. The
only visible articles of property consisted of an iron stew-pan,
a steel trap, an axe, and a quantity of skins.

Motioning to his companion to seat himself on the floor,
Hark proceeded with some alacrity to prepare a meal. In
the first place he drew from a magazine of sundries, hidden
in one corner of his tent, several pieces of jerked venison
dried so hard as to be nearly of the consistency of wood, but
which, by the by, was by no means unpalatable; and placing
them before his guest, signified that he might commence operations; an intimation which Mr. Lee, with the assistance
of a pocket-knife, obeyed without hesitation. Hark then
retired, and having kindled a small fire in a ravine near the
tent, produced the carcase of a fat opossum, which he cut up
and placed in the stew-pan. In a few minutes the savoury
mess was in a condition to be placed before the traveller;
and although totally unseasoned, and destitute of the accompaniment of bread or vegetables, the famished wayfarer did

ample justice to the cookery of Hark, who sat by, and refused
to partake, until the hunger of his guest was appeased.

This was the proudest day of the life of Hark the snake-
killer.   Unused to kindness, and accustomed from the earliest
dawn of reason to consider men as his enemies, this was
probably the first time that he had ever enjoyed the luxury
of doing good from motives entirely voluntary.   He was in
company with a gentleman of fine appearance, and, to his apprehension, of superior intelligence, who treated him as an
equal.   Although an aristocrat by birth, property, and association, Mr. Lee was naturally good-humoured, and his habits
as a sportsman and man of pleasure had thrown him frequently into contact with the lower classes of society, and
this we suppose to be generally true of those who engage in
sensual pleasures, or in what is more commonly called dissipation.   And it is, if we mistake not, a national characteristic, that our gentlemen can, when circumstances render it
convenient, adapt themselves with perfect ease to the society
of their inferiors in education and manners.   Mr. Lee, therefore, without much effort, had the tact to treat our friend
Hark as an equal, simply by avoiding any supercilious show
of aversion or airs of superiority; and the consequence was
that he rose every moment in the esteem and affection of
this uncouth boy, who soon began to venerate him as a superior being.

It was now dusk, and our traveller had no choice left but
to spend the night under the miserable shelter which he had
found so opportunely.   Indeed, contrasting his present situation with the gloomy terrors of the forest, and the disquie-
tude which he had experienced within the last twenty-four
hours, he found great room for congratulation, and recovered
his natural flow of spirits sufficiently to converse freely with
Hark, whose reserve began imperceptibly to wear away.

While they were thus engaged, the dog all at once showed
symptoms of agitation, pricking his ears, then crawling out

of the tent and snuffing the air, and at last uttering a low
sharp whine, and hastily retreating back to his master with
his hair bristling and his limbs trembling. Hark, always
alive to fear, looked at his dumb companion and at his guest
with a ghastly expression of terror on his sallow features.
Mr. Lee would have spoken, but the boy cautioned him to be
silent, and creeping to the aperture of the lodge reconnoitred
the surrounding shades with the cunning of a wary hunter.
George followed, and was about to step from the lodge when
his companion caught his arm and whispered "Indians!"
Footsteps could now be heard passing around; they were the
wily steps of the cautious savage treading softly as if aware
of the vicinity of a foe; but the rustling of the leaves and the
cracking of the dried twigs betrayed them to the ears of the
attentive listeners. Then a low signal-cry was heard, which
was answered by another from a different direction. A party
of Indians, painted for war, was seen scattered about, moving
silently through the bushes, or standing in the attitude of
eager and watchful attention, with their hands upon their
weapons and their dark eyes gleaming with ferocious avidity.
It was evident that they had traced their victims to this spot,
and were now anxiously seeking the place of their concealment. Suddenly, Hark uttered a piercing scream, and rushing forward a few steps, pushed aside the bushes so as to
disclose the entrance of the lodge to the Indians.

"Traitor!" exclaimed Mr. Lee as he sprung after him,
convinced by this action that the wretched boy had betrayed
him into an ambuscade, and intending, under a sudden
impulse of passion, to strike him to the ground. But a
momentary glance induced him to abandon the suspicion.
Before him stood a tall Indian, whose superior air and dress
announced him to be a leader, with his rifle pressed to his
shoulder as if in the act of taking aim. His keen eye had
discovered the faces of the whites through some slight opening of the intervening foliage, and he was deliberately pre-

7

paring to fire with a deadly aim, when Hark perceiving his
intention, leaped towards him to implore mercy, throwing
himself on his knees, and regarding his savage captor with
looks of intense agony. Lee stood behind him unarmed and
embarrassed; while the Indians, dashing through the bushes
with the most terrible yells, and brandishing their tomahawks,
crowded about their victims, prepared to glut their vengeance
by immolating them upon the spot. But the chief restrained
them, making a brief but peremptory explanation in a
language unknown to the prisoners, but which probably suggested a respite from instant death only as a prelude to a
more lingering and dreadful fate.

Ferocious as this band of savages appeared to the eye of
Lee, to whom the scene was new, an experienced observer
would have remarked in their deportment a more than
ordinary degree of moderation. The Indians, like all other
unlettered men, act from impulse. A battle always whets
their appetite for blood; and they visit upon the lives of their
unfortunate captives the ill-humour occasioned by their own
fatigues, losses, or sufferings. They are cruel always when
excited, and often without excitement; and sometimes from
mere caprice treat their prisoners with lenity and even
kindness.

It happened that the captors of Lee were in a good
humour. They had perhaps made a successful inroad upon
the whites, or had met with no occurrence lately to awaken
resentful feelings. The fine horse of Mr. Lee, the gun, the
axe, and the skins of Hark, constituted in their estimation a
prize of no small value, and their ready tact enabled them to
see at a glance that their prisoners were not persons of warlike habits. Some or all of these reasons operated to protect
the captives from ill usage, and they were marched off to the
shore of the Ohio, where the Indians embarked in canoes that
were concealed among the willows, and crossed to the opposite
bank, where they encamped.

At an early hour the following morning the whole party prepared to march; but not until some of the warriors evinced a disposition to amuse themselves at the expense of Hark. The diminutive size and queer looks of the half-civilized youth attracted their attention, and they indulged their drollery by forming themselves into two parallel lines, and making the disconcerted snake-killer march backwards and forwards between them. As he passed along one would prick him in the side with the point of his knife, and when the frightened boy turned his head towards his tormentor another would trip him by placing an obstacle in his path. One of the tallest of the braves led him to a tree, against which he placed him, while with a tomahawk he marked his diminutive height accurately upon the bark; then measuring and marking his own height upon the same tree, he pointed out the difference to the amused warriors, who laughed vociferously at this specimen of wit.

George Lee joined heartily in the laugh occasioned by the ludicrous appearance of his new acquaintance, but it was not long until he became himself a subject of merriment. Among the spoils was a large iron kettle, into which the Indians had packed their provisions, and when the march was about to be commenced, it was determined to make our friend George the bearer of this burden. In vain did he remonstrate, both by emphatic signs and imploring language, assuring them that he was a gentleman, unused to labour, and totally unable to carry such a burthen; the Indians persisted in placing the kettle on his head, and the unfortunate gentleman, willing to try the virtue of obedience, and afraid to refuse, moved forward. But although his head had always been considered hard in one sense of the word, it did not prove so in the present instance, and after proceeding a few steps he began to falter, and showed a desire to set down his load. A very muscular savage, a surly, malicious-looking ruffian, advanced towards him, and brandishing his war-club

ordered him to proceed.   George, without understanding the
language, readily comprehended the meaning of the Indian,
and turning towards him exclaimed, in a tone of vexation,
"I say, my good fellow, if you think it's so mighty easy to
carry this load, you had better try it yourself." The Indian
raised his club to strike, but George, who was a theoretical
boxer and a man of spirit, threw the kettle from his head, .
suddenly darted upon him, wrested the club from his grasp,
and throwing it from him struck his assailant with his fist.
The Indians shouted applause, formed a circle, and encouraged
their companion to continue the battle; and the latter, who
could not refuse without disgrace, sprung furiously upon the
rebellious prisoner.   Though stout and active, he found his
full match in Lee, who was a young man of large frame, in
the prime of manhood, and accustomed to athletic exercises.
He was much stronger than the savage, while the latter was
his superior in cunning.   Thus matched, the battle was
severely contested for several minutes, when George, by a
lucky blow, stretched his adversary upon the ground, to the
infinite amusement of the bystanders, who made the forest
ring with their acclamations, while they taunted their beaten
comrade with the severest irony.

Lee now rose considerably in the estimation of his
captors; the kettle was suspended upon a pole and carried by
two of the party, and our friend accommodated with a lighter
load.

They had not proceeded far when they reached the margin
of a broad and rapid stream, which they prepared to cross by
fording.   To this evolution Hark evinced great repugnance;
for although accustomed to dabble in marshy pools, he could
not swim, and was marvellously afraid of deep water. The
Indians, who became more and more amused with his untoward vagaries, drove him into the water before them with
shouts of merriment.  The stream was about waist deep to
the men, who waded firmly through without difficulty; not

so Hark, whose chin floated like a cork upon the surface, while his feet, scarcely touching the bottom, were frequently swept by the force of the current from under him, and the terrified urchin completely immersed—until he was relieved, and again placed in a perpendicular attitude.

The Indians, either from a sense of the ludicrous, or from the pleasure of giving pain, found such rare sport in the sufferings of Hark, that they no sooner reached the shore than they determined to repeat the exhibition; actuated by the same spirit which induces the spectators at a theatre to *encore* some precious piece of buffoonery. Hark was therefore commanded to retrace his steps to the opposite bank, attended by a warrior, whose duty was to keep the performer's head above water, but who mischievously bobbed it under the surface whenever a suitable opportunity offered. Having thus recrossed and returned, the savages, satisfied for the present, prepared to resume their journey. Such are some of the sports of the Indians, by which they enliven the brief intervals of enjoyment, few and far between, that succeed the solitary labours of the chase and the butcheries of war, the gloomy nights of watching, and the long days spent in brooding over meditated violence and insatiable revenge.

Hark, though greatly terrified, was not much fatigued by his late exertions, for he was as hardy as a pine knot, and accustomed to exposure to the elements. He was therefore soon rested, and was leaning carelessly against the stem of a young tree, when the singular expression of his countenance attracted the attention of the Indians, who are quick and accurate observers of physiognomy. His eye, usually dull, was now lighted up, and keenly fixed upon some object at a short distance off in the woods. His lips were compressed, and the muscles of his vacant countenance in perceptible motion. He seemed to be drawing himself up like some crouching animal preparing to spring on its prey. Suddenly he darted forward towards a large black-snake which was slily dragging its shining folds over the dry leaves, and seizing the reptile by the neck with one hand, whirled the long body in the air over his head, as a child would flourish a whip-lash. Then he suffered it to coil itself round his arm and neck, and disengaging it, threw it into the air, catching it as it fell. This he repeated frequently, always taking care to seize the animal dexterously so near the head as to prevent the possibility of its biting. At length, he dropped on his hands and knees, and fixing his teeth in the back of the creature's neck, shook it violently as a terrier dog worries a rat; and finally taking the head in his hand, he rose and lashed the trees with the long flexible body of his victim, until he dashed it to pieces, exhibiting in the latter part of this singular exercise a degree of spite and fury altogether foreign from his ordinary indolence of manner. The Indians, in the mean while, gazed at this novel achievement with delighted admiration, clapping their hands and shouting applause; and when Hark rested from his labours, some of the oldest warriors patted him on the head, and exclaimed in broken English, " good!" "velly good!" They forthwith conferred upon him a sonorous Indian name, which, being interpreted, signified "He that kills snakes," and treated him afterwards with lenity, and even favour.

It was very evident that the Indians were neither in haste nor fearful of pursuit; for they loitered by the way, stopping at particular places, and examining for signs, as if expecting to fall in with some other war party of their own tribe. At length, towards evening, they reached the brow of a hill, where a small mark was discovered, which had been made by chipping a portion of the bark from a sapling with a tomahawk; and at a distance, in the low ground, a thin column of smoke was seen wreathing above the trees. Here they halted, cut a large pole, which, after stripping off the bark, they painted with several colours, and then planted in the ground. They now cut a lock of hair from the head of each of the pris-

oners, and after braiding them, placed them in a medicine
bag, which they hung upon the pole ; and endeavoured to explain by signs and broken English, that these locks represented
the prisoners whom they intended to adopt into their tribe.
All things being ready, the chief shouted with a loud voice,
uttering certain peculiar yells, by which they intended to convey to their tribe the intelligence of their successful return,
and the number of their prisoners.   Then they formed a
circle round the pole, and joining hands with each other and
with the prisoners who were now taken into companionship,
danced round it, singing and leaping with great vivacity.

After this exercise had continued about half an hour, they
were joined by some of their companions whose smoke they
had seen, and the whole party marched off in great ceremony
to the camp, where Mr. Lee witnessed a spectacle which filled
him with astonishment and horror.   What this was will be
explained in a future chapter.

## CHAPTER XVII.

THE course of our narrative now brings us back to Jenkins' Station. William Colburn, the brave youth who effected the escape of Mr. Lee, was the same hunter to whom the reader was introduced at the carriers' encampment in the Allegheny mountains. He knew the ruffians by whom he was surrounded, and having saved a stranger from their clutches, retired silently to his lodging, little apprehensive of any danger to himself. But his situation was not without peril, which, however he might be disposed to despise it, occupied his thoughts; while the interest that he felt in the stranger, who seemed to have been thrown upon him for protection, concurred to drive sleep from his pillow. The apartment which he occupied was a mere loft, the same which Mr. Lee had just left, immediately above the room in which the noisy ruffians were assembled. Their loud conversation had now ceased, and they seemed to have thrown themselves on the floor to slumber. After some time he heard a slight noise in the apartment below, succeeded by a faint murmur of voices; then a step could be distinguished, as of one slowly ascending to his chamber. He snatched his hunting-knife from the chair beside his bed, and concealing it under the bed-clothes, feigned sleep. A person entered and approached the bed which had been occupied by Lee. A short silence ensued, then a blasphemous expression of disappointment escaped the intruder,

who now partially threw aside a cloak which had concealed a
dark lantern, and a dim light gleamed over the apartment.
Having satisfied himself that the bed before him was empty,
the ruffian turned hastily to that of Colburn, whose placid
features indicated the calmness of profound slumber. The
ruffian laid his hand upon his knife, gazed for an instant with
resentful malignity, and then hastily retired, but not until the
youth had recognised the savage countenance of Patterson.
Colburn heard him enter the room below, and arising lightly
from his bed placed his ear to a crevice in the floor and heard
one of the party exclaim,

"Gone !"

"Ay," replied Patterson, "gone, hook and line."

A confused whispering ensued, from which Colburn could
gather nothing; but directing his eye to the crevice, he saw
Patterson point his finger upwards, and concluded that the
conversation related to himself.

A moment afterwards one of the party remarked, "*He*
knows something about it."

Patterson, with a tremendous oath, replied, "He knows
more than he shall ever tell."

A long consultation ensued, which ended with Patterson's
saying, "Not to-night—it will not do—but to-morrow he
must be taken care of."

During this time Patterson had applied himself several
times to the whiskey-bottle, and becoming much intoxicated,
began to curse his companions as villains and cowards.

"It was you," said he, "that put me on this—I never
attempted the like before—I have stood by you and protected
you in all your villainy—but you know I have always said I
would never be concerned in taking life—I never have done
it before—this is the first time—and when the act come to be
done, you all backed out and left me to do it—but this is the
last time—I shall never lift my hand against a man in the
dark again—"

7*

"Yes, you will," said a coarse voice; and the speaker followed by another person entered the room.

"Harpe!" exclaimed several voices.

"Ay—that's my name; I am not ashamed to own it."

"You ought to be," rejoined Patterson, "for if ever there was a bloody-minded villain——"

"That's enough," said Harpe fiercely, "you and I know each other, and the less we say of one another the better."

"I never killed a man," said Patterson.

"Because you haven't the courage," cried Harpe; "but you pass counterfeit money and steal horses—and besides that, don't I know something about a man's that just gone from here, and another that's asleep," pointing significantly upwards.

Patterson saw that Harpe had been eavesdropping, and felt the necessity of compromising matters.

"I was only joking, Mr. Harpe," said he: "what you do is nothing to nobody but yourself—go your ways, and I'll go mine."

"I am willing to do you a good turn," replied Harpe, "and you must do me one; that lad up there must be—— you understand—or else you must quit the country—and there's another that I missed in the woods, that must be hunted up in the morning—help me, and I'll help you."

Colburn had been satisfied, until now, that he was safe for the night. Being the son of a respectable farmer in a neighbouring settlement, whose courage and enterprise were well known, and being popular himself, he was aware that Patterson and his gang would not dare to molest him under the roof of Jenkins, where a deed of violence could not be perpetrated without the risk of discovery. Had he been a stranger, his situation would have been hopeless; the chances of detection would in that case have been few, and the danger of retribution small, compared with the consequences that would result from an injury to himself. That an attempt would be made in the morning to waylay him in the woods, where no witness would be present, he saw was probable, and to escape that danger required all his ingenuity. But the arrival of the Harpes, and the disclosures he had heard, convinced him that he was placed in imminent peril.

At the time of the escape of the Harpes from justice in the manner formerly related, their names were unknown in Kentucky. They were strangers in the country, and the aggression for which they were then in custody was the first that they were known to have committed. Since then, a series of shocking massacres had given them a dreadful notoriety. They had passed through the whole length of the scattered settlements of this wild region, leaving a bloody track to mark their ruthless footsteps. They spared neither age nor sex, but murdered every unprotected being who fell in their way. What was most extraordinary, they appeared to destroy without motive or temptation. Plunder was a secondary object; the harmless negro and the child were their victims as often as the traveller or the farmer. A native thirst for blood, or a desire of vengeance for some real or imaginary injury, seemed to urge them on in their horrible warfare against their species. They had escaped apprehension thus far, in consequence of the peculiar circumstances of the country, and by a singular exertion of boldness and cunning. Mounted on fleet and powerful horses, they fled, after the perpetration of an outrage, and were heard of no more, until they appeared suddenly at some distant and unexpected point to commit new enormities. Their impunity thus far was the more astonishing, as the people of the frontier have always been remarkable for the public spirit, alertness, and success with which they pursue offenders, who seldom escape these keen and indefatigable hunters.

Colburn was aware that from such enemies he had no chance of escape but in immediate flight, and hastily putting on his clothes, he had the good fortune to slip out of the

house unperceived. A few minutes afterwards, a loud halloo-
ing from beyond the stockade announced the arrival of other
travellers; and Captain Jenkins soon appeared, introducing
a lady and gentleman into the common room, which served
as a receptacle for all the guests, gentle, simple, or compound,
whom chance or inclination brought to this primitive hotel.
The lady was Miss Virginia Pendleton, and the gentleman
Colonel Hendrickson, her uncle—an elderly man, of plain,
but peculiarly imposing exterior. He was spare and muscular, and, though past the age of fifty, seemed to be in the
vigour of strength and activity. His person was erect, his
step martial, and somewhat stately. His features, sunburnt
and nearly as dark as those of the Indian, were austere, and
announced uncompromising firmness. There was in his
deportment towards Miss Pendleton a mixture of parental
kindness with the punctilious courtesy observed by the gentlemen of Kentucky towards all females, as well those of
their own families as others. There was even a more than
ordinary degree of polite observance in his attentions, which
might have arisen, in part, from a spontaneous admiration of
the womanly graces of his lovely ward, and have flowed in
part from sympathy for her misfortunes. These feelings
produced a kind of fatherly gallantry, a mixture of delicacy
and respect with fondness and admiration, which blended
harmoniously with the plain but dignified and gentlemanly
air of the veteran pioneer. They were followed by two
negroes, a man and maid servant, who, having removed the
outer garments of their master and mistress, retired to the
kitchen.

The arrival of Colonel Hendrickson struck the ruffian
party who were assembled round the fire with awe, for he
had long been a terror to evil-doers. They shrunk back to
make room for the travellers, while Micajah Harpe drew
Patterson out of the apartment, and disclosed to him a tremendous scheme of diabolical revenge. Representing the

advantage which would accrue to themselves by ridding the
country of Colonel Hendrickson, an active magistrate and a
man of military skill and intrepidity, he proposed not only
to murder him and his fair ward, but to destroy all evidence
of the foul act by including Jenkins and all the inmates of
the house. Patterson started back in horror at this proposal.
The felons who sometimes infest our frontiers have generally
an aversion against deeds of violence, and seldom practise on
the lives of those they plunder; Patterson, though dissipated,
unprincipled, and a hardened depredator, had never dipped
his hands in blood. But human nature is always progressive
in depravity or in virtue. The heart of man is continually
becoming strengthened in principle, or callous to the dictates
of conscience; and he who embarks in criminal pursuits can
affix no limits to his own atrocity. Some recent occurrences
had rendered Patterson more than ordinarily reckless, and
stirred up his vindictive passions; he was disappointed, excited, and intoxicated—and the foul compact was made.

Supper was prepared for the travellers, and placed upon the
table. Colonel Hendrickson led his niece to the ample board,
and as soon as they were seated, bowed his head, which was
slightly silvered with age, and in a manly, solemn voice,
implored the blessing of Divine Providence. At that moment, while the uncle and niece sat with eyes bent downwards, the two Harpes appeared in the door, and deliberately
aimed their rifles at the unconscious travellers. Their fingers
were already on the triggers—their eyes, gleaming hellish
vengeance, were directed along the deadly tubes with unerring skill, and another second would have rendered all
human aid unavailing, when each of the ruffians was felled
by a powerful blow from behind. The rifles went off, sending
the bullets whistling over the heads of those who had been
doomed to death. Patterson and some of his gang rushed
to the rescue of their confederates, while the assailants,
snatching the guns from the grasp of the prostrate ruffians,

passed rapidly over their bodies, and Fennimore and Colburn
stood by the side of Colonel Hendrickson, who in an instant
comprehended the scene, and acted warily on the defensive.
They were all brave and athletic, and although opposed to
thrice their numbers, the gentlemen thus accidentally thrown
together, stood erect, fearless, alert, and silent. There is a
dignity in courage which awes even opposing courage, and
subdues by a look the mere hardihood which is unsupported
by principle. The ruffians had crowded tumultuously into
the room; but when Colonel Hendrickson and his two
friends, who were all armed, advanced to meet them, they
faltered. Harpe, who was again on his feet, with a voice of
desperation and the fury of a demon urged them to the
attack; but they stood irresolute, each unwilling to commit
himself by striking the first blow, and fearful of being the
foremost in assailing men who stood prepared to sell their
lives at the dearest price; and when Colonel Hendrickson,
in a tone of the most perfect composure and in the most
contemptuous language, commanded them to retire, with
bitter reproaches on their baseness, they slunk away, one by
one, until the two Harpes, finding themselves deserted,
retreated, muttering horrible imprecations.

The doors were now secured, and the arrangement being
made that one of the party should act as a sentinel while the
others slept, alternately, the travellers separated, but not until
Colonel Hendrickson returned to Colburn, who was his neighbour, and to Mr. Fennimore, whom he now saw for the first
time, his hearty thanks and commendations for their gallant
interference. Miss Pendleton, in acknowledging her acquaintance with the young officer, extended her hand with a
cordiality which evinced her gratitude, and having introduced
him to her uncle, retired.

## CHAPTER XVIII.

ON the following morning, Miss Pendleton met the young officer who had a second time been instrumental in saving her life, with some embarrassment. She had seen him first in the spring-day of her happiness and the pride of her beauty, and had mentally awarded to him that preference over most other men of her acquaintance, which the heart so readily accords to a pleasing and amiable exterior. He was associated in her mind with the last of her days of joy, and with the dawn of her misfortunes. She had twice witnessed his courage, voluntarily and generously exerted in her behalf; and if she acknowledged to herself the existence of no more tender feeling, she felt that she at least owed him a debt of gratitude. His abrupt departure from Virginia, at a time when his own conduct had seemed mysterious, and when some explanation seemed to be due to herself, or to the representatives of the deceased Major Heyward, surprised and perplexed her. She had ascertained that he was related, in what degree she knew not, to the guardian of her youth, and his interests had been placed in painful opposition to her own. These recollections passed hastily through her mind, and she met him with a flushed cheek and a constrained manner, very foreign from the usual easy frankness of her deportment. But she saw in him the same traits of character which at first won her confidence—the same calm self-possession, cheerful conversation, and open countenance; and the thin clouds of suspicion which

had cast a momentary shadow over her mind, floated rapidly
away.

After an early breakfast, the whole party mounted and
commenced the journey of the day, for in new countries,
ladies as well as gentlemen travel only on horseback.  They
were not without their apprehensions that the Harpes, who
were desperate and unrelenting villains, might endeavour to
take revenge for the disappointment of the preceding night
by firing upon them from some covert in the woods; but
Colonel Hendrickson, confident that his name and standing
would deter their late confederates from joining in any such
attack, considered his party sufficiently strong to repel any
attempt that might be made upon it.  But every precaution
was used to ensure safety; the gentlemen, who were all provided with rifles, loaded them carefully, and the little company was arranged with all the precision that would have
attended the march of a squadron of cavalry.  Fennimore
managed, as young men are apt to do in such cases, to place
himself by the side of Miss Pendleton, the other two gentlemen
took the van, while the servants brought up the rear.  Their
way led through the same lonesome expanse of forest which
had been traversed by Mr. Lee, when suddenly ejected from
the hospitable roof of Captain Jenkins, in the manner related:
a vast wilderness, rich in the spontaneous productions of
nature, but in which the travellers could not expect to see a
human being, or a dwelling, until their arrival at their place
of destination.

In travelling, many of the restraints of social intercourse are
necessarily laid aside ; and those whose lots are thus for the
time being cast together, find it expedient as well as agreeable
to render themselves acceptable to each other.  There is a
race of islanders, who, in travelling, become even more unsocial, morose, and supercilious, than they are at home; but
the ordinary effect of this occupation upon human nature is
such as we have suggested ; and well-bred persons, in particu-

lar, always bring their politeness into active exercise, when the necessity of the case renders this accomplishment a virtue. And at the risk of being accused of national vanity, we will assert that our own countrymen are the best travellers in the world, the most affable, patient, and cheerful, and the least incommoded by accidental hardships. An occasion like the one before us is particularly calculated to produce the effects to which we have alluded—when the long and lonesome way exhibits a wild but gloomy monotony of scenery, and a sense of danger unites the parties in the bond of a common interest.

Thus felt the young and grateful pair of riders, who had, besides, so many reasons for entertaining a strong interest in each other. Mr. Fennimore exerted all his powers in the endeavour to render himself agreeable, and people who try to please most generally succeed, for the art of pleasing depends almost entirely upon the will; and the young lady with that admirable tact, in the possession of which her sex is infinitely superior to ours, displayed her conversational powers with more than ordinary vivacity and eloquence. We shall not set down what passed, because we were not there; and if we had been, it would ill become us to give publicity to those sprightly and unpremeditated sallies which were never intended for other ears than those to which they were addressed, but flowed spontaneously from young hearts in the glow of unrestrained feeling. Tradition has only preserved the fact, that although they rode forth from the woodland fortress, on a bright sunny morning, as stately as a hero and heroine of chivalry, it was not long before they were laughing and chatting like people of flesh and blood and wit and feeling.

They had travelled for some hours when the experienced eye of Colonel Hendrickson discovered the fresh track of a horse in the path before them. On dismounting and examining more closely, it appeared that several horses had entered the path at this place and passed on in the same direction

pursued by our travellers; and one of the tracks was pro
nounced by Colburn to be that of the horse of Patterson.
That the gang whose villainy they had so much cause to dread,
should have taken the same direction with themselves, and at
the same time should have avoided the beaten path for so
great a distance, were circumstances so suspicious as to leave
little doubt of a design to attack them at some point, which
was now probably near at hand. In the irritation of the moment, nothing would have pleased these gentlemen more
than to have marched directly upon the ruffians; but a proper care for the lady under their charge rendered more prudent measures advisable; and, after a short consultation, it
was determined to abandon the road and to endeavour to
avoid the danger by taking a circuitous route through the
forest. They now proceeded rapidly through the woods, observing all the precautions of a warlike party; avoiding the
thickets and low grounds, and keeping along the ridges and in
the most open woods. This mode of travelling was extremely
arduous, for they were now obliged to pass over many in-
equalities of ground, and to surmount a variety of obstacles.
At one moment they leaped their horses over the trunk of a
fallen tree, at another they climbed a steep hill; sometimes
deep ravines were to be crossed, and sometimes low branches,
or the great grape-vines swinging from tree to tree obliged
them to bow their heads as they passed along.

After riding several miles in this manner, guided only by
that knowledge of natural appearances which enables the experienced hunter to ascertain the points of the compass,
under almost any circumstances, they arrived at the bank of
a deep creek, which was not fordable except at the spot where
it was crossed by the road they had forsaken, and where the
robbers would be most likely to await their approach. As
there are several modes of passing over streams, practised by
backwoodsmen, they rode along the bank consulting as to the
most practicable expedient, when they reached a place where

a large tree had fallen across the creek, affording the very facility which they desired. Few ladies, however, would have possessed sufficient courage and dexterity to have walked over this natural bridge. The banks of the creek were extremely high, and the trunk of the fallen tree was still further elevated by the large roots at the one end, and the immense branches at the other, so that its distance from the water was so great, as to render it unpleasant to look downwards. But Virginia had a mind which could not be daunted by ordinary dangers, and stepping nimbly upon the log, she walked with a firm step along its round and narrow surface, and reached the opposite shore in safety. The saddles and baggage were carried over by the same way. The greatest difficulty was to cross the horses, for the banks were so steep and miry, as to render it impossible to get them into the water. By dint of coaxing, pushing, and whipping, however, all the animals were forced in, except that belonging to Colburn; and after swimming part of the way, and floundering through mire the remainder, they struggled up the opposite bank, where Colonel Hendrickson and Fennimore stood to receive them.

Colburn had remained alone, and was about to send over the last horse which was still fastened to a tree, when the rapid tramp of horses' feet was heard upon the dry leaves, and he had barely time to unloose his steed and spring upon its back, when Patterson and his confederates came sweeping towards him at full speed. To cross the creek with his horse was now impossible; to abandon the animal and seek safety for himself on the other side would have been but the work of an instant, but Colburn loved his horse, and had too much spirit to give him up to an enemy. Besides, the heroic idea occurred to him at the moment, of making a diversion in favour of his friends, by drawing the pursuit upon himself. Catching up his rifle which leaned against a tree, he shouted to his companions to take care of themselves, and turning towards the pursuers, flourished his weapon round his head in bravado, and dashed off through the forest. The outlaws saw that the party which had crossed the creek was beyond their grasp, as it was but a few miles to Colonel Hendrickson's settlement, which could be reached by the fugitives before they themselves could accomplish the tedious process of crossing with their horses; nor were they willing to attempt the passage in the face of two resolute men armed with rifles. Their whole fury, therefore, was turned towards Colburn, and uttering a volley of execrations, they put spurs to their horses, and went off at full speed in pursuit of the young forester.

Colburn, well mounted and admirably skilled in all the arts of the hunter, had little doubt of being able to evade his enemies by speed or artifice; and guided only by the sun, and by his knowledge of the country, pressed onward through the trackless forest. Relying on the great strength of his steed, and his own superior horsemanship, he often chose the most difficult ground, leaping over ravines, plunging down steep declivities, or dashing through dense thickets where thorns and tangled vines seemed to render it impossible for any animal to pass; and he had the satisfaction of seeing more than one of his pursuers thrown from their horses, while others were left in the rear. Still they kept upon his track, with the unerring sagacity of woodsmen.

Patterson, who, although the largest man, was best mounted, soon left his comrades, straining forward to overtake the young hunter; while Colburn, confident of success, and anxious only to separate his pursuers and keep them in his rear, so as to prevent their surrounding or intercepting him, held up his horse, to husband his powers for a long race. But he had judged too meanly of the animal ridden by Patterson, who soon came in sight, uttering a loud yell when he beheld the young forester, and madly urging his steed over every obstacle. Still the advantage was in favour of Col burn, who, being the lightest rider, and mounted on a fine-blooded animal, led the outlaw through the most intricate ways, passing dexterously through thickets apparently impenetrable, plunging into deep morasses, and leaping ravines which seemed impassable.  The latter pursued with spirit, sometimes gaining a view of his adversary, and sometimes falling in the rear.

At one time an accident had nearly decided the contest, for Colburn's horse became entangled in a close thicket of hazel and grape-vines, and the outlaw came near enough to discharge his rifle deliberately, and with so true an aim that the ball passed along the side of the hunter inflicting a severe though not a dangerous wound.  The young man extricated himself from the tangled brushwood, reined up his horse, and turning towards his enemy waved his hat in the air, shouted in derision, and then rode on with unsubdued alacrity.  At last, in leaping over the trunk of a fallen tree, his horse sprained an ankle and Colburn found that it was impossible to retreat any longer.  A gentle swell of the ground concealed him at that moment from Patterson, who had stopped to reload his rifle, and hastily pushing his horse into a clump of bushes he crouched behind a tree to await the coming of his foe.  In a few minutes Patterson came in sight, pressing eagerly forward with his heels closed into his horse's flanks, his eye gleaming with fury and his countenance animated by the excitement of an anticipated triumph.  When he arrived within a few paces of the spot where Colburn stood concealed, the latter stepped boldly out, directly in front of the advancing horseman and presented his rifle.  Patterson with a powerful arm reined up his horse, dropped the bridle and threw his gun to his shoulder; and before he could fire the young forester's ball passed through his body, and the wretch fell forward with a deep groan upon his horse's neck. Instantly recovering his strength, he raised himself in his stirrups and charged upon Colburn with his rifle presented ; but the latter no longer avoiding the combat darted nimbly upon his foe, and throwing his arms around him dragged him from the saddle. For a moment they struggled fiercely upon the ground ; the ruffian abandoning his gun drew his knife ; but Colburn parried the stroke and at the same time disengaging himself seized the loaded rifle of his adversary and stood on the defensive. Patterson attempted to rise, but his career of crime was ended !

The young forester now caught the outlaw's horse, which stood trembling beside his own disabled animal, and having re-loaded his rifle continued his retreat. He was pursued no further. The ruffian gang were struck with panic when they reached the spot where their comrade lay in his gore, a mangled corpse. They had perhaps carried their scheme further than had been at first intended, and they now feared the consequences of their audacious attempt. The remains of Patterson were hastily buried at the lone spot where he had fallen ; and the unprincipled companions of his guilty life, dispersing in different directions, sought safety in concealment or flight.

Colonel Hendrickson and his young friends had been greatly shocked on beholding the peril in which Colburn was placed when surprised, as we have narrated. But it was impossible to render him any assistance, and when the sounds of the pursuit died away, they recommenced their journey with heavy hearts. They soon regained the road which they had left in the morning, and descending from the high grounds struck into a rich flat through which a deep creek was sluggishly meandering. On their right hand the Ohio, smooth and transparent as a mirror, suddenly burst upon their view. They stopped and gazed for a moment with delight—for there is something so cheerful in the appearance of a beautiful sheet of water, that the same scenery which had seemed gloomy without it, became, with this addition, gay, brilliant, and romantic. The western bank of the river was low and fringed to the water's edge with trees, whose long limbs dipped into the current, while their shadows stretched far over the stream, and pictured the exact contour of the shore upon the green surface. Nearer to them the beams of the setting sun fell upon the water, tinging it with a golden hue. There was a softness and repose in this landscape that were irresistibly charming; no living object was to be seen, not a leaf moved, not a sound was heard; all was serene and silent.

Their path now pursued the course of the river for a short distance, then turning from it at right angles crossed the creek by a deep ford. They had nearly reached the fording-place, when their horses pricked their ears, snorted aloud, and stopped trembling in the path. At the same instant the travellers discovered that they were beset on all sides by a party of Indians, hideously painted, who had risen from an ambuscade, and stood around with their rifles pointed, and their black eyes gleaming with a hellish triumph. They uttered a terrific yell when they beheld their victims; our travellers saw their ghastly smiles, their murderous looks, their flashing knives, and felt in anticipation the tortures of a lingering death. A single glance satisfied them that it was impossible to reach the ford, as the largest body of the savages stood in that direction, while on either hand they were so stationed as to cut off all hope of retreat. One of superior stature stood in the path a few paces before them, laughing with demoniac exultation as he took a deliberate aim and discharged his rifle. This was the signal of attack; several others fired at the same time, and a number of tomahawks whistled around the heads of the assailed party.

Colonel Hendrickson and Mr. Fennimore closed up on each side of Miss Pendleton, endeavouring to shield her with their own persons, and beating back the assailants with the most desperate courage. But they were overpowered by numbers. Colonel Hendrickson was dragged to the ground. Fennimore received a wound which caused him to reel in his saddle. A faint and sickly numbness was creeping over him. At this instant his horse wheeled suddenly and plunged into

the thicket.　He rushed through the savage band, who in vain
attempted to arrest his flight, and in a moment stood on the
margin of the creek.　The bank was perpendicular, arising to
a considerable height above the water; but the noble animal
without hesitating leaped forward and alighted in the turbid
stream, about midway from either shore.　A few powerful
struggles brought him to the opposite side, which was steep,
but less precipitous than the other.　Clambering up the bank
he soon reached the level of the plain, and darted through the
forest with the swiftness of an arrow, bearing his rider
wounded and nearly insensible beyond the reach of pursuit.

# CHAPTER XIX.

THE place to which Mr. Lee was conducted by his captors was situated in a secluded valley among a range of low hills. At a spot from which the underbrush had been cleared away, so as to form an open space, shaded by tall trees, a number of Indian warriors armed and painted for war were arranged in a circle and seated upon the ground. In the centre, strongly bound to a tree, was a man of large stature, whose face was painted black,—an indication, as Lee recollected to have heard, that the prisoner was doomed to death. Near the victim was a lady also bound, in whom the eye of our young friend instantly recognised the companion of his childhood, the idol of his heart, the long-loved Virginia Pendleton!

The warriors of the newly arrived party were received with much ceremony by their friends, with whom they took their seats, while Mr. Lee and Hark were placed within the circle. A conversation ensued, in which only the older and more conspicuous of the warriors participated. They spoke with deliberation but with much emphasis, and from their pointing frequently towards the east, it was inferred that they were severally relating to each other the incidents of the late predatory excursion.

Their attention was then directed towards their prisoners, and the interest with which they referred to him who was bound to the tree, who was Colonel Hendrickson, showed that

8

they exulted in his capture with no ordinary degree of triumph. One of the warriors approached him and addressed to him a speech in which he seemed to pour out a volume of eloquent hatred, contempt, and ridicule upon the defenceless captive, often brandishing his tomahawk as he spoke, and describing with gestures too significant to be mistaken, the tortures that were proposed to be inflicted. The unfortunate gentleman eyed him with perfect composure, and listened to his speech without showing the least appearance of fear or irritation. Several warriors then placed themselves in front of the captive, and prepared to throw their tomahawks.

Lee, whose good-nature and chivalrous feelings began to be warmly enlisted, now sprung up, and rushing towards the victim exclaimed to the torturers, "Gentlemen! gentlemen Indians! consider what you are about—don't murder the gentleman! If he has done you any harm, I'll be security that he shall make you ample satisfaction;" while poor Virginia shrieked and buried her face in her hands. In a moment George Lee was at her side; "Virginia! dear Virginia!" he cried, "don't be alarmed—they shall not touch you—I'll fight for you while there's a drop of blood in my veins!" But the Indians did not intend to slay their prisoner. Paying no attention to the distress of his friends, which only afforded them amusement, they threw their tomahawks, one after another, in such a manner as to strike them into the tree immediately over his head, each striving to come as near as possible to the mark without actually hitting it. Others came and threw spears in the same mode, and a variety of other means were used to torture and intimidate their victim, and to induce him to degrade himself by showing some symptom of alarm. But all to no purpose: Colonel Hendrickson was well acquainted with the habits of his enemies; he had prepared himself to die, and faced his savage persecutors with the composure of intrepid resignation.

The feelings of his companions in misfortune may be better

imagined than described. The unhappy Virginia, though her
high spirit enabled her to display a show of resignation, felt
herself bowed down by this unexpected calamity. The calm
fortitude of her brave relative, while it won her admiration
and stimulated her courage, made her heart bleed for the
sufferings of one so worthy of a nobler fate. Mr. Lee had
ceased to entertain any fears for his own safety, but his love
for Virginia, and his native goodness of heart, induced him to
sympathise deeply with his fellow-sufferers; while Hark, who
had withdrawn himself from observation as much as possible,
was lying on the ground, coiled up, gnawing a bone that had
been thrown to him, and hiding another which he had stolen,
casting stealthy and watchful glances around him all the while,
as if in constant dread of harm, but lying so motionless that
his eye alone afforded the slightest indication of his apprehension.

At length the shades of night closed in, and the warriors
prepared for repose. Colonel Hendrickson remained tied to
the tree; Miss Pendleton sat not far from him on the ground,
but no intention was shown of offering her any thing to lie
upon, or any covering to protect her from the night air. Lee
was more favoured, for, as the Indians happened to have
several blankets among the plunder recently taken, one of
these was thrown to him. Our friend George immediately
threw his blanket over the shoulders of Virginia, and obliging
Hark to resign a similar present that had been made to him,
was enabled effectually to protect the young lady from the
cold. The Indians interposed no objection to these arrangements; though they look upon acts of gallantry with sovereign contempt, they know how to estimate a humane
action, and thought none the less of George Lee for this
sacrifice of his own comfort in favour of *a woman of his
tribe.*

Silence reigned throughout the camp. Not a sound was
heard but the footsteps of the armed sentinels, who moved

incessantly about, watching the prisoners with jealous eye,
and listening with intense eagerness to catch the most distant
sound which might announce the approach of an enemy.   As
they glided slowly in the shade of night, rendered still deeper
by the thick shadows of the overhanging forest, and but
slightly relieved by the faint glow of an expiring fire, they
seemed more like spectres than human beings.   Colonel Hendrickson remained in a standing posture, bound securely and
painfully to a great tree which was probably destined to be
his place of execution.   He knew that the Indians more frequently carry to their villages the prisoners destined to death
by torture, in order that the women, the children, and the
whole tribe may participate in the horrid entertainment and
derive instruction in the dreadful rites of cruelty.   A conformity with that custom might procure him a reprieve for a
few days, though it would enhance the tortures that inevitably
awaited him; while a more speedy death on the spot they
then occupied would cut off all hope of rescue.   Occupied
with such reflections, it was impossible to sleep; but though
denied repose, he was not without consolation.   Colonel Hendrickson was a Christian; and in this trying hour, when
enduring torture and anticipating a lingering and excruciating
death, he submitted with the most perfect composure to the
will of the great Disposer of all events.   He prayed silently
but with fervour and sincerity, in the full belief that he was
heard, and that his was "the fervent effectual prayer of the
righteous," which availeth much to the humble petitioner.
His devotional feelings became quickened and elevated by
this exercise, until at last the overflowings of his heart burst
from his lips in audible and eloquent language.

Virginia, who dozed, but did not sleep, raised her head
when these solemn accents struck her ear.   The embers of a
nearly extinguished fire threw a faint glare over the figure of
Colonel Hendrickson and rendered his features distinctly
visible, while an impenetrable veil of darkness hung around

The forms of the Indian warriors could be barely distinguished as they reposed on the ground and raised their heads at this unexpected interruption. Their dim outlines only could be faintly traced in the uncertain light, except where here and there a scattered ray fell upon the harsh visage of a savage warrior, and for a moment lighted up the ferocious lineaments. The only object upon which the expiring blaze threw its beams directly was the victim prisoner, whose person resembled the prominent figure in a gloomy and deeply shaded picture. His appearance was strikingly sublime. His large frame, placed thus in bold relief, and dimly illuminated, assumed gigantic dimensions to the fancy of the beholder. His face was serene and tranquil, his full, bold eye meekly raised towards heaven. Neither fear nor resentment marked his features; all was hope, confidence, and calm self-possession. His voice was full and manly; his enunciation deliberate, though impassioned; his language, the bold, the beautiful, the affecting phraseology of the holy scriptures. Even the eye of the savage was attracted by this picturesque and striking spectacle exhibited in the lone wilderness and at the midnight hour, and all gazed upon it in wonder and in silence. They knew their prisoner to be a distinguished warrior, before whose arm some of the most renowned of their tribe had fallen; and when they heard his solemn voice, beheld his dignified composure, and saw him in the act of holding converse with the Master of life, under circumstances so calculated to impress the imagination, they regarded him as a being under supernatural protection, and were filled with awe. And although they would have felt a dread in approaching him at that moment, they were the more determined to rid themselves as soon as possible of so hated and so powerful a foe.

Gradually the fire became extinguished, a thick cloud gathered over the camp, and total darkness shrouded the spot. The voice of the prisoner ceased, the warriors sunk again to their slumbers, and all was silent. The sentinels renewed their vigilance, and as their eyesight could now avail nothing, other precautions were used to prevent any attempt to escape on the part of the prisoners. It was near daybreak, when Colonel Hendrickson felt a hand passing slowly from his feet upward along his person—and then another hand which evidently grasped a knife. He knew that almost every Indian had some individual quarrel to avenge upon the white men, which he broods over in secret until a favourable opportunity enables him to satiate his appetite for vengeance; and he supposed that some warrior who had lost a relative in battle, was now about to take that revenge which is so grateful to their lust of blood. Brave as he was, a chill crept over him, and the blood almost ceased to flow in his veins as he felt the hand of the murderer cautiously seeking out, as he supposed, the vital spot, into which he might plunge his weapon with the certainty of reaching the life of his victim. The point of the knife was pressed to his back, and he expected to feel the steel passing through from that direction, when the cord that bound his hands was suddenly cut, and in a moment he stood free from his bonds. His unknown friend glided away with a step as noiseless as that with which he had approached; and the released prisoner had now to exert his own ingenuity in effecting his escape.

His determination was soon made. To attempt to release his companions would endanger all their lives; and should he succeed in escaping with them from the camp, it was next to impossible that such a party could elude the pursuit of a large number of skilful warriors, who would follow them at the break of day, which could be little more than an hour distant. But he was himself a woodsman; hardy, cunning, and swift of foot: with a start of an hour, he believed he could outstrip the fleetest of the savage warriors, and bring a rescue to his friends, whose lives were probably not in immediate danger. He stole silently from the camp, passed the sentinels, and in a few minutes was rapidly making his way through the forest, with unerring skill, towards the waters of the Ohio.

Great was the astonishment and bitter the imprecations of the savages, when they discovered, at the first dawn of day, the escape of their prisoner. They were almost frantic with disappointment and fury, and were ready to sacrifice their remaining prisoners to their rage. Suspicion very naturally fell upon them as having been instrumental in the escape of Colonel Hendrickson; but after a close examination it did not appear that Mr. Lee or Miss Pendleton had moved. At length a track, different from that of an Indian, was discovered near the tree to which the victim had been tied, and a yell of rage was uttered by the whole gang. It was the track of Hark Short, the snake-killer, who, it was now perceived, was also missing.

# CHAPTER XX.

NO sooner were these discoveries made, than the greater portion of the warriors set out in immediate pursuit of the fugitives, while a few remained to guard the prisoners. Mr. Lee and Miss Pendleton were now seated near each other, and for the first time had the opportunity of conversing together; and the latter addressing her former playmate with the frankness due to so old an acquaintance, expressed her regret for his misfortune, while she could not help congratulating herself on having a friend near her at so trying a period.

"Ah, cousin Virginia!" exclaimed George, "how willingly would I bear captivity, or even death, to do you a service!"

This speech savoured too much of gallantry for the time and place, and Miss Pendleton looked very grave.

"Dear Virginia," continued George, "don't be cast down; they will not have the heart to do you any harm. I have been a brother to you all my life—you have been kinder to me, and dearer to me, than a sister—and they shall not separate us, while I have a drop of blood in my veins."

"Thank you, cousin George," was all that Virginia could reply, while the tears started from her eyes. This touching proof of affection went to her heart, and her noble nature enabled her to comprehend the full extent of the sacrifice that her kind-hearted companion was willing to make for her. Had that affection flowed only from the friendship of the playmate of her early years, it would have been most grate-

ful to her feelings; but sensible as she was that it resulted
from a hopeless passion, which she could not encourage without insincerity, nor without cherishing hopes which she felt
could never be realized, it distressed and pained her. She
endeavoured to change the subject, but the single-hearted
George always came back to the same point, and continually
exclaimed, "Poor Virginia!" "Dear cousin Virginia!" "To
think that *you, you,* should be here, a prisoner among savages!"

At length a new thought seemed to strike him; and starting up suddenly, he beckoned the Indian to him, who seemed
to have been the chief person in the party by which be was
taken. This person had seemed to claim George as his own
prisoner, and had treated him with a show of kindness. To
him Mr. Lee now offered to give any ransom which might be
demanded, for the liberty of Miss Pendleton, assuring the
Indian of his ability to comply with any contract which he
might make. The Indian, who spoke a little broken English,
readily understood the proposition, and listened to it with
interest.

"Hugh!" said he, "how much?"

George, who was no great hand at making a bargain, and
was besides too much in love to think of standing upon trifles,
replied eagerly that he would give all he was worth for her
liberation.

"Velly good!" replied the Indian, perfectly comprehend-
ing the offer, "how much—how much you got?"

George told him that he owned a thousand acres of land;
and the Indian shook his head, and, swinging his arms with a
lordly contempt, as he pointed to the vast forest around
them, gave the Virginian to understand that he had land
enough.

The Indian then inquired if he had any "*whiskee.*"

George had no whiskey, though his cellar at home contained some very choice liquors; but said he had money

8*

enough buy to boat-loads of it, and promised to give his captor much as would keep the whole tribe drunk for a month.

"Hugh! velly good!" exclaimed the delighted Indian, who then inquired for tobacco.

"Plenty, plenty, my dear fellow," cried George, who thought he was making a fine bargain, "I raise ever so much on my own plantation every year. You shall have as much as you can use all your life!"

"How much hos?" inquired the warrior.

"Horses! no man in Virginia has more horses or finer ones. I have more than forty on my plantation now, as fine blooded animals as ever you saw."

"How much?" inquired the Indian, who had caught the meaning sufficiently to see that a large number was intended to be expressed, but without understanding exactly how many.

George was at a loss how to explain, until the Indian directed him to hold up his fingers. He then held up both hands to express ten. The Indian nodded. Lee repeated the operation, and the Indian nodded with still greater satisfaction; and this dumb show was carried on until Mr. Lee had signified that he was willing to give forty horses, in addition to the whiskey and tobacco before stipulated, for the ransom of the lady of his heart.

Avarice is a passion which exists in some form in every state of society; the Indian can make all the other feelings and propensities of his nature bend to his interest as well as the most civilized inhabitant of a commercial city. The wealth of George Lee had its usual effect upon his captor. Naturally distrustful, he had some misgivings as to the sincerity of so generous an offer, and he could hardly conceive how one man could be so rich as to possess so many horses and such a quantity of whiskey and tobacco; but then Lee had an ingenuous countenance and a rather imposing person and appearance, and, upon the whole, the Indian felt disposed to credit his word. Inasmuch, however, as he had proffered freely thus far, the crafty savage determined to try how far he might extort from the liberality of his captive; and he again inquired if Mr. Lee had nothing more to offer.

George considered and muttered aside, "Yes, I have a great gang of negroes—but I can't give them to be roasted and eaten by the savages—no, plague on it, I couldn't have the heart to send my black people here"—and he prudently replied that he had nothing more to give.

The warrior shook his head and intimated that unless more was offered he should marry the lady himself.

"Heaven forbid!" exclaimed the terrified lover, "take all I have,—take my farm! take my black people! I have a hundred likely negroes; you shall have them all!"

"Nigger!" said the Indian, "velly good—help squaw to make corn—how much nigger?"

George had now to go through the tedious process of counting his fingers, frequently stopping, in hopes that the cupidity of the savage would be satisfied without taking all; but the latter possessed that faculty of the wily gambler or the experienced merchant, which enables its possessor to judge from the countenance of the subject under operation whether he is still able to bear a little more depletion, and continued to shake his head until George declared that the black people were all counted. He then coolly remarked that he should keep the woman himself.

George flew into a rage, and then burst into tears—"You unconscionable rascal!" he cried, "will nothing satisfy you? I offer you all I have in the world for the liberty of this lady. I am willing, besides, to stay and serve you myself all my life. Set her free, you avaricious dog, and I will stay and be overseer for you among my own negroes!"

"The white man has a forked tongue," replied the warrior calmly: "when he offered horses, whiskey, and tobacco for his squaw, I thought he was honest. White men are fools;

they will give all they have for a palefaced woman.  But
when the white man offers to sell himself to be a servant to
the Indian women, and to send his squaw back to the thirteen
fires, I know that he speaks lies."

So saying, he walked off.  But the overture had a good
effect.  The idea of procuring a valuable ransom for Miss
Pendleton determined the Indians to treat her with kindness.
A lodge of mats was prepared for her, and she soon found
herself placed in a situation of comparative comfort.  She
was not an inattentive listener to the preceding conversation.
The solicitude and generosity of Lee affected her deeply.
But she was generous herself, and noble natures know how to
receive as well as to confer obligations.  Conscious that her
warm-hearted friend was offering no more than she would
have freely given to redeem him or any other human being
from so dreadful a fate, she did not attempt to interfere until
he proposed to become a slave himself.  Then she exclaimed,
" No ! not so—George—cousin George Lee—dear George—"
but he heard her not, and in the vehemence of his exertions
in her behalf he lost perhaps the tenderest words that she
had ever addressed to him since the days of their childhood.

But however Miss Pendleton's heart might have been
awakened to sensations of gratitude, she felt that this was not
the time nor place to indulge them ; and in the exhausted
state of her mind and body she readily and hastily accepted
the shelter prepared for her, and throwing herself, stupefied
with sufferings of various kind, upon a mat, endeavoured to
to find repose.  She had sunk into a feverish slumber, when
she was awaked by the noise of loud and triumphant shouting.
The camp was again crowded with Indian warriors ; the party
which had gone in pursuit of the fugitives was returned ; they
had overtaken Colonel Hendrickson, and that unfortunate
gentleman was again a prisoner.  His fate was now sealed.
The determination which had originally been formed of carrying him to the village of the captors to be publicly sacrificed

was now abandoned; and the savages determined to gratify their eager thirst for his blood by torturing him at the stake without further delay. He was again bound, and preparations were made for the awful solemnity. Some of the savages employed themselves in painting their faces and bodies, to render them the more terrific; others were whetting the edges of their tomahawks and knives; and some were endeavouring to excite their own passions and those of their companions to the utmost pitch of fury by hideous yelling, by violent gesticulations, and by pouring out bitter execrations upon their defenceless prisoner.

"I saw you in the dark and blood ground," cried one, drawing the back of his knife, in mockery, across the throat of the victim—"You killed my brother there, and I will have your heart's blood!"

"You slew my son," shrieked a hoary-headed savage; "his bones lie unburied in the villages of the white men, his scalp his hanging over the door of your wigwam—but his spirit shall rejoice in the agonies of your death!"

"You led the warriors of your tribe to battle," exclaimed a young warrior, as he flourished his tomahawk over the head of the veteran pioneer, "when the long knives met the red men on the banks of the big river—my father fell there— your foot was on his neck—I will trample on your mangled body. The wolf shall feed upon your flesh—the bird of night shall flap her wings over your carcase, and the serpent shall crawl about your bones!"

"Revenge is sweet!" shouted one.

"Revenge! revenge!" echoed many voices.

"It is good and pleasing to the spirit of the warrior to witness the death-pang of the enemy he hates!" exclaimed another human monster.

"The white man is our enemy!"

"He is the serpent that stung our fathers!"

"He is the prowling fox that stole away our game!"

" He is the hurricane that scattered our wigwams and destroyed our corn-fields!"

" He drove us from our hunting-grounds, and trampled in scorn upon the bones of our fathers!"

" His knife has drunk the blood of the red man; the blood of our women and children is on his hands!"

" Let him perish in torture!"

" Let him be slowly consumed by fire!"

" The great Spirit will laugh, when he sees the white man writhing in agony!"

" The spirits of our fathers will rejoice—they will shout and clap their hands in the world of shades, when they hear the shrieks of the white warrior."

These exclamations were uttered severally by different individuals in the Indian tongue, with which Colonel Hendrickson was acquainted, in the emphatic tones of savage declamation, and with that earnestness of gesticulation which renders their eloquence so impressive. There were others who addressed the victim in coarser language, loading him with opprobrious epithets, and pouring out the bitterness of their malignant hearts in copious streams of vulgar invective. And now the wood was piled about the victim; torches were lighted and blazing brands snatched from the fire, and the hellish crew, flourishing them around their heads, danced round the prisoner with that malignant joy with which devils and damned spirits may be supposed to exult in the agonies of a fallen soul.

At length a chief stepped forward and commanded silence. " White man," said he, " are you ready to die?"

"I am!" replied the brave Kentuckian, in a calm tone: " The white man's God has whispered peace to my soul."

" Can the God of the white man save you from torture? Can he prevent you from feeling pain when your flesh shall be torn, when your limbs shall be separated, one by one, from your body, and the slow flames shall scorch, without consuming, your miserable carcase?"

"My God is a merciful God," replied the undaunted pioneer; "his ear is ever open to the prayers of those who put their trust in him. He has filled my heart with courage. I have no fear of death—blessed for ever be the Lord God of Israel!" Then raising his eyes upward, he exclaimed, with devout fervour, "Make haste, O God, to deliver me; make haste to help me, O Lord. Let them be ashamed and confounded that seek after my soul: let them be turned backward, and put to confusion, that desire my heart!"

Virginia, who had thus far endeavoured to restrain her feelings, now rushed forward, and gliding rapidly through the circle of warriors, threw herself upon her uncle's bosom, exclaiming in frantic accents, "Let us die together!" while George Lee, who had gazed on the preceding scene with stupid wonder, sought to follow her, determined to share her fate. Being prevented, he swore that it was "the most infamous transaction he had ever witnessed, and that if he got back to old Virginia, he would have satisfaction, at the risk of his life."

And now the whole fury of the savage band was ready to be poured upon their devoted but heroic prisoner, when the report of a single rifle rang through the woods, and the principal chief, who stood alone, received a death-wound. A volley instantly followed, and every ball being aimed by a skilful hand at a particular object, brought one of the Indian warriors to the ground; in another minute, a band of hardy backwoodsmen, headed by Fennimore and Colburn, rushed into the camp. Before the Indians had time to array themselves for battle, the bonds of Colonel Hendrickson were cut, and Fennimore had passed one arm round Miss Pendleton, while he prepared to defend her with the other.

The assailants rushed upon the savage band, and hewed them down with desperate valour. Colonel Hendrickson

snatched up a war-club, and plunged into the thickest of the
fight. Nor was George Lee backward; he first sought Virginia, and finding her supported by the young soldier, he
caught up a weapon, and mingled in the battle with more
hearty good-will than he had for some days shown for any
operation in which he was called upon to join, except that
of eating. The valour and skill of the backwoodsmen soon
prevailed. It was impossible to withstand their fury. Colonel Hendrickson seemed a new man; he shouted until the
woods resounded with his battle-cry, and his friends, animated
by the sound of his voice, returned the yell, and pressed on
with determined vigour. They literally cried aloud and
spared not. The Indians sounded their terrific war-whoop;
but that cry, so dreadful to the white man, so full of thrilling
horror to the hearts of the borderers who have heard it in the
lone hour of night, breaking in upon the repose of the wilderness, and ringing the death-knell of the mother and the infant, was drowned in the louder shouts of the Kentucky
warriors.

The first fire had reduced the savages to a number less
than that of the assailants, and they now stood opposed to
men who were their superiors in bodily strength, their equals
in courage and in all the arts of border warfare. Thus over-
matched, they maintained the fight for but a little while,
when they began to give back; the whites still pressed on,
cutting them down with the most revengeful hostility at
every step. The battle soon became a massacre, for the
Kentuckians not having lost a single man, the disparity of
force was becoming greater every moment; and those who
had so often witnessed the scenes of savage barbarity, or
mourned over the affecting consequences of that unsparing
warfare, now dealt their blows with unrelenting animosity.

So long as the battle raged round the spot where Miss
Pendleton stood, Fennimore joined in it, supporting her with
his arm and shielding her with his body, while he performed

a soldier's duty with his sword. But when the Indians began to give way he withdrew from the fight, and gave his whole attention to his fair charge. Not to George Lee; animated with a newly-awakened fury, smeared with blood, and shouting like a madman, he rushed forward among the foremost, beating down the stoutest warriors with his war-club, and taking full satisfaction for all the fright, the sufferings, and the hunger he had endured. While thus engaged he saw the Indian who had captured him and had saved his life struck down by a sturdy backwoodsman, who was aiming the death-blow at his prostrate foe.

"Don't strike!" cried George, "that's a good fellow—he treated me well——"

But he spoke to deaf ears; the tomahawk fell, and the only Indian in whom he had seen any thing to conciliate his good-will slept with the mangled dead.

"Bless me," cried George, "what a bloody business! They are all alike—Indians and Kentuckians—a blood-thirsty set."

Having uttered this moral reflection he drew his gory hand across his brow to wipe off the big drops of perspiration. The battle swept on past him like a heavy storm which no human hand can stay, and his momentary pause gave him time to look round. The ground was strewed with the dead and dying; wherever he turned his eye it fell on distorted features and gaping wounds, from which the crimson current still flowed. He stepped forward and the blood gurgled under his footstep. Groans and convulsive breathings fell upon his ear. His heart sickened at the scene of horror, and he slowly retraced his steps to the camp-fire of the vanquished Indians.

Colonel Hendrickson and young Colburn, who fought side by side through the whole contest, were the last to relinquish the pursuit. The veteran seemed to be animated with a supernatural strength and activity, and to be actuated by an inhuman ferocity. Wherever his blow fell it crushed; but his fury was unabated. Blood seemed to whet his appetite for blood. As he struck down the last enemy within his reach he halted, and his eye seemed to gloat upon the victims of his revenge. His cheek was flushed, his nostrils distended, and his muscles full of action—like those of a pawing war-horse. In a moment this excitement began to subside, and he exclaimed, "God forgive my soul the sin of blood-guiltiness!"

Colburn looked at him with astonishment. The veteran turned towards him and said, "Young man, I have this hour shown how frail are our best intentions. I was once a soldier of some note. But when I became a Christian, and felt the obligation to love all men and forgive my enemies, I determined to fight no more except in defence of my home or country. I even prayed that I might have strength to forgive an injury which had rankled in my bosom for years. You were too young to remember my boy—my only son, who was butchered in my presence by this very tribe. Dearly did I revenge his death, and devoutly did I afterwards pray that I might forgive it. For years have I disciplined my feelings so severely that I had thought the last spark of hatred was extinguished, and that my last days would glide away in charity with men, in peace with God. When I stood a prisoner bound to the stake, and expecting a miserable death, I endeavoured to subdue every vindictive feeling. I prayed that I might die the death of the righteous, and felt that peace which the world cannot give nor take away. When it pleased God to cut my bands asunder, it was my right and my duty to defend the life which He spared, and the friends who were dear to me. But no sooner did I raise my armed hand than all my former feelings of vengeance against the race who had slain my child were kindled up. Hatred, long smothered, broke forth with implacable fury, and I tasted the sweets of revenge. It was a bad, a wicked feeling. It is a dreadful, an unholy passion. Take warning from me, my young friend; never let the passion of revenge find a place in your bosom. It will poison your best enjoyments, destroy your noblest feelings, and make shipwreck of your purest hopes. God preserve you from hating as I have hated, from suffering as I have suffered!"

# CHAPTER XXI.

SEVERAL days had succeeded the termination of the adventure described in our last chapter, and the parties were all assembled at the mansion of Colonel Hendrickson. This was a house somewhat larger than ordinary, built of hewn logs after the plain but comfortable fashion of the country. There was not the slightest attempt at ornament, but every thing was substantial and neat; and a stranger might see at a glance that it was the abode of hospitality and abundance. A large farm lying around consisted of extensive fields newly cleared, whose deep rich soil was now heavily loaded with luxuriant crops of tobacco and corn. A large number of negroes, decently clothed, cheerful and contented, were engaged in the various labours of agriculture.

The Colonel's family consisted of himself, his wife, and an only daughter, a beautiful girl of eighteen, who combined in her person and manners the truly feminine gracefulness, the easy politeness, the cordiality and frankness, so remarkably characteristic of the ladies of Kentucky, who unite, with singular tact and elegance, the noble independence and generous kindness of their country with the gentleness and delicacy appropriate to their sex.

This young lady was now walking arm in arm with William Colburn on the beautiful lawn in the front of the house. It was one of those fine autumnal days which are thought to be peculiar to the western country, when the atmosphere is

mild and in a state of perfect repose, the leaves of the forest
are tinged with a variety of rich and gorgeous but pensive
hues, and every natural object wears the sober drapery and
the serene aspect of the departing year. The sun shone
brightly, the soft warm air created a delightful sense of lux-
urious enjoyment; and the young couple that sauntered
together, conversing in expressive glances and tones of con-
fiding affection, were not the least interesting objects in the
picturesque landscape.

Miss Pendleton sat at a window with Mr. George Lee.
This young gentleman was as much in love as ever, and as
difficult to be persuaded that it was not altogether possible
and proper for his fair relative to return his passion. It was
beyond the power of language and the art of logic to convince
him that he had not the best claim to her affections. He was
a gentleman of good family and had an ample estate; he had
been her companion from infancy, and had loved her from the
first dawn of reason. These arguments he now urged for
the hundredth time, with all the eloquence of which he
was master, not forgetting to insist on the priority of his
suit.

"Who is there, cousin Virginia, who has loved you as
long as I have? or who will ever love you half as much?
When we were children, did I not climb the tallest trees in
the woods at the risk of my neck, to gather grapes for you,
or to catch young squirrels or birds for you to play with?"

"I am inclined to think, cousin George, that you had a
natural propensity for such feats, which required but little
stimulus to bring it into action."

"There it is, again! I have been trying all my life to
convince you of my love for you—and you will never believe it."

"Do not do me injustice; I have always known your feelings—have always been sincerely grateful for your kindness;
have always valued and prized your friendship—"

"Friendship! there it is, again—it is a shame to call such devoted love as mine by the cold name of friendship. I love you better than my own life; I have shown that."

"You have indeed," replied Virginia, with much emotion, "and I should be most ungrateful not to be deeply affected by your kindness, by an affection so long continued and disinterested. But it is painful, Mr. Lee—"

"Don't, don't call me *Mr. Lee*. You know, Virginia, I can never stand that. Refuse me, if you will—but don't treat me as a stranger."

"I was only going to remark, how painful it is to see you persevere in a suit which I have never encouraged—and which I have so often—so very often—declined. I feel towards you, cousin George, all the affection of a relative; if you were my only brother, my feelings and sentiments in regard to you could hardly be different from what they are. More than this we cannot be to each other."

"There it is, again—that is just the way you always wind up. I can't for my soul understand you. *Why*, if you love me so much, will not you marry me?"

Miss Pendleton, though grieved, and even shocked at the perseverance of her generous but silly lover, could not repress a melancholy smile as she replied, "Because there is a great difference, George, between sisterly affection and that love which is necessary to happiness in marriage."

"Well, I cannot for my life see that. I love you like a brother—yet I wish to marry you, to live for you, to die for you, to do any thing for you that would make you happy."

"But if marrying you would not conduce to my happiness, what then?"

"Dear Virginia, you could not help being happy. I should be devoted to you. I have a large fortune, a fine house, plenty of servants, and every thing that heart could wish."

"Let us drop the subject, Mr. Lee, now and for ever."

George rose and walked across the room.

"So you have determined not to marry me?"

"I have always told you so."

"Virginia, it is not for myself that I care. It is for your happiness that I am interested. I cannot bear to leave you here in this cabin, in these wild woods, and in the neighbourhood of those dreadful savages. Say you will go back to the Old Dominion, live with my mother, and be my sister; let me divide my fortune equally with you; and I will never again ask you to be my wife."

She was deeply affected. She had always known that this simple young man, although almost an idiot in intellect, was generous and sincerely attached to her. She had seen him forsake an affluent home and pleasures to which he was fatally addicted, to follow her to the wilderness. She had been the innocent means of leading him into captivity and suffering. There he had shown his devotion to her in the most extravagant yet touching offers of self-sacrifice. All this passed rapidly through her mind; and his last offer brought tears into her eyes.

"No, George," said she, rising and offering her hand, which he grasped with a lover's eagerness, "I cannot accept your offer, nor is it necessary—I cannot be your wife, but if ever I should need a friend or a brother I will frankly apply to you —if ever I shall be destitute of a home or a protector, most willingly will I seek them under your mother's roof." So saying she left the room.

While this scene went forward, Colonel Hendrickson and Mr. Fennimore were engaged in close consultation in the garden. Mr. Fennimore, after communicating the facts with which the reader is already acquainted, proceeded as follows:—

"Major Heyward having satisfied me that my mother had no legal claim upon him, added that he had already made his

will, by which he had bequeathed his whole estate to Miss
Pendleton, who had been brought up as his adopted child,
and who, having been reared in the expectation of being his
sole heiress, could not now be disinherited without injustice.
Nor could his affection for her, which was that of a father,
permit him to make any disposition of his fortune to the pre-
judice of her interest.   But he desired to be reconciled to my
mother, and spoke of making some provision for her.

"That will, you are aware, has been lost.   I am the heir
at law of my uncle, and I have come to you, as the legal
guardian of Miss Pendleton, to say that I intend to fulfil
strictly his intentions.   This instrument contains a formal re-
linquishment and transfer to her of all my right, title, and
claim, to the whole of my deceased uncle's estate.   This was
one of the objects of my visit here ; the other to bring to justice the murderer of Major Heyward, who I am satisfied is
Micajah Harpe, and who, with the assistance of our friend Mr.
Colburn, I have traced to this neighbourhood."

"That paper," replied the Colonel, "I shall not accept
without consulting Miss Pendleton.   I had determined to
divide my own property equally between her and my daughter.   I shall apprize her of my intention, and let her decide
for herself on your offer."

"But I hope, my dear sir, that you will advise her that it
is her duty to accept that which of right belongs to her."

"If my advice is asked," said Colonel Hendrickson, "I
will give such as I think it becomes my niece to accept.   You
are the proper heir to your uncle.   Had he left all his property to her, he would have done wrong ; and I shall certainly
not advise her to avail herself of your generosity."

## CHAPTER XXII.

A HAPPY company was assembled that evening at the mansion of Colonel Hendrickson, consisting of the agreeable and interesting personages mentioned in the last chapter, together with several young people who had dropped in during the afternoon, and who were, of course, expected to spend the night. For in this region of generous living and abundant hospitality, a visit of a few hours is a thing not to be thought of; the fashion of *making calls*, which furnishes such pleasant occupation to a city belle, is not practised; and a young lady always carries with her, on such occasions, a wardrobe that will serve for at least a week.

Colonel Hendrickson was comfortably seated in his armchair, by the side of an immense fire-place, filled with one of those enormous piles of wood which the Kentuckians build up, in the hospitable desire of giving a warm reception to their friends; while the door was judiciously left wide open, to admit a free circulation of frosty air. The apartment was spacious, and the plain old-fashioned furniture, consisting of a few articles, each of which was particularly large and inconvenient, was such as may be readily imagined by those of my readers who are acquainted with the habits of the more wealthy of the pioneers; and those who have not that advantage, may fancy it what they please—for it has little to do with the story. One article, however, must not be passed over, because it was characteristic of the times of the country

9

—this was a bed, covered with a snow-white counterpane, and surrounded by a fine suit of curtains; for as cabins—by which we mean log houses—however large, contain but few apartments, all of them are occupied as sleeping-rooms, and the common sitting-room is always my lady's chamber. One consequence of this fashion is, an excessive, and even ostentatious neatness, rendered necessary by the fact, that every apartment is open to the inspection of visitors; and another is, that the mistress of the mansion must be an early riser, that her room may be put in order before breakfast, and the visitors must retire early at night, to avoid encroaching upon her regular hours.

There was an engraved portrait of General Washington hanging over the fire-place, and above it a rifle, with a powder-horn and shot-pouch. Of the rest, it is enough to say that the whole interior of this primitive dwelling bore evidence that it was the residence of comfort and abundance—that it was the habitation of a fine, liberal old gentleman, and a handsome, neat, industrious, stately, old lady. It was, as we have seen, and this worthy couple were both revolutionary patriots, who, having served their country well in their respective departments, were now enjoying their laurels in content and competency. The worthy lady, who sat in the the corner opposite to her husband, diligently plying her knitting-needles, still retained traces of great beauty, and wore an air of demure sedateness, mingled with a feminine, lady-like grace, and contrasted finely with the bold, manly, countenance of her lord. She was a dear old lady; few of the girls were as handsome, and none of them looked half so natural. Her soft eye beamed with benevolence, the charities of life were in her smile, and even her snow-white cap had a matronly and Christian-like appearance which invited respect. Over the back of her chair hung the almanac for the current year, conveniently at hand for frequent reference; on whose margin might be seen numerous marks, made with a

pencil, or still oftener with the point of a needle, denoting
certain days on which remarkable events had happened in
the family, such as the birth of a negro or a brood of chickens,
or the sale of a crop of tobacco, and marking the times in the
age of the moon most proper for planting particular seeds,
or shearing sheep, or weaning children.

When supper was announced, the whole party was seated
round a large table, loaded with substantials, well cooked,
and piping hot. Other people may know the luxury of good
eating, but the Kentuckians practise it. Before the master
of the house was an ample dish of fried chickens, dressed with
cream and parsley, a little farther up were venison steaks,
then fried ham; then there was cold ham, and chipped beef,
and sausages, and, better than all, there was a fine dish of
*hominy*, and a noble pile of sweet potatoes. Of the eatables
composed of bread-stuffs, served in various shapes, no one
who has had the misfortune to be *raised* north of Mason and
Dixon's line can form an adequate conception. The biscuits,
white, light, spungy, and smoking hot—the wheat bread, smoking hot—the corn bread, smoking hot—and the cakes, almost
red hot—these are luxuries which defy the power of description, and the excellent qualities of which can only be estimated
truly by that infallible test which the old adage supposes to
be necessary in reference to a pudding. There was no lack
of sweetmeats and pastry; but the pride of the feast were the
great pitchers of milk—sweet-milk, sour-milk, and buttermilk; for, after all, milk is the staff of life, and is a thousand
times better than the cold water so much lauded by modern
philosophers. There were other good things; but we shall
content ourselves with mentioning a capital cup of coffee, and
leave the reader to form his own conclusions as to the comforts of a tea-table in the backwoods.

After supper, when the company were again ranged about
the fire, the conversation took a lively turn; hunting, war,
and love naturally became the leading subjects. The old,

when they are benevolent, love the conversation of the young. Genuine simplicity of character is always shown in a relish for hearing the sentiments and witnessing the joys of youth. Persons of the strongest minds often read children's books with interest, and mingle with delight in their sports. Colonel Hendrickson was one of those. Although dignified in his manners, and even austere in his appearance, he could unbend and win the eager attention of a youthful circle by his cheerful sallies. On this evening he was in high spirits, and joined freely in the mirth of his guests.

"I will tell you," said he, "a very singular *hunting adventure*, which happened when Mrs. Hendrickson and I were both young people——"

"Mr. Hendrickson," interposed the venerable lady mildly, but with a little spice of one having authority, "I would not tell that story now."

"Why not, my dear? It is a good story."

"But you have told it so often, Mr. Hendrickson."

"No matter for that, my dear; our guests have never heard it."

## A Hunter's Tale.

"You must know," said he, while the young folks all assumed the attitude of eager listeners, "that my father was a wealthy farmer, in the western part of old Virginia. We lived near the mountain, and I learned to hunt when I was a mere boy. We had plenty of servants, and I had little else to do than to follow my own inclination. At fourteen I used to break my father's colts, and had gained the reputation of a daring rider; at the same age, I could track a deer as successfully as the most experienced hunter; and before I was grown, I had been a volunteer against the Indians. At sixteen I began to get fond of going to see the young ladies; so that between my gun, my father's colts and the girls, I was in a fair way of growing up a spoiled boy. Things went on in this way until I was twenty-one; then the Revolution came on, and saved me. War is a good thing in some respects. It furnishes employment for idle young men. It brings out the talents, and strengthens the character of those who are good for any thing; and disposes of many who would otherwise hang upon society, and be in the way of better folks. I joined a company that was raised in the neighbourhood, and was made an officer; and off I went, in a gay suit of regimentals, mounted on a fine horse, with a capital rifle in my hand, and a heart full of patriotism, and courage, and love. Perhaps you all want to know who I was in love with?"

Here the old lady began to fidget in her chair and threw a deprecating look at her spouse, who nevertheless proceeded:

"I was just of age, and my old dame there was seventeen, when the war broke out. Our fathers' estates joined, and we had known each other intimately from childhood. She was generally allowed by every body—"

"Mr. Hendrickson," exclaimed Mrs. H., "I would leave *that* out."

"To be remarkably handsome," continued the Colonel, "and what every body says must be true. She was really, although I say it myself, a *very great beauty*."

"Well, I declare—you ought to be ashamed, Mr. Hendrickson!" interrupted the lady; but the husband, who was used to these scattering shots, very composedly continued his story.

"She was a regular toast at the barbacues, and General Washington, then a Colonel, once drank her health at a county meeting."

This reminiscence was better received by the worthy matron, who took a pinch of snuff, and then left the room; not without throwing a look of pride and affection at her good man, as she passed; but as the tale was becoming rather personal, as respected herself, she remained absent until near the close of it."

"I cannot say that we ever fell in love with each other; for our mutual affection commenced with childhood, grew with our growth, and filled our hearts so gradually, that it may be said to have formed a part of our natures. As for courtship, there was none; I rode to meeting with Caroline every Sunday, went with her to the races and barbacues, danced with her at every ball, and spent half of my time at her father's house. When returning home late in the evening, after an absence of several days, I used to stop at her father's, or at my own, just as happened to be most convenient, and felt myself as welcome at the one house as at the other. But no explanation had taken place. When equipped for service, the last thing I did before I marched away, was to go there in my new regimentals, to take leave. She wept, but my mother and sisters did the same, and I thought nothing of it at the time.

"I was gone more than a year, was in several engagements, and went through a great variety of hardship and suffering. We were poorly paid, badly fed, and terribly thrashed by the regulars while learning the discipline which enabled us to beat them in return. At length our company was completely destroyed; some were killed, some taken prisoners, some got sick, and a few got tired of being patriots. The remainder were discharged, or transferred into other companies; and I obtained leave of absence. I had lost my horse, spent all my money, worn out my clothes, and had no means of travelling, except on foot. Patriotism, young gentlemen, was a poor business then, and is not much better now. Like Falstaff's honour, it will not set a limb; and I found to my sorrow that it would not keep out cold or furnish a barefoot soldier with a pair of shoes. But it warmed the hearts and opened the doors of all true whigs, and I generally procured a meal and a night's lodging at the close of each day's travel under the roof of some friend to the cause of liberty.

"I had lately thought a great deal about Caroline. It was not until I parted from her that I knew how necessary she was to my happiness. I now recollected her remarks, and recalled with delight the amusements in which we had participated together. When lying upon the ground in my cheerless tent, or keeping guard at some solitary outpost, I amused the weary hours in forming plans for the future, in which she was always one of the *dramatis personæ*. When any thing agreeable occurred, I longed to tell it to her; and when in trouble I could always fancy how entirely she would enter into my feelings, and how tender would be her sympathy could she be at my side. I had no doubt that her sentiments were similar to my own; yet, when I recollected that no disclosure had been made or pledge given on either side, and that she was not even bound to know of my attachment, I condemned myself for having taken no precaution to secure a treasure without which the laurels I had won would be valueless and life itself a burden.

"In order to get home I had to pass the door of Caroline's father; and I determined to stop there first, curious to know whether I should be recognised in my wretched garb, and how I should be received. I was as ragged a rebel as ever fought against his unlawful king. I had no shoes on my feet, my clothes were faded, torn, and dirty, my long hair hung tangled over my face, I had been without a razor for some time, and this scar which you see on my cheek was then a green wound, covered with a black patch. Altogether I looked more like a deserter or a fugitive from a prison-ship than a young officer. The dogs growled at me as I approached the house, the little negroes ran away, and the children of the family hid behind the door. No one recognised me, and I stood in the hall where most of the family were assembled, like some being dropped from another world. They were engaged in various employments; as for Miss Caroline, she spinning upon a large wheel in the farther end of the room; for young ladies then, however wealthy their parents, were all taught to be useful. She looked at me attentively as I entered, but continued her work; and I never felt so happy in my life as when I saw her graceful form and her light step while she moved forward and backward, extending her handsome arm and displaying her pretty fingers as she drew her cotton rolls into a fine thread. The ingenuity of woman never invented a more graceful exercise for showing off a beautiful figure than spinning cotton on a large wheel.

"I thought she looked pensive; but her cheek was as blooming as ever, and her pretty round form, instead of being emaciated with grief, had increased in stature and maturity. I felt vexed to think that she was not wretched, that her eyes were not red with watching, nor her cheeks furrowed with tears. I endeavoured to speak in a feigned voice, but no sooner did the tones meet her ear than she sprung up, eagerly repeated my name, and rushing towards me, clasped both my hands in hers with a warmness and frankness of affection which admitted no concealment and left no room for doubt. The whole family gathered round me, and it was with some difficulty that I tore myself away.

"When my good mother had caused me to be trimmed, and scrubbed, and brushed, I felt once more the luxury of looking and feeling like a gentleman. I passed a happy evening under my native roof; and the next morning early shouldered my rifle for a hunting excursion. My friends thought it strange that, after the hardships I had recently undergone, I should so soon evince a desire to engage in this fatiguing sport. But I had different game in view from any that they dreamed of. I took a by-path which led to the residence of a certain young lady, approaching it through a strip of forest which extended nearly to the garden. Caroline

was in the garden. I thought she was dressed with more
than usual taste, and she certainly tripped along with a
livelier step than common. I leaped the fence, and in a
moment was at her side. I shall not tell what passed, nor
how long we stood concealed behind a tall clump of rose-
bushes—nor how much longer we might have continued the
*tête-à-tête*, if the approach of some one had not caused Caroline
to dart away like a frighted deer, while I retreated to the
woods, the happiest fellow in existence.

"I strolled through the forest thinking of the pleasant
interview, recalling the soft pressure of the hand that had
trembled in mine, the exquisite tones of the voice that still
murmured in my ear, and the artless confessions that remained
deeply imprinted on my heart. It was some hours before I
recollected that in order to save appearances I must kill some
game to carry home. How many fat bucks had crossed my
path since I was musing upon this precious little love-scene,
I know not; I had wandered several miles from my father's
house, and it was now past noon.

"Throwing off my abstraction of mind, I turned my attention in earnest to the matter in hand, and, after a diligent
search, espied a deer quietly grazing in an open spot in full
view. I took aim, touched the hair-trigger, and my gun
snapped. The deer, alarmed, bounded away; and not being
very eager, I renewed the priming and strolled on. Another
opportunity soon occurred, when my unlucky piece again
made default,—the priming flashed in the pan, but no report
followed. As I always kept my rifle in good order, I was
not a little surprised that two such accidents should follow in
quick succession—and I began to consider seriously whether
it might not be an omen that my courtship would end in
a mere flash. Again and again I made the same attempt, and
with a similar result. I was now far from home, and night
was closing around me; I could not see to hunt any longer,
nor was I willing to return home without having killed any

9*

thing.   To sleep in the woods was no hardship, for I had long
been accustomed to lodging upon the hard ground in the open
air; indeed, I had been kept awake most of the preceding
night by the novel luxury of a feather-bed.   Accordingly I
kindled a fire and threw myself on the ground.   I never was
superstitious; but my mind was at that time in a state
of peculiar sensitiveness.   My return home, the sudden relief
from privation and suffering, the meeting with my family,
and the interview with Caroline, had all concurred to bewilder
and intoxicate my brain; and as I lay in the dark shade of
the forest, gazing at the few stars that twinkled through the
intervals of the foliage, some of the wild traditions of the
hunters occurred to my memory, and I persuaded myself that
a spell had been placed upon my gun.   When I fell asleep I
dreamed of being in battle unarmed, of hunting without ammunition, and being married without getting a wife :—the
upshot of the whole matter was, that I slept without being
refreshed.

"I rose, and was proceeding towards a neighbouring
spring, when a strain of singular music burst upon my ear.
It was so wild, solemn, and incoherent, that I could make
nothing of it, and became more and more convinced that I
certainly was bewitched; but determined to see the end of
this mysterious adventure, I hastened towards the spot from
which the sounds proceeded.   As I approached, the tones
became familiar, and I recognised a voice which I had known
from childhood.   I had rested near the foot of a mountainous
ridge, at a spot where a pile of rocky masses rose in tall
cliffs abruptly from the plain.   Against the bald sides of these
precipices the rising sun now shone, lighting them up with unusual splendour.   On a platform of rock, overhung by jutting
points, from which the sound of the voice was returned by
numerous echoes, knelt a superannuated negro, whom I had
known from my infancy.   From my earliest recollection, he
had been a kind of privileged character, wandering about the

country, and filling the various offices of fiddler, conjurer, and preacher. Latterly he had quit fiddling, and taken to philosophy, most probably because ambition, the last infirmity of noble minds, had induced him to seek higher honours than those achieved by the triumphs of the violin. The old man was engaged in his morning devotions, and was chanting a hymn at the top of his voice, with great apparent fervour and sincerity. I made up my mind in a moment that he was the very conjurer who had placed a spell upon my gun, and perhaps upon my courtship; for he had long served as a kind of lay-brother at the altar of Hymen, and was famous for his skill in delivering *billet-doux*, and finding out young ladies' secrets. Moreover, his name was Cupid. As soon as his devotions were concluded, I approached and disclosed with perhaps more seriousness of manner than I felt, and certainly with more than I would have acknowledged, the mysterious conduct of my gun, which was as good a rifle as ever a man put to his shoulder, and my suspicions that some necromancy had been practised. The old man was overjoyed to see me, for I had danced to his violin many a long night; he uttered some very profound and philosophic moral reflections upon the rapidity with which little boys grow up into big men—complimented me upon my improved appearance and safe return from the wars, and assured me that I looked '*mighty sogerfied*.' Then proceeding to inspect my unlucky weapon, he first examined the lock, then drew the ramrod, and having searched the barrel, handed it back, exclaiming, with a most sarcastic grin,

"'Please goodness! massa Charley, how you *speck* your gun go off, '*out* no powder?'

"The truth broke upon my mind with the suddenness of an explosion. I stood with my finger in my mouth like a boy caught in a forbidden orchard, a lover detected in the act of swearing allegiance upon his knees, or an author whose wit has flashed in the pan. The simple fact was, that in the pleasure of courting, and the delight of winning my old dame there, who, plain as you see her now, was, as I said before, in her young days, allowed to be a great beauty, I had totally forgot to load my gun! But old Cupid kept my secret—I kept my own counsel—Caroline kept her word, and I have always had reason to consider that as the best hunt I ever made."

## CHAPTER XXIII.

WHEN Colonel Hendrickson had concluded his story, it was found that the hour of retiring to repose had arrived. Mrs. Hendrickson arose and placed a large family bible and a hymn-book upon the table ; for these worthy people, as we are happy to say is the case with a great many families in this region, never separated for the night without bowing down together in worship. The Colonel read a chapter in the holy book, selected a hymn, in the singing of which the whole circle joined, and then kneeling down prayed with fervour and solemnity. There is no worship which impresses the imagination and warms the heart like that of the family. When in the silent hour of night those who are joined together by consanguinity and affection kneel together—when the father prays for his children and dependents—there is a touching interest and a moral beauty in the scene ; and we know not how any who profess the doctrines of Christianity can neglect so serious a duty, or deny themselves so delightful a pleasure.

Just as they were about to retire, a loud barking of the dogs announced the arrival of other visitors, who proved to be a party of boys, sons of the neighbouring farmers, going to hunt the raccoon. They had called to borrow the Colonel's favourite dog, who was famous at catching these animals. Mr. George Lee, delighted with any thing in the nature of sport, immediately proposed to the other gentlemen to join

the party, but they declined participating in any amusement
which was considered as being more properly suited to boys.
But George was not to be balked in his humour. A refusal
from Virginia Pendleton had always the effect of driving him
to the sports of the field with renewed ardour, and he now
joined the lads in their excursion with hearty good will.

The party consisted of a number of lads, some of whom
were nearly grown, and others quite small. They carried
axes and blazing torches, and were followed by a number of
dogs. On reaching the woods, the dogs scattered in different
directions in search of their game; and the human animals
strolled carelessly along, waiting for a signal from their brute
companions. The atmosphere was still, but frosty; it was a
clear and starlight night, but the heavy mass of decaying
leaves that still clothed the tops of the tall trees, rendered
the darkness impenetrable, except where the torches carried
by the hunters threw a bright glare immediately around
them as they passed along. The stillness that reigned through
the forest was profound. As the hunters moved, the leaves
rustled under their footsteps, and their voices breaking in
upon the repose of nature seemed to have an unnatural loudness; and when they stood still to listen, nothing could be
heard but now and then a distant faint sound of the tread of
a dog, leaping rapidly over the dried vegetation, or the scream
of an affrighted bird. They pursued no path, but strolled
fearlessly through the coverts of the forest, directed only by
their acquaintance with the local features of the country.
They often paused to listen. The dogs continued to hunt,
taking wide circuits through the forest, and returning at long
intervals, one by one to their masters, as if to report progress or
to ascertain what had been the success of others. All at once
a barking was heard, falling upon the ear so faintly, as to
show that it proceeded from a distant spot. It came from a
single dog, and announced that he had fallen upon the scent
of a raccoon; and in a few minutes a change in the tones of

the animal which became more lively, intimated that he had
chased the game to its hiding-place. The other dogs, on
hearing this sound, all rushed eagerly towards the spot from
whence it procceded, followed by the hunters at full speed.
They found the successful dog sitting at the foot of a large
honey-locust tree—or as the boys expressed it, "barking up
a honey-locust," with every appearance of triumphant delight.

The first thing which was now done, was, to collect a
quantity of fallen limbs, which were piled into a large heap,
and lighted by means of the torches that had been brought
for this purpose. In a few minutes an intense blaze shot upwards, throwing a brilliant glare of light upon the surrounding scene; and the animal for whose capture these preparations were made, was seen standing on a bough forty feet
from the ground, endeavouring to conceal itself, while it gazed
downwards in alarm and wonder. A loud shout announced
the delight of the party on beholding their game, the dogs
evinced an equal degree of pleasure, and it would have been
hard to tell which animals—the human or canine—experienced the greatest degree of enjoyment in the sport.

The young men now threw off their coats and began
with their axes to cut down the tree in which their prey
had taken refuge. It was several feet in circumference; but
that which would have been considered, under other circumstances, a laborious task, was cheerfully undertaken in the
eager pursuit of amusement. Blow after blow fell upon the
solid trunk in quick succession, and the woods re-echoed the
rapid and cheerful strokes of the axe. Two of the hunters
wielded the axe on opposite sides of the tree, striking alternately with regular cadence, and with such energy and skill
that every blow made its appropriate impression; others relieved them, from time to time, by taking their places, while
the smaller lads continued to supply fuel to the fire. At
length the work was so nearly accomplished that a few more

blows only were required to complete it, and all of the party,
except those engaged in chopping, retired to the side of the
tree opposite to the direction in which it was expected to fall,
gathering together all the dogs, and holding them fast by
main strength, to prevent them from running under the falling
tree, and being crushed by its descent.   Nor was it an easy
matter to restrain the eager animals, for no sooner did the
great tree begin to totter and creak, than they began to whine
and struggle, showing the greatest impatience to rush forward
and seize their prey, as soon as he should reach the ground.
The tall tree slowly bowed its top, trembling for a moment
as if balanced, then cracking louder and quicker, and at last
falling rapidly, tearing and crushing the boughs that intercepted its downward progress, and stretching its enormous
length on the ground with a tremendous crash.   The neighbouring trees, whose branches were torn off, and whose tops
were disturbed by the sudden rush of air accompanying the
fall of so large a body, bowed their heads over their prostrate
comrade, waved their splintered limbs, and then relapsed into
their original state of majestic repose.

No sooner did the tree strike the ground, than the raccoon
darted from among its quivering branches and bounded away
pursued by the whole yelling pack of dogs and boys.   And
now there was shouting and scrambling.   Surrounded by so
many foes, the raccoon was soon brought to bay by a young
dog, who paid dearly for his inexperience, for the enraged
animal turning suddenly, struck his sharp teeth into the head
of the dog, who yelled lustily with pain ; this occupied but
a second ; the raccoon resumed his flight, and the beaten dog,
whining and bleeding, slunk away.   Again and again was
the hard-pressed animal obliged to face his pursuers, who now
headed him in every direction that he turned, and more than
one dog felt his keen bite.   The human tormentors crowded
around, interfering no further than by encouraging the dogs
with loud shouts ; and the sport went bravely on, until the

raccoon suddenly springing at the trunk of a large tree, clambered up, and with a few active bounds placed himself out of the reach of his pursuers.

Another fire was now kindled under the second tree, which happened to be of a less formidable size than the first, and the undefatigable hunters went to work again with their axes. The raccoon was less fortunate than before, for when the tree fell, he was completely surrounded by his enemies, who took care to prevent him from again " *treeing*." It was astonishing to see the fierceness and success with which this small animal defended himself against so many adversaries of superior size; the sharpness of his teeth, and the quickness with which he snapped, rendered his bite severe, and his sagacity in seizing upon the most vital and sensitive parts of the bodies of his assailants was remarkable. He sprung often at' the eye, the lip, and throat of the dog who ventured to engage him; and it is always observable that a dog who is a veteran in such affairs, or as the hunters say, " an old 'coon dog," has a face covered with scars, an effect probably produced by the skill of the canine animal, in protecting the rest of his body, by presenting his front only to his foe. It was impossible, however, to contend long against such unequal numbers; several of the dogs were sent yelling out of the fight; but at last one more experienced and bolder than the rest rushed in, seized the brave little animal by the throat, and in a moment worried him to death. The whole combat, though lively, fierce, and eventful, lasted but a few minutes.

The dogs were again sent out, and soon succeeded in chasing another victim into a tree, and the same proceedings were thereupon had, as a lawyer would say, as in the case aforesaid; and in the course of the night several raccoons were taken in a similar manner, so far as respected the kindling of fires and chopping down trees. In other particulars, however, there was a considerable variety of incident. A veteran old male raccoon fought like a determined warrior, and sold his

life dearly, while one of smaller size, or of the softer sex, fell
an easy prey. Sometimes the unhappy animal was crushed
to death by the fall of the tree in which it had taken refuge;
and sometimes after an immense tree had been felled with
great labour, it was found that the wily game had stolen away
along the interlocking branches, and found refuge in the top
of another. Then the fires were renewed, and the bright
glare usually enabled the hunters to discover the fugitive
closely nestled in a fork, or at the junction of a large limb
with the body of a tree, where it lay concealed until curiosity
induced it to show its face in the sly endeavour to take a peep
at the operations going on below, or some slight motion betraying a protruding paw or the quivering tip of the tail.
Occasionally the young dogs committed the disgraceful mistake of "treeing" a lazy fat opossum in the branches of a
slender sapling, from which it was quickly shaken down and
beaten to death ignominiously with clubs.

The hunters were nearly satiated with sport, when it happened that the dogs on striking a trail went off with great
vivacity, following it to a considerable distance, to the surprise
of their wearied masters; for the raccoon runs slowly, and on
finding itself pursued, immediately climbs a tree. On they
went, full of hope, the scent growing more and more fresh,
and the dogs barking louder and with greater animation as
they proceeded, until the game was driven to a tree. The
fire was lighted, when the trembling of a bough showed that
the animal was springing from one tree to another, where new
operations were commenced, and the axes were striking mer-
rily, when an alarm from the dogs was heard, and it was found
that the wily game after stealing from tree to tree had descended to the ground and dashed off. Away went the dogs
and boys again in higher spirits than ever, for the ingenuity
and boldness of the animal showed that nobler game was now
started, and that they were on the trail of a wild-cat, who was
so closely pressed as to be again obliged, after a gallant run

of about half a mile, to take refuge in the branches of a tall
oak which happened to stand apart so that the animal could
not leap into a neighbouring tree. Fires were now lighted all
round the spot, so that a considerable space was illuminated
with a brilliancy as great as that of noon-day; the cat was
seen, with back erect and glaring eyeballs, looking fiercely
down; the axes were plied with renewed vigour and the oak
was soon prostrated. Greater precautions were now used to
prevent the escape of their prey; the youths armed with clubs
formed a large circle and the dogs rushed in from different
directions. The enraged animal sprung boldly out, bounding
with vigorous leaps, showing his white teeth and growling
defiance. The dogs highly excited dashed fearlessly at their
prey, and a hot engagement ensued, for they had now to cope
with one of the most ferocious brutes of the forest—one
which, though not large in size, is muscular, active, cunning,
and undauntedly fierce. Fighting with teeth and claws, he
inflicted deep wounds on his eager assailants. Growling, barking, hissing, and shouting, were mingled in horrible discord.
Dried leaves and earth and fur were thrown into the air, and
the slender bushes were crushed and trampled down by the
maddened combatants. Surrounded and attacked on all sides
the furious cat fought with desperation. Sometimes springing suddenly up over the heads of his assailants he alighted
on the back of a dog, fixing his teeth deep in the neck, driving
his sharp claws into the throat on either side and bearing down
the agonized and suffocated animal to the earth; and sometimes overthrown, and fighting on his back, bitten and worried
from every direction, he sprang at the throat of one of his
tormentors, sunk his deadly fangs into the jugular, nor released
his hold until the dog quivered with the pangs of death; until
wounded, torn, bleeding, and exhausted, he was overpowered
by numbers. Thus ended, in triumph, a most *glorious hunt.*

The night was nearly wasted, and the sportsmen, now several miles from home, began to retrace their steps. After

proceeding a short distance they divided into several parties, each taking the nearest direction to their respective habitations. One of the youths agreed to accompany Mr. Lee to Colonel Hendrickson's; and our friend George, after expressing the delight he had experienced in the "capital sport" which they had enjoyed, bade them a hearty good-night and marched off with his young guide through the dark and now silent forest. Fatigued with several hours of severe exercise they sauntered slowly along, and as the hunter walks habitually with a noiseless tread, their footsteps fell silently on the leafy carpet of the forest. The death-like repose of the woods afforded a strong contrast to the fires which had lately gleamed, and the sounds of conflict that had awakened the echoes of the wilderness. Although the darkness was almost impenetrable, the guide moved forward with unerring skill, keeping the direct course without deviation, climbing over hills on whose summits the star-light glimmered faintly through the foliage, or descending into vales where not a gleam of the light of heaven broke in upon the solitary travellers.

At length they crossed their former track at a spot where one of the fires had been lighted. The fuel had been heaped up at the foot of a dead tree of considerable magnitude, and as the pile had been great and the heat intense, the flames had enveloped the trunk, extended upwards to the branches and lighted the whole fabric in a blaze of glowing fire. They first saw this beautiful sight from the summit of a neighbouring hill, from which, though still distant, it was distinctly visible —a tree of fire, standing alone in the dark forest! The trunk presented a tall column of intense redness, round which the flames curled and rolled, giving to this majestic pillar of fire the appearance of a waving motion; while the branches and twigs were all lighted up and completely enveloped with the glowing element, and parts of them were continually breaking off and falling to the ground like drops of blazing liquid. As they stood gazing at this splendid exhibition, several

figures were seen moving in the light close to the burning
tree, which were ascertained to be those of men and horses;
and the hunters felt their curiosity excited by the appearance
of horsemen in this solitary place at such an hour. Mr. Lee
proposed to approach them and ascertain their character; and
the guide, equally inquisitive, consented, with some hesitation,
and after suggesting the propriety of using caution. Deeds
of violence had lately been perpetrated; and the young forester
whispered that for some days past, when the men of the
family were at work in the fields at some distance from the
house, his mother had kept the doors fastened all day, and if
she heard a footstep approaching hid her children and armed
herself with a rifle before she looked out to ascertain the character of the visitor. The butcheries of the Harpes had filled
the whole country with dread.

Thus prepared, they advanced cautiously towards the fire,
and came sufficiently near to distinguish two men, stout, ill-
looking, and completely armed. They frequently looked suspiciously around, and listened like men expecting to be pursued and resolved to be on their guard; and as they stood
exposed in the broad glare of the light, there could be no
doubt that they were the identical ruffians who had disturbed
the peace of these new settlements, and against whom the
whole community was about to rise in vengeance. Each of
them held by the bridle a fine horse panting as if from a hard
ride. There was another person with them, to whom one of
the men was speaking in earnest and authoritative language,
and who was recognised at a glance by Mr. Lee as his late
companion, Hark Short the snake-killer.

After conversing a few minutes the men mounted their
horses and rode rapidly away, plunging their spurs into the
sides of their spirited steeds and riding over obstacles and
through brush with fearless and careless speed. Mr. Lee
waited until they were out of hearing, and then advanced to
the fire to speak to Hark; but the boy on hearing his foot-

steps ran nimbly away, without waiting to ascertain who it was that approached; and the hunters resumed their home-ward way, which led in a direction opposite to that taken by the Harpes.

## CHAPTER XXIV.

IT was nearly noon when Mr. Lee rose the following morning. He found Colonel Hendrickson and all his guests waiting for him to accompany them in a ride to the house of a neighbouring gentleman, where they had engaged to dine. When he communicated the intelligence of having seen the Harpes on the preceding night, the gentlemen expressed great regret at not having heard it sooner, and determined to go in a body the next day in pursuit of the ruffians.

The horses were soon at the door, and the gay party began to mount, each of the young gentlemen selecting a favourite fair one for his own special charge, as is customary and proper in all well-regulated parties of pleasure. Mr. Lee, who considered that he had a prescriptive right to wait upon Miss Pendleton, was advancing to assist her to mount her horse, when he perceived that Mr. Fennimore had already taken her hand; and turned back, jealous, mortified, and almost determined that he would not join the company. The blood mounted into his cheeks, and his brow lowered, as he stood irresolute—a momentary passion of rage struggling in his bosom, against his native good-humour and habitual politeness.

Colonel Hendrickson saw his embarrassment, and with ready politeness endeavoured to remove it.

"Mr. Lee," said he, "I must show you a few acres of fine tobacco, as we ride along. I suspect you are a good judge

of such matters; your father, if I recollect, was a famous
tobacco raiser."

George bowed, and silently walked with his host towards
their horses.

"Cousin George," said Miss Pendleton, with one of her
sweetest smiles, as he was stalking sulkily by her horse's
head, "will you have the goodness to arrange that rein for
me?"—the cloud passed from his brow, as he placed his hand
on the bridle—"not that one, George, the other—thank you
—there—that is exactly right—you are going with us, cousin
George?" and, bowing gracefully, she rode off, escorted by
Mr. Fennimore; while George Lee, completely conciliated
by this little manœuvre, swore, internally, that she was the
sweetest creature in the world, and that Fennimore deserved
to be shot.

As the gay company filed off in couples, Mr. Lee and the
Colonel lingered in the rear; the latter pointed out his tobacco
crop, his corn, and his turnips, talked of his horses, and then
turned the subject to hunting, and told some stirring anecdotes
of backwoods adventure. George listened until he became
interested, and, before the ride was over, had recovered his
usual spirits. But still he was not satisfied. To give up
Virginia was sufficiently painful, but to see another carry off
the bright prize was more than his slender stock of philosophy
could bear.

They found a large party assembled to dinner. We shall
not stop to count the roasted pigs and turkeys, the juicy
hams, the fat haunches of venison, the bowls of apple-toddy,
and the loads of good things on which they were regaled.
More important matters lie before us, and urge us forward to
the sequel of this history.

After dinner, when the gentlemen were strolling in the
open air, Mr. Lee whispered to Mr. Fennimore that he
wished to converse with him in private, and led the way to a
retired place. Fennimore noticed his discontented air, and

an expression of defiance on his features, and followed him in silence, wondering what was to be the subject of their secret conference. When entirely out of hearing of the rest of the company, Mr. Lee demanded, in a haughty tone,

"I wish to know, sir, whether you intended to affront me by your conduct this morning?"

"Most certainly not," replied Mr. Fennimore, in a cheerful tone. "I am even ignorant of the circumstance to which you allude."

George had invited his rival to this conversation in the determination to quarrel with him at all events. The conciliatory tone of Fennimore disarmed him for a moment; but having, like most men when acting under the influence of passion, predetermined not to be satisfied, he returned to the charge.

"Do you say, sir, that you do not consider it an affront, to have stepped between me and a lady that I was about to conduct to her horse?"

"If I had done so intentionally, I should say I had been guilty of great rudeness."

"Then you assert that you did not do it purposely?"

"I do, sir," replied the officer, composedly; "and I will add——"

"Well, sir?" exclaimed George, pricking up his ears and expecting to hear a defiance which would lead to the result that he wished to provoke.

"I will add, with great pleasure, that if unintentionally I was guilty of such seeming rudeness, it is due to my own character and to your feelings that I should ask your pardon."

A soft answer turneth away wrath. George was too much of a gentleman, and had too much native good-humour, not to be reconciled by the politeness and good sense of these replies. He gave his hand to Fennimore, and then walked up and down for some time in great embarrassment.

10

" And so you won't quarrel with me ?" said he, at last.

" Not willingly, Mr. Lee," replied Mr. Fennimore, laughing ; " I have seen such evidences of your prowess lately, that I would much rather fight by your side than against you."

" Would you do me a favour, Mr. Fennimore ?"

" With a great deal of pleasure, sir."

" Then just insult me, if you please ; say any thing that I can ask satisfaction for ; do any thing that I can take offence at, and I will thank you as long as I live."

" I am sorry I cannot gratify you, Mr. Lee," replied Fennimore, much amused ; " but really I like you too well to feel any desire to forfeit your friendship."

" Well, if you will do nothing else to oblige me, will you go to the woods, and let us shoot at each other, for amusement ?"

" Excuse me, Mr. Lee," replied Fennimore, in the best humour possible.

" Tell me one thing, if you please, sir, and I have done— are you in love with Virginia Pendleton ?"

" How shall I answer you ?" replied Fennimore ; " to say I am, might argue presumption ; to say I am not, would show a want of taste."

" Well, sir, allow me to put you on your guard. It is useless to court her. She will not have you. I have been courting her these ten years, and have offered myself fifty times. It is perfectly useless, sir, to court her. I know her well—she is determined not to marry. She is the finest woman ever raised in Virginia—but she will not marry any man—I have ascertained that."

" I thank you, Mr. Lee, for your friendly warning ; and should I be unsuccessful, I shall recollect that I have ventured contrary to a friend's advice."

" Recollect another thing, if you please, sir—I have a prior claim to that lady's affection, which I will maintain at the risk of my life."

"Nay, but, Mr. Lee——"

"Excuse me, sir,—I have made up my mind on that point; any man who marries Virginia Pendleton must fight me first."

So saying, Mr. George Lee walked off, leaving Fennimore a little provoked, and very much amused; though, upon re-flection, he felt only sympathy for this amiable young man, who, with an excellent heart and the most gentlemanly feel-ings, was betrayed by the weakness of his intellect and his perseverance in a hopeless passion into the most extravagant absurdities.

# CHAPTER XXV.

THE Harpes had heretofore escaped punishment in consequence of a variety of peculiar circumstances. The
scene of their barbarities was still almost a wilderness, and a
variety of cares pressed on the people. The spoils of their
dreadful warfare furnished them with the means of violence
and of escape. Mounted on fine horses, they plunged into
the forest, eluded pursuit by frequently changing their course,
and appeared unexpectedly, to perpetrate new enormities, at
places far distant from those where they were supposed to
lurk. More than once were the people lulled into security
and the pursuit of the ruffians abandoned by the supposition
that they had entirely disappeared from the country—when
the conflagration of a solitary cabin, and the murder of all its
inmates, awakened the whole community to lively sensations
of fear, and horror, and indignation.

Miss Pendleton heard of these atrocities with shuddering.
Thrice had she seen one of these assassins, under circumstances
calculated to excite the most dreadful apprehensions. On
each occasion his hand was raised against her life, and his
malignant scowl seemed to announce the existence of some
deadly feud against her. But why she should thus be an object of vengeance and pursuit, she was totally unable to discover, or even conjecture.

In the meanwhile, the outrages of these murderers had
not escaped public notice, nor were they tamely submitted

to. The governor of Kentucky had offered a reward for their heads, and parties of volunteers had pursued them; they had been so fortunate as to escape punishment by their cunning, but had not the prudence to fly the country or to desist from their crimes.

On the morning after these wretches had been seen by Mr. George Lee, the intelligence arrived of their having murdered a woman and all her children. The vengeance of the whole community was now roused to the highest pitch, and it was determined to raise parties and hunt down the murderers. Horsemen were seen traversing the woods in every direction, eagerly beating up all the coverts, and examining every suspicious place where it was supposed the outlaws might lurk.

A man named Leiper, who had some renown as an active and successful hunter, and who was both muscular and brave, headed a small party. The ruffians were encamped in the woods, at an obscure wild spot, distant from any habitation; and were seated on the ground, surrounded by their women and children, when the hunters came so suddenly upon them, that they had only time to fly in different directions. Micajah Harpe, the larger of the two brothers, sprung upon a fine blooded horse, that he had taken from a traveller but a day or two before, and dashed off, pursued by the whole party; while his brother, not having time to mount, stole silently away among the brushwood, and escaped notice.

Micajah, who was kept in view by the pursuers, spurred forward the noble animal on which he was mounted, and which, already jaded, began to fail at the end of five or six miles. The chase was long and hot, and the miscreant continued to press forward; for although his pursuers had one by one dropped in the rear, until none of them were in sight but Leiper, he was not willing to risk a combat with a man so strong, and bolder than himself, who was animated by a noble spirit of indignation against a shocking and unmanly outrage.

Leiper was mounted on a horse of celebrated powers, which he had borrowed from the owner for this occasion.  At the beginning of the chase he had pressed his charger to the height of his speed, carefully keeping on the track of Harpe, of whom he sometimes caught a glimpse as he ascended the hills, and again lost sight of him in the valleys and the brush. But as he gained on the foe, and became sure of his victim, he slackened his pace, cocked his rifle, and deliberately pursued, sometimes calling upon the outlaw to surrender.

It was an animating, but fearful sight, to behold two powerful and desperately bold men, armed, and mounted on gallant steeds, pursuing each other so closely as to render it almost certain that a mortal struggle must soon ensue.  At length Harpe's horse, having strained all his powers in leaping a ravine, received an injury which obliged him to slacken his pace, and Leiper overtook him.  Both were armed with rifles.  When near enough to fire with certainty, Leiper stopped, took deliberate aim, and shot the retreating ruffian through the body; the latter, turning in his saddle, levelled his piece, which missed fire, and he dashed it to the ground, swearing that it was the first time it had ever deceived him.  He then drew a tomahawk, and waited the approach of Leiper, who, nothing daunted, drew his long hunting-knife, and rushed upon his desperate foe, grappled with him, hurled him to the ground, and wrested the weapon from his grasp. The prostrate wretch, exhausted with the loss of blood, conquered, but unsubdued in spirit, now lay passive at the feet of his adversary

Leiper was a humane man, easy, slow-spoken, and not quickly excited, but a thorough soldier when his energies were aroused into action.  Without insulting the expiring criminal he questioned him as to the motives of his late atrocities.  The murderer attempted not to palliate or deny them, and confessed that he had been actuated by no other inducement than a settled hatred of his species, whom he had

sworn to destroy without distinction, in revenge for so,ce
fancied injury. He expressed no regret for his bloody deeds.
He acknowledged that he had amassed large sums of money,
and described some of the places of concealment; but as
none was ever discovered, it is presumed he did not declare
the truth. Leiper had fired at Harpe several times during
the chase, and wounded him; and when Harpe was asked
why, when he found Leiper pursuing him alone, he did not
dismount and *take a tree*, from behind which he could have
inevitably shot him as he approached, he replied that he had
supposed there was not a horse in the country equal to the
one he rode, and that he was confident of making his escape.
He thought also that the pursuit would be less eager, so long
as he abstained from shedding the blood of his pursuers. On
the arrival of the rest of the party the wretch was dispatched,
and his head severed from his body. This bloody trophy was
then carried to the nearest magistrate, before whom it was
proved to be the head of Micajah Harpe; after which it was
placed in the fork of a tree, where it long remained a revolting object of horror. The spot is still called *Harpe's Head*,
and the public road which passes near it is called the Harpe's
Head Road.

Colonel Hendrickson and his friends had ridden out to
join in the pursuit, and had been scouring the forest some
hours when they met a party who informed them of the
death of Harpe, and they turned their horses' heads home-
wards. They were passing over a high but level tract of
country, whose surface was undulated by gradual swells and
covered with a thick growth of timber; to their right was a
hilly, broken tract, called " *The Knobs*," in which these villains had often harboured. In front of them was a region of
open, brushy land, destitute of trees, and which seemed to
have been lately a wild prairie, with no other covering but
grass. Mr. Lee, whose feelings seemed to be less social than
usual, was riding by himself in advance of the party; when

at a spot where two roads crossed he was surprised to see Hark Short leaning against a tree in an attitude of fixed attention. He was so completely absorbed as not to be at all conscious of the approach of Mr. Lee, until the latter spoke to him.

"What's the matter, Hark?" said he: "have you found a big rattlesnake?"

Hark started as he heard the voice, and looked timidly round. His features, usually melancholy, now wore an expression of fear and horror. Without answering the questions of Mr. Lee, he raised his eyes wildly; and George looking upward in the direction indicated by the glance of the boy, beheld the bleeding head of Harpe! For a moment he felt his own faculties bewildered, and a shuddering sensation crept over him as he gazed at this shocking spectacle; but a recollection of the crimes of the delinquent who had been punished in this summary manner changed the current of his feelings, and he exclaimed sharply,

"Is the boy mad?—is it so strange a thing that a murderer should be put to death?"

Hark only groaned and looked perplexed.

"This wretch was an acquaintance of yours, it seems— you appear so much concerned about him that I am inclined to have you taken up as an accomplice."

"No, don't—don't, if you please, stranger," exclaimed Hark.

"Then tell me why you seem so much interested in the death of that murderer."

"Who—that gentleman?" inquired Hark stupidly, pointing to the mangled relic.

"Yes, that miscreant, who has been put to death for his crimes,—what do you know about him?"

"Well, I don't know *nothen* in *peticklar*."

The other gentlemen now rode up, and on learning the subject of conversation insisted that the boy should disclose all the particulars that he knew respecting the ruffians, of whose history little was known.

"I never saw that gentleman," said Hark, "till since I came out here to Kentuck."

"But I understand," replied Colonel Hendrickson, "that a lad who I have reason to believe was yourself assisted these ruffians in escaping when arrested some weeks ago, and went off with them."

"Anan !" exclaimed the lad.

Colonel Hendrickson repeated, and explained what he had said.

"'Spose I did cut the strings—was there any harm in that ?"

"Certainly—aiding in the escape of a prisoner is a criminal offence; and it is my duty as a magistrate to bring you to punishment for it."

"Would you punish me for cutting the strings when the Indians had *you* tied to the pole to be roasted ?"

This was an appeal which was not easily parried. The Colonel acknowledged his obligations to Hark, and at once disclaimed any intention of arresting him, but on the contrary offered him his protectien.

"And now," said he, "I want you to tell me all that you know about Harpe."

"Will you let me go arter that ?"

"Yes."

"Won't you beat me afore you turn me loose ?"

"No, my lad, nobody shall touch you. You did me a good turn at the risk of your life, and I will repay it at the risk of mine, if necessary."

"Well—I never seed Harpe, as I know on, in peticklar, till that night."

"Had you never heard of him ?"

"Well—not in peticklar—only what mammy said."

"What did she say ?"

10*

" She told me 'Kage Harpe was a powerful bad man.  She·
used to get mad and curse him a hour."

" Did she ever tell you any thing that he did ?"

" Not in peticklar—only that he killed every body that he
got mad at—and that he would kill her and me if he got a
chance."

" Why should we wish to kill your mother ?"

" I axed her that myself, but she wouldn't tell me."

" Why then did you release Harpe, when you saw him for
the first time in custody ?"

" I couldn't help it."

" Why not ?  Come, tell us all about it—nobody shall
hurt you."

" Well—Harpe told me that he was my father !"

" And then you cut him loose ?"

" Yes—wouldn't you cut your daddy loose, if any body
had him tied ?"

" Hark," said George Lee, " you must go with me to Virginia, and live with me—I will take care of you."

" I reckon I can't go."

" Why not ?"

" 'Cause I don't want to."

" Would you not like to live in a fine house, and have
plenty to eat, and nothing to do ?"

" I don't like to live in houses."

" You don't ! what is your objection ?"

" Well—I can't say in peticklar—only I'd rather live in
the woods.  I can do just as I please in the woods, and be as
happy as a tree-frog."

So saying, Hark began to move off.  He cast a look of
terror towards the remains of his inhuman parent, as he retired.  It was not affection, nor regret which chained his
glance to this revolting object; but a kind of instinct—a
superstitious reverence for the only remaining being whose
blood was kindred to his own, mingled with a dread of human

punishments, that seemed to have been instilled into him in infancy, and which was the master-spring of all his actions. He quickened his pace on finding himself at liberty, walked rapidly away, and never was seen again in that region ; nor is it known, with any certainty, whatever became of Hark Short, the snake-killer. It is most probable that he perished in the wilderness; although it is altogether possible that he may still be killing reptiles on some distant frontier of our vast country.

A company of people now arrived, who had in their possession a number of articles which had been found in the camp of the Harpes. Among the rest was a small tin case, which was filled with papers. Mr. Fennimore having hastily looked over this, expressed a wish to examine it more at his leisure; and it was accordingly placed in his charge. The fatigued woodsmen separated, and Colonel Hendrickson conducted his friends once more to his hospitable mansion.

Their arrival was joyfully welcomed by the family, who had been under great apprehensions during their absence. Miss Pendleton, though much shocked at some of the particulars which they related, could not but feel relieved when she heard that the enemy of her peace was no more. Fennimore, who had concealed from his friends, as they rode home, an interesting discovery which he had made, advanced to her with a face beaming with joy, and, presenting to her a parchment, remarked,

"I am happy, Miss Pendleton, to have it in my power to restore to you this document. It is the will of my uncle Heyward, and places you in full possession of all his estate. Allow me to congratulate you on your good fortune."

"I do not know, Mr. Fennimore, whether I ought to accept the bounty of my uncle, which, by making me rich, deprives you of your natural inheritance."

"Happily for us both," replied the officer, "that is a question which need not now be argued; Major Heyward, who had the undoubted right to dispose of his own property, has made the decision, and we have only to acquiesce."

Mrs. Hendrickson, who seldom spoke except when spoken to, but who, with the sagacity peculiar to her sex in matters relating to the heart, had made some shrewd observations on the deportment of these young people towards each other, now remarked in her quiet way,

" If there is any difficulty about the property, perhaps you had as well let *me* keep that instrument until you can devise some plan for holding the estate jointly."

Virginia blushed deeply; and Fennimore, very gaily, handed the parchment to Mrs. Hendrickson.

" On those terms, madam," said he, " I most cheerfully deposit this document in your keeping, and shall, on my part, submit the controversy to your decision."

George Lee, when he heard that the *will* was found, danced and capered about the room like a boy, wished his cousin Virginia joy a hundred times, and shook Fennimore cordially by the hand, swearing that he was the cleverest fellow in all Kentucky; but when he saw what he considered proof positive that Fennimore was a successful candidate for the hand of her who had so long been the object of his affections, he left the room, and began to make immediate preparations for his return to his native State.

# CHAPTER XXVI.

### THE CONCLUSION.

SEVERAL years had passed away since the occurrence of the events recorded in the preceding pages. Captain Fennimore and the fair Virginia had been married, and were residing near to Colonel Hendrickson. William Colburn was united to the Colonel's only daughter, and was settled in the neighbourhood; and as no evidence to the contrary is before us, we are authorized in believing that both these couples were enjoying the most uninterrupted matrimonial felicity.

The best friends, however, must sometimes part; and Captain Fennimore found it necessary to leave his pleasant home and his agreeable wife to attend to the affairs of their joint estate in Virginia. The farm formerly occupied by Major Heyward was rented out, but the tenant had erected a house on a part of the land distant from the spot where the former mansion had stood. Captain Fennimore feeling a desire to revisit the place where his uncle had resided and his wife had grown up from infancy to maturity, rode over one day to the ruins of the old house. The lane was still kept open, but was grown up with weeds and briers. The lawn around the house preserved something of its former verdure and beauty, but the garden was overrun with bushes, whose wild and tangled limbs were strangely mingled with the remains of a variety of rare and ornamental shrubs. Indigenous thorns and domestic fruits grew side by side, and wild flowers mingled their blossoms with those of exotic plants. There is nothing so melancholy as such a scene, where luxury and art are beheld in ruin, and their remains revive the recollection of departed pleasures. There has always seemed to me to be something peculiarly desolate in the appearance of a deserted garden, where the spot once adorned with taste, and cultivated with assiduous care, has been suffered to run into wilderness. Nowhere are the efforts of nature and art so harmoniously blended as in the garden; nowhere does embellishment seem so appropriate or labour so productive. There is something quiet, and innocent, and peaceful about the beauties of a garden that interests the heart, at the same time that the senses reap enjoyment.

While Captain Fennimore was strolling pensively about, he discovered a horseman riding up the avenue towards the same place. On reaching the large gate which opened into the lawn, the person halted, and remained sitting on his horse. Fennimore supposing that it might be some one who had business with himself, walked slowly towards the gate; but before he reached it, and while concealed from the stranger by a cluster of bushes, he was surprised to hear the voice of the latter, as if in conversation with another person.

"She is not at home, eh?" said the voice; "well, tell her I called, boy, d'ye hear?—tell her Mr. George Lee called."

Fennimore, curious to know to whom Mr. Lee was speaking, advanced a few steps so as to see without being exposed himself; and was surprised to find that no person was within sight but themselves. Mr. Lee was mounted on a fine horse, and completely armed with a sword, a pair of large pistols, and a rifle. He wore his father's revolutionary uniform coat, buff waistcoat, and cocked hat, and, thus accoutred, formed an imposing figure. His countenance wore the blush of habitual intemperance, together with the mingled wildness and stupidity of partial derangement. After sitting silent for a few minutes, he drew his sword and exclaimed,

" Gentlemen, I pronounce Virginia Pendleton to be the most beautiful woman ever raised in the Old Dominion, and I am ready to make good my words. You understand me, gentlemen! There she sits at her window—she has made a vow that she will never marry, and I stand here prepared to cut any gentleman's throat who shall dare to pay her his addresses. Gentlemen, shall we hunt to-morrow? Pass that bottle, if you please, Mr. Jones—no heeltaps. My compliments to Miss Pendleton, boy, d'ye hear? and tell her I called to inquire after her health."

Then drawing himself up, he saluted with his sword, and sheathed it, took off his hat, bowed towards the spot where the house had been, and kissed his hand; after which he wheeled his horse about, and rode with a slow and stately pace down the avenue.

Poor George! he had fallen a victim to the evil example of an intemperate father and the intrigues of an ambitious mother. With a heart tenderly alive to the best charities of human nature, and a disposition easily moulded to the purposes of those with whom he associated, he might readily have been trained to respectability and usefulness, and although he could never have become a brilliant man, he might have been what is far more important, an amiable and worthy citizen. But his weak intellect, assailed by the seductions of pleasure on the one hand, and by dazzling schemes of ambition on the other, became unsettled, and at last totally destroyed. His vigorous constitution enabled him long to outlive the wreck of his mind, and he continued for many years to visit the ruins of Major Heyward's mansion, dressed in the fantastic habiliments which we have described. He remembered nothing which occurred after his ill-starred journey to the frontier; and the events of his early life were mixed up in his memory in the most singular confusion. He continued to be the devoted lover of Virginia Pendleton, and nothing ever ruffled his temper except the mention of her marriage, which he always denied with indignation, as an insult to her and himself; while the recollections of his early love were mingled with visions of bacchanalian orgies, and with hideous dreams of bloody encounters with the savages. Many years afterwards, when his cheeks were furrowed and his hair gray with premature old age, he might be still seen, mounted on his sleek hunter, clad in his ancient uniform, with his hair powdered and his long queue neatly tied, riding with stately grace every day along the old avenue, paying his imaginary morning visit to the idol of his heart. He was followed by an old negro valet, as gray and nearly as stately as himself, who humoured all the fancies of his master, until it was supposed that the faithful black began to be tinctured with the madness which he had affectionately humoured, and spoke of Miss Virginia Pendleton with the most unaffected gravity, long after that lady was the mother of a numerous and thriving colony of young Kentuckians.

Mrs. Lee mourned over the disappointment of all her hopes in the bitterness of unavailing repentance. When our errors affect only ourselves, the pang of remorse may be borne with patience; but when they have extended to those we love, and our own conviction comes too late to restore peace to the bosoms we have ruined, the cup of wretchedness is fatally poisoned for the remainder of a miserable life. She never smiled, and was never seen to weep, and bore the sufferings which only a woman's love can know, with a dignified resignation, of which woman's fortitude is alone capable.

# PART SECOND.

# CONTENTS.

# THE BACKWOODSMAN.

THE beautiful forests of Kentucky, when first visited by the adventurous footsteps of the pioneers, presented a scene of native luxuriance, such as has seldom been witnessed by the human eye. So vast a body of fertile soil had never before been known to exist on this continent. The magnificent forest trees attained a gigantic height, and were adorned with a foliage of unrivalled splendour. The deep rich green of the leaves, and the brilliant tints of the flowers, nourished into full maturity of size and beauty by the extraordinary fertility of the soil, not only attracted the admiration of the hunter, but warmed the fancy of the poet, and forcibly arrested the attention of the naturalist.

As the pioneers proceeded, step by step, new wonders were discovered; and the features of the country, together with its productions, as they became gradually developed, continued to present the same bold peculiarities and broad outlines. The scale of greatness pervaded all the works of nature. The noble rivers, all tending towards one great estuary, swept through an almost boundless extent of country, and seemed to be as infinite in number as they were grand in size. The wild animals were innumerable. The forest

teemed with living creatures, for this was the paradise of the
brute creation. Here were literally "the cattle upon *a*
*thousand* hills." The buffalo, the elk, and the deer roamed
in vast herds, and all the streams were rich in those animals
whose fur is so much esteemed in commerce. Here lurked
the solitary panther, the lion of our region, and here prowled
the savage wolf. The nutritious fruits of the forest and the
juicy buds of the exuberant thickets reared the indolent
bear to an enormous size. Even the bowels of the earth exhibited stupendous evidences of the master hand of creation.
The great limestone beds of the country were perforated
with spacious caverns of vast extent and splendid appearance, many of which yielded valuable minerals; while the
gigantic bones found buried in the earth, far exceeding in size
those of all known animals on the globe, attested the former
existence in this region of brutes of fearful magnitude.

Such were the discoveries of the first adventurers; such
the inducement which allured them onward, and inclined them
to linger in these solitudes, enduring the severest privations,
and beset by dangers which might have shaken the firmest
manhood. But the pioneers were men whose characters were
not now to be formed in the school of adversity or danger.
They were the borderers already trained to war and the
chase upon the extensive frontiers of our country; men cra-
dled in the forest, and accustomed from their infancy to the
bay of the prowling wolf and the yell of the hostile Indian.
Trained to athletic sports and martial exercises, their military
propensities were cherished throughout their whole lives, and
became engrafted in their nature. Martial habits mingled in
all their rural pursuits. If they travelled or walked abroad,
it was with the wary step and jealous vigilance of the Indian:
with an eye continually glancing into every thicket, and an
ear prepared to catch the slightest alarm of danger. They
slept upon their arms, and carried their rifles to the harvest-
field, to the marriage-feast, and to the house of worship.

Simple, honest, and inoffensive in their manners, kind and just to each other, they were intrepid, fierce, and vindictive in war. Under an appearance of apathy, with a gait of apparent indolence, and with careless habits, they were muscular and hardy, patient of fatigue, ardent in their temperament, warm-hearted and hospitable. They were the borderers of Virginia and North Carolina, where they had long formed a rampart between the less warlike inhabitants and the savage tribes. In the war of the revolution they had engaged with ardour; but while the acknowledgement of our national independence brought peace to the rest of our country, it left the frontiers still embroiled with the savages.

The backwoodsmen, therefore, when they first emigrated into the western forests, had not to learn the rude arts of sylvan life, nor to study the habits of the Indian and the beast of prey. These were enemies with whom they had long been familiar, and with whom they delighted to cope.

They lived in cabins hastily erected for temporary shelter, and as hastily abandoned when a slight allurement at some distant spot invited them to change their residence. Their personal effects were of course few, and their domestic utensils rude and simple. Their horses, their rifles, and their herds, constituted their wealth; and with these they were prepared at a moment's warning to push farther into the wilderness, selling their habitations for a mere trifle, or abandoning them to any chance occupant who might choose to take possession, and conquering for themselves a new home from the panther and the Indian.

In the settlement of Kentucky, the pioneers emigrated singly, or in small parties. Unused to congregate in large bodies, unless on special occasions, and unaccustomed to military discipline, they chose to rely for defence on their own personal courage and vigilance. The boldest went foremost, traversed the country fearlessly, and having selected the choicest spots, however remote from other settlements, built their cabins, surrounded them with palisades to protect them from the Indians, and set all enemies at defiance.  Others followed and settled around them, forming little communities, detached from each other, and each organized independently, for its own defence; and it was not until these insulated settlements extended so as to come into contiguity, that the arm of government was felt and the mild operation of law diffused.  In the mean while the vast deserts by which they were separated retained their pristine wildness, traversed in common by the Backwoodsman and the Indian, who never met without a conflict, which was usually of the most exterminating character.

The ferocity of the Indian was not likely to be tamed, nor his animosity to the white man to be conciliated, by this state of things.  He had to do with men who had long been taught to consider the savage as a natural enemy, as hateful as the serpent and as irreconcilable as the wolf; men whose ears had been accustomed from infancy to legends of border warfare, in which the savage was always represented as the aggressor, and as a fiend stimulated by hellish passions, and continually plotting some detestable outrage or horrible revenge. Most of them had witnessed the Indian mode of warfare, which spares neither age nor sex; and many of them had suffered in their own families, or those of their nearest friends. They were familiar with the capture of women and children, the conflagration of houses, and the midnight assassination of the helpless and decrepid: and they had grown up in a hatred of the perpetrators of such enormities, which the philanthropist could hardly condemn, as it originated in generous feelings, and was kept alive by the repeated violation of the most sacred rights and the best affections.

As the settlements expanded, the wealthy and intelligent began to follow the footsteps of the pioneer.  Virginia, the parent State, had rewarded the patriotism of many of her distinguished revolutionary officers, by large grants of land in Kentucky, and some of these emigrated among the early settlers. Many young gentlemen with elevated views and liberal educations, followed ; and some of those who thus came with the rifle in hand, and commenced their professional career amid the commotion of the battle-field, have since been widely known to fame, as among the most distinguished lawyers and statesmen of the nation.

There were others of a character still more essentially peaceful, who at an early period braved the dangers and privations of that unsettled region, stimulated by a noble and self-denying sense of duty. While the tomahawk and firebrand were still busy ; when to travel from one settlement to another required the courage and hardihood of the hunter ; the ministers of the Gospel penetrated into the wilderness, and zealously pursued their sacred calling in defiance of every danger. They learned to endure fatigue, to provide for their wants, and to elude the common enemy, with the sagacity of woodsmen ; and those of them who lived to enjoy the dignity of grey hairs, and the luxury of peaceful times, could narrate a series of strange adventures, and " hair-breadth 'scapes," such as seldom occur in the lives of the clergy.

The incidents of the following tale have their date at a period when the settlements, though still detached, began to be so strong as to be considered permanent. Some of them were now regularly organized, and felt no longer any dread of predatory incursions of the neighbouring savage. The one particularly in which the scene is laid, had experienced a long interval of uninterrupted peace ; agriculture was beginning to flourish, and the civil arts had been introduced. The woodsmen still retained their cabins, pursued the wild game for a livelihood, and joined in distant expeditions against the savages, and in defence of feebler settlements ; while a number of the class who might more properly be called farmers, and several intelligent and wealthy families, had moved into the neighbourhood. Civil institutions had been introduced

11

and the spirit of improvement was awake. The sound of the axe saluted the ear in every direction; roads were opened; magistrates had been appointed, and were assuming the authority of their stations; and females who had heretofore confined themselves within doors, brooding over their offspring, like watchful birds, and who had found even the sacred fortress of woman, the fireside, no protection from violence, now felt at liberty to indulge the benevolent propensity for visiting their neighbours, and talking over the affairs of the community, which is said by those acquainted with human nature to be peculiar to the sex.

Among other novelties, a *camp meeting* was about to be held for the first time. This popular mode of worship was familiar to the emigrants from Virginia and North Carolina, where it had long been practised, and found highly beneficial and convenient in new settlements, where public edifices had not yet been erected, and where private habitations were too small to accommodate worshipping assemblies; and the effort now about to be made for its introduction in the west, was hailed as a happy omen for the country. The spot was selected with great care; the whole neighbourhood united in clearing the ground, erecting huts, and making the most liberal arrangements for the accommodation of the concourse which was expected to be assembled. For the convenience of obtaining water, a place was chosen on the margin of a small rivulet and near a fine spring. The ground was a beautiful elevation sloping off on all sides and crowned with a thick growth of noble forest trees. The smallest of these together with all the underbrush were carefully removed, leaving a few of the most stately, whose long branches formed a thick canopy at an elevation of fifty feet from the ground. The camp was laid off in a large square, three sides of which were occupied by huts, and the fourth by the *stand* or pulpit. The whole of the enclosed area was filled with seats roughly hewed out of logs.

A busy scene was presented on the day before the meeting commenced, occasioned by the arrival of the people, some of whom had travelled an immense distance. The larger number came on horseback, some in wagons and some in ox-carts. They were loaded with beds, cooking utensils, table furniture and provisions. These articles, however, were chiefly furnished by the inhabitants of the vicinity, who claimed the privilege of entertaining strangers. The persons resident in the immediate neighbourhood had each erected his own hut, with the intention of accommodating, besides his own family, a number of guests; large quantities of game had been taken, beef, pigs, and poultry had been killed, and the good wives had been engaged for several days in cooking meat and preparing bread and pastry. The loads upon loads of good things for the body which were accumulated were marvellous to behold; not that there was any indulgence of luxury or extravagant display, but as was very judiciously remarked on the occasion by a veteran hunter, "it took a *powerful chance of truck* to feed such a *heap of folks*," and the generous Kentuckians, accustomed to practise the most liberal hospitality, could not be backward on a public occasion.

The meeting commenced on Thursday and lasted until Monday, the whole of each day being occupied with religious exercises. At daylight in the morning the voice of prayer was heard in each hut, where the families were separately assembled, as such, for worship. Shortly afterwards the fires were kindled around the encampment, and a few of the females were seen engaged in cooking. A few individuals then collected on the seats in the area and raised a hymn; others joined them, and the number swelled gradually until nearly the whole company was collected. They sang without books; the pieces being those of which the words were generally known. Some of the tunes were remarkably sweet, and and thus sung in the open air under the broad canopy of

heaven, and as it were in the immediate presence of the great
Object of all worship, were indescribably solemn and affecting;
some were peculiarly wild, and some cheerful; many of them
being the beautiful airs of popular ballads, which were in this
manner appropriated to Divine worship. The balmy freshness of the morning air, the splendour of the rising sun, the
stillness of the forest and the wild graces of the surrounding
scenery gave a wonderful interest to this voluntary matin service. It was thus our first parents worshipped their Creator
in Paradise, thus the early Christians assembled in groves and
secluded places; and so close is the union between good taste
and religious feeling, that while civilized nations have set
apart the most splendid edifices for worship, ruder communities, in a similar spirit, assemble for the same purpose at the
most genial hour and the most picturesque spot. The heart
powerfully excited by generous feelings always becomes
romantic; the mind elevated by the noble pursuit of a high
object becomes enlarged and refined; and although such impulses may be temporary, the virtuous actions which they
produce have a tendency towards the soft, the graceful, and the
picturesque in their development. After the morning hymn,
the preachers ascended the *stand*, and service was performed
before breakfast. The rest of the day, with the exception of
short intervals for refreshment, was filled in the same manner.
But nothing could exceed the solemn and beautiful effect of
the meeting at night. The huts were all illuminated, and
lights were fastened to the trunks of the trees, throwing a
glare upon the overhanging canopy of leaves, now beginning
to be tinged with the rich hues of autumn, which gave it the
appearance of a splendid arch finely carved and exquisitely
shaded. All around was the dark gloom of the forest, deepened to intense blackness by its contrast with the brilliant
light of the camp.

But we must hasten to our narrative. On Sunday morning a company consisting of three persons was seen approach-

ing the camp-ground. The elder of these who rode alone in advance of the others, was Mr. Singleton, a gentleman who had recently emigrated from Virginia. He was a farmer, a well-educated man, in easy circumstances, who not being religious nor in any manner connected with the sect under whose auspices the meeting was held, contented himself with participating no farther in its proceedings than by being a regular and respectful attendant on the daily services. Miss Singleton, his only daughter, and Edward Overton, her affianced lover, were his companions. They were to be married in a fortnight from this time. It is unnecessary to inform the erudite reader that the young lady, who was just turned of seventeen, was beautiful and interesting, and her lover tall and handsome. Had they been otherwise their lives might have slept in oblivion, with the fame of the "mute inglorious" rustics in Gray's Elegy. Dennie, who has been called the American Addison, once amused himself by criticising an advertisement of a man who had stolen "a *chunky* horse," and with such a lesson before our eyes, we should hardly venture upon a *chunky young man* for a hero, or a hard-favoured lady for a heroine. The decree of literary ostracism by which short gentlemen have been banished from the pages of fiction, is, in our humble opinion, unjust, believing, as we do, that to be an interesting young man and a tender lover it is by no means necessary to possess the corporeal altitude of a grenadier. For the homely and the dull we put in no plea: it is a standing rule among writers, having a laudable care of their own fame, not to waste their midnight oil upon ugly or insipid people. The reader is therefore desired to understand distinctly, that the young couple now introduced, were not only worthy and amiable, but were in point of appearance all that the most romantic peruser of these veracious pages could rationally desire.

As they rode slowly along, they were deeply engaged in conversation; but it was easy to see from the sedate demean-

our of Ellen Singleton, that the subject was suited to the day
and the occasion. She was naturally gay and volatile; but
latterly her thoughts had been turned to the subject of religion;
and as the day approached when she was to take upon her the
vows of wedlock, and to enter upon new and solemn duties,
she felt more and more the necessity of directing her life
agreeably to the precepts of the Gospel. To these virtuous
resolutions a new impulse had been given by the exercises of
the camp-meeting. Her heart was sensibly awakened, and
her judgment fully persuaded; and after serious reflection and
preparation she was now ready to make a profession of her
faith by uniting herself with the church, and assuming those
engagements which are imposed upon the disciples of the Redeemer. These duties she expected to take upon her that
day; and Edward Overton felt deeply affected as he noticed
the solemn tone, the deep conviction, and the firm determination of her mind; for however a false shame may sometimes
induce the concealment of devotional feelings, under the mistaken notion that they will be considered as the evidence of
weakness, the truth is, that a young lady is never so interesting in the eyes of her lover as when conscientiously engaged
in the performance of her duty.

The senses of a young man are easily excited by beauty,
wit, gaiety, and the thousand attractions of feminine loveliness, but there must be moral energy and pure principle to
secure his affections. Edward had admired Ellen when he
saw her in the pride of beauty and the flush of overflowing
spirits; he had long known her to be refined and generous,
and loved to contemplate her soft attractions and delicate
graces; but he now witnessed the operations of her mind
under a new aspect, and when he saw the good sense, the
energy, and the strength of principle which supported her in
the determination to act up to her sense of duty, his love rose
to a sentiment of devotion. Formerly Ellen had been in his
eyes a beautiful vision, floating along in the tide of youthful

enjoyment; but now that she had assumed an individuality of character, asserted her independence as a moral agent, and acknowledged her accountability to God, she became invested with a dignity which gave an almost angelic sacredness to her charms.

On that day the concourse was greater than it had been before; and those who had been for years accustomed to the solitude of the forest, to alarm, toil, and privation, felt their hearts elevated with a new species of joy and gratitude, when they found themselves surrounded by their countrymen, and united with them in social and sacred duties. With many of them the Sabbath had long passed unhonoured and even unnoticed, and its public acknowledgment called them back to holy and happy feelings; for there is in the observance of this day something so noble, so heart-cheering, so appropriate to the most virtuous impulse of our bosoms, that even the thoughtless cannot divest themselves of its influence. It is, to all who submit to restrictions, a day of repose, when "the weary are at rest, and the wicked cease from troubling;" a day from which care and labour are banished, and when the burthens of life are lightened from the shoulders of the heavy laden. But to him who sincerely worships at the altar of true piety, and especially to one who has been led in infancy to the pure fountains of religion, the return of the long-neglected Sabbath brings up a train of pure and ecstatic recollections. To all it was the harbinger of peace, security, and civil order.

It was delightful to see a whole community, who but recently had assembled only at the sound of the bugle, or by the glare of the beacon fire, now coming together, by a spontaneous impulse, to mingle their hearts and voices in the rational and solemn exercises of religion. Insulated as that congregation was from the rest of mankind, the individuals composing it felt as if they were reunited with the great human family, when they resumed the performance of

Christian duties, and knelt before the Redeemer of men in common with all Christendom on his appointed day. Many of them had reared the altar of worship in their own families, and the sweet accents of praise had been heard ascending through the gloom of the forest, mingled with the fiendish sound of the war-whoop and the dissonant yell of the beasts of prey, and they had seen days of moral darkness, of bodily anguish, of almost utter despair, when it seemed as if their prayers were not heard, and that God had abandoned that land to the blackness of darkness for ever. But now he had set his bow in the heavens; his altar was publicly reared and his presence sensibly felt; and they who believed in the reality of religion felt assured that a sign was given them that they should not be destroyed from off the face of the land. Never did those simple and affecting words seem more appropriate, "How beautiful upon the mountains are the feet of him that bringeth tidings that publisheth peace."

In the evening, when Mr. Singleton and his daughter were about to return home, Edward Overton hastened to join them. Ellen had that day been among the number who became attached to the church, and, deeply absorbed in devotional feelings, had abstracted her senses and thoughts from all other subjects. Edward had watched her with deep emotion, and he now approached her with a feeling of reverence, such as he had never felt towards her before. She extended her hand and spoke to him with her usual kindness of manner, but in a tone in which seriousness was mingled with unwonted tenderness; and as he assisted her to mount her horse, whispered to him not to accompany them. "I cannot converse with you this evening, Edward," said she; "I wish to be alone, and I am sure that you will gratify me —come to-morrow." He saw the propriety of her request, and pressing her hand affectionately bade her adieu, with a promise to visit her early the next morning.

The sun had just set as Mr. Singleton and his daughter

left the camp-ground, but having only a short distance to go they were in no haste. It was a serene evening in September. The air was still and soft, and the sky had that richness and brilliancy of colour which travellers describe as peculiar to the genial atmosphere of Italy. The leaves still hung upon the trees, and some of them retained their verdure, while others were tinged with yellow, brown, or deep scarlet, giving to the foliage every variety of hue. The wild fruits were abundant. The grape-vines were loaded with purple clusters. The persimmon, the paw-paw, and the crab-apple hung thick upon the trees, while the ground was strewed with nuts. Ellen, who was fatigued with the confinement of the day, enjoyed the exercise and the balmy air of the evening, and felt that the passing moments were among the most delightful of her life. They were in unison with her feelings and emblematic of her situation: she had passed the joyous spring of life, and a season of riper enjoyment, of serene quiet, and useful virtue, was pictured to her fancy in agreeable perspective.

They had nearly reached home when they met one of their neighbours, with whom Mr. Singleton wished to converse for a few moments; he therefore stopped, desiring Ellen to ride slowly forward. Absorbed in her own reflections, and not dreaming of danger, she gave the rein to her spirited horse, which, impatient to return to his stable, quickened his pace imperceptibly, and she was soon out of sight of her parent. But their dwelling was now in view, and she felt no alarm until her horse suddenly stopped and snuffed the air, as if in great terror. She had heard of the keenness of scent by which these animals discover the approach of an Indian, and the affright that they evince on such occasions; and feeling confident that nothing but the vicinity of a savage or some ferocious beast could thus alarm her gentle nag, she attempted to rein him up in order to return to her father. But the horse stood as if fixed to the ground, trembling and snorting

11*

with an accent of agony; and before she could form any
other resolution, a party of Indians, lying in ambush on each
side of the road, rushed forward and dragged her from her
horse, while the high-bred animal, becoming frantic with
terror, tore the bridle which they had seized from their
grasp, and made his escape at full speed.

The savages having secured their prize, immediately
began to retreat towards their towns at a rapid pace, forcing
the afflicted girl to exert her utmost strength to keep up with
them.   It soon, however, grew dark, and they proceeded at a
more deliberate gait, but still pursued their journey through
the whole night, groping their way amidst dense thickets
beset with thorns and briars, and over ravines and the trunks
of fallen trees, with ease to themselves, but with brutal violence to the delicate frame of their captive.   Poor Ellen had
need now of all the consolations which the religion that she
had just professed could afford.   She had been told that day
that she would meet with afflictions that would try her faith,
but that God would never forsake those that believed
on him; and she now threw herself entirely upon Him for
protection.   She prayed earnestly and sincerely, and felt a
conviction that she was heard.   Her courage rose with confidence, and she went forward without a murmur, resigned to
meet her fate whatever it might be.   Ellen, too, was naturally
a girl of good sense and high spirit, and while she humbly
relied upon divine protection, saw also the propriety of exert-
ing herself; and knowing that the Indians would soon be
pursued, she deliberately laid plans to retard the retreat and
disclose their path.   Keeping up an appearance of diligence
and obedience, she contrived to linger at the various obstacles
which obstructed their way, while she employed herself,
whenever she could do so without attracting notice, in tearing
off small pieces of her dress, and dropping such articles as
she could dispense with in places where they would be likely
to attract attention.   The darkness of the night favoured this

scheme; her reticule, handkerchief, &c., were thus strewed by the way, and in brushing through the thickets she broke the twigs with her hands as signals to her pursuers.

The morning added to her griefs. The warrior who claimed her, and who seemed to be the leader of the party, having led her during the night by thongs of skin bound round her wrists, now removed the bands, and seemed to contemplate his prize with complacency. He assured her in broken, and barely intelligible English, of a kind treatment, and promised that if she behaved well, he would make her his wife. When Ellen shook her head in alarm, as if dissenting from this matrimonial arrangement, he said, "May be, you think I cannot support you. That is a mistake. The *Speckled Snake* is a great hunter. My lodge is on the bank of a great river, where the water is cold, and the big fish love to swim. The plains all round my village are covered with deer and buffalo. The stars in the heavens are not so many as the cattle on our hunting-grounds. The white man does not come there to destroy every thing that the Great Spirit made for his red people, like the hurricane when it sweeps through the woods. I can outrun the elk; I am stronger than the buffalo; I am more cunning than the beaver. They call me the *Speckled Snake*, because I can conceal myself in the grass, and so my enemies step on me before they see me. I have only three squaws. I can support another very well, and my lodge is big enough for three or four more. You need not be afraid of my women treating you ill. I will beat them unmercifully if they strike you. My squaws fear me; I whip them severely when they quarrel with each other. Women need a great deal of whipping."

Late in the morning they halted to eat and rest. Ellen had no appetite for food. She had now been walking for fourteen hours without cessation, over hills and through swamps and thickets. Her feet were swelled and lacerated, and her hands and arms torn with briars. Worn down by extreme

fatigue and mental exhaustion, she began to suffer intense
thirst and violent pains.    But her bodily afflictions were
light in comparison with the gloomy anticipations of her
mind, and the shock already inflicted on her sensitive heart.
She found her companions more brutal and loathsome than
even prejudiced description had painted them.    They had
urged her forward with pointed sticks, and would have beaten
her, had she not endeavoured to anticipate their wishes.    They
devoured their raw and almost putrid meat with the gluttony
of beasts ; and exhibited altogether a ferocity which seemed
to belong to fiends rather than to human beings.    The idea
of remaining in their power was dreadful ; death, she thought,
would be infinitely preferable to such captivity.    Like all
generous minds, she had, too, in the moment of her severest
sufferings, a sympathy for others which was more poignant
than her own afflictions.    She thought of her father, who had
no child but herself, and whose heart would be wrung with
intense agony by this event ; and of Edward Overton, the
devoted lover, whose affections were so closely linked with her
own, and pictured to herself the misery they would endure
upon her account.    Still her courage remained strong, and
her confidence in Heaven unshaken ; and, as her captors swallowed their hasty meal, she sunk upon her knees, clasped her
hands together, and with a countenance beaming calm resignation, engaged in audible prayer, while the Indians gazed at
her with a wonder not unmingled with awe.

Here we shall leave her for the present, while we introduce another character to the reader's acquaintance.    At a
distance of some fifteen or twenty miles from the place of
holding the religious meeting above alluded to, a solitary hunter was "camped out" in the woods.    He had selected a spot
in a range of low broken hills, on the margin of an extensive
flat of wet alluvion land, to which the wild grazing animals
resorted at this season, when the grass and herbage were beginning to wither upon the uplands.    His camp was simply

a roof resting on the ground, formed by leaning stakes of wood together, so as to make them meet at the top, and covering them with bark. It was not more than four feet high, and intended only to accommodate a single person in a reclining posture ; and was placed in a thicket, so concealed by vines and branches, as not to be discoverable, except by close inspection, while the aperture, which supplied the place of a door, commanded a view to some distance in front. Not far from it was an Indian war-path, leading from the flat to the uplands ; and the hunter seemed to have purposely placed himself in a position from which he would be likely to see tho war parties of the savages, should any pass, without being discovered by them.

The hunter was a man of middle height, not remarkably stout, but with a round built, compact form, happily combining strength with activity. His countenance was mild and placid, showing an amiable and contented disposition; and his eye was of a quiet, contemplative kind. The muscles of his face were rigid and strongly developed, and his complexion darkened by long exposure to the weather ; but there was no lines indicating violent or selfish passions. It was a bold, manly countenance, but the prevailing expressions were those of benevolence and thought. There was an archness, too, about the eye, which showed that its possessor was not deficient in humour. He was evidently a man of strong mind, of amiable propensities, and of great simplicity of character. The quiet courage of his glance, the self-possession and calm vigilance of his manner, together with a certain carelessness and independence of mien, would have pointed him out as a genuine pioneer, who loved the woods, and was most happy when roaming in pursuit of game, or reclining in his solitary retreat, with no companion but his faithful dog. Nor was this fondness for the silence of the wilderness the result of unsocial feelings : the hunter loved his friend, and enjoyed the endearments of his own fireside ; but he forsook them in the same spirit in which the philosopher retires to the seclusion of his closet—to enjoy unmolested the train of his own reflections, and to follow without interruption a pursuit congenial with his nature. Though unacquainted with books, he had perused certain parts of the great volume of nature with diligent attention. The changes of the seasons, the atmospherical phenomena, the growth of plants, the habits of animals, had for years engaged his observing powers; and without having any knowledge of the philosophy of schools, he had formed for himself a system which had the merit of being often true, and always original.

On the same night in which Ellen Singleton was captured by the Indians, the hunter whom we have described slept in his camp. It was dark, but perfectly still, and his slumbers were undisturbed until near the dawn of day, when his dog, which lay on the outside, suddenly started up and uttered a low whine. The watchful hunter, accustomed to awake at the slightest alarm, raised his head and listened. The dog snuffed the air for a moment, and then crept cautiously into the camp, as if to apprise his master of approaching danger. The latter seized his rifle and crept from the place of concealment, while the dog, with bristling hair, crouched on the ground uttering at intervals a low suppressed moan, intended only for the ear of his master.

The hunter looked cautiously around, and having satisfied himself that no enemy was within striking distance, directed his scrutiny to a spot where the war-path crossed the summit of a small knoll which was bare of timber, and beyond which the blue sky could be seen. As he watched, a human figure was seen dimly traced on the horizon, passing rapidly over the summit of the knoll along the Indian trail. Another, and then others followed, until the hunter had counted seven; but their forms were too indistinct to enable him to make any guess as to their character. He had other data, however, upon which to form a judgment. "Indians?" muttered he to himself, "yes, Drag would not crouch between my feet trembling and whining, and bristling like a scared pig, if he did not scent a red-skin. I can almost think I smell them myself. They have been in some devilment now, the abominable wretches! How they sneak off like thieves!" Then while the last figure was in sight, he placed his mouth against a hollow tree to give a more sepulchral tone to his voice, and imitated the screech of the owl. The figure halted, and uttered a low short sound resembling a different note of the same bird; but the hunter continued his mournful serenade in loud prolonged accents, until the human prowler, apparently satisfied that it was the night-song of the real bird, and not the signal of a friend, resumed his silent march. An owl, the tenant of a neighbouring oak, and who was the identical music master of our hunter, took up the strain with increased vivacity, but in a tone so nearly resembling that which had just ceased, as to have deceived the nicest ear, and the hunter resumed his reflections.

"Well, I've fooled them—and not the first time either. They are my old acquaintances, the Mingoes; and that is the signal of the Speckled Snake—the prince of mischief—the head devil of his tribe. Oh, the beggarly cut-throat villains! If I had Billy Whitley here now, or Simon Kenton, or Ben Logan, the way we'd fix these seven Indians would be curious. Some honest man's cabin is blazing now, I warrant, and his wife and children butchered. It is *ridic'lous*, I declare. They have no more bowels of compassion than a wolf. But after all, the Indians have some good qualities. They are prime hunters, I will say that for them, and they are true to one another. I don't blame them a grain for their hatred to the Long Knives. That game is fair, for two can play at it. But their thirst for human blood, and their cruelty to women and children is ridiculous. It does no good to nobody, and is ruinous to the pleasant business of hunting; for a man cannot take a little hunt of a month or two, without the danger of having his cabin burnt, and his family murdered in his absence. Well, it is no use for me to sit here; I'll take another nap, and look after the Speckled Snake in the morning."

At the first appearance of daylight the hunter sprang from his bed of skins. No time was required for the toilet, for he had slept with all his accoutrements about him, and came forth equipped at all points. He was clad in dressed buckskin, fitted closely to his form, and so arranged as to protect every part of his person from the thorns and briars which might assail it in passing rapidly through the brushwood of the forest. Under one arm hung a large powder-horn, which had been selected for the beauty of its curve and texture, carefully scraped and polished and covered with quaint devices traced with the point of the hunter's knife; under the other was suspended a square pouch of leather, containing flints, patches, balls, steel, tinder, and other "little fixens," as a backwoodsman would call them, constituting a complete magazine of supplies for a protracted hunt. On the belt supporting the pouch in a sheath contrived for the purpose, was a hunter's knife, a weapon with a plain wooden handle, marvellously resembling the vulgar instrument with which the butcher executes his sanguinary calling. From a crevice in a neighbouring rock where it had been artfully concealed, our pioneer supplied a small wallet with a store of dried venison, in order to be prepared for a march of several days, should occasion require. A broad leathern belt, secured round the waist by a strong buckle, confined the whole dress and equipment and supported a tomahawk.

Thus clad and prepared for action the hunter, after carefully examining the priming of his rifle, scraping the flint, and passing his eye along the barrel to see that all was right, strode off towards the place where he had seen the Indians. "To think of their having the impudence to walk along a footpath like white people," muttered he; "they must know that if they have been in mischief the settlements will be raised, and the horsemen will follow this trail. They didn't keep it long, I judge, but only fell into here on the broken ground to get along a little faster." Having reached the path, he examined it closely, but the hard ground afforded him but little satisfaction, and he proceeded cautiously towards a rivulet, or, in the vernacular of the country, *a branch*, that meandered along the foot of the hill. Here he was again disappointed, for the Indians had cunningly diverged from the path, and crossed the water by a log, leaving no trace of their footsteps. "Aye, they are cunning enough," soliloquised the hunter, "I couldn't expect them to cross the branch at a ford, like a mail-carrier in the settlements. But they can't fool me; I have not been raised in the woods to be outwitted by a gang of thieving Mingoes. The Speckled Snake is famous for these tricks, and has done his best, there is no mistake about that; but no animal that moves upon feet can walk these woods without making a sign.

"Well, it is a pleasant life that the hunter leads, after all, though it is a hard one," continued he, as he opened his collar, bathed his face and hands in the clear stream, and seated himself on a log to enjoy the cool morning air. "Nature did not make these clear waters and beautiful woods merely for the use of treacherous Indians,—no, nor for land speculators and pedlars. Here is quiet and repose, such as they know nothing of who toil in their harvest fields or bustle about in crowded cities. And what is the use of all their labour? The enemy steals into the settlement, and in a moment their stacks, their barns, and their houses are all in flames, or the pestilence walks abroad in the city, and they die by hundreds, like the Indians in a hard winter. The hunter avoids both extremes: he lays up provisions for the winter, but does not accumulate so much property as to tempt the Indian to rob, or the lawyer to fleece him. It makes me sorry when I go into the settlements, where the people are getting so crowded that there is

no comfort, and where there is so much strife.  It is so with
all animals: confine cattle in a yard and they will hook each
other, or chickens in a coop, and they will peck out each
other's eyes.  But there is no stopping them; the pedlar's
carts will be along over this very spot before many years, and
the time will come when there will not be a buffalo in Kentucky.  It is bad enough now.  There are settlements already
where a woodsman cannot find his way for the roads and
farms."

At this moment the tread of a horse was heard.  The
hunter threw his rifle over his arm, and stepped behind a large
tree to be prepared for friend or foe.  In a moment, Edward
Overton made his appearance, dashing along the war-path.
His horse was panting and covered with foam, his dress torn,
and his countenance haggard.  The hunter emerged from his
concealment to meet him.  They were strangers to each
other, but no time was lost in useless ceremony or unnecessary questions, and Edward soon related the catastrophe of
the preceding evening.

"Mr. Singleton's daughter, eh?" said the hunter coolly;
"I have heard tell of the gentleman, though I never saw him.
Very much of a gentleman, I expect—he came from Culpep-
per—I killed a deer once in sight of his plantation—though I
never saw the man to know him.  Well, the way these Indians act is curious."

"Shocking!" exclaimed the youth, "this atrocious act ex-
ceeds all former outrages."

"Well, I can't say as for that," replied the hunter, "though
I am sorry for the young woman—they took my own daughter
once, and I feel for another man's child.  But where is your
company?"

"I became separated from them in the woods, and accidentally struck this path."

The hunter then related what he had seen, and the youth,
elate with new hope, urged an instant pursuit.

"There are six or seven of them, and but two of us," said the hunter.

"No matter if there were a hundred," replied the impatient Overton, " she is suffering agony, and every moment is precious. Even now she may be at the stake."

" That is true. The savages treat their prisoners very ridiculous sometimes. But, young gentleman, I see you carry a fine-looking rifle,—can you handle it well."

" As well as any man. Never fear me—I will stand by you. I would die a thousand deaths for that dear girl."

"I reckon you would; I see it in your eye. If there is not good Virginia blood in you, I am mistaken. The misfortune is, that a man can only die once, however willing he may be to try it over again. Well, there is nothing gained without risk—and I feel for this poor child. Don't be in a fret, young man, I am just waiting to let you take breath. I will go with you provided you will obey my instructions. Now, mark what I say ; hitch your horse to that tree, and leave him—examine your priming and pick your flint—then fall into my track, tread light, keep a bright eye out, and say nothing. It will be curious if we two cannot out-general a half-a-dozen naked Mingoes."

The former apathy of the hunter's manner had entirely vanished. The excitement was sufficient to call out his energies. His eye was lighted up with martial ardour, his lips were compressed, and his step firm and elastic. Without waiting for farther parley, he dashed forward with a rapid stride, followed by his young and not less gallant companion. With unerring sagacity he struck at once into the trail of the enemy. "Here is plenty of *Indian sign*," said he, pointing to the ground, where the youth could see nothing, " and a beautiful plain track it is—almost as plain as some of the roads in the *Old Dominion*—there is the place where they crossed the branch, on that log, and here is the print of a woman's foot, a small slender foot with a shoe on, such as the

ladies wear in the old settlements—it is narrower than our
women's shoes that we make in these parts—there is the other
foot without a shoe—she has lost one, poor thing—and there
is a drop of blood on that leaf!"

Overton groaned, the tears started from his eyes, and his
limbs trembled with emotion.

"Keep cool, young man—be a soldier—no one can fight
when he is in a passion.  Blood for blood is the backwoodsman's rule.  We shall have them at the first halt they make.
They cannot travel all the time, without stopping, no more
than white folks."

The hunter now advanced with astonishing rapidity, for
although his step seemed to be deliberate, it had a steadiness
and vigour which yielded to no obstacle.  His course was as
direct as the flight of a bee, and his footsteps, owing to a peculiar and habitual mode of walking, were perfectly noiseless,
except when the dry twigs cracked under the weight of his
body.  His eye was continually bent on the ground, at some
distance in advance of his course; for he tracked the enemy,
not so much by the foot-prints on the soil, as by the derangement of dry leaves or growing foliage.  The upper side of
a leaf is of deep green colour and glossy smoothness; the
under side is paler, and of a rougher texture, and when turned
by violence from its proper position, it will spontaneously
return to it in a few hours, and again expose the polished surface to the rays of light.  The hunter is aware of this fact,
and in attentively observing the arrangement of the foliage
of the tender shrubs, discovers, with wonderful acuteness,
whether the leaves retain their natural position.  So true is
this indication, that where the grass is thick and tangled, a
track of lighter hue than the general surface may be distinctly
seen for hours after the leaves have been disturbed. The occasional rupture of a twig, and the displacing of the branches in
the thickets afford additional signs; and in places where the
ground is soft, the foot-prints are carefully noticed.  Other

cares, also, claimed the attention of the woodsman. His vigilant glance was often thrown far abroad. He approached every covert, or place of probable concealment, with caution, and sometimes when the trail passed through dangerous defiles, where the enemy might be lurking, suddenly forsook it, and taking a wide circuit, struck into it again far in advance. Thus they proceeded for three hours, with unremitting diligence and silence, when the pioneer halted.

"Here are fresh signs," said he, "the enemy are at hand; sit down and let us take breath."

The youth, whose confidence in his guide was now complete, obeyed in silence. The hunter again examined his arms.

"This is a charming piece," said he, in a low voice, "she never misses when she has fair play. It is a pleasant thing to have a gun that will not deceive you in the hour of danger. But then a man must do his duty, and have every thing in order."

Overton had been accustomed all his life to hunt occasionally for amusement. He was a young man of considerable muscular powers, and possessing the high spirit and the aptitude in the use of weapons, which are so characteristic of the youth of his country, was no mean proficient in the exercises of the forest. He now followed the example of his guide. They laid aside their coats and hats, drew their belts closely, and began to advance slowly, taking every step with such caution as not to create the slightest sound. They soon reached the summit of a small eminence, when the backwoodsman halted, crouched low, and pointed forwards with his finger. Overton followed with his eye the direction indicated, and beheld with emotions of indescribable delight, mingled with agony, the object of his pursuit.

At the root of a large tree sat the Indians, hideously painted, and fully equipped for battle, voraciously devouring their hasty meal. At a few yards distant from them knelt

Ellen, in the posture already described, awaiting her fate
with all the courage of conscious innocence and all the resignation of fervent piety. Overton's emotion was so great that
the hunter with difficulty drew him to the ground, while he
hastily whispered the plan of attack, a part of which had been
concerted at their recent halt. "Let us creep to yon log, and
rest our guns on it when we fire. I will shoot at that large
warrior who is standing alone—you will aim at one of those
who are sitting; the moment we have fired we will load again,
without moving, shouting all the while, and making as much
noise as possible;—be cool—my dear young friend—be cool.
Take it quiet and comfortable." Overton smothered his feelings, and during the conflict emulated the presence of mind of
his companion.

They crept on their hands and knees to the fallen trunk of
a large tree, which lay between them and the enemy, and
having taken a deliberate aim, the hunter gave the signal, and
both fired. Two of the savages fell, the others seized their
arms, while the heroic Kentuckians reloaded, shouting all the
while. Ellen started up, uttering a shriek of joy, and rushed
towards her friends. Two of the enraged Indians pursued,
with the intention of despatching her, before they should
retreat. Edward Overton and his companion rushed to her
assistance. One of the Indians had caught her long hair,
which streamed behind her in her flight, and his tomahawk
glittered above his head, when Edward rushed between them
and received the blow, diminished in force, on his own arm.
Undaunted, he threw himself on the bosom of the savage, and
they rolled together on the ground in fierce conflict. The
hunter advanced upon his adversary more deliberately, and,
practising a stratagem, clubbed his rifle. The Indian, deceived
into the belief that his piece was not charged, stopped, and
was about to throw his tomahawk, when the backwoodsman,
adroitly bringing the gun to his shoulder, shot him dead.
Two other foemen remained, and were rushing upon the intrepid

hunter, when the latter perceiving that the struggle between Overton and his antagonist was still fierce and doubtful, hastened to his assistance, and with a single blow of his knife decided the combat. Edward sprung up, reeking with blood, and stood manfully by his friend, prepared for a new encounter ; but the parties being now equal in number, the two remaining savages retreated.

In another moment Miss Singleton was in the arms of the heroic Overton. We shall not attempt to describe the joy of the two lovers. Ellen, who had thus far sustained herself with a noble courage, and whose resignation to her fate, dictated by an elevated principle of religious confidence, had won the admiration of her savage captors, and perhaps preserved her life, now felt the tender affections of the woman resuming their gentle dominion in her bosom. The faith, the hope which had supported her, though resulting from rational deductions, had been almost superhuman in their operation ; but the gratitude to Heaven that now swelled her heart, and burst in impassioned eloquence from her lips, was warm from the native fountains of sensibility. Sudden deliverance from all the horrors by which she had been surrounded, was in itself sufficiently joyful ; but it came infinitely enhanced in value, when brought by the hand of her lover ; and when Edward Overton found that, though fatigued and bruised, she had suffered no material injury, his joy knew no bounds.

As for the hunter he was engaged, like a prudent general, in securing the victory. He had carefully reloaded his gun, and having with his dog pursued the fugitives for a short distance, to ascertain that they were not lurking near, began to inspect the bodies of the slain and collect their arms.

"Not a bad morning's work," said he, "here are four excellent guns, tomahawks, and knives. Some of our people want arms badly, and these will just suit."

As he surveyed the field of battle, a flush of triumph was on his cheek ; but it was evident that his paramount feelings

were those of a benevolent nature, and that his sympathies
were deeply enlisted.

"There they sit," said he, glancing at the young couple,
"as happy as a pair of blackbirds in a new ploughed furrow.
This has been a sorrowful night to both of them, but they
will look back to it hereafter with grateful hearts. They did
not know before how much they thought of each other."
He then approached the young lady, and with the kindness
of a father inquired into her sufferings and wants, and began to provide for her comfort.

In a few minutes a shout was heard, and another hunter,
clad like the first, joined them. "Ah, here you are," exclaimed the new comer, as he gazed at the scene of action ;
"the work's all done, and here's the Speckled Snake as cold
as a wagon tire. I have been on the trail all the morning."

"Pity but you had been here," replied the first hunter,
"we have had a smart brush, I assure you."

"A pretty chunk of a fight, I see ; there's no two ways
about that. I knew the crack of your rifle when I heard it,
and hurried on. But I couldn't get here no sooner, no how.
Well, there's always plenty of help when it's not wanted.
The woods is alive with rangers."

"Is my father among them ?" inquired Miss Singleton.

"Oh, yes—and the old gentleman is coming along *pretty
peart,* I tell you. I took a short cut about a mile back, and
left them. I never saw such a turn out, no how. The camp-
ground was emptied *spontenaciously* in a few minutes after
the news came. How do you stand it, Miss ?"

"I am dreadfully bruised. but no bones are broken," replied Ellen, smiling.

"That is a mere *sarcumstance,*" replied the rough son of
the forest, waving his hand ; "it's a mercy, Miss, that the
cowardly *varments* hadn't *used you up body-aciously.* These
Mingoes act *mighty redick'lous* with women and children.
They aint the *raal true grit,* no how. Vile on them ! they

ought to be essentially, and particularly, and *tee-totally obflis-
ticated* off of the face of the whole *yeath*."

A party of horsemen now arrived, among whom was Mr.
Singleton. A litter was soon prepared for the rescued lady,
who was borne on the shoulders of men, in joy and triumph,
to the settlement, and found herself repaid for her sufferings
by the assiduous attentions and affectionate congratulations
of her friends and neighbours. When Mr. Singleton had
heard the particulars of the rescue, he pressed the happy
Overton to his bosom, and looked round for the brave hunter,
to whom he owed so deep a debt of gratitude, but he was no
where to be seen. On the arrival of the horsemen, he had
given the trophies of the fight in charge to one of them, and
retired with his companion. Mr. Singleton was deeply cha-
grined, for he felt a sense of obligation to the generous backwoodsman, which, as he knew that no other compensation
would be received, he wished to acknowledge.

" Where can he have gone ?" exclaimed he, "I *must* see
him !"

" You will hardly have that pleasure to-day," replied one
of the company. "No one ever saw *him* sitting down to
*chat* when there were Indians about. He is on the trail of
the two that fled, and will have them before he sleeps."

No sooner was this communication made, than a party set
out to join in the pursuit, and it was afterwards understood
that they overtook the veteran pioneer, only in time to participate in the last scene of the tragedy of that eventful
day.

Ellen Singleton recovered her health rapidly, and the wedding took place on the day that had been appointed. Agreeably to the hospitable custom of this country a general invitation was given, and the whole neighbourhood was assembled.
They had already collected when Mr. Singleton joined
them in company with the veteran woodsman, the most conspicuous character in this legend. He was now dressed like

12

a plain respectable country gentleman. His carriage was erect, and his person seemed more slender than when cased in buckskin. Though perfectly simple and unstudied in his manners, there was nothing in them of the clownish or bashful, but a dignity, and even an ease approaching to gracefulness. His countenance was cheerful and benevolent, and in his fine eye there was a manly confidence mingled with a softness of expression which afforded a true index of the character of the man. His hair, a little thinned and slightly silvered with age, gave a venerable appearance to his otherwise vigorous and elastic form. His agreeable smile, his well-known artlessness of character and amiability of life, as well as his public services, rendered him a universal favourite, and his entrance caused a murmur of pleasure.

"I have had some trouble," said Mr. Singleton, "in finding our benefactor, whose modesty is as great as his other good qualities. But as the happiness of this occasion would have been incomplete without him, I have persevered. And now, my friends and neighbours, allow me to acknowledge publicly my gratitude for his intrepid conduct on the late mournful occasion, when my only child was rescued from a dreadful captivity by his generous interference; and to exert the last act of my parental authority by decreeing that the first kiss of the bride shall be given to the *pioneer of the west*—the Patriarch of Kentucky."

"Thank you," replied the veteran, "but as I have no wish to take such a liberty with any gentleman's *wife*, I shall apply *now* for my reward to *Miss Singleton*, leaving it to *Mrs. Overton* to compensate a certain brave young gentleman, to whom she owes a great deal more than to me."

And so the matter was settled, greatly to the satisfaction of all parties.

# THE DIVINING ROD.

O N a pleasant evening in the autumn of the year 18——, two travellers were slowly winding their way along a narrow road which led among the hills that overhang the Cumberland river, in Tennessee. One of these was a farmer of the neighbourhood—a large, robust, sun-burnt man, mounted on a sleek plough-horse. He was one of the early settlers, who had fought and hunted in his youth among the same valleys that now teemed with abundant harvests; a rough, plain man clad in substantial homespun, he had about him an air of plenty and independence which is never deceptive, and which belongs almost exclusively to our free and fertile country. His companion was of a different cast—a small, thin, gray-haired man, who seemed worn down by bodily and mental fatigue to almost a shadow. He was a preacher, but one who would have deemed it an insult to be called *a clergyman;* for he belonged to a sect who contemn all human learning as vanity, and who consider a trained minister as little better than an impostor. The person before us was a champion of the sect. He boasted that he had nearly grown to manhood before he knew one letter from another; that he had learned to read for the sole purpose of gaining access to the Scriptures, and, with the exception of the hymns used in his church, had never read a page in any other book. With considerable natural sagacity and an abundance of zeal, he had a gift of words which enabled him at times to support his favourite tenets with a plausibility and force amounting to something very nearly akin to eloquence, and which, while it gave him unbounded sway among his own followers, was sometimes not a little troublesome to his learned opponents.

His sermons presented a curious mixture of the sententious and the declamatory, an unconnected mass of argument and assertion, through which there ran a vein of dry original humour, which, though it often provoked a smile, never failed to rivet the attention of the audience. But these flashes were like sparks of fire struck from a rock; they communicated a life and warmth to the hearts of others which seemed to have no existence in that from which they sprung, for that humour never flashed in his own eye nor relaxed a muscle of his melancholy, cadaverous countenance. Yet that eye was not destitute of expression; there were times when it beamed with intelligence, moments when it softened into tenderness; but its usual character was that of a visionary, fanatic enthusiasm. His ideas were not numerous, and the general theme of his declamation consisted of metaphysical distinctions between what he called "head religion" and "heart religion," the one being a direct inspiration, and the other a spurious substitute learned from vain books. He wrote a tract to show it was the thirst after human knowledge which drove our first parents from paradise, that through the whole course of succeeding time *school larning* had been the most prolific source of human misery and mental degradation, and that colleges, bible societies, free masonry, books, the holy alliance, and the inquisition, were so many engines devised by king-craft, priest-craft, and school-craft to subjugate the world to the power of Satan. He spoke of the millennium as a time when "there should be no king, nor printer, nor Sunday-

school, nor outlandish tongue, nor vain doctrine—when men
would plough, and women milk the cows, and talk plain English to each other, and worship God out of the fulness of their
hearts, and not after vain forms written by men." In short,
this worthy man was entirely opposed to the spread of religious knowledge. "When a man has *head religion*," he
would say, "he is in a *bad fix* to die—cut off his head, and
away goes his soul and body to the devil." The remainder
of his character may be briefly sketched. Honest, humane,
and harmless in private life, impetuous in his feelings, fearless
and independent by nature, and reared in a country where
speech is as free as thought, he pursued his vocation without
intolerance, but with a zeal which sometimes bordered on in-
sanity. He spoke of his opponents more in sorrow than in
anger, and bewailed the increase of knowledge as a mother
mourns over her first-born. He was of course ignorant and
illiterate; and with a mind naturally vigorous and capable of
high attainments, his visionary theories, and perhaps a slight
estrangement of intellect, had left the soil open to superstition, so that while at one time he discovered and exposed a
popular error with wonderful acuteness, at another he blindly
adopted the grossest fallacy. Such was Mr. Zedekiah Bangs.
His innocent and patriarchal manners ensured him universal
esteem, and rendered him famous far and wide, under the title
of Uncle Zeddy; while his acknowledged zeal and sanctity
gained for him in his own church, and among the religious
generally, the more reverend appellation of Father Bangs.

Our worthy preacher, having no regular stipend—for he
would have scorned to preach for the lucre of gain, cultivated
a small farm, or as the phrase is, *raised a crop* in the summer
for the subsistence of his family. During this season he min-
istered diligently among his neighbours; but in the autumn
and winter his labours were more extensive. Then it was
that he mounted his nag, and rode forth to spread his doctrines, and to carry light and encouragement to the numerous

churches of his sect.  Then it was that he travelled thousands of miles, encountering every extreme of fatigue and
privation, and every vicissitude of climate, seldom sleeping
twice in the same bed, or eating two meals at the same place,
and counting every day lost in which he did not preach a ser-
mon.  Gentlemen who pursue the same avocation with praise-
worthy assiduity in other countries, have little notion of the
hardships which are endured by the class of men of whom
I am writing.  Living on the frontier, where the settlements
are separated from each other by immense tracts of wilderness, they brave toil and hunger with the patience of the
hunter.  They traverse pathless wilds, swim rivers, encamp
in the open air, and learn the arts, while they acquire the
hardihood of backwoodsmen.  Such were the labours of our
worthy preacher ; yet he would accept no pay ; requiring only
his food and lodging, which are always cheerfully accorded,
at every dwelling in the west, to the travelling minister.

Among his converts was Johnson, the farmer, in whose
company we found him at the commencement of this history.
Tom Johnson, as he was familiarly called, had been a daring
warrior and a hunter in the first settlement of this country.
When times became peaceable he married and settled down,
and, as is not unusual, by the mere rise in value of his land
and the natural increase of his stock, became in a few years
comparatively wealthy with but little labour.  A state of
ease and affluence was not without its dangers to a man of his
temperament and desultory habits ; and Tom was beginning
to become what in this country is called a " Rowdy," that is
to say, a *gentleman of pleasure*, without the high finish which
adorns that character in more polished societies.  He " swap-
ped" horses, bred fine colts, and attended at the race paths ;
he frequented all public meetings, talked big at elections, and
was courted by candidates for office ; he played *loo*, drank
deep, and on proper occasions " took a *small chunk* of a fight."

Tom " got religion" at a camp-meeting, and for a while

was quite a reformed man. Then he relapsed a little, and finally settled down into a doubtful state, which the church could not approve, yet could not conveniently punish. He neither drank nor swore: he wore the plain dress, kept the Sabbath, attended meetings, and gave a cordial welcome to the clergy at his house. But he had not sold his colts; he went sometimes to the race-ground; he could count the run of the cards and the chances of candidates; and it was even reported that he had betted on the high trump. From this state he was awakened by Father Bangs, who boldly arraigned him as a backslider. "You've got *head religion*," said the preacher, "you're a Sunday Christian—on the Sabbath you put on a straight coat and your long face, and serve your Master—the rest of the week you serve Satan; now it doesn't take a Philadelphia lawyer to tell, that the man who serves the master one day and the enemy six, has just six chances out of seven to go to the devil; you are *barking up the wrong tree*, Johnson,—take a fresh start and try to get on the right trail." Tom was convinced by this argument, became a changed man, and felt that he owed a heavy debt of gratitude to the venerable instrument of his reformation, whom he always insisted on entertaining at his house when he visited the neighbourhood. On this occasion, the good man having preached in the vicinity, was going to spend a night with his friend Johnson.

As the travellers passed along, I am not aware that either of them cast a thought upon the romantic and picturesque beauties by which they were surrounded. The banks of the Cumberland, at this point, are rocky and precipitous; sometimes presenting a parapet of several hundred feet in height, and sometimes shooting up into cliffs, which overhang the stream. The river itself, rushing through the deep abyss, appears as a small rivulet to the beholder; the steamboats, struggling with mighty power against the rapid current, are diminished to the eye, while the roaring of the steam and the rattling of wheels come exaggerated by a hundred echoes.

The travellers halted to gaze at one of these vessels, which was about to ascend a difficult pass, where the river, confined on either side by jutting rocks, rushed through the narrow channel with increased velocity.   The prow of the boat plunged into the swift current, dashing the foam over the deck.   Then it paused and trembled ; a powerful conflict succeeded, and for a time the vessel neither advanced nor receded.   Her struggles resembled those of an animated creature. Her huge hull seemed to writhe upon the water.   The rapid motion of the wheels, the increased noise of the engine, the bursting of the escape-steam from the valve, showed that the impelling power had been raised to the highest point.   It was a moment of thrilling suspense.   A slight addition of power would enable the boat to advance,—the least failure, the slightest accident, would expose her to the fury of the torrent and dash her on the rocks.   Thus she remained for several minutes; then resuming her way, crept heavily over the ripple, reached the smooth water above, and darted swiftly forward.

"Them sort of craft didn't use to crawl about on the rivers, when we first knew the country, brother Johnson," said the preacher.

" No, indeed," returned the other.

"And more's the pity," continued the preacher; "does not the apostle caution us against the inventions of men ? We had vain and idle devices enough to lead our minds off from our true good, without these smoking furnaces of Satan, these floating towers of Babel, that belch forth huge volumes of brimstone, and seduce honest men and women from home to go visiting around the land in large companies, and talk to each other in strange tongues."

"I am told," said Johnson, "that some of them carry tracts and good books, for the edification of the passengers."

"Worse and worse !" replied the preacher; "tracts ! what

are they but printed snares for the soul? There was no printing-office in Eden—oh no! and when all the creatures of the earth were gathered into the ark, there was no missionary, male or female. But go thy way," he exclaimed, raising his voice, "thou floating synagogue of Satan! soon shall the time arrive when there shall be neither steamboat, nor Sunday-school, nor other devices of vain philosophy!"

"Others of these boats," said the farmer, "have cards and music and wine, with every sort of amusement on board."

"These are bad things," returned the preacher; "men and women should not drink rum, nor swear, nor gamble, nor make uncouth noises with outlandish instruments; but all these are not so bad as tracts—for these former are open ene-mies, while the latter catch a man's soul asleep under a tree, and kidnap him when he is *camped out* afar from home."

"In our day, father, the merchants were well enough satisfied to *tote their plunder* upon mules and pack-horses. And that puts me in mind of a story that happened near about where we are riding."

"What is that, brother Johnson?"

"In an early time some traders were crossing the country, and aimed to make the river at the ford just below this. They had a great deal of money, all in silver, packed upon mules, for in them days we hadn't any of this nasty paper money."

"No—nor much of any sort," said the preacher slyly.

"If we hadn't," replied the farmer sturdily, "we had what answered the purpose as well. I mind the time when tobacco was a legal tender, and 'coon-skins passed currenter than bank-notes does now. In them days, if a man got into a chunk of a fight with his neighbour, a lawyer would clear him for half-a-dozen muskrat skins, and the justice and constable would have scorned to take a fee, more than just a treat or so. But you know all that—so I'll tell my tale out, though I reckon you've heard it before?"

12*

" I think I have," said the other, " but I'd like to hear it
again—it *sort o'* stirs one up, to hear about old times."

" Well, the traders had got here safe with their plunder,
when the news came that Indians were about.  There was no
chance to escape with their loaded mules; so they unloaded
them, and buried the money somewhere among these rocks;
and then being light, made their escape.  So far, the old settlers all agree; but then some say that the Indians pursued
on after them a great way into Kentucky, and killed them all;
others say that they finally escaped; the fact is, that the people never came back after the money, and it is supposed that
it lies hid somewhere about here to this day."

" Has not that money often been searched after ?"

" Oh, bless you, yes; a heap of times.  Many a chap has
sweated among these rocks by the hour.  Only a few years
ago, a great gang of folks came out of Kentucky and dug
all around here as if they were going to make a crop; but to
no purpose."

" And what, think you, became of the money ?"

" People say it is there yet."

" But your own opinion ?"

" Why, to tell you my opinion *sentimentally*," replied
Tom, winking and lowering his voice, "I don't believe in
that story."

" How ?" exclaimed the other incredulously.

" It's just a tale—a mere *noration*," said Tom, "there's *no
two ways* about it."

" Indeed ! how can you think so ?"

" Why, look here, father Zedekiah,—I know very well,
that every man, woman, and child, within fifty miles, thinks
there is certanily a vast treasure buried in these rocks; but
when I almost as good as know to the contrary, I am not
bound to give up my opinion."

" Very right, that's just my way; but let us have your
reasons."

"I have fought the Indians myself," said the farmer, "and I know all their ways. They never come out boldly into the open field and take a fair fight, fist and skull, as Christians do; but are always sneaking about in the bushes studying out some devilment. The traders and hunters understand them perfectly well; the Indians and they are continually practising devices on each other. Many a trick I've played on them, and they have played me as many. Now it seems to me to be *nateral*—just as plain as if I was on the ground and saw it—that them traders should have made a *sham* of burying money, and run off while the Indians were looking for it."

"That's not a good argument, brother Johnson."

"I have great respect for your opinion," replied the farmer, "but on this subject I have made up my mind—"

"So have I," interrupted the preacher; and reining his horse he fell in the rear of his companion, as if determined to hear no more.

Johnson, in broaching this subject, had not been aware of the interest it possessed in the mind of his friend. The fact was, that Bangs in his visits to this country had frequently heard the report alluded to, and it was precisely suited to operate upon his credulous and enthusiastic mind. At first he pondered on it as a matter of curiosity, until it fastened itself upon his imagination. In his long and lonesome journeys, when he rode for whole days without seeing a human face or habitation, he amused himself in calculating the probable amount of the buried treasure. The first step was to fix in his own mind the number of mules, and as the tradition varied from *one* to *thirty*, he prudently adopted the medium between these extremes. He found some difficulty in determining the burthen of a single mule, but to fix the number of dollars which would be required to make up that burthen was impossible, because the worthy divine was so little acquainted with money, as not to know the weight of a single coin. For the first time in his life he lacked arithmetic, and

found himself in a strait in which he conceived that it might
be prudent to take counsel of a friend.

Near the residence of the reverend man dwelt an industrious pedagogue. He was a tall, sallow, unhealthy-looking
youth, with a fine clear blue eye and a melancholy countenance, which at times assumed a sly sarcastic expression that
few could interpret. In the winter, when the farmers' children had a season of respite from labour, he diligently pursued his vocation. In the summer he strolled listlessly about
the country, sometimes roaming the forest with his rifle,
sometimes eagerly devouring any book that might chance to
fall into his hands. Between him and the preacher there was
little community of sentiment; yet they were often together;
the scholar found a source of inexhaustible amusement in the
odd, quaint, original arguments of the divine, and the latter
was well pleased to measure weapons with so respectable an
opponent. They never met without disputation, yet they
always parted in kindness. The preacher, instead of wondering with the rest of the neighbours, how "one small head
could carry all he knew," derided the acquirements of his
friend as worse than vanity; and the latter respectfully, but
stoutly, maintained the dignity of his profession.

It was not without many qualms of pride that the worthy
father now sought the schoolmaster, with the intention of
gaining information which he knew not how to get from any
other source. Having once made up his mind, he acted with
his usual promptness, and unused to intrigue or circumlocu-
tion, proceeded directly to the point.

"Charles," said he, "can you tell me how many dollars a
stout mule might conveniently carry?"

"Indeed I cannot."

"Do none of your trumpery books treat of these
things?"

"They do not, Uncle Zeddy; but they lay down the
principles upon which such results may be ascertained."

"Very well; let us see you resolve the question by your arithmetic."

"You must give me the data: what is the burden of a mule?"

"Can't tell; never backed one in my life."

"Well, let us see:—we will say that a stout animal of this class might easily carry you and me, with all our books, money, and learning; now we cannot rate our two selves at more than two hundred and fifty pounds, and for our luggage, tangible and intellectual, we may set down ciphers; a dollar weighs an ounce, and there the question is stated; if one dollar weighs one ounce, how many dollars will it take to make two hundred and fifty pounds? Work it by the rule of three, and there is the answer."

The preacher's eyes glistened as he saw the figures; a long deep groan, such as he was in the habit of heaving upon all occasions, whether of joy or sorrow, burst involuntarily from him.

"Charles, my son," said he, gasping for breath, and lowering his voice to whisper, while his eyes, riveted upon the sum total, seemed ready to start from their sockets, "suppose there were fifteen such mules?"

"In that case," replied the pedagogue carelessly, as he multiplied his former product by the sum named, "in that case the result would be so much."

"Read the figures to me," said the preacher, groaning again, "I am not certain that I can make them out."

"It is only about forty-five thousand dollars."

"Only! oh the blasphemy of learning! Young man, the wealth of Solomon was nothing to this—yea, the treasures of Nebuchadnezzar were as dust in the balance compared with this hoard!" and he walked slowly away, muttering, "It is too much! it is too much!"

It was indeed a vast sum! more than the honest Zedekiah had ever thought or dreamed of; and to a mind like his, confined

heretofore to a single subject, it developed a new, an immense
field of speculation. He seemed to have opened his eyes upon
a new world. He conjured up in his mind all the harm that a
bad man might do with so much money; and trembled to
think that any one individual might, by possibility, become
master of a treasure so great, as to be fraught with destruction to its possessor, and danger to the whole community in
which he lived. He thought of the luxury, the dissipation,
the corruption that it might lead to; and rising gradually to
a climax, he adverted to the ruinous and dreadful consequences, if this wealth should fall into the hands of some weak-
minded, zealous man, who was misled by false doctrines:
how many Sunday-schools it would establish, how many
preachers it would educate, how many missionaries it would
send forth, to disseminate a spurious *head religion* throughout
the world!

Turning from this picture, he reflected on the benefits
which a good man might with all this money confer on his
fellows. Ah! Zedekiah, now it was that the tempter who
had been all along sounding thee at a distance, began to lay
a regular siege to thy integrity! Now it was that he sought
to creep into the breast, yea, into the very heart's core, of
worthy Zedekiah. He had always been poor and contented.
But age was now approaching, and he could fancy a train of
wants attendant upon helpless decrepitude. He glanced at
the tattered sleeve of his coat, and straightway the vision of
a new suit of snuff-coloured broadcloth rose upon his mind.
He thought of his old wife who sat spinning in the chimney-
corner at home; she was lame, and almost blind, poor woman! and he promised to carry her a pound of tea and a
bottle of good brandy. In short, the Reverend Mr. Bangs
set his heart upon having the money.

Such was the state of matters, when the conversation
occurred that I have just related. It was again renewed at
Johnson's house that night after a substantial supper, and

ended, as such conversations usually do, in confirming each party in his own opinion. Indeed, the old man had that day got, as he thought, a clue which might lead to the wished-for discovery. He had heard of an ancient dame who, many years before, had dropped mysterious hints, which induced a belief that she knew more of this subject than she chose to tell.

On the following morning, the preacher rose early, saddled his nag and rode forth in search of the old woman's dwelling, without apprising any one of his intention. He soon found the spot, and the object of his search. She was a poor, decrepit, superannuated virago, who dwelt in a hovel as crazy, as weatherbeaten, and as frail as herself. She was crouched over the fire smoking a short pipe, and barely turned her head as the reverend man seated himself on the bench beside her.

"It's a raw morning," said the preacher.

" I've seen colder," was the reply.

"So have I," returned Zedekiah, and there the *tête-à-tête* flagged. The old man warmed his hands, stirred the fire with his stick, and being a bold man advanced again to the charge.

" Pray, madam, are you the widow Anderson ?"

" That's my name ; I'm not ashamed to own it," replied the woman sullenly.

" You're the person then that I was directed to ; I wished to get some information on a particular subject."

" Aye ; you're after the money too, I suppose—the devil's in all the men !"

" The devil never had a worse enemy than I am," said the old man archly.

"I don't know who you are," replied the woman, " but you may travel back as wise as you came."

The preacher mentioned his name, his vocation, and the object of his visit. The virago, in spite of her ill-nature, was evidently soothed when she learned that her visitor was no less a person than the Reverend Mr. Bangs. " Who'd have thought that the like of you would come on such an errand ?" said she ; " well, well, it's little I know, but you are welcome to that."

Now came the secret. The husband of Mrs. Anderson had been a water-witch, a finder of living fountains. These he discovered by the use of the divining rod, which is well known to possess a virtue in the hands of a favoured few, of which it is destitute when used by others. Anderson wielded the hazel twig with wonderful success, and became so celebrated that he was sent for far and near to find water. Inflated with success, he became ambitious of higher distinction and greater gain. He imagined that the same art by which he discovered subterranean fountains, would enable him to find mineral treasures in the bowels of the earth. He fancied his fortune already made by the discovery of mines of precious metals ; the hidden silver on the shores of the Cumberland would of itself repay his labours. He put all his ingenuity in requisition, and busied himself for years in endeavouring to find a wand that would " work" in the vicinity of minerals, as the ordinary *divining rod* operates in the neighbourhood of water. In the latter process, much depends on the kind of wood of which the rod is composed ; the hazel, the peach, the mulberry, and a few others, all of rapid growth, are the most approved. Proceeding upon the same principle, he endeavoured to find a tree or shrub which should possess an attractive sympathy for metals. Success at length crowned his operations ; he found a tree whose branches had the desired virtue. He discovered veins of iron ore in the surrounding hills, and had announced to his wife that he was on the point of finding the buried money, when death, who respects a water-witch no more than a beggar or a king, arrested his career.

But when she came to speak of the manner of his death, her voice faltered. She had often warned Anderson that it was dangerous to meddle with hidden treasures. They were generally protected by supernatural beings, who would not allow them to be removed with impunity ; and several persons who had been engaged in the same search, before Anderson, had been alarmed by appearances which caused them to desist. One day he came home to his dinner in high glee, and throwing aside his rod, for which he declared he had now no further use, he swore he would have the money before he slept. It was deposited, he said, in a certain cliff, which was very difficult of access, and which he was determined to visit that afternoon. It was midnight before he returned. He crawled into his cabin and sunk with a groan on the floor. His wife struck a light and hastened to his assistance, but he was speechless, and soon expired. His body was covered with bruises, and the general opinion was that he had been precipitated from the rocks by some invisible hand.

The rod remained in the possession of his wife, but its existence was a secret to all others. Fear had prevented her from ever trying its efficacy, and inasmuch as it was useless to herself, she took the wise and spirited resolution that no other person should profit by its virtues, and uniformly turned a deaf ear to the applications frequently made by those who, knowing the habits of her husband and his researches in relation to the matter, applied to her for information. She now presented to the preacher the long-treasured wand, the bark of which having been peeled off, it was impossible to discover from what tree it had been taken.

For several days after this event the reverend man continued to traverse the neighbourhood, carefully concealing himself from observation, and exploring with the *metallic rod* every spot where it was probable the treasure might be hidden, and particularly the cliffs near to Anderson's cabin. One day he returned to the house of Johnson with a look of triumph, and desiring a private interview with his host, informed him that he had found the spot ! It was so situated that he

could not reach it without assistance, and having described the
place accurately to his friend, he concluded by offering him a
liberal share, if he would accompany and aid him.   To his
surprise, Johnson briefly and peremptorily refused.

Offended at the obstinacy of the farmer, Father Bangs
left his house.   On the road he met a stranger travelling on
foot, with whom he entered into conversation, and finding
him prompt and intelligent in his replies, he engaged him as
an assistant, and appointed a spot at which they were to
meet on the following morning.

At the hour appointed Uncle Zeddy proceeded to the rendezvous, where the stranger soon appeared, bearing on his
shoulder an immense coil of rope.   They proceeded to a tall
cliff, which, springing from the margin of the river, towered
into the air to the height of two hundred feet.   The summit
on which they stood presented a table surface of a rock, to
which they had ascended by a gentle acclivity.   Few ventured
to the edge of that precipice, for its verge, projecting over the
river, overhung it at such a fearful distance that the boldest
trembled as they looked into the abyss.   The face of the
precipice as viewed from the opposite shore seemed to be
nearly perpendicular, the slight curve by which the summit
projected over the water, being not observable from that
direction; and about one-third of the way down might be
seen the mouth of a cave, which was deemed inaccessible to
all but the birds of the air.   The preacher, after due consideration, had arrived at the conclusion that the money was in
this cave; and having fastened the cable about his own waist,
he required his assistant to lower him into the gulf.

It would have been edifying to have seen the courage
with which that old man passed over the verge, and the steady
eye with which he looked upon the deep abyss, the jutting
rocks, and the foaming torrent below; while his companion,
having passed the end of the rope round a tree, advanced to the
edge of the rock, and gazed after him with wonder.   Uncle

Zeddy found no difficulty in descending : but on getting opposite to the mouth of the cave, it was no small exploit to
achieve an entrance, for as the cable hung perpendicularly
from the projecting peak, he found himself swinging in the
air, several feet in advance of the face of the rock.   The only
chance for it, was to swing in by an horizontal movement,
and to do this it was necessary first to give the rope a motion
like that of a pendulum.   It was not easy to produce this
effect, for as the preacher hung suspended by the middle, like
the golden fleece, it was difficult to throw his weight in the
desired direction.   This, however, was at last accomplished ;
and, after swinging to and fro half an hour, Uncle Zeddy succeeded in grasping the rock at the opening, and drew himself
into the cave.

The cavern was small, and our worthy adventurer soon
satisfied himself that the cavern did not contain the object
of his search.   The sides were all of solid rock, without a
crevice or other place of concealment.   Being ready to return, he gave the signal agreed upon, by jerking the rope ;
he waited a few minutes and jerked again—and again—and
again, but without success.   Was it possible that his assistant
could be so depraved as to abandon him ?   He crept to the
mouth of the aperture, and looked out.   Under different circumstances he could have enjoyed the rushing of the water,
and the pleasant fanning of the breeze as it swept along the
valley.   But now the wind seemed to murmur dolefully, the
waves looked angry, and the cragged rocks had a fearful aspect of danger.   He shuddered at the thought of being forsaken to die of hunger.   He shouted, and his voice echoed
from rock to rock.   An hour, and another hour, passed.   A
steamboat came paddling along, and he screamed for help.
The crew looked up ; they saw the cable, and a man's head
peeping out of the cavern at a dizzy height above them, and
shouted loud in admiration of his daring exploit.   He waved
his neckcloth in the air and uttered piteous cries, but they

understood him not, and only shouted and laughed the louder
as they beheld what they supposed to be the antic bravadoes
of some daring hunter. The boat passed on. Night came,
and he gave himself up for lost. The sun rose and he was
still a prisoner. The morning wore away wearily; loss of
sleep, hunger and terror, had nearly worn the old man out—
when he felt the rope move! A thrill of joy passed through
his chilled frame. He sprung to his feet and jerked it violently. The signal was successful; he felt that a strong and
steady arm was drawing him, as it were, from the grave, into
the regions of the living. In a few minutes he passed over
the verge, and found himself in the arms of Johnson. The
latter, alarmed at the unusual length of his friend's absence,
had set out in search of him, and knowing his plan of visiting
the cave, had hastened to this spot, where, finding the cable
attached to a tree, he was so fortunate as to save the life of
his friend in the manner described. The assistant had
absconded with the preacher's horse.

When Father Bangs was a little recovered from his terror,
he said, "I have not found what I went for, but I have discovered something that convinces me I am not far from the
spot. It was here that Anderson met his fate."

"How did you find that out? there was a heavy fall of
rain the night of his death, and we could afterwards find no
marks to satisfy us where he fell.

"As I passed over the edge of the cliff I found this watch
lying in the crevice of the rock. It seems to have been a long
time exposed to the weather, and must have been in Anderson's pocket when the demon, or whatever it was, cast him
over."

"You still believe in this story, then?"

"I have seen nothing to shake my belief; but I begin to
feel *sort o'* dubious that if there be any money buried here, it
is not altogether lawful for any but the right heirs to search
after it. Anderson was punished for making the attempt,

and you see what *a fix* I am in. This thought came over me while I lay confined, and I trembled for the young man whom I left on the rock, lest he should have been spirited away or brought to an untimely end."

"He has been spirited away by that good horse of yours, and if he ever comes to a violent death it will be under the gallows."

"Well, be it so; but my own confinement and suffering I cannot but think, was meant as a punishment."

"Have your own way," said the farmer; "if you do but quit money-hunting, I am satisfied; but I must say, when I hear you talk of spirits and such like, that I am sorry to find you are still *barking up the wrong tree.*

# THE SEVENTH SON.

I HAD a classmate at college whose name was Jeremy Geode. Circumstances threw us together at that time, and we became attached friends. We occupied the same room and the same bed, and freely communicated to each other our most secret thoughts. I am not philosopher enough to account for the principle of attraction which operated upon us; the adhesion was very strong, but the cause that produced it was as deeply hidden from my feeble power of perception as the properties of the loadstone. I once read a very learned and unintelligible book of philosophy, from beginning to end, for the purpose of finding out why it was that two human beings should be stuck together like particles of granite : but I had my labour for my pains. The reason was inscrutable ; stuck together we were, and yet never were two individuals more unlike each other. We were perfect antipodes, and our friendship a moral antithesis. My readers will enter fully into the perplexities which this subject afforded me, when I inform them that my friend was dismally ugly, while I was not only a great admirer of beauty, but in my own opinion, at least, very good-looking. He was a sloven, I was neat and dressy. He loved books, I loved men—particularly those of

the feminine gender.   He was devoted to figures, and so was
I—but then his affections settled upon the figures of arithmetic and geometry, while mine were running riot among
those of the cotillion.   He was studious, grave, and unsocial,
and I gay, volatile, and fond of company.   I could talk by
the hour about any thing, or about nothing, while my friend
was taciturn, seldom opening his remarkably homely mouth
except to utter a syllogism or demonstrate a problem.   There
were occasions, it is true, when his eloquence would burst
forth like the eruption of a volcano.   I have seen him rant
like a stump orator over a geological specimen, or pour forth
metaphors in all the exuberance of poetic phrensy, while com-
menting upon the wonders exhibited in the structure of a
poor, unfortunate musquito which had fallen into his clutches.
Strange as it may seem to those who are unacquainted with
the organization of such minds, he was a wit of the highest
order.   A sly inuendo, a sententious remark, a playful sarcasm, uttered with the most inflexible gravity, would excite
in others a paroxysm of laughter, while he was apparently
unconscious of any feeling akin to mirth.   That he enjoyed
his own exquisite vein of humour and the humour of others,
I have now no doubt, for every man who possesses any strong-
ly-marked faculty of the mind experiences a high degree of
pleasure in its exercise.   But he passed for a misanthrope, an
unfeeling, selfish man, who, wrapped up in the abstraction of
his own mind, had no sympathies in common with his fellow-
creatures; and he was willing to pass under any character
which might secure him from intrusion, and leave him at
liberty to pursue the leadings of his own genius.   His equa-
nimity under these surmises, and under all the crosses of life,
was absolutely miraculous; the truth was, that his vigorous
understanding and native good temper enabled him to look
down upon the accidents that vex other men.   I alone suspected that he was kind and generous, because I had seen his
eye moisten and the rigid muscles of his face relax as he

perused the tender epistles of a doating mother; though it was only in after years that I learned that he earned his own subsistence and that of his parent by the labours of his pen, while he pursued his college studies. I could have wept when this fact came to my knowledge, and when I recollected how I had sometimes ridiculed his parsimonious habits and his unceasing devotion to labour.

Another trait in the character of my friend shall be chiefly noticed. Although he diligently eschewed the company of women, and regarded men with careless indifference, he seemed so perfectly enamoured of the society of children and other irrational animals, that I sometimes suspected him of being a believer in the Pythagorean doctrine of transmigration. When fatigued with mental exertions, he would steal off to join his little playfellows on the green beyond the town, which was their place of evening resort. There he would be seen stretched upon the grass, gazing at them with an eye of interest and of complete satisfaction. The youngsters quickly struck up an acquaintance, and cleaved to him with instinctive affection. They soon learned to bring him their hats and coats to take care of when they drew them off for play; he became the umpire in their contests and the peacemaker in their disputes; and he might often be seen with the whole *posse* around him, the smallest hanging on his knees and his great shoulders, and the biggest forming a dense circle, with open eyes and mouths, while he related some strange legend or explained the curious phenomena of nature. These facts were not generally known in college; and it was well for him—for had the erudite and dignified Sophomores detected him in such childish pursuits, my friend Jeremy Geode would undoubtedly have been put in Coventry. He had a mocking-bird, too, in a cage, a martin-box at his window, and an industrious family of silk-worms in a small cabinet. A lean, hungry, ferocious-looking cat, whose love of mice or of mythology had brought her to college, who had been expelled

13

from one room, and kicked out of another, and suffered martyrdom in so many shapes, that, but for the plurality of her
lives, she would long since have ceased to exist, at last took
refuge in our room.   She entered with a truly feline stealth
of tread, and sought concealment with the cowardice of conscious felony.   But no sooner did she attract the eye of Jeremy, than a mutual attachment commenced, a single glance
revealed to each a kindred spirit; in a few hours puss was
running between the student's feet; before the close of the
day she was reposing in his lap, and a firm friendship was ce-
mented.   Under his care she grew fat, social, and contented,
and justice requires me to say, that a more intelligent or better behaved cat never inhabited the walls of a learned insti-
tion.

   After the completion of our college course, we commenced
the study of our respective professions.   Now it was that a
principle of repulsion began to operate, which carried us per-
petually in opposite directions.   Our minds, which had heretofore, to some extent, inhabited the same sphere, began to
diverge, as it were, from a common centre, so that we entered
upon the great theatre of life by different paths.   My friend,
who was cautious and plodding, betook him to the dusty turn-
pike of science, carefully noting the indications of the innumerable finger-posts and mile-stones, which have been set up
by the industry of sundry worthy men on either side of that
great highway.   He was willing to reach the ultimate point
of his ambition by the beaten road, which experience had
marked out.   Wisdom's ways are said to be pleasant ways,
and all her paths peace, and I dare say he found them so; but
I must confess that I had not sufficient taste to discern wherein that peace and pleasantness consisted.   I betook myself to
that flowery path, which, without having any particular source
or destination, meanders through the regions of fancy and the
resorts of pleasure.   But I was unwilling, at first, to part with
my friend; I grieved to see his youth withering in monastic

seclusion, and his energies wasted in a severe course of unproductive studies.

"What do you expect to gain," said I to him, one day, "by this incessant toil of the mind, this rigid self-denial, this total abstraction from the ordinary pursuits of youth?"

"Knowledge!" was his laconic reply.

"And will the accumulated stores of knowledge be worth so dear a purchase? Are you not acting the part of the miser who keeps up a mass of useless wealth, at the expense of all the courtesies of life, and all its enjoyments? Is this a rational way of spending time?"

"I like it," said he.

I was nettled at his perfect composure. "So does your cat like sleep," I exclaimed, "and pardon me for saying that I see little difference"—I was going to say, "between you and your cat," but I had the grace to modify the comparison —"between dozing over the fire, or over musty books."

"The books are far from musty," replied he very placidly, "and as for poor puss, she is quite happy and respectable, in her way."

"But, my dear Geode, to what end is this slavery of mind?"

"Usefulness."

"Usefulness? to whom, pray?"

"To myself, to my country, to mankind."

"And the reward? Come, tell us that. What do you expect in return for becoming the benefactor of an ungrateful world?"

"The approbation of good men and of my own conscience."

He had reason and virtue on his side, and my logic would hold out no longer. I was awed, but not convinced; and we parted.

My friend studied medicine, a choice upon which I had often rallied him as growing out of his love for the occult sciences; for with his more solid acquirements he had mingled an acquaintance with alchemy, witchcraft, and all the mystic lore which is found in black-letter books.  He could draw horoscopes and tell fortunes like an adept, and so gravely would he talk upon such subjects, that had it not been for a lurking roguishness of the eye, which he could never wholly command, I should have feared that he was in earnest. I chose the science of law, because this profession is considered the path to office and honour.  I had no relish for the drudgery of a practising attorney.  Framing declarations and exploring the intricacies of law reports had no attractions for me.  My ambition soared higher; and I imagined, as multitudes of young men do, who crowd to the bar in the hope of leading a life of ease and dignity, that my labours would cease, and my triumphs begin, with my maiden speech. In common with all who have been deluded by this fallacy, I have discovered my error.  The labours of the lawyer who pursues his profession with energy are as severe as those of the farmer or mechanic, while his pecuniary gains are less certain.  But then the farmer is a drudge and the mechanic is not an *esquire.*  The legal profession confers a patent of gentility on its members; they are *gentlemen* of the bar; and the man who wishes to become a gentleman by a short cut, and to remain one during life, has only to procure a license to practise in a court of record, which confers an indefeasible title to that distinction, whatever may be the properties of his body, mind, or estate.

But I sat down, not to write of myself, but to indite the veritable history of Doctor Jeremy Geode, who, having obtained his diploma with great distinction, emigrated to the Western States.  He called to take leave of me, previous to his departure.  A suit of mourning announced that he had lost his mother, the only human being in memory of whom he would have thought it necessary to exhibit this outward symbol of grief.  " I nursed her," said he, " in her last illness, and received her blessing.  It was mournful to sever so dear a tie; but I felt that I had gained, in her approbation of my conduct, a richer legacy than any that the whole earth could bestow." He spoke of his future prospects with confidence, though with that peculiar bashfulness with which a modest young man, accustomed to seclusion, faces the world for the first time. There is no sight more touching to a considerate heart, than to behold a highly gifted and ingenuous youth embarking in the voyage of life with no companion but enterprise and indigence. Bright may be his career and noble his triumphs, but the chances that those buoyant hopes, those modest graces, those virtuous emotions, which render youth so engaging, will be blighted by vice, by disappointment, and by sordid cares, are so many, as to fill the benevolent heart with trembling apprehension.

Doctor Geode settled in an obscure town, far in the wilderness. It was a village newly laid out upon the borders of an extensive prairie; a beautifully undulating plain, fringed with wood, and dotted with picturesque clumps and groves of trees. The grass, as yet but little trodden, exhibited its pristine luxuriance, and a variety of gorgeous flowers enlivened the scene. The deer still loitered here, as if unwilling to resign their ancient pastures, and at night the long howl of the wolf could be heard, mingled with the fearful screechings of the owl. The village was composed of log-cabins, and was, with the neighbourhood around it, inhabited chiefly by backwoodsmen—a race of people, who, delighting in the chase, and devoted to their wild, free, and independent habits, precede the advance of the denser population, and keep ever on the outskirts of society. Ardent, hospitable, and uncultivated, the stranger is as much delighted with the cordial welcome he finds at their firesides, as he is struck with their primitive manners, their singular phraseology, and their original modes of thinking. Accustomed to long journeys, to frequent changes of residence, to protracted hunting expeditions, to swimming rivers, and encamping in the woods, they bear fatigue and exposure with the patience of the Indian: their figures of speech are numerous, and drawn from natural objects; and they have a fund of that intelligence which arises from extensive wanderings, from a close observance of nature, and from habits of free discussion, mingled with the simplicity induced by the absence of literature.

A few months passed away delightfully with Doctor Geode. He roamed the forests and the prairies with the eagerness of one who had fallen upon a new world, more beautiful than that of his nativity. He walked and rode, hunted and fished, not for sport, but in search of scientific truth. The cabin which he occupied as a study soon grew into a museum of natural curiosities. Every day brought some novel and interesting subject under his investigation. The treasures of knowledge which he had accumulated over the midnight lamp, seemed now to swell and burst forth into life, as the exuberant flower springs from the folds of the bud. The world around him was teeming with living and beautiful illustrations of those abstruse principles that had been gathered into his memory with so much toil and arranged with so much care. Not a wind blew nor a shower fell, not a flower regaled his senses with its gaudy beauties or rich perfumes, without filling his mind with a sensation of pleasurable emotion. To him the phenomena of nature were all eloquence and music and symmetry. He had studied these things in the closet as mere abstractions, but now they came before him as sensible objects, bearing the stamp of reality, and glowing with the freshness and beauty of life.

But in the midst of these pursuits, my worthy friend entirely forgot to employ the ordinary means of getting into practice. He made no display of his skill nor courted the acquaintance of any of his neighbours. No flashy advertisement extolled the merits of Doctor Geode and informed the public that he was their humble servant. A wily competitor, taking advantage of this improvidence, represented my

erudite friend as an insane gentleman, who roamed about
gathering roots and catching prairie flies, and the neighbours
felt no inclination to consult a mad doctor. His own habits
confirmed these mercenary slanders. His homely face was
pale and sallow; his thick black beard was often allowed to
remain a whole week unshaven; and in his total carelessness
of every thing relating to his own comfort, he sometimes
walked from his shop to his lodgings without his hat, or with
one boot and one shoe. His collection of stuffed birds, im-
paled insects, and pickled reptiles might well bring his sanity
in question with those who could see no advantage in this
hideous resurrection of dead bodies. Moreover, he had tamed
a crow, a bird held in particular aversion, in consequence of
its depredations upon the corn-fields, and pronounced by a
popular verse to have been,

> "Ever since the world began,
> Natural enemy of man;"

and a black cat, who of her own accord had taken up her
residence with him, was his constant companion. He soon
found himself avoided, like a mad dog in a populous town, or
a freemason in the enlightened State of New York. Week
after week rolled away, and not a patient called the skill of
Doctor Geode into requisition. He wondered at this circumstance, and perplexed himself with vain endeavours to conjecture the reason. He saw that he was even shunned, but his
modesty as well as his independence prevented him from inquiring into the cause. In the mean while his finances were
exhausted, and poverty, with all its inconveniences and mor-
tifications, stared him in the face.

There is one truth, as regards the moral government of
this world, to which there are few exceptions; it is that good
deeds always have their reward. So it happened to my
friend. He was one day induced to enter a solitary cabin,
in the outskirts of the village, by hearing, as he passed, the

groans of a person who seemed to be in pain. A decent widow, who supported a large family by her labour, was suffering under a high fever and in a state of delirium. Beside her sat a fair-haired girl, about fourteen years old, the daughter of a neighbouring gentleman, bathing her temples and vainly endeavouring to soothe her torture. Without asking any questions, the humane physician rendered such assistance to the sufferer as her case required; nor did he quit her bed side till every alarming symptom was removed. The young girl, who at first shrunk back in alarm, was soon drawn to his assistance by the kindness of his tones, and now witnessed his promptitude and success with astonishment. He continued to attend from day to day until his patient was completely restored, and then refused any compensation for what he considered a slight and a voluntary service. Being an intelligent woman, who had been accustomed to attend the sick, she readily discovered, from his tender manner and skilful prescriptions, that he was no ordinary man; and she now, in the warmth of her gratitude, revealed to him the arts by which his competitor had deprived him of the confidence of the public.

Doctor Geode never did things like other men. Instead of getting angry, he was amused at the ingenuity of his rival, and at his own ridiculous predicament. He was born *too far east* to be overreached by a specious pretender; and as his necessities were at that moment particularly pressing, he soon devised a plan for present relief, and for the utter discomfiture of his rival. Although his bashfulness and habits of abstraction had kept him aloof from an intercourse with his neighbours, he had not been inattentive to their traditions and modes of thinking; while he spoke little, he had listened and observed much. Some of their superstitions had struck him as remarkably amusing, and he was even then preparing an essay on this subject. With these landmarks to assist him, his scheme was soon digested. Having prepared a neat card,

and drawn upon it a circle and a triangle with red ink, he proceeded to trace over it several words in the Greek character.
He then advertised that "Doctor Jeremy Geode, the seventh
son of a celebrated Indian doctor, would cure all diseases, by
means of the wonderful Hygeian Tablet, or Kickapoo Pana-
cea, of which he was sole proprietor." It was a happy
thought! the virtues of *a seventh son* have long been well
known; and however our sturdy borderers may dislike their
savage neighbours, the *Indian doctor* has always been in high
repute among them.

The reputed lunatic was at once elevated into an inspired
mediciner; the crow, the black cat, and the collection of natural curiosities became objects of respectful curiosity. In
vain did the *regular* physician of the village denounce him as
an impostor; in vain an incredulous few professed their entire disbelief. The doors of the seventh son were soon
crowded with the halt and the sick. Among the first that
came was Mr. Jones, the father of the fair-haired girl, a gentleman of information and property; a frank, hospitable
man, who had taken up a favourable opinion of the doctor,
and who became now, by his daughter's account of the incident she had witnessed, warmly engaged in his interest.
What passed at the interview need not be repeated: Mr.
Jones at its conclusion exhibited evident symptoms of having
enjoyed a hearty laugh, and Doctor Geode had received some
new views of Western character. They remained firm friends,
and Mr. Jones never spoke of the seventh son but in terms
of high respect.

The success of the mystic tablet was triumphant, and its
fame spread far and near. Nauseating and dangerous drugs
were decried as useless and pernicious. It even became a
matter of general remark and wonder, that people should be
so stupid as to swallow deadly poisons, while health could be
so much more cheaply purchased by looking at a card.
Faith alone was requisite to give efficacy to the spell. It is

13*

true that the charm sometimes failed ; but this was always attributed to the unbelief of the patient, and the doctor forthwith proceeded to treat such cases *secundum artem*, concealing the fact that he used the subtile minerals of the pharmacopœia, and leaving the world to suppose that he practised only with the simples gathered in his botanic excursions. The consequence was that his practice spread not only through the country around, but an immense number of patients were brought to him from a distance. As for the *regular* physician, he was obliged to quit the village.

Happening to pass through that region, when the fame of Doctor Geode was at its zenith, I was astonished to hear the name of my old classmate, of whom I had lost sight for some years, coupled with miraculous cures by faith; and I determined to pay him a visit. Muffled in my cloak, and disguised still further by the alteration that time had made in my features, I entered his dwelling. It was a spacious loghouse, divided into several apartments, all of which, except one, were occupied by the sick. In the audience room, if I may so call it, sat the doctor; his black beard, which he had suffered to grow, overhanging his breast, and his raven locks almost concealing his features; while his mountainous nose, his calm but piercing eye, and his sarcastic lip, revealed to me, at a glance, my former classmate. He was surrounded by a group of persons who sought relief from real or imaginary diseases.

"I have a desperate *misery* in my side," said one.

"I've got the *billiards* fever," groaned another.

"I am *powerful weak*," drawled a third.

"My limbs are *sort o'* dead like," whined a fourth.

"Oh, doctor, I've got the *yaller janders* powerful bad; I feel *jist* like I'd *naaterally* die off; and I can't *hope* myself, no how."

"Can you cure the rheumatiz?"

"I've an inward fever."

"Doctor, my *peided* cow is in a *desput bad fix* with the *holler* horn."

"Ah, Doctor Geeho, you never *seed sich* a poor afflicted *crittur* as I be, with the misery in my tooth; it seems like it would *jist* use me up *bodyaciously*."

"Oh, doctor, doctor, I've got the shaking *ager* so mighty bad, I aint no account, no how."

"Mr. Geehead, I wish you'd look at my boy; he's got in the triflingest way you ever *seed ;* he can't larn his book, and does nothing but jeest tell lies and steal, *study*, all the time; he aint in his right mind, no how."

"Canst thou minister to a mind diseased?" inquired I in a feigned tone. His quick eye, which had more than once rested on me, since I had entered the room, was turned hastily towards me in eager scrutiny. Failing to penetrate my disguise, he civilly inquired my business.

"I know," said I in a mock heroic tone, "that knowledge is thy idol, usefulness thy creed, the approbation of good men thy reward. I seek advice."

"Your complaint?" he inquired in a tremulous voice, for he more than suspected who was his visitor

"The *cacoethes scribendi.*"

"Oh, *si* sick *omnes !*" exclaimed the seventh son, waving his hand over his valetudinarian levee, who stood gasping in awe at this outlandish dialogue.

"It hath afflicted me from my youth," rejoined I.

"Get you gone," cried he in a tone of grave sarcasm, while a joyful recognition sparkled in his eye, "Get you gone, it is a loathsome, incurable disease, which criticism may correct, but the grave only can remove. It hath afflicted the world for ages, carrying with it revilings and jealousies and war. It maketh a man lean in flesh and poor in substance. A hollow eye, a sunken cheek, a soiled finger, and a tattered coat, are its symptoms."

"I crave a private consultation, learned doctor," said I,

and accordingly, after dismissing his patients, he led me into
his *sanctum* and embraced me with the fervour of affectionate
friendship.

I remained with him that day, and we consumed nearly
the whole night in conversation. After he had recounted his
adventures, I inquired how he, whose moral principles I knew
to be rigid, could justify himself in assuming a character which
did not belong to him.

" There is less of imposture," he replied, " in the character
which I have assumed than you imagine ; my father was a
physician, and I am his seventh son."

" But is it right to delude the ignorant, and give your
sanction to an idle superstition ?"

" I will not say that it is right.   Nothing is right but
truth and plain dealing.   Yet I am not prepared to say that
it is morally wrong to do good to men through the medium
of their own weakness.   One half of the diseases which afflict
mankind are imaginary, and should be treated as such.   I practise upon this rule, and have found *faith* quite as valuable as
physic."

" But is it possible that you can pursue this life with satisfaction ?"

" So far as there has been any deception in it, it has been
irksome.   But it has afforded me a fund of amusement, and
has given me an insight into the human heart which I consider invaluable.   I have acquired an intimate acquaintance
with the peculiarities of a most original people ; have seen
the workings of superstition in one of its most powerful forms ;
and have closely studied one of the most curious incidents of
the mysterious connection between mind and matter."

" Then you have some confidence in your system ?"

" Oh yes : how can I help it ?   I have seen the sturdy
hunter, who could face the painted Indian or wrestle with a
hungry wolf, quailing under a fancied or unimportant disorder, and suddenly at my bidding, by a mere volition of will,

resuming his vigour and returning to his manly exercises; I
have seen the drooping maiden, who withering like the
autumn leaf, call back her smiles and bloom, by a simple
exertion of faith. I must acknowledge, however, that my
plan has been extended further, and continued longer than I
intended. It was embraced partly in jest, partly under the
goadings of stern necessity. My success astonished me. I
saw no way to retreat. I was doing good to others and enrich-
ing myself. I am now possessed of a sufficient sum to establish me wherever I please. Besides, the bubble must soon
burst; ours is not a country nor an age in which delusion can
live long."

I left him on the following morning. Shortly afterwards
he abandoned the scene of his success, after presenting the
mystic tablet to the poor widow, who had proved so valuable
a friend to him in the hour of adversity, and instructing her
in the real secret of its efficacy.

\*　　\*　　\*　　\*　　\*　　\*　　\*　　\*　　\*

Three years had passed away since the interview just
related, when one day Doctor Geode, who was now a *regular*
physician of high standing, in a city not far from that of my own
residence, entered my room. I was astonished at the change
which a short time had wrought in his person and appearance.
He was now in his thirtieth year, and had just reached the
vigour of manhood. He was plainly but neatly dressed.
Good living and active employment had clothed his muscles
with flesh, and brought a healthy bloom to his cheek. The
sharp angles of his face had become rounded, and the clouds
of care were dispersed. The clownish manners of the student
had given place to the deportment of a plain, intelligent
gentleman. A smile of benevolence and placid contentment
sat upon his features; and I thought him by no means so
ugly as he had been in his youth.

"Come," said he, " will you join me in a trip to —— ?"

"For what purpose?"

"During my residence there, I had a friend who treat⟋ ⟍
me with kindness.　He had penetrated my disguise by his
own sagacity, but appreciated my motives, kept my secret
with inviolable honour, and promoted my influence with all
his influence.　I was his family physician.　He is dead, and
his only daughter, the fair-haired girl whom I told you of, is
about to be deprived of her inheritance by a designing relative.
My intimacy with the family has put me in possession of
facts, which are unknown to her, but which in my opinion will
establish her claim.　She is a mere child, poor thing, and does
not know her own rights.　Come, you have the dyspepsia, I
am sure; I prescribe a long journey."

Who could resist the temptation of a tour to the frontier
in company with such a man?　"The seventh son shall be
obeyed," said I; and the next morning found us on our way.
The journey was delightful.　The doctor was full of anecdote
and brimful of science: both of which he poured out in
copious streams.　His former taciturnity had given place to
conversational powers of a high order.　It had never been
been constitutional, but was the result of circumstances.　His
youth had been silently and diligently employed in acquiring
the knowledge which now burst forth in rich exuberance; and
he reminded me of the tree that in the winter stands bare,
solitary, and ungraceful, but in due season bears the leaf, the
blossom, and the fruit.　His inquisitive mind was continually
on the stretch.　I was struck with his various information,
his affability, and colloquial skill.

We reached the broad prairies, and the region of thinly
scattered population, and having procured horses, struck into
the wilderness.　The wide and beaten road was changed for
the path that winded over the plains or among the tangled
woods.　We forded the little streams, and crossed the rivers
in canoes, driving our horses before us.　Instead of meeting
the travelling carriage, the stage, and the loaded wagon, we
encountered the solitary hunter in his blanket-coat, treading

along with the stealthy step of a cat and the watching glance
of the wary Indian.   We lodged no longer at the inn, attended
by assiduous servants, but slept at the settler's cabin, and
sat as equals at his board.   Two more days would have
brought us to ——, when my friend was taken ill.   The
attack was severe, and he thought his own case doubtful.
There was no physician in the neighbourhood, and he himself
was unprovided with such medicines as were suitable to his
case.   The fever was raging and the pain intense.   It was
one of those cases in which the crisis approaches rapidly.
Two days passed, and he hourly grew worse.   I was almost
frantic.   At length the man of the house told us of an old
woman, who had lately settled in the neighbourhood, who
was "a desperate good doctor."

"There was a right smart chance of sickness when she
came into the settlement," continued the man, " a heap of
people called on her—she had abundance to do, and she flew
round among the folks mighty *peart*, I tell you.   The way
she fixed 'em was the right way, there's no mistake in it.   I
wouldn't give her for naary high larnt marcury doctor I ever
see, no how."

" But this is an extreme case."

" No matter," replied the hunter cheerfully—" if the man
was as cold as a wagon-tire, provided there was any life in
him, she'd bring him to ; there's no two ways about it."

My friend smiled.   " Send for the woman !" I exclaimed,
" she may tell us of some remedy."   A boy was accordingly
mounted on the fleetest steed, and soon returned with the
female Æsculapius.   There was nothing peculiar in her
appearance, except that she wore a large black veil, which
completely concealed her features.   She required to be left
alone with the patient, but as I insisted on being present at
the interview, an exception was made in my favour.   She
approached the bed, felt the sufferer's pulse, and passed her
hand over his forehead, while the doctor, who seemed to re-

cognise the skilful touch of the practitioner, mechanically put
out his tongue. The woman turned to me and said in a low
voice, "I can do nothing for this gentleman—he is very ill.
and requires a greater physician than I am."

"Do your best," exclaimed I.

"Ah, sir, I have little skill in medicine. I am but a poor
weak woman; a very humble instrument in the hands of
Providence. I can do nothing here. This man needs medicine."

"If you mean to say, that you do your work by a spell, I
insist upon your trying it."

"Very willingly," said the woman meekly, and then raising her voice, she exclaimed, "let no one speak."

She next turned to her patient, and said, "Sick man! do
you believe that I can raise you from this bed of pain?"

The doctor, who, even in the hour of extremity, seemed to
retain his relish for *hocus pocus*, nodded his head, while I felt
an unaccountable awe creeping over me.

"Then look upon my face," continued she in a solemn tone,
throwing back her veil, and displaying in her right hand the
identical tablet of Doctor Geode, "and look upon this tablet
of health, and these mysterious figures, and charmed words,
drawn upon it by the hand of the seventh son of a celebrated
Indian doctor—look on them, and believe, and be restored."

This was more than the doctor could stand. No sooner
did he behold the workmanship of his own hands and the
pupil of his tuition, and witness the whole acting of that
curious scene, of which he had been the inventor, than he
burst into an immoderate convulsion of laughter. The woman gazed in amazement, for in the altered features of her
patient she did not recognise her master. I ran to him in
alarm; but he continued to laugh, rolling from side to side,
throwing up his long arms, and screaming as if distracted.

As soon as he was composed enough to speak, he exclaimed,
"Give her a fifty-dollar note, Charles! Go, go, good woman,

you have done your duty well—go now, but do not leave the house !"

"Can it be possible," continued he, as the wondering woman closed the door after her, "can it be that there are two Richmonds in the field ? No, it is my own veritable spell, and my very deputy herself !" And then he laughed again, until the whole house re-echoed the sonorous peal. The big drops rolled from his forehead. "See there !" he exclaimed, "behold the work of the *faith doctor;* here we have been labouring these two days to break this obstinate fever, and to produce a perspiration, and lo ! the cunning woman has wrought the desired change in a moment !" And it was exactly so ; the violent muscular action, and the sudden revolution in the patient's train of thought, had produced instantaneous relief. A profuse perspiration, succeeded by a gentle slumber, relieved the most violent symptoms. When he awoke he asked for the doctress. "I knew I was safe," said he, "as soon as I saw her face. She has a lancet and a box of calomel pills in her pocket. No man need die of a bilious fever when these are near. I lost mine on the road. Send her in." It is only necessary to add, that after a few days' careful attention from the old lady, who was really an admirable nurse, he was able to resume his journey.

In consequence of this detention, we arrived at the place of our destination too late to be of any service to the daughter of Doctor Geode's former friend, in her lawsuit. The cause had been tried, and decided against her. My worthy fellow-traveller bore this disappointment with less patience than was usual with him. He took it to heart, and brooded over it. Every day he went to see the young lady, to console her, and to try to devise some means to reassert her rights.

After a few visits, the doctor began to talk, in a very dignified strain, of the moral excellence and mental acquirements of his young friend ; at the close of one week he pronounced her a *natural curiosity,* and before the end of the

second, he assured me solemnly that she was a *phenomenon*.
He had discovered a new scientific truth, namely, that in five
years a slim girl of fourteen may be metamorphosed into a
full-grown lovely woman.

"Why, Charles," said he, "there is nothing in all the arcana
of nature to be compared with it; the bursting of the gorgeous butterfly from its chrysalis, the expansion of a beautiful
flower, nor any of the most wonderful changes in the material world cannot equal it."

"What's the matter now, doctor?"

"Matter enough, sir; matter for curious thought. Here
is this little girl, who, when I saw her last, was dressed in cotton homespun, wore a sun-bonnet, and ran on errands for her
father—a little slight thing, as pale as a lily and as timid as
a fawn. She sat in the corner knitting while her father and
I conversed, and never raised her eyes or uttered more than
one syllable at a time. I used to carry young birds, flowers,
and pictures to her, as I would to any other child. Now she
is a woman, as beautiful as Hebe, as hospitable as was her
own warm-hearted father, and as rational as an M.D. She is
a remarkable specimen—"

"If she is a specimen," interrupted I, "I can easily guess
her fate. She will hardly escape so industrious a collector
as yourself. Take her home, doctor, and place her in your
cabinet; she would be worth a thousand dried flies or pickled
snakes." The doctor put on his hat and walked off. I saw
that it was all over with him.

At the end of the third week of our stay, I began to grow
impatient; but my friend's "phenomenon" still engaged all
his thoughts; and where is the ardent lover of science who
would have been willing to relinquish so interesting a subject
of investigation? He was anatomising the young lady's affections with as much patience of research as he would have
bestowed on the complete skeleton of a mastodon. I popped
in upon them one day unexpectedly, as they stood conversing

at a window, and before I was observed or had time to retire, I heard her say in a tremulous tone:

"Indeed, Doctor Geode, I hardly know what to say—it is
so sudden—so—so very unexpected—so—"

"I will tell you what to say; say Yes."

The young lady covered her face, and uttered neither yes
nor no.

"I see through your case," continued the determined doctor, "all that it requires is *faith*. As I used to ask my
patients here, I now ask you, have you faith *in me*?"

"It requires no exertion of credulity to believe that Doctor Geode is all that is noble and excellent," and then she
placed her hand in his. The lover took it respectfully, and
evidently at a loss what he ought to do next, mechanically
laid his finger upon her pulse as if he expected to find
thoughts of love and vows of truth throbbing in the arterial
system.

I suppose I laughed, for they both turned towards me.

"Ah, Charles! what, eavesdropping? well, no matter—
let me introduce you to Mrs. Jeremy Geode that is to be.
We shall be married to-morrow, and the next day bid adieu
to the frontier."

The wedding took place accordingly; and I need scarcely
inform the intelligent reader that my friend is now one of the
best and happiest of husbands, and is enjoying in the meridian
of life the rich harvest of prosperity and honour, which crowns
a youth of virtue, industry, and self-denial.

# THE MISSIONARIES.

O N a fine morning in May, 18—, two of those large boats in which families emigrating to the west descend our rivers, were seen floating down the Ohio. Built of rough, heavy timber, and intended to move only with the current, those unwieldy vessels lay silent and motionless on the wave that bore them gently towards their destination. At a small village—or rather at a spot intended to be occupied as such—the boats were brought to the shore and moored, and the passengers began to mingle with the people whom curiosity had drawn to the landing-place. It was a missionary family, proceeding to its station among the Osage Indians, that halted thus in the wilderness, to receive a foretaste of the scenes that awaited them in the distant forest.

The place at which they had stopped was a level plain, of rich alluvion, from which the timber had been cleared for the space of a mile along the river, and nearly that depth into the forest. A cluster of cabins recently built of rough logs, to which the bark still adhered, presented to the eyes of our travellers a specimen of human existence more nearly approaching the rudeness of savage life than any thing they had

yet seen.   There was nothing here to recall to memory their
own lovely homes—the beautiful villages of New England.
There was no green spot shaded with venerable trees, hallowed
to the repose of the dead—no church pointing its spire to
heaven, and offering a holy refuge to the living.   Here were
no rural embellishments indicating taste, and neatness, and
enjoyment—no domestic trees, no honeysuckle bowers, nor
any of those ornaments which beautify the village and give
to the humblest cottage an air of elegance.   Gardens, and or-
chards, and meadows, there were none, nor any dwelling that
seemed to have been endeared to a human being by the name
of *home*.   The ground, newly cleared, was thickly set with
stumps, and covered with a rank growth of weeds.   The frail
and unsightly cabins, standing apart from each other, and destitute of out-houses and enclosures, seemed to be, as they
really were, the temporary residence of an unsettled people.
But cheerless as this spot appeared to those who had been accustomed to all the comforts and many of the luxuries of life,
it was such as all new towns in the west had once been ; such,
perhaps, as the hamlets were on the shores of the Atlantic,
where the voices of the pilgrims first ascended in prayer to
Him who had brought them in safety out of the land of per-
secution.

And yet the scene was not destitute of attraction.   Art
had done little to spoil and nothing to embellish it, but nature
had been prodigal of her bounties.   As the travellers stood
on the bank, they beheld the "beautiful river," for miles
above and below them, rolling gently along with a surface as
smooth as polished crystal.   The shores were slightly curved,
swelling out on the one side and receding upon the other, so
as to exhibit a series of long and graceful bends.   The banks,
as far as the eye could reach, were low and subject to inundation by the spring floods, but the vegetation which formed
their chief beauty was rich beyond description.   Springing
from a deep alluvion soil, the forest trees reared their im-

mense trunks to an amazing height, while their interwoven branches and foliage formed an impenetrable shade. The hues of the forest were as various as they were beautiful. Here was the melancholy cypress, with a dark trunk and sombre leaf, and the tall sycamore with a stem of snowy whiteness and a foliage of light-green. The poplar, the elm, the maple, and the gum, with numerous other trees, exhibited every variety of verdure between these extremes. The dog-wood and the red-bud, countless in number, decked the whole scene with their rich blossoms, the former of pure white, and the varieties of the latter glowing with all the shades between a pink and a deep scarlet. Then there was the locust, rich in fragrance as in hue, the delicate catalpa, the yellow flower of the tulip-tree. The graceful cane covered the ground, the willow fringed the stream, the vine crept to the tops of the tallest trees, and the mistletoe hung among the branches. The luxuriant soil, while it loaded itself with a gigantic vegetation, gave a depth and vividness to the colouring of the landscape, that imparted a peculiar strength and character to the scene. But if the eye was charmed, there was a loveliness, a stillness, and a silence reigning throughout this scene that touched the heart. The very beauties that delighted, and the quietness that soothed, testified that man was a stranger here, and told the traveller that he was alone with his God.

Such were the feelings of the missionaries as they gazed on this gentle stream and its wild shore. They had left their homes and their friends, their pious companions, their cherished relatives, and the scenes of their childhood, and were going beyond the confines of civil society, to dwell with the savage in his own wild woods. As they travelled to the west, they had seen the traces of civilization becoming every day more faint—every day they had found the villages ruder and more distant from each other—until at last they had reached the abodes of the hunter, where the rifle and the axe furnished the means of subsistence and of defence. An im-

mense tract of wilderness was yet to be traversed, before
they could reach the scene of their future labours, and they felt
sad to think how seldom the smile of a countryman or the
voice of a brother would cheer them on their way.   Their
spirits sunk, as they looked at the boundless extent of forest:
gorgeous as it was to the eye, it was still but a blooming
desert, containing nothing to warm the heart or cherish the
affections.   Every object around them was strange, and they
felt like exiles wandering far from the land of their birth.

These were trials, however, that had been anticipated; and
it was easy to see in the mournful countenances of these humble Christians, as they wandered along the shore, that a hea-
vier visitation was pending over them, than those which were
necessarily incident to their situation.   One of their companions, a beloved sister, was about to breathe her last sigh.   The
messenger of death had arrested her in the wilderness; giving
a solemn warning to those who journeyed with her, that
although they had forsaken the haunts of men, they had not
escaped the casualties of human existence.   Even here, where
nature bloomed so fresh, where every surrounding object
teemed with youth and vigour and fragrance, the messenger
of fate would reach its victim.   Bound on a mission of love
and bearing the tidings of life to thousands, they also bore
with them the evidence of their own mortality.   Death was
silently pursuing their footsteps, watching his own appointed
time to claim the tribute which all must pay to the insatiate
king of terrors.

The situation of the dying missionary was soon known to
the villagers, and a few of them went to offer in their homely
way the offices of hospitality; but they came too late; the
sufferer was too feeble to be removed, and the mourning
strangers said that they needed nothing from human kindness
but a grave for their companion.   The visiters were deeply
affected.   The death-bed exhibits at all times a solemn and
touching scene, and though of daily occurrence its frequency

does not destroy its fearful interest. There are few who reason coldly in the chamber of dissolution ; and the imagination
is easily excited by any incidental circumstance which brings
an additional pang to the parting of the living and the dying.
The present scene was one of no ordinary interest. The sufferer was a young and delicate female. A husband watched
over her pallet, and two lovely children, unconscious of the
loss they were about to sustain, were with difficulty withheld
from her embrace. The severing of hearts wedded in love—
the parting of a mother from her infant children—are events
which the most callous cannot view without emotion ; but on
ordinary occasions there is a melancholy pleasure in the reflection that the survivors will often visit the grave of the deceased, to drop the unseen tears of affection. Even this mournful consolation was now wanting ; and those who sorrowed,
felt that when the soul of their friend should have departed
they must abandon her earthly remains, retaining no relic of
her whom they had dearly loved. Her tomb would be on
the wild shore, where no kindred ashes slept, and where they
who dwelt near the spot could only point it out as a *stranger's
grave.*

The solemn moment had arrived when none affected to
doubt the truth which was too evident, or sought to detain
the spirit in its earthly abode. That spirit had begun to assume its celestial character, and was already invested in the
eyes of the beholders with the attributes of a brighter existence. An angel seemed to be lingering among men, as if
unwilling to sever too rudely the cords of affection with
which she had been united to human beings. She spoke little,
but her words showed that her thoughts partook of the change
she was about to undergo. Her affections alternately lingered on the earth and soared towards a better existence.
The bosom of the saint swelled with a holy joy—but the
heart of the wife and mother clung to the dearly cherished
objects of its purest and strongest earthly passion.

14

The mission family embraced a number of persons of both sexes, and it was gratifying to see in their deportment how efficient is religion in the hour of sorrow. Though deeply afflicted, there was a decent composure, a quiet humility, and an entire resignation, in all their words and actions. They spoke not of death as the loathsome companion of disease, or the precursor of corruption, but as the natural consummation of all earthly beings. They sorrowed not for her who was going to a better world, but for those who remained. Their voices were firm and cheerful—and even the timid soul that was fluttering in the hope and fear, and joy and sorrow, of the dying moment, acquired calmness from the serenity of others.

Such was the day. Evening came, and the sufferer still lived. Prayer and hymn were heard at intervals throughout the night, but all else was silent ; and at a late hour, they who cast a look at the shore, beheld a dim light still emanating from the chamber of death, and appearing as a bright speck in the surrounding gloom—like the lingering soul, whose feeble radiance still gleamed in the dark " valley of the shadow of death."

The following day was the Sabbath. At the dawn, the villagers hastened to the boats. The missionaries were already engaged at their morning devotions. The voice of prayer was heard ascending through the stillness of that quiet hour. The accents were low and trembling, but distinctly audible. The speaker alluded to her whose spirit had gone to the mansions of the blessed, and prayed for the bereaved husband and the orphan children ; and the villagers then knew that she in whose fate they had felt so deeply interested suffered no longer. After a moment's pause the notes of sacred song were heard floating over the tide—so sweet, so mournful, that every heart was touched and every eye moistened.

At sunset the same day the remains of the stranger were borne to the place of burial by her late companions, followed by the inhabitants of the village. A large Indian mound in the rear of the town had been selected, as the only spot not subject to inundation. The grave was opened on the summit of its eminence, and here was the body of a Christian female deposited among the relics of heathen warriors. The inhabitants and the mission family stood around with their heads reverently uncovered while one of the missionaries addressed them—then some one raised a hymn, and the whole company joined, chanting with solemn fervour, as if a flood of devotional feeling had burst spontaneously from every bosom at the same instant—and when they all knelt upon the mound, it was not from any signal or invitation given by man, but God touched their hearts, and as the song of praise ceased, they all involuntarily prostrated themselves before His throne.

When the people rose, and the officiating minister had dismissed them with the usual benediction, the widowed husband stepped forward, leading one of his children in each hand. For a moment he stood by the newly filled grave, gazing on it with an agony which he strove in vain to subdue. In a broken voice he thanked the people of the village for their kindness, and committed the remains of his wife to their protection. He begged them to mark and remember the place of interment, in order that " if hereafter a stranger in passing through their village should ask them for the grave of Maria ——, they could lead him to the spot."

# THE INDIAN WIFE'S LAMENT.

THE Indian tribes who reside near the Falls of Saint Anthony, have a tradition of one of their females, who drowned herself in a fit of jealousy. Her husband, to whom she was tenderly attached, had, after their fashion, which permits a plurality of wives, introduced a second female into his wigwam, which so mortified the heroic woman, who had prided herself in being the sole possessor of his affections, that she calmly placed herself and her children in a canoe, and floated over the cataract, singing her death-song.

SHE launched her frail bark on the swift-rolling stream,
And sang her death-song with a maniac scream,
That pierced the lone caves of that desolate shore,
And rose o'er the din of the cataract's roar.

The bald eagle sprang from his perch at the sound,
And, poised high in air, circled watchfully around;
The panther crouched low in his brush-covered bed,
The timid deer rushed from her thicket and fled.

She saw not the eagle, she marked not the deer,
The echo that scared them was mute to her ear,
So wild was her sorrow, so wretched her doom,
She seemed a lone spirit escaped from the tomb.

Her babes clung around her with timorous cry,
Alarmed with the glance of her fierce rolling eye,
And still o'er those dear ones impassioned she hung,
And madly she kissed them, as wildly she sung:

"Oh, children forsaken! wife, mother forlorn!
The heart that should cherish has spurned ye in scorn;
Expelled from his bosom, and banished his door,
The father, the husband, shall clasp us no more.

"How blest were the days of my youth, when in pride
I climbed yonder mountains, or bathed in this tide;
When I chased the young fawn to its woodland retreat,
And snatched a rich plume from the gay paroquet.

"But happier far when I roamed through the shade,
Companion of him who with pride I obeyed;
His quiver I carried, his game I secured,
 I shared all his triumphs, his toils I endured.

"He was strong as the oak, he was straight as the reed,
No warrior could match him in courage or speed,
So true was his arrow, so sharp was his spear,
The Otto and Pawnee-Loupe met him in fear.

"How faithful, how fond, how enduring my love,
These tears and the pangs of a broken heart prove·
Do I dream! no, these pledges too dearly proclaim,
How happy I was, and how wretched I am.

"Had he died, I had mourned him with many a tear,
His son should have wielded his bow and his spear,
His daughter in songs should have honoured his name,
Every vale, every mountain, had rung with his fame.

"Ah, subtle destroyer! he charmed as the snake,
Who basks on the mountain or lurks in the brake:
He stung like the reptile! the poison is sure,
No herb can relieve me, no sorcery cure.

"False traitor! who won and caressed to destroy,
Oh could I but hate thee, I still could know joy,
But spurned and degraded, this heart is so frail,
Love remains where deep hate and revenge should prevail.

"One spirit we worship, one chief we obey,
One bright sun gives lustre and warmth to our day,
One mate has the eagle, the turtle one love,
I am proud as the eagle, and true as the dove.

"Oh think not to tread in your pride o'er my grave!
I will sleep with my babes buried deep in the wave,
Where thou canst not follow—unworthy to be
A husband, a father, to them or to me.

"If stung with remorse, thou shalt seek for my tomb,
To mock at my weakness, or mourn o'er my doom,
Thy voice shall be drowned in the cataract's roar,
And my spirit be vexed with thy false vows no more!"

As she sung, the sad strain came prolonged o'er the cliff—
Every cave, as in sympathy, echoed her grief,
So deep each response, as it murmured along,
No mortal e'er heard so terrific a song.

And onward the bark swiftly glides o'er the spray,
No hand gave the motion, or guided the way,
But headlong through breakers it swept as the wind,
No pathway before it, no trace left behind.

A moment it paused on the cataract's brow,
Then sunk into fathomless caverns below,
And the bark, and the song, and the singer, no more
Were seen on the wild wave, or heard on the shore!

# A LEGEND OF CARONDELET;

## OR, FIFTY YEARS AGO.

THERE is no knowledge so valuable as a knowledge of the world. Thousands have grown gray in the acquisition of learning, without ever getting the slightest insight into the human character, while many seem to be born with an intrinsic perception of the workings of the human heart. There is a something called common sense, which books do not teach, but which, nevertheless, is worth more than all the lore of antiquity. A man may starve with his head full of Latin and Greek, while a single grain of common sense operates like the presence of the prophet of old upon the widow's cruse. The fortunate individual who is born with this desirable quality, bears a charmed existence, and glides along in the voyage of life with an ease that surprises his companions. There is a thriftiness about such persons which is almost miraculous; like those hardy plants that spring up in the crevices of the rock, they flourish in the midst of barrenness, when every thing perishes around them.

To this class belonged Timothy Eleazer Tompkinson, the

14*

hopeful heir of a worthy mariner, whose domicil was situated in a small seaport of New England, but who, being almost constantly abroad, was obliged to leave his only son to the care of a maiden aunt and to the teaching of a public school. This amiable youth exhibited, even in childhood, some of the touches of the disposition which adhered to him through life. He liked salt water better than attic wit; and loved to steer his little boat, in the most stormy weather, around the capes and headlands of the neighbouring sea-coast, better than to trace out the labyrinths of a problem, or to wander among the shoals and quicksands of metaphysics. In his tenderest years, he launched his bark upon the ocean with the temerity of a veteran pilot; and when the gay breeze swept along, and the waves danced and sparkled in the sun, his little sail might be seen skimming over the surface like a sea-bird. Often as he strolled off in the morning might the shrill voice of his aunt, the worthy Miss Fidelity Tompkinson, be heard hailing him with, "Where are you going, Timmy dear?" "Don't go near the water, dear;" and as often would he toss his head and march on, smiling at the simplicity of his watchful guardian and marvelling at the timidity of women. In vain did the village pedagogue remind him that time flies swifter than a white squall, and that in the voyage of life there is but one departure, which, if taken wrong, can never be corrected. Tim would listen with a smile, and then placing his tarred hat on one side of his head, stroll off whistling to the beach.

At sixteen it was concluded that the years and gifts of Timothy rendered him a suitable candidate for college honours, and his name was accordingly entered upon the books of a celebrated institution. Here he was soon distinguished; not for Latin or logic, but for cleverness, ingenuity, and gymnastic feats. He never was a great talker, but, on the contrary, expressed himself with a laudable brevity, and with that idiomatic terseness of language which is common along shore, where a significant sea-phrase answers all the purpose

of a long argument; and he reasoned, plausibly enough, that
one who employed so few words, had little use for any other
tongue than his own, which afforded a copious medium for
the conveyance of his slender stock of ideas. In the mathematical sciences, he was better skilled. Few could estimate
with more accuracy the number of superficial yards between
his own chamber and a neighbouring orchard, or calculate
with more nicety the difference of distance between these
points upon a direct line, or by the meanders of a number of
obtuse angles. He knew the exact height of every window
in the college edifice, and the precise force required to elevate
a projectile from the college green to the roof of the tutor's
boarding-house. He knew precisely the angle at which an
object could be presented to the retina of a professor's eye,
and was acquainted with the depth of every intellect and the
measure of every purse in the Senior class. In short, however deficient in Athenian polish, he had all the hardihood of
a Spartan youth, and was especially gifted with that thrifty
quality called common sense. He was a lucky boy, too.
Though foremost in every act of mischief, he was always the
last to be found out or punished; and though he never studied, he always managed to glide unnoticed through the college
examinations, or to obtain praise for productions which were
strongly suspected to be not his own. In difficulty or danger,
he was sure to have a device to meet the exigency, and was
so often successful on such occasions, that his companions
compared him to the active animal, which, when thrown into
the air, always lights upon its feet.

It will be readily imagined that our hero gained but few
scholastic attainments; yet he was, nevertheless, a general
favourite. He was blessed with the finest temper in the
world. His good nature was absolutely invincible. Although
the very prince of mischief, none suspected him of malice. In
the midst of a bitter reproof he would smile in the professor's
face; and the student who treated him with insolence was,

perhaps, the first to receive some kind act from his hand. If the faculty frowned upon him, he had the *faculty* of turning the storm into sunshine, and of averting punishment by a well-timed jest or compliment. Every body loved Tim, and Tim loved every body. He hated study; but then he liked college, because the students were jolly fellows, and the professors took flattering kindly, and stood quizzing with that patience which is the result of long endurance.

How long these halcyon days would have lasted, and whether the name of Timothy Eleazer Tompkinson would have been numbered among the alumni of the college, is now beyond the reach of conjecture; for just as he had attained his twentieth year, the news came that his father had discharged the debt of nature, leaving all his other debts unpaid, his sister fortuneless, and his son a beggar. Our hero paid the tribute of a tear to the memory of his departed parent, and more than one drop attested his sympathy for the desolate condition of his kind aunt. But he soon brushed the moisture from either eye, and as the good president condoled with him in a tone of sincere affection, he acknowledged with a smile that his case might have been much more desperate.

"The worst of it is," said the reverend principal, "that you will not be able to take out a degree."

"I shall be sorry to quit college," replied the youth, "but as for the degree, that is neither here nor there."

The president shook his head and took snuff, while Tim cast a sidelong glance out of the window, gazing wistfully over the green landscape, which was now decked with the blossoms of spring, and longing to rove uncontrolled about that beautiful world, that seemed so redolent of sunshine, and flowers, and balmy breezes.

"It is a sad thing," said the president, "for a young man to be cast upon the cold charity of the wide world."

"The wider the world is the better," said Tim; "it is a fine thing to have sea-room; and as to its coldness, I don't regard that; a light heart will keep a man warm in the stiffest northeaster that ever blew."

The worthy president applied his handkerchief to his nose, then wiped his spectacles, and wondered how marvellously the wind is tempered to the shorn lamb.

"Thou hast a bold heart," said the president, "still I cannot bear to see you cast forth without a profession."

"Oh, never mind that; I'm all the better without it. To a man without a farthing in his pocket, a profession is only an incumbrance, which forces him to wear good clothes and talk like a book. I shall put out into the world as light as a feather, and float along with the breeze."

Arguments were thrown away upon the common sense of our hero, who was already panting to exercise among men the same devices which had smoothed all the asperities of college life, which had won him the affection of his fellow-students, and gained even the kindness of his superiors.

"There goes," said the president, as he gazed after him, "the shrewdest boy and the greatest dunce that ever left college—the most obstinate, yet the most conciliatory spirit."

Obstinate as he was, there was one point on which he yielded. He abandoned a long-cherished intention of going to sea, upon the earnest solicitation of his aunt. It was the only request from his sole remaining relative. She had nursed his infancy with unceasing kindness; she now leaned upon him for support, and her tears were irresistible. But in abandoning the ocean, he stipulated for free permission to roam at large over the wide expanse of his native country, and in a few days after the intelligence had arrived of his father's death, he was seen leaving his native village with an elastic step, with a staff in his hand, and a small portmanteau under his arm.

Here I must leave my hero for the present, and ask the gentle reader to accompany me to the pleasant village of Carondelet, or, as it is more commonly called, Vide Poche, on the margin of the Mississippi. Although now dwindled into

an obscure and ruinous hamlet, remarkable only for its outlandish huts and lean ponies, it was then the goodly seat of a
prosperous community.   It is situated on the western shore
of the river, in a beautiful little amphitheatre, which seemed
to have been scooped out for the very purpose.   The banks
of the Mississippi at this place are composed of a range of
hills rising abruptly from the water's edge.   The town occu-
pies a sort of cove, formed by a small plat of table land, surrounded on three sides by hills.   The houses occupy the whole
of this little area, including the hill-sides ; and are models of
primitive rudeness, carelessness, and comfort.   They were
sometimes of stone ; but usually of framed timber, with mud
walls ; and all the rooms being arranged on the ground floor,
their circumference was often oddly disproportioned to their
height.   In a few of the better sort, spacious piazzas, formed
by the projection of the roof, surrounded the buildings, giving
to them both coolness and a remarkable air of comfort.   The
enormous steep roofs were often quadrangular, so as to form
a point in the middle, surmounted by a ball, a weathercock,
or a cross.   Gardens, stocked with fruit trees and flowering
shrubs, encompassed the dwellings, enclosed with rough stone
walls, or stockades made by driving large stakes in the ground.
The dwelling stood apart, having each its own little domain
about it ; and when it is added that the streets were narrow
and irregular, it will be observed that the whole scene was
odd and picturesque.

The inhabitants presented, as I suppose, a fair specimen of
the French peasantry, as they existed in France previous to
the first revolution.   They had all the levity, the kindness,
and the contentment which are so well described by Sterne,
with a simplicity which was perfectly childlike.   Though subject at the date of our tale to a foreign king, they were as
good republicans as if they had been trained up in one of our
own colonies.   They knew the restraints and distinctions of a
monarchy only by report, practising the most rigid equality

among themselves, and never troubling their heads to inquire how things were ordered elsewhere. The French commandants and priests, who ruled in their numerous colonies, had always the knack of giving a parental character to their sway, and governed with so much mildness, that the people never thought of questioning either the source or extent of their authority; while the English invariably alienate the affections of their colonists by oppression. The inhabitants of Vide Poche were all plebeians; a few who traded with the Indians had amassed some little property; the remainder were hunters and boatmen—men who traversed the great prairies of the West, and traced the largest rivers to their sources, fiddling and laughing all the way, lodging and smoking in the Indian wigwams, and never dreaming of fatigue or danger.

To return to our story. It was a sultry afternoon in June. Not a breath of air was stirring—the intense glare of the sun had driven every animal to some shelter—the parched soil glowed with heat, and even the plants drooped. There was, however, a pleasant coolness and an inviting serenity among the dwellings of the French. The trees that stood thick around them threw a dense shade, which contrasted delightfully with the glaring fierceness of the sunbeams. The broad leaf of the catalpa and the rich green of the locust afforded relief to the eye; bowers of sweetbrier and honeysuckle, mingled with luxuriant clumps of the white and red rose, gave fragrance to the air, and a romantic beauty to the scene.

In the cool veranda of one of the largest of those dwellings, sat a round-faced, laughing Frenchman. Near him sat Madame, his wife, a dark-eyed, wrinkled, sprightly old lady; and at her side was a beautiful girl of seventeen, their only daughter. The worthy couple had that mahogany tinge of complexion which belongs to this region; as to the young lady, politeness compels me to describe her hue as a brunette—and a beautiful brunette it was—fading into snow-white upon her neck, and deepening into a rich damask on her round smooth cheek. The ladies were sewing; and the gentleman was puffing his pipe with the composure of a man who feels conscious that he has a right to smoke his own tobacco in his own house, and with the deliberation of one who is master of his own time.

While thus engaged, their attention was attracted by the apparition of a man leading a jaded horse along the street. The stranger was young and slender; his dress had once been genteel, but was much worn, and showed signs of recent exposure to the weather. The traveller himself was tanned and weather-beaten, his hair tangled, and his chin unshaved; while the sorry nag, which he led by the bridle, had just life enough left in him to limp upon three legs. Worn down with fatigue, and covered with sweat and dust, the new comer halted in the street, as if unable to proceed, and looked around in search of a public house. Of a boy, who passed along, he inquired for a tavern; but the lad, unable to understand him, shook his head. He put the same question to several others, with no better success; until Monsieur Dunois, the gentleman whom we have described above, seeing his embarrassment, stepped forward and invited him into his porch.

The stranger was no other than our friend Timothy Eleazer Tompkinson, who, in the course of a few months, had made his way from New England to Louisiana. It is unnecessary to recount the various expedients by which he maintained himself upon his journey. He was a lawyer, a doctor, or a mechanic, as occasion required. At one place, he pleaded a cause before a magistrate; at another, he drew a tooth; for one man he mended a lock; for another he set a timepiece; and by these and similar devices, he not only supported himself, but procured the means to purchase a horse, saddle, and bridle. Arrived at the frontier of Kentucky, his restless spirit still urged him forward, and he determined to strike across the wilderness to the French settlements, on the Mississippi. The distance was nearly three hundred miles, and the whole region through which he had to travel was uninhabited, except

by Indians. Unaccustomed to the forest, he must have perished, had he not encountered a solitary hunter, who, pleased
with his free and bold spirit, voluntarily conducted him
throughout a considerable part of the route, taught him how
to avoid the haunts of the savages, and instructed him in some
of the arts of forest life. For the last two days he had wandered without food; and both himself and his horse were
nearly exhausted when he reached the Mississippi, where some
friendly Indians, of the Kaskaskia tribe, had ferried him across
in their canoes. The arrival of a stranger at this secluded
hamlet, by land, was quite an event, and little else was talked
of, this evening, at the tea-tables of Carondelet.

M. Dunois, who had traded and travelled, valued himself
highly on his knowledge of the English language, which he
had attempted to teach to his daughter; and he no sooner
discovered that this was the vernacular tongue of the stranger,
than he opened a conversation in that dialect. The cork was
drawn from a bottle of excellent claret, a pitcher of limpid
water from the fountain was brought, and our hero having
moistened his parched lips, and seated himself in the coolest
veranda of Vide Poche, felt quite refreshed. The following
dialogue then ensued:

"Pray, sir," said Timothy Eleazer, with his best college
bow, "can you direct me to a tavern?"

"Tavern! *vat* you call? *eh? Oh la! d'auberge*—no,
Monsieur, *dere* is no tavern *en Vide Poche*."

"That is awkward enough—what shall I do? my horse
must be fed, and I am almost starved."

"*Eh bien?* you will have some *ros bif*, and somebody for
eat your *cheval! n'est ce pas?*"

"I need food and lodging, and know not where to go."

"*Fude! vat* is *fude*, Marie? Ah ha! *aliment. Sacre!*
Monsieur is *hongry; Loge!* here is *ver* good place, *chez moi.*
You shall stay *vid* me. *Ver* good *loge* here, and plenty for
eat you, *et votre cheval.*"

Timothy " hoped he didn't intrude ;" but a man who has
been lost in the woods is not very apt to stand on ceremony ;
and as he glanced at the symptoms of plenty which surrounded
him, at the good-humoured hostess, and at the fair Marie, a
spectator would have judged that his fears of intrusion were
overbalanced by feelings of self-gratulation at having fallen
into the hands of such good Samaritans.  He soon found that
the hospitality of this worthy family was of the most substantial kind.   In a moment his tired nag was led to the stable,
and our hero, so lately a wanderer, found himself an honoured
and cherished guest.

The air of Vide Poche agreed well with him.  The free
and social habits of the French were exactly to his taste.
Although their pockets, as the name of their town implies,
were not lined with gold, there was plenty in their dwellings
and cheerfulness in their hearts.

He was delighted with the harmony and the apparent
unity, both of feeling and interest, which bound this little
community together.   They were like a single family ; their
hearts beat in unison, " as the heart of one man."  There was
but one circle.   Though some were poorer than others, they
all mingled in the same dance ; and as none claimed superiority, or attempted to put others to shame by affecting a show
of wealth, there was little envy or malice.   All were equally
illiterate, with the exception of Mons. Dunois and the priest,
who had travelled, and who spoke, the one Latin, and the
other, as we have seen, English.   But so far from assuming
any airs on account of these attainments, they were the plain-
est and most sociable men in the village, and were reverenced
as much for their benevolence as for their superior knowledge.

All this chimed so well with the feelings of Mr. Timothy
Eleazer Tompkinson, that he resolved forthwith to engraft
himself upon this cheerful and vigorous stock.  The next
thing was to choose a profession ; but he had too much common sense to suffer so small a matter as this to cause him

any embarrassment. I am not aware of the precise motive which determined him to embrace the practice of physic. It might have been benevolence, or a conviction of special vocation for the healing art; but I rather attribute it to a motive which I suspect too often allures our youth to become the disciples of Æsculapius, namely, the occult nature of the science, which enables an adroit practitioner to cover his ignorance so completely as to defy detection. Timothy had discovered that when he practised law, any spectator could expose the fallacy of his arguments; when he mended clocks, they often refused to go; but the case was different with his patients; if, in spite of his drugs, they refused *to go*, it was well for them and for him; and if they *did go*, nobody knew whom to blame. To say the truth, he never presumed to " exhibit" any drug more active than charcoal, brickdust, or flour; and his success had heretofore been quite marvellous.

He therefore took the earliest opportunity of disclosing to his host that he was a physician, and was disposed to exercise his calling for the benefit of the good people of Carondelet.

"*Eh bien!*" exclaimed M. Dunois, "*un medecin! ver* good; *ver mosh* fine *ting* for Vide Poche; *vat* can you cure?"

" Oh, I am not particular; I can cure one thing almost as well as another."

" You can cure every *ting, eh?—de fevre, de break-bone, de catch-cold—dat* is fine *ting,* you shall stay *chez Vide Poche.*"

So the question was settled.

Had there been a newspaper in Carondelet, the name of Doctor Timothy Eleazer Tompkinson, "from the United States," would, doubtless, have figured in its columns. But as there was no such thing, our hero resorted to other means of acquiring notoriety. In the first place, having procured a suitable cabin, the whole village was searched for vials, and gallipots, and little boxes, and big bottles, which, being filled with liquids and unguents of various hues, were " wisely set for show," at the window. But the greatest affair of all was

a certain machine, for the invention of which Doctor Tompkinson ought to have had a patent. This was no other than
a wheel, turning on an axis, and surrounded by an immovable
rim, within which it revolved.  Upon the wheel Timothy
wrote the name of every disease which he could recollect, as
well as every dreadful accident to which flesh is heir; and on
the rim he inscribed the cures.  When the remedy for any
disorder was required, the wheel was set in motion, and on
its stopping, the cure was found opposite the disease.  The
honest villagers crowded to see " the magic wheel," and vied
in their courtesies to its fortunate possessor, who was rising
fast into celebrity, when his prospects were clouded by an
untoward event.

In the midst of the village stood the chapel—a low, oblong
building, whose gable end was presented to the street, and
behind which was a cemetery, where all the graves were
marked by great wooden crosses, instead of tombstones.
Here the good Catholics repaired every morning and evening
to perform their devotions, and confess their peccadilloes to
the priest.  Hither one morning, at an earlier hour than
usual, was seen repairing the fair Marie Dunois, with a step
as light as the zephyr and a face radiant as the dawn.  Kneeling beside the worthy old man, who placed his withered hand
upon her raven locks, she began in a low, earnest tone to
unburthen her mind.  Suddenly the ecclesiastic started from
his seat, exclaiming,

" Ah, the insolent! how did he dare to make such an
avowal ?"

" He meant no harm, I assure you, father," replied Marie.

" How do you know that ?"

" He told me so, with his own mouth.  He said that he
valued my happiness more than his own ; and that he would
rather swallow all the physic in his shop, than offend me."

" Very pretty talk, truly!  Do you not know that he is a
heretic, and that no reliance can be placed in him ?"

"Very true, Father Augustin, but then he is so agreeable."

"Besides, he is a Yankee; and does not understand your language."

"Oh, I understand him very well; and he says he will teach me to speak English. Don't you think him very handsome, Father Augustin?"

"I am afraid, my child, that this adventurer has imposed too much upon your youth and innocence."

"No, indeed, Father Augustin, I am old enough to know when a gentleman is sincere, and all that. Don't you think Doctor Tompkinson plays beautifully on the flute? and on the violin, he plays almost as well as you, father."

"Pshaw! go, go, I shall inform your parents."

"Oh dear, I have no objections to that; they will feel highly honoured by Doctor Tompkinson's partiality for me."

Nevertheless the pretty Marie blushed and cast down her eyes when she met her father at breakfast that morning, and no sooner was that meal despatched than she hastened to her own room. Presently came Father Augustin, and after an hour's conference, Monsieur Dunois, evidently much agitated, sallied forth in search of our hero.

"*Vel, sair!*" he exclaimed as they met, "I *ave* found you out! I *ave catch de Yankee!*"

"How?"

"How! you *ave* court my daughter; *dat is how! sacre!* you *ave* make love *avec ma Marie, dat* is how enough, *Monsieur docteur.*"

"My dear sir, pray be composed, there is some mistake."

"*Dere* is no mistake. I *vill* not be *compose*—I *will* not be *impose, too! diable!* Suppose some *gentilhomme* court *ma Marie contrair* to my *vish*, shall I sit down *compose?*"

"Really, sir, I see no reason for this passion," replied the cautious Timothy, who saw his advantage in keeping cool.

"*Sair, I ave raison*," exclaimed the enraged Frenchman; "I *ave* too *mosch raison. Vous etez traitre!* you are *de* sly

*dem rogue !* You very pretty *docteur !* very *ansome* Yankee
*docteur !* can you no mix *de physique,* and draw *de* blood,
*vidout* make love *avec* all *the French gal ?*"

" I assure you, sir, the ladies have misconstrued something
that I have said merely in jest———."

" *Jest ! vat* is *jest ? ah ha ! raillerie ; fon—vat, sair,* you
court *ma fille* for *fon ?* very *ansome fon !* you make love *avec*
*de French gal* for *fon, eh ?* Suppose *bam bye* you marry some
of *dem* for *fon ! diable !* Suppose, maybe, I break all your
bone, for *fon, vid* my *cane, eh,* how you like him ?"

" My dear sir, if you will tell me coolly what you complain of, I will endeavour to explain."

" *Sair,* I complain for many *ting.* I sorry for you make
love *avec ma fille, vidout* my leave—*dat* is *von ting ;* I very
*mosch incense* for you court *ma chile* for *fon—dat* is *nodder*
*ting ; den* I *ave raison* to be *fache* for you *faire la cour a* two,
*tree* lady all same *tem.*"

The last of these accusations was unjust. Timothy had
not really intended to pay his devotions to more than one
lady. But the females all admired him, and in their confidential conversations with the priest, who was no great con-
noisseur in the affairs of the heart, spoke of him in such high
terms of approbation, as to induce the holy man to believe
that he was actually playing the coquette. What Monsieur
Dunois and the priest believed, soon became the belief of the
village ; and the men all condemned, while the ladies sympa-
thized with, the ingenious stranger. The doctor, of course,
changed his lodging ; and ceased to have any intercourse with
Mademoiselle Dunois, except by means of expressive glances
and significant pressures of the hand as they met in the
dances, which occurred almost every evening.

Things now looked gloomy ; our friend Timothy lost his
practice ; and a fortunate circumstance it was for him, as
well as for those who might otherwise have been his patients.
He now had leisure to make hunting excursions, and expedi-

tions upon the water; and his skill in the management of a boat, as well as his courage and address in every emergency, soon gained him friends. His vivacity, his versatility and promptness, won daily upon his comrades; he became a daring hunter, a skilful woodsman, and a favourite of all the young men of the village.

Such was the posture of affairs, and Doctor Tompkinson was sitting one evening in his lonely room, *quite out of patients,* as a punster would say, when he was called in haste to visit a young lady who had met with the misfortune of having a fish-bone stuck in her throat. The priest had exercised all his skill—the old ladies had exhausted their recipes without effect; and, as a last resort, it was determined to consult Dr. Tompkinson and the magic wheel. Our hero, with great alacrity, brushed the dust from the neglected machine, set it in motion, and waited patiently until it stopped, when opposite to the word " choking" was found " bleeding." The doctor, somewhat perplexed, repeated the experiment; but, the result being the same, resolved to obey the oracle, and trust to fortune. Having prepared his bandages and lancet, he repaired to the sufferer, who, opening her eyes and beholding the operator brandishing a bright instrument, and naturally supposing that the part affected would be the first point of attack, and that her throat would be cut from ear to ear, uttered a terrific scream, and—out flew the bone! "St. Anthony! what a miraculous cure!" exclaimed the priest.

"Ste Genevieve! what a noble physician!" cried all the ladies.

And the whole village of Vide Poche was alive with wonder and loud in praise of the consummate sagacity of the young American. Never did a man rise so suddenly to the highest pinnacle of public favour—never did Doctor Tompkinson shake so many hard hands, or receive so many bright smiles and courtesies, as on this evening. The news soon flew to the tea-table of Monsieur Dunois, who had already begun to repent of his harshness to our hero, and whose ardent feelings, easily excited, now prompted him into the opposite extreme.   Seeing the object of his solicitude passing his door, while the first. gush of returning kindness was flowing through his heart, he rushed out and caught him in his arms. "*Ah, mon ami!*" exclaimed he, "I *ave* been *mistake!* I *ave* been *impose!* you are *de grand medecin!* you shall marry *avec* my *gal!*" and without waiting for any reply, he dragged him into the house.

Shortly after this event, the smartest and merriest wedding that ever was seen in Carondelet was celebrated under the hospitable roof of Monsieur Dunois, and our hero became the happy husband of the beautiful and artless Marie. On that night, every fiddle and every foot in Vide Poche did its duty; even the priest wore his best robes and kindest smile at the marriage feast of the lucky heretic.   Mr. Tompkinson immediately abandoned the practice of physic; the magic wheel disappeared; and he embarked in business as an Indian trader.  Here his genius found an appropriate field. With his band of adventurous boatmen he navigated the long rivers of the West to their tributary fountains; he visited the wigwams of tribes afar off, to whom the white man was not yet known as a scourge; he chased the buffalo over plains until then untrodden by any human foot but that of the savage, and returned laden with honest spoil.   Year after year he pursued this toilsome traffic; until, having earned a competency, he sat down contented, and waxed as fat, as lazy, and as garrulous as any of his townsmen.   He grew as swarthy as his neighbours, and as he wore a *capot* and smoked a short pipe, no one would have suspected that he was not a native, had it not been for his aunt, the worthy Miss Fidelity Tompkinson, who occupied the best room in his mansion, and who resolutely refused, through life, to eat *gumbo*-soup, to speak French, or to pay any reverence to that respectable man, the priest.

# THE INTESTATE;

## OR JERRY SMITH'S WIDOW

---

I LEFT my residence in Kentucky a few years ago, and proceeded to Baltimore, for the purpose of transacting some
business with a mercantile house, with which I had been extensively concerned.   No one knew the object of my journey;
because, being a bachelor in easy circumstances, I was under
no obligation to disclose to any person more than I thought
proper.   I left my farm under the direction of a manager, with
the expectation of returning in a few weeks.   On my arrival
in Baltimore, I found that it would be necessary to proceed
to New Orleans.   The vessel in which I embarked, after being
baffled and detained by head winds, at length sprung aleak,
and we were obliged to put into Havana.   Here various delays occurred, and as I could neither talk Spanish, play billiards,
nor smoke cigars, the time hung so heavy upon my hands,
that I soon fretted myself into a bilious fever.   In this condition my captain left me, without so much as saying good-bye;
and when at last I reached New Orleans by another vessel, I
found the person with whom my affair had been intrusted,
was absent and not expected to return in several weeks.
There was no alternative left me, but either to abandon the

15

object of my voyage, and risk the entire loss of a large sum, or by remaining expose my constitution, already debilitated and predisposed to disease, to the dangers of a sickly climate. Unfortunately I adopted the latter course.

I found the weather as hot here as in Cuba, the language as incomprehensible, and the billiard-tables quite as devoid of interest. The sickly season was fast approaching, and as I determined not to escape disease by flight, I endeavoured to avoid it by precaution. It is amusing enough to those who can look on from a distance, to see the various expedients by which men endeavour to contend with death; as if the great destroyer was a foe who could be eluded by cunning or baffled by force. The yellow fever assailed the inhabitants; I felt the malady, or I thought I felt it creeping slowly into my system, and resorted to every preventive which my own reason, or the experience of others, suggested. I first tried the San-grado plan; drank water, ate vegetables, and suffered phle-botomy. But I soon found that I could not endure starvation, nor carry on the functions of life without a due supply of the circulating medium. I resorted to stimulants and tonics— a mint julep in the morning, bitters at noon, and wine after dinner; but, alas! with no better success; for every time I looked in the glass, I discovered, by my sallow visage, that the enemy was silently making his approaches. My eyes became jaundiced, my pulse heavy, my skin dry, and my complexion received a new coat of yellow every day, deep-ening at first into a delicate orange, then to a saffron, and lastly to a copper-colour; until I began to fear that I was actually degenerating into a Spaniard, a Quarteroon, or a Cherokee.

"Coming events throw their shadows before,"

and on this occasion the shadows that tinged my face were but too prophetic. The dreaded fever came at last, and I sunk into a state of helpless and hopeless misery, which none can truly estimate but those who have felt its poignancy. I was a stranger, far from home; in a climate tainted with disease; and attacked by a disorder supposed to be fatal. That malady, among other distressing characteristics, has one which is peculiarly aggravating. I know not whether others are similarly affected, but to me a fever brings a state of excitement and sensitiveness, which produces the most exquisite torture. My whole nature is subtilized—every feeling is quickened—and every sense sharpened into a painful acuteness of perception. The judgment is weakened, but the imagination acquires a supernatural activity; the body sinks, but the spirit is feelingly alive. Such was my state. In the early stages of my disease, a thousand wild visages were in my brain. I made rhymes; repeated pages of Latin, although in a moment of sanity I could not have connected a sentence; I saw people whose faces had been forgotten for years; I called up events which had transpired in my childhood; I planned novels, composed essays, and devised theories; I fought battles; I recalled the joys and repented the sins of my whole life. I was a madman, a philosopher, a devotee, and a wag, in the same hour. At one moment I prayed fervently; at another I dropped the doctor's nostrums in my sleeve, and amused myself with inventing ingenious answers to deceive him, and feigning symptoms which did not exist. I jested, moralized, groaned, wept, and laughed; and found in each new mood that came over me, a pang as agonizing as that which I had suffered in the one that had passed. Such is fever! excruciating bodily pain, with a brilliancy and strength of intellectual vision, which looks back to infancy, and forward to eternity, and around upon the whole scene of life, while the mental eye is crowded with images, whose number and vividness weary and distract the brain. Loss of strength, stupor, and melancholy, succeeded. I thought of home, of myself, and of death; and my visions assumed every day a deeper and more death-like hue.

There was one object which intruded into all my dreams. I need only name its character, in order to enlist the sympathy of every tender-hearted reader. It was a young widow— for whom I felt a particular regard, and to whom—if I must speak out—I was engaged to be married on my return home. She was my first love. I had paid my addresses to her before her marriage, but was too bashful to declare myself explicitly; and while I balanced matters in my own mind, and sought by the gentlest hints to disclose my passion, she by some fatality—by mere accident, as I have since understood—married a certain Jeremiah Smith! a fellow for whom and for whose name I had always entertained a sovereign and special contempt. I did not blame her for marrying, for that was her privilege;—but to wed a fellow named Jerry! and of all the Jerries in the world to pitch upon Jerry Smith, a dissipated, silly profligate, not worth a cent in the world, was too bad! It was flying in the face of propriety, and treating her other lovers, who were numerous, with indignity. Poor girl! she had a sad time of it, for Jerry treated her worse than a brute; but at the end of two years he had the grace to pop off, leaving her penniless and as pretty as ever. It was a long time after her widowhood before we met; I would not call on her, and as to courting Jerry Smith's widow, that seemed out of the question. But when we did meet, she looked so sad and so beautiful, and smiled so pensively, and talked so sweetly of old times, that all her power of fascination over me revived. I began to visit her, thinking of nothing more at first than to show her my superiority over Jerry Smith, and to convince her how great a slight she had shown to my merits in selecting him. But, in trying to make myself agreeable to the widow, she became so very agreeable to me, that in spite of all my former resolutions I offered her my hand, which was accepted with the most charming grace imaginable. This was just before my journey, and as that could not be postponed, we agreed to but off the wedding until my return.

Such was the beautiful vision that had smiled upon me through all my wanderings; but which was now presented to my distempered fancy, arrayed in the brightest colours. In vain did I sometimes try to banish it; I thought of my business, my farm, my negroes, my tobacco—but anon came the graceful widow, with that same smile and blush that she wore when she faintly murmured "no," and expressively looked "yes"—there she was, hanging fondly over me, and chiding my delay.

This could not last for ever; and just when every body thought that I was about to die, I grew better, and to my great joy was put on board a steamboat bound to Louisville. For a day or two I continued to recruit; change of air, scene, and food did wonders: but the happiness of a speedy recovery was not fated to be mine. I had embarked in a steamboat of the largest class, on board of which were four hundred passengers. The weather was excessively hot, there were many sick among us, and the atmosphere between the decks soon became impure. The yellow fever was said to be on board; and our comfortless situation was rendered dreadful by the panic that ensued. I relapsed, and was soon pronounced past recovery. I had the yellow fever, and was considered a fatal bearer of contagion. It was thought proper to remove me from the boat, and to abandon me to my fate, rather than endanger the lives of others.

I was accordingly put on shore; but when or how it happened I know not. I have a faint recollection of being lowered into the yawl, and seeing people gazing at me; I heard one say, "He will die in an hour;" another inquired my name; one voice pitied me; and another said I had made a happy escape from pain. I thought they were about to bury me, and became senseless in an agonizing effort to speak.

When I had recovered my consciousness I found myself in

a cabin on the shore of the Mississippi. A kind family had
received and nursed me, and had brought me back to life after
I had been long insensible. They were poor people, who
made their living by cutting firewood to supply the steamboats;—a lean and sallow family, whose bilious complexions
and attenuated forms attested the withering influence of a corrupted atmosphere. They had the languid southern eye, the
heavy gait and slow speech of persons enervated by burning
sunbeams and humid breezes.

For two weeks I was unable to rise from the miserable
pallet with which their kindness had supplied me. I counted
every log in the wretched cabin—my eye became familiar
with all the coats, gowns, and leathern hunting-shirts that
hung from the rafters—I noticed each crevice—and set down
in my memory all the furniture and cooking utensils. For
fourteen long summer days my eyes had no other employment but to wander over these few objects again and again,
until at last nothing was left to be discovered, and I closed
them in the disgust occasioned by the sameness of the scene,
or strained them in search of something new until my eyeballs ached. But I had no more feverish dreams, and when I
thought of the widow Smith, it was with the delight of a newly
awakened hope, and with the confidence that better days and
brighter scenes awaited me at home.

At last I was able to crawl to the door and to see the sun,
the green trees, and the water. It was a most refreshing sight,
although the landscape itself was any thing but attractive.
The cabin stood on the bank of the river in a low alluvion
bottom. It was surrounded and overhung by a forest of immense trees, whose tall dark trunks rose to the height of sixty
or seventy feet without a branch, and then threw out their
vast lateral boughs and heavy foliage so luxuriantly as entirely
to exclude the sun. Beneath that dense canopy of shade
were long, dark, and gloomy vistas, where the Indian might
well fancy himself surrounded by the spirits of his departed

14

friends. The soil itself had a dismal aspect; the whole surface had been inundated but a few weeks past; the fallen
leaves of last year, saturated and blackened by long immersion,
were covered with a thick deposit of mud, and the reeking
mass sent up volumes of noxious vapour. Before the house
was a naked sand-bar sparkling and glowing with heat. In the
middle of the river was a large *sawyer*, an immense log, the
entire trunk of a majestic oak, whose roots clung to the bottom, while the other end, extending down the stream, rose to
the surface, the current giving it a heavy and eternal motion;
now uprearing some twenty feet of the huge black mass above
the surface, and then sinking it again in the water with the
regular swing of a pendulum. I gazed for hours at that per-
petual seesaw, wondering what law of nature governed its exact
vibrations. Here the hideous alligator might be seen, rocking
through half a day as if in the enjoyment of an agreeable recreation; while droves of those animals, sporting in the stream
or crawling on the beach, roared like so many bulls, filling
the whole forest with their bellowings. Added to those
sounds were the braying of the wolf, the croaking of innumerable frogs, and the buzz of myriads of musquitoes. Under
any other circumstances I should have thought myself in a
pandemonium; but I had in the last few weeks endured so
much pain, passed through so many horrors, and trembled so
often and so long upon the brink of the grave, that I enjoyed
the sun, the breeze, and the verdure, even with these dismal
accompaniments. I was even agreeably situated; for so
great and so pleasing was the change in having my mind
relieved from its abstraction, that I could gaze placidly for
hours upon natural objects of the most common description
and converse with interest on the most trivial subjects. Of
all forms none are so hideous or so terrifying as the horrible
creations of a distempered imagination.

For another fortnight I remained contented, gradually gaining strength; and then finding myself again able to travel, I

took my passage in a steamboat for Louisville. The river was now extremely low, and we advanced slowly, sometimes running aground upon the sand-bars, and always getting forward with difficulty. At length we reached our port, and I sprung with delight upon the soil of Kentucky. Among the steamboats lying along the shore, dismantled and laid up for the season, was the vessel in which I had embarked at New Orleans, a feeble invalid, and which had left me almost a corpse.

My baggage consisted of several well-filled trunks; one of which, a common black leather travelling trunk, I had purchased at New Orleans and packed with articles of finery for my intended bride. On setting me ashore at the wood-cutter's, the captain of the boat had been careful to land my several chattels, and I now proceeded with them to a hotel in Louisville. My baggage was carried into a bar-room crowded with gentlemen, and I had scarcely time to turn round, when a lank, agile Frenchman, with tremendous whiskers, darted forward, and seizing my black trunk, seemed to be about to appropriate to his own use all my nuptial presents.

"That is my trunk, sir," said I.

"Aha, sair! you say dat your tronk? By gar, sair, dat is *not* your tronk!"

"Excuse me, sir, it is undoubtedly mine."

"Ah! ma foi! I shall not excuse you, sair! By gar, sair, if you say dis your tronk you no gentiman."

As he said this he jerked a key from his pocket, thrust it into the lock, threw open the disputed trunk, and to my utter consternation, and the infinite amusement of all others present, displayed a magazine of "sundries" as undoubtedly French as his own accent.

"Dare! vat you say now, sair?" he exclaimed triumphantly, as he threw out the contents, "you say dat your coat? dat your waistcoat? your fiddle-string? your musique note?

your every ting ! by gar, sair, you no gentiman, if you say dat your tronk !"

"I ask your pardon," said I, "the trunk is not mine ; but there is a strange mystery in this affair, which I cannot pretend to unravel."

"Ah, very much mystery, for some oder gentiman get my tronk, and make me wear my linen in dis hot contry for five six week !"

"The fault is not mine ; I purchased a trunk at New Orleans so nearly resembling that one, that if I was not convinced by the contents, I would still think it mine. I am sorry to have been the innocent cause of any inconvenience to you."

"Very well ; I buy my tronk at New Orleans too—dat how he look so much alike ; very sorry for you, sair : but I cannot let you have my tronk, indeed, sair."

I stood mortified and confounded ; cutting a very awkward figure in the presence of a large company, who viewed this odd adventure with astonishment. I began almost to doubt my own identity, and to fancy myself transformed by magic into somebody else. It seemed as if my ill luck was never to cease. I dreaded lest this incident should prove prophetic, and as I had seen my trunk transformed under my very nose into the trunk of another gentleman, I feared that I might find my widow changed into another man's wife. I was somewhat relieved by the captain of the steamboat, who had witnessed this scene, and who now stepped forward and informed me that my trunk, which had been exchanged by mistake, was on board his boat.

Feeling in no mood to visit any of my acquaintances, I directed my course to the counting-house of a merchant, upon whom I held a draft. On handing it to his clerk, he returned it, observing,

"The drawee of this bill is dead, sir ; and we have instructions not to pay it."

15*

" I am the drawee," returned I.

"There must be some mistake," replied the clerk **very**
coldly ; "Mr. M——, in whose favour that bill is drawn, is
certainly dead.   We have it from his heir."

" Heir ! don't you suppose, sir, that I am the best judge
whether I am dead or alive !"

" Can't say, sir—sorry to dispute any gentleman's word—
but my orders—"

"Sir, you don't only dispute my word, you deny my existence—don't you see me, and hear me, and can't you feel me ?"
said I, laying my long, cold hand upon his soft, white palm.

" Very sorry," repeated the book-keeper, withdrawing his
hand as if a viper had touched it, " but my principal is absent
—I act under instructions—and Mr. M——'s account is closed
in our books."

" This is the strangest turn of all," said I to myself, as I
stepped into the street.   " I am dead—my heir has entered
upon the estate—the widow mourns over my grave !   Very
pretty, truly !   I shall next be told that this is not Kentucky,
and that I am not, and never was, Edward M——."

Angry and dispirited, I turned into a public reading-room
and sought for a file of newspapers published in my own
neighbourhood.   I looked for an old date, and soon found—
my own obituary ! and learned that in my untimely death
society had been deprived of a useful member; my kindred,
of an affectionate relative; and my servants, of a kind master !
Upon further research, I stumbled upon a notice from my
administrator—the next of kin—inviting all my debtors to
settle their accounts.   I saw no announcement of the widow's
dissolution—and concluding that her strength of mind had
enabled her to survive my "untimely death," I determined to
set out for home instantly, as well to relieve the burthen of
her sorrows, as to resume the privilege of collecting my own
debts.

After a tiresome journey, I arrived on the night of the

third day in my own neighbourhood. Concealed by the darkness, I reached my own door without being recognised. Two of my negro men stepped up to the carriage as it stopped, and of them, in a disguised voice, I inquired for myself, by my Christian and surname.

"Bless you, sir," replied one of them, "old master's dead and buried long ago!"

"And who is your master now?"

"Why, young master,—old master's nephew, Mr. Charles."

I stepped out of the carriage, and the negroes no sooner beheld my form in the moonlight than they shouted, "A ghost! old master's ghost!" and scampered into the house. I entered after them, but could not obtain an audience of any human being. My servants fled when they perceived me, screaming with surprise and terror. I followed them to the kitchen. It was deserted by all but an old palsied woman. She reminded me that she had been my nurse, that she had served me faithfully all my lifetime, and begged my spirit not to injure her. She asked me affectionately what troubled me, and promised to do any thing in her power to enable me to repose quietly in my grave. She told me I had been a good and kind master, and that all my people liked me while I lived, and besought me not to make them hate my memory, by haunting them after my death. And finally she told me that the spirit of a gentleman *like me*, who had been *well raised*, might find some better employment than that of disturbing a peaceable family and scaring a parcel of poor negroes. I was too much affected to make any reply to old Elsey, and turning from her, stepped into the house. In the hall stood a gentleman and lady, who had been drawn thither by the uproar. They were the "next of kin" and—the widow Smith! The former, being a man of spirit, stood his ground, but the lady screamed and fled.

"Will you be good enough to tell me, sir," said I, "whether I am dead or alive?"

"We have mourned your death," said my nephew, with an embarrassed air, "but I am happy to find that you are alive, and most sincerely welcome you home."

"Supposing the fact to be that I am alive," said I, "will you do me the kindness to tell me whether I am master of this house?"

"Surely you are, and—"

"Do not interrupt me; you are my administrator, I find; do you claim also to be my guardian? these characters are not usually doubled."

"I claim nothing, sir, but an opportunity to explain those matters which seem to have offended you so deeply."

"Then, sir, being master here, and having neither administrator nor guardian, I desire to be alone."

The young man looked offended, and then smiled superciliously, as if he thought me insane, and turning on his heel walked off.

I retired to a chamber, and having with some difficulty drawn my servants about me and convinced them of my identity, took supper and went to bed. About the widow I made no inquiry; circumstances looked so suspicious that I dreaded to hear the truth.

In the morning I rose late. I sallied forth and gazed with delight upon my fields, my trees, and the thousand familiar objects that are comprised within that one endearing word—*home.* My negroes crowded about me, to welcome me, inquire after my health, and tell me all that had happened to them. Passing over these matters as briefly as possible, I proceeded to probe the subject nearest my heart, and—what think you, gentle reader, was the result?—the widow Smith was married to the "next of kin!" They had left my house at the dawn, that morning.

I have only to add that I have entirely recovered my health and spirits; and that as Jerry Smith's widow has twice slipped through my fingers, undervalued my character, slighted my affection, and at last married that wild scamp, my nephew, whom I had before thought of disinheriting, I am determined that neither of them shall ever touch a dollar of my money; and to effect this laudable object I am resolved not to live single, nor die *intestate.*

# MICHEL DE COUCY.

A TALE OF FORT CHARTRES.

———◆◆◆———

ON a pleasant day in September, 1750, two horsemen were
seen slowly winding their way along the road leading by
the margin of the Mississippi river, from the French village
of *Notre Dame de Kaskaskia*, to Fort Chartres.   One of them,
who appeared to be about forty years of age, was a man of
gay and martial appearance.   He wore an elegant military
undress, and rode gracefully on a fine and high-mettled horse.
He was the commandant of Fort Chartres, and in virtue of
that office, governor of the French settlements in Illinois,
which he ruled with a power little less than despotic, but with
a mildness that savoured more of parental than of sovereign
authority.   His companion was the superior of the convent
of Jesuits at Kaskaskia, of whose personal appearance we
have no accurate account; but we suppose that he was a tall,
lank, homely man, with a cunning, mysterious, austere look,
such as monks and superiors of convents usually wear on
public occasions, and who, while he ruled his own little community with a high hand, acquired considerable influence in
the affairs of the colony by his deferential deportment towards
the commander of his majesty's forces.   The riders were fol-

lowed by a small train, which seemed to be paraded rather
for show than for protection, consisting of half a dozen gaudily
dressed huzzars, mounted on the small fiery horses of the
country, which, having run wild in their early years, retained
ever after their original impatience of restraint.

Their way led through that beautiful plain which is now
called the American bottom, an extensive tract of rich, flat,
alluvial soil, which lies along the eastern shore of the Mississippi and Illinois, and reaches from the river to the bluffs,
and which is justly regarded as containing the greatest body
of fertile land in this country, or perhaps in the universe.
Part of this plain is covered with timber, the remainder is
open prairie, and the whole interspersed with groves of vine
and native fruit. Here are to be seen the indigenous productions of this climate in the greatest variety and highest perfection. The tallest cotton-wood and sycamore trees, which
rear their enormous shafts to an amazing height, are covered
with vines equally aspiring, while the thickets are matted
together with smaller vines, and loaded with innumerable
clusters of fine grapes. Our travellers beheld groves of the
wild apple, whose blossoms in the spring season fill the air
of this region with a delightful fragrance, and whose limbs
were now bending under loads of useless fruit. They saw
hundreds of acres covered with the wild plumb, of which
there are many varieties, deepening in colour from a light
yellow to a deep crimson, and the ripe fruit of which now
hung in amazing quantities, and in appearance rich and beautiful beyond description. The walnut, the peccan, and other
fine nuts abounded, the whole combining with the remarkable
beauty of the autumn sky in this country, and the serenity
and mildness of the atmosphere, to fill the mind with ideas of
luxury and plenty.

The plain, which at some places spreads out to the breadth
of twelve miles, was confined to a narrow strip, at the point
now travelled by the riders whom we have described, and

their path, which sometimes approached the river, at others. wound along the foot of the bluffs, a ridge of abrupt hills rising perpendicularly to the height of more than a hundred feet, and supposed to have been anciently washed by the Mississippi. Advancing into the Prairie de Rocher, they beheld an open plain, bounded on one side by the river, and on the other by a tall barrier of solid rock, whose summit projects over its base, and whose highest points, which are beautifully rounded, are covered with rich soil and prairie grass, and here and there ornamented with a single tree. At the foot of this rock, and extending thence to the river, was a large village, called, in reference to its situation, the village of Prairie de Rocher. Adjoining this was a large enclosure called the " Common Field," which was held in severalty by the inhabitants, each of whom owned a greater or less number of acres, according to his ability, and the whole of which was surrounded by a common fence without partitions. Each person cultivated his own part, and had a right to pasturage at proper seasons in proportion to the quantity of his land; and the whole business of fencing, tilling, and pasturing, was regulated by village ordinances, and conducted with a harmony which is not known to have existed in any other community similarly situated. Lots in the " Common Field" were held by purchase or grant from the French crown, the rest of the ground in and around the village was held by the inhabitants *in common*, and portions of it were reduced to private property by a simple procedure. When a young man married, or a person wished *to settle* in the village, an instrument of writing was drawn and signed by all the inhabitants, vesting in him the fee-simple of a lot for building, and equal rights with the others in their common property. But we detain the reader too long from the gay and gentle company who were about to honour the rustic villagers with their august presence.

They had passed the Common Field, now covered with a

ripening crop of Indian corn, and were entering the village
when their attention was attracted by a crowd of persons assembled in front of the cottage of Michel de Coucy.   Honest
Michel himself, who when at home usually sat under a
spreading catalpa before his own door, with a red cap on his
head, and a short black pipe in his mouth, the very emblem
of content and placid composure, now stood in the midst of
the concourse, weeping, raving, and threatening, with the most
vehement gestures.   He was a small, thin, dark man, with
black hair, and an eye that he might have been suspected of
inheriting from the aborigines, had not his character been so
genuinely French as fully to redeem the purity of descent.
He was as honest as gay, and as contented a soul as ever
breathed, famed for the simplicity and benevolence of his character, as well as for a vein of humour, which rendered him at
all times an agreeable companion.   In fact, to smoke his pipe,
to do kind actions, and to tell pleasant tales and sly jests,
seemed to be the business of his life, his other occupations
being of secondary importance.   Born in the wilds of Canada,
and reared in the woods and upon the water, he was equally
at home, whether paddling his canoe to the sources of our
largest rivers, or wandering alone through the trackless forest.
After his emigration to the borders of the Mississippi, his
chief occupation became that of a boatman, and none pulled
a better oar or sung with truer cadence the animating notes
of the boat song than Michel de Coucy.   The Canadian boatmen are the hardiest and merriest of men; if their boat is
stranded they plunge into the water in all weathers, diving
and swimming about as if in their native element; if it
storms, they sleep or revel under the protection of a high
bank, and whether pulling down the stream, or pushing labo-
riously against it, the shores ring with their voices.   One will
recount his adventures, another will imitate the Indian yell,
the roar of the alligator, the hissing of the snake, or the chat-
tering of the paroquet; and anon the whole will chant their

rude ditties concerning the dangers of rapids, snags, and sawyers, or the pleasures of home, the vintage, and the dance. Michel was an adept at all these things, and he loved them as a Cossack loves plunder, or a Dutchman hard work and money. He was the darling of the crew, for he could skin a deer, cook a fish, scrape a chin or a fiddle with equal adroitness, and always performed such offices so good-humouredly, that his companions, in compliment to his universal genius, kept it in continual employment. When the boat was in motion he was always tugging at the oar or the fiddle-bow, when it landed, and the crew sat round their camp fire, he cooked, sung, and told merry stories; on Sunday he shaved the whole company, even at the risk of neglecting his own visage, and was after all the merriest and most respectable man in the boat. With all this, Michel was temperate and careful of his earnings, which he shrewdly husbanded in a leathern purse during every voyage, and handed over on his return to his wife, who hid them under the floor of their cabin. Such talents could not fail to bring honour and promotion to their possessor; Michel became popular among his comrades, and having acquired experience in his craft, in a few years rose to the charge of a boat and the title of captain.

Having acquired a decent competency by the time he reached the meridian of life, Michel thought it expedient, and his wife thought so too, that he should consult his own comfort for the rest of his days. He therefore abandoned his frail cabin, which in truth was beginning to stumble about his ears, and built a goodly house with substantial mud walls, surrounded on all sides by cool piazzas, and planted his yard full of catalpas and black locusts. He purchased a large lot in the common field, and took unto himself herds of black cattle and droves of French ponies.

Michel, however, still loved the water, and like a sprightly spaniel, could be induced to leap into it upon the slightest invitation. He continued to make a voyage of three or four months annually, and spent the remainder of his time in cultivating his crop, smoking his pipe, attending the king-balls, and playing the fiddle. He had his crosses like other men: his chimney often smoked, and Madame Felicité, his wife, sometimes got out of temper; his cattle occasionally had the murrain, the frost nipped his corn, and more than once he lost both boat and cargo by running on the snags and sawyers of the Mississippi. But none of these things ever disturbed the placid spirit of Michel; a single shrug, and a " *Sacre !*" were the strongest symptoms of emotion which ever were elicited from him by such disasters, and he would most frequently smile, and exclaim in the moment of misfortune, " *C'est toute le même chose.*" It is said that he could even bear the breaking of a fiddle-string, a lecture from his wife, or a public admonition from the priest for not going to confession, with the same composure which he preserved on less provoking occasions. He had his joys, too, and these greatly predominated. His wife was an excellent manager, made charming *gumbo soup*, and could interpret dreams; his daughter, Genevieve, was as fair as the swans that sailed on the Mississippi; and his neighbours loved him. He was head man at the balls; for as they had no hireling fiddlers in those days, the honourable office of musician was filled in turn by such heads of families as were blessed with musical ears and limber elbows; and none touched the violin so cleverly as Michel, who continually cheered the dancers with his voice, as he kept time with head and feet. Happy days of equality and glee! when every man who owned a cabin, a car, and a pony was a French gentleman, when the evening gun of the fort and the matin bell of the chapel were daily heard; and the song and dance prevailed, wherever a plank floor, a French girl, and a fiddle could be paraded.

Such being the character and standing of worthy Michel de Coucy, it is not surprising that the whole village of Prairie de Rocher should have been astonished at beholding him in the attitudes of rage and grief, swearing and wailing, and beating the air with his clenched fists; nor that even such august personages, as the commandant of Fort Chartres and the superior of the Jesuits at Notre Dame de Kaskasia, should marvel thereat. Nor was Michel a man whose sorrows would be slightly viewed by his neighbours; he had as large a house, as much land, and as many horned brutes and ponies as the best of them; and a man in easy circumstances is always sure of sympathy when in trouble. Michel, moreover, was popular; and when the voice of distress issued from his cottage, every one ran to condole with him; even the commandant and the superior of the Jesuits felt it incumbent on them to rein up their steeds and inquire the cause of this unusual disturbance.

It seems that Michel having been many years employed as a carrier of merchandise for others, began at last to think that he might as well freight his boat upon his own account; and had for the last two or three years dabbled pretty extensively in the ticklish business of buying and selling. The long-cherished hoard of Spanish dollars, which his wife had buried under the cabin-floor, had been transferred, when he removed to his new house, to a similar place of deposit, a plank having been left unfastened for that express purpose. But when he embarked in traffic, those silver coins were exchanged for furs, the furs for goods, wares, and merchandise, and the latter for notes of hand and fair promises. Still Michel and his wife were content; for the nominal sum secured by fair words and due-bills trebled the actual amount that had been disbursed in hard money, and they doubted not that it would all come in, in due time. But in the mean while he had entered into some pecuniary engagements which could be discharged only with cash, and found himself in an embarrassing situation. He had never before owed money, and had now to face a creditor for the first time! In this dilemma, being unwilling to publish his situation to his own

neighbours, he bethought himself of a certain Pedro Garcia,
a Spaniard, who lived on the opposite side of the river, in
a wilderness track of broken country, where no law was
known, and where the military arm of the French authority
could scarcely reach him.   This Pedro was a black-whiskered,
ill-looking fellow, who had amassed a large fortune, nobody
knew how.   He had a farm, and a good many slaves; he
traded with the Indians, who hated him, and went often to
New Orleans, were he lost and won large sums by gambling,
and was more than once in the hands of the police.   Nobody
liked Pedro; the French had little to say to him, and the Indians looked with distrust at the long dirk which he carried
rather ostentatiously in his bosom.   But Michel wanted money, and Pedro had it, and without more ado, the distressed
Frenchman applied to the Spaniard for a loan.   Pedro, who
knew that Michel was abundantly able to repay him, and
saw that he was only hard pressed at the moment, in conse-
qnence of his reluctance to call upon those who owed him,
readily advanced the sum required, taking Michel's bond for
the amount, payable at the end of six months, with usury.

The six months soon rolled round, and Michel was not
prepared to pay his bond.   He had waited from day to day
in the vain hope that his debtors would discharge their dues;
and at last finding that they did not come forward voluntarily, he deferred from hour to hour the disagreeable task of
dunning them, because it was so abhorrent to his feelings,
that he could not muster sufficient resolution to undertake it.
The day of payment came, and with it came Pedro Garcia,
and Michel was constrained to acknowledge that he could not
fulfil his engagement.   Garcia knit his black brows and
swore like a trooper, and although his debtor spoke fairly and
humbly, and made liberal propositions, the relentless creditor
would take nothing but his money, and forthwith hied to the
civil magistrate of the village..   The minister of the law
heard the application with surprise, and expressed in emphatic

language his astonishment that a subject of Spain should think of suing a subject of the Grand Monarque, within the territory of France, and above all that he should have the assurance to propose to employ an officer of the French crown, in so flagrant an act of contumacy. "The laws of France," said this worthy functionary, "are made for the benefit of the French people and the honour of their king, and not for Spaniards, and my duty is to administer those laws to my fellow-subjects, not to foreigners. Go, you are not under my jurisdiction—I know nothing of you,—and am only in doubt whether your attempt to employ the laws of my country against a Frenchman is not a high misdemeanour."

Pedro, finding that he could obtain no satisfaction from the civil authority, determined to resort to the military, and as the commandant was absent, laid the matter before his lieutenant. This gentleman called to his assistance the chaplain, a very worthy priest, who having been long attached to the army, was experienced in questions of *meum* and *tuum*, and being thus fortified, proceeded to hear the complaint, and examine the papers of Pedro Garcia.

"*Ma foi!* what is this?" exclaimed Captain de la Val, as he glanced his eye over the unlucky instrument of writing, laid before him by the Spaniard.

"It is Michel de Coucy's bond, for the sum I loaned him," replied the plaintiff.

"*Diable!* how shall I know this to be a bond, seeing that it is written in an unknown tongue?"

"It is Spanish, a language which your excellency no doubt speaks with the elegance and propriety of a native Castilian."

"You do my excellency unmerited honour, and must permit me to inform you, that *officially* I am not to be presumed to know any other language than my own."

"The purport of the instrument," said Garcia, "may readily be ascertained by means of an interpreter."

"Indeed !" exclaimed the officer, "can you not also provide a deputy-commanding officer to perform the rest of my
duty ?   If I must read your papers by proxy, I may as well
decide in the same way."

"Captain de la Val," said the priest, "takes a very proper and nice distinction.   The first step in the adjustment of
a controversy is to ascertain the true intent and meaning of
the contract between the parties litigant, and it would ill become the dignity of any high tribunal to entrust the decision of that important point to an irresponsible agent."

"What shall I do ?" inquired the alarmed money-lender.

"That I cannot tell," replied the officer ; "of this, however,
I am clear, that a paper written in Spanish can be of no
validity in a French court, for there would be an obvious
absurdity in requiring the ministers of justice, whether civil or
military, to decide on that which they cannot read."

"Besides," said the priest, who began to envy the wisdom
of the captain, "his most Christian Majesty has appointed
notaries whose business it is to draw such writings between
parties, and as this paper was not drawn by a proper notarial
scribe, we cannot know whether it is in due form of law."

"What matters it about form," said the Spaniard, "if the
writing contains a substantial promise ?"

"My son," replied the chaplain, "you do not understand
these matters.   If a man makes a verbal engagement, the
form thereof is not material, because in that case the creditor
trusts to the honour and honesty of the debtor, and the latter
is bound in conscience not to abuse that confidence ; but if
the parties reduce their contract to writing, the creditor re-
poses his trust, not in the virtue of the other party, but in the
binding operations of the law, and if the work of the law is
not made secure, the creditor must lose thereby, for he looked
to that only for his payment."

"My bond is sufficient in law," contended Pedro; "it is in
the form used by our Spanish notaries."

"Worse and worse," exclaimed the priest; "if his excellency the commanding officer should undertake to decide upon the validity of a writing authenticated by a Spanish functionary, it would doubtless be considered by his most Cathalic Majesty as a very indelicate interference, inasmuch as he would be enforced, not only to weigh the language and construe the laws of Spain, but to look into the acts of the civil magistrates of that nation ; and the consequence might be a war between two Christian princes."

Pedro Garcia, though he could not comprehend how the settling of a dispute between himself and Michel de Coucy could become the cause of war between two European kings, began to think that possibly he had mistaken his remedy, and making a sulky bow was about to retire, when Captain de la Val called him back and said,

"Senor Garcia, it is well known that Michel is no scholar, how then could he execute that bond ?"

"He has made his mark," replied the other, showing the cross at the foot of the bond.

"Aha ! but that same cross might stand with equal propriety for the name of any Catholic in Christendom."

"But I can prove by the notary that Michel made it."

"Like enough; but Michel does not understand Spanish, how then could he know the contents of that paper ?"

"It was interpreted to him."

"But how can I know that it was interpreted correctly ? In short," continued the officer, "I am induced to believe that this document is a forgery, and that it is my duty to lodge you in the guard chamber, until the return of the commandant."

"And if it be a forgery," added the priest, "there is little doubt in my mind that the counterfeiting the sign of the cross is an offence against our holy church, and of much higher grade than a common forgery."

Pedro, finding that the aspect of his case grew darker every moment, and fearing that he might be in the end handed over

16

to the inquisition, began to supplicate for mercy, and being permitted to retire, hastily made good his retreat, marvelling at the strange turn in his affairs, which, from a simple creditor of Michel de Coucy, had converted him into an enemy of his Holiness the Pope and his most Christian Majesty the King of France.

Michel, who, when he saw Pedro take the road to Fort Chartes, had suspected his business, and hastily followed him, entered the quarters of Captain de la Val during the conference above described; and standing respectfully with his cap in his right hand, his left stuck in his waistband, and his mouth wide open, listened in mute admiration of the wisdom and nice sense of justice displayed by the priest and officer. As Pedro retired, he slipped after him, and, tapping him on the shoulder as he passed out of the main gate, said triumphantly, "*Bon jour*, Senor Garcia, your bond is too small—it will not cover the sore place! it is not worth a sous! Now come to my house when you get in a good humour and I will make a new bargain to pay you all I owe, and give you the word of honour of a French gentleman, which, Father Felix says, is better than a Spanish bond." Pedro paused a moment and laid his hand on his dirk—then turned on his heel and retired, without deigning to reply.

When he reached home he was half inclined to turn back and embrace Michel's offer, but still believing that a bond, good or bad, was better than any parol engagement, he hastened to his friend the notary, on his own side of the river, and having informed him of all that had passed, requested him, when Michel should next cross into their territory, to have him arrested for his debt. To his surprise, the notary declined interfering in the business, highly extolling the good sense and courtesy displayed by the French functionaries, and declaring that he knew no law under which a Spaniard could sue a Frenchman, and that at all events it was extremely proper and decorous that the officers of France should abstain from

meddling in matters of such high import, which ought to be
left to ministers plenipotentiary, or to the crowned heads
themselves.

"Then the long and short of the matter is," said Pedro,
as he retired, "that I am to be cheated out of my money;"
and he forthwith prayed to all the saints of whom he had any
knowledge, to visit with special maledictions, the heads of
Michel de Coucy, Chevalier Jean Philippe de la Val, Father
Felix the priest, and all others directly or indirectly concerned
in preventing him from recovering the amount nominated in
his bond, with interest thereon, at the rate of ten per cent.
per annum until paid.

People who live on the frontier imbibe very accurate
notions of justice, and adopt summary modes of obtaining
it; and Senor Pedro Garcia, not being a man to sit down
quietly after a loss, and finding the door of the law closed
against him, began to cast about for some other remedy.
After brooding over the matter for several days, he at length
devised a plan; and getting into his canoe in the night, paddled secretly over to the Illinois shore, where he remained
concealed in a thicket, until Genevieve, the daughter of
Michel, passing that way alone, he sallied out, and making her his prisoner, carried her off, leaving a placard in
these words, "Meshell Coosy! French rascal! pay me my
money, and you shall have your daughter!" Genevieve was
a beautiful child of twelve years of age, the pride of the village, and the darling of her parents. She had seen Pedro
before, and always with repulsive feelings; and when she
found herself rudely seized by him, sued piteously for mercy,
believing that he would sell her to the Sioux, the English, or
the Long Knives, "of whom by parcels she had something
heard,"—or to some other outlandish people, to be eaten at
a great war-feast. Pedro, without regarding her cries, bore
her to a secluded place, among the broken hills, and, summon-

ing a score of his associates and dependents, prepared to make a stout resistance in case of pursuit.

When Michel discovered the outrage committed against him, in the person of his child, on whom he doated, he was inconsolable; not only were his parental feelings awakened, but his sense of honour was touched to the quick. He wept, raved, swore strange oaths, and vowed bitter vengeance. All who were acquainted with him knew that, gentle as he was, he was brave; he had been accustomed to face danger from his childhood; and when they heard the deep imprecations which he now poured forth, they were satisfied that Pedro would pay dearly for the cruel insult he had perpetrated. The whole male population of the village immediately volunteered to accompany him to the rescue; and the distressed father, after thanking them with tears of gratitude, urged them to arm themselves without delay. It was at this juncture that the commandant and the superior of the Jesuits opportunely arrived, and having heard of the circumstances, Michel was enjoined to proceed no further in his plan of revenge, the commandant promising to take immediate measures for the restoration of his daughter.

Michel, who, believing that in wisdom, power, and goodness the commandant was second only to the king, was greatly composed by this assurance, and although his fellow-villagers continued to be ripe for an immediate inroad into the wilderness where Pedro lurked, he restrained their ardour, and passed the night in more tranquillity than could have been expected. Early on the following morning he received a summons to attend the commandant at Fort Chartres, which was distant two miles from the village; and set out, with Madame Felicité, in one of those commodious vehicles, half-chaise and half-cart, which were fashionable among the Canadian French of those days, and are still to be seen in daily use among their descendants, at the famous village of *Vide Poche*, otherwise called Carondelet, in Missouri.

Fort Chartres was at that time the largest and most extensive fortification owned by the French in America, and was the seat of government for all their settlements in Illinois. Its shape was a regular quadrangle, with bastions at the angles, the sides of the exterior polygon being four hundred and ninety feet in extent; and the walls, which were two feet and two inches thick and twelve feet high, were built of stone, and plastered over. It was pierced all round, at regular distances, with loopholes for musketry, and had two port-holes for cannon in each face, and two in the flanks of each bastion. If any of my fair readers, who are desirous to know the exact description of this celebrated fortress, should be anxious to ascertain what is meant by "an irregular quadrangle with bastions at the angles," I am happy to inform them that they may obtain an exact idea of the figure intended to be described, by laying on the table before them an old-fashioned square pincushion, of which one side is a little longer than the other three, with large tassels at the corners. Such was precisely the shape of Fort Chartres. Within the walls were extensive buildings of stone, for the accommodation of the garrison :— a fine house for the commandant, quarters for the officers, and barracks for the soldiers, together with a great magazine, a chapel, and a snug cell for the priest, who officiated here, and at the village of Fort Chartres adjacent. This was the strong hold of power and the seat of festivity ; here, on all suitable occasions, were assembled the rank, beauty, and fashion of the colony ; and here could be paraded as many handsome French girls as one could wish to behold.

Michel entered the main gate of the fort, with a countenance of sorrow, far different from his usual gaiety, when he came to head-quarters an invited guest ; and his feelings could be with difficulty restrained when he beheld the dark visage of Pedro Garcia. The latter had been induced to give his attendance by a missive from the commandant, assuring him of a safe-conduct to and from the fort, and that all amicable

means would be used to settle the unfortunate difference between Michel and himself.   Being naturally bold and impudent, and finding, too, that the delicate little Genevieve was
withering like a plucked flower, and was at best a troublesome guest,—he came at the summons, and stood confronted
with the incensed Frenchman.   There, too, came all the relations of Michel and Felicité, and divers other of the villagers,
burning with indignation—there stood Captain de la Val,
Father Felix, the magistrate, and the notary, as dignified and
complacent as if nothing had happened—and there sat several
aged chiefs of the Kaskaskia tribe, in grave and solemn expectation, wondering at the levity of the whites, who could
hold a counsel on a matter of such high import, without making
presents, tendering the wampum, and smoking the great pipe.

The commandant examined the bond, heard the evidence
and the decisions of his lieutenant, and of the civil officers on
both sides of the river.   He pronounced the conduct of all the
functionaries, civil and military, to have been highly decorous
and proper, and hoped that, in future, no Spaniard would
presume to sue a Frenchman without his leave first had and
obtained.   He censured Pedro for the violent capture of the
innocent Genevieve, and finally decreed that the latter should
be safely returned to her parents, that Michel should pay to
Pedro the principal borrowed without interest, the latter being withheld as a fine for the violence committed in the French
territory, and that both the parties litigant should stand committed until this sentence should be fully complied with.
Pedro remonstrated against the latter part of the decree, as
a breach of his safe-conduct, but the commandant decided
that he had guaranteed his safety in *going* and *coming*, but
he had not precluded himself from fixing the length of time
during which he should have the pleasure of Senor Garcia's
company.   The latter, finding himself entrapped, made a
merit of necessity, and despatched an order for the little
Genevieve, who was soon given to her parents' arms.

We cannot describe their joy, nor the spontaneous burst of sympathy which ran through the assembly, when the lost child was restored. The Indians, who had sat motionless as statues throughout the whole scene, preserving an inflexibility of muscle which nothing could change, rose when they beheld this affecting meeting, and said to each other, "Very good." One of them then stepped forward, and addressing the commandant, said, "Father, we came to see you do justice; we opened our ears, and our hearts are satisfied. The cunning black serpent crawled into the nest of the turtle, and stole away the young dove; but our father is an eagle, very strong and brave; he is wiser than the serpent; he has brought back the young dove, and the old turtles sing with joy. Father, we are satisfied, it is all very good. We bid you farewell." Then advancing to the commandant, each of the chiefs gave his right hand, and stalked out of the audience chamber, without deigning to notice any other person.

As for Michel, he had now no difficulty in paying his debt; for those who owed him, when they found that his misfortune had grown out of their own delinquency, immediately raised among them the sum required; and Michel retired well satisfied, but convinced of three truths, which he continued to maintain through life: first, that French laws surpass all others in wisdom and justice; second, that Spaniards with black whiskers are not to be trusted; and third, that it is safer to bury money under the floor than to embark it in traffic; and he thereupon made a vow to his patron saint, that whenever the leathern bag should be replenished, it should be restored to a place of deposit, there to remain as a talisman against the like misfortune in future.

NOTE.—This tale was suggested by an incident which really occurred in the early history of the French settlements in Illinois. A lady was still living there, a few years ago, who had been captured when a child by a creditor of her father, and carried to the opposite side of the river, where she was detained until the debt was arranged. Although the country on both

sides of the river was under the same jurisdiction, some amusing negotia-
tions took place, in consequence of the ignorance of the parties of that fact
and of their respective rights.    In our picture, the French officers are supposed to have humoured the mistake for the joke of the thing, as well as for
the sake of rescuing the child from durance.    There were no newspapers in
those days, and the schoolmaster was not abroad, wherefore honest Michel
and his friends may be pardoned for supposing that the King of Spain
ruled the western side of the Mississippi.

# THE EMIGRANTS.

THE events of the present little tale which I am about to relate, occurred some ten or fifteen years ago, when the western states were yet in their minority, and pretended not to vie in wealth or population with their blooming and accomplished sisters in the east. It is true, that our people had some vague notions of their own importance, and would sometimes talk of their *birth-rights* and their *future greatness* in a strain that would make a stranger stare. Accustomed to the contemplation of great mountains, long rivers, and boundless plains, the majestic features of their country swelled their ideas, and gave a ting of romance to their conceptions. The immense cotton-woods and sycamores that overhung their rivers, the huge alligator that bellowed in the stream, and the great mammoth bones imbedded in their swamps became familiar standards of comparison; while their long journeys over boundless plains teeming with the products of nature, gave them exalted notions of the magnificence of their country. One would have thought they were speaking in parables, who heard them describing the old thirteen states as a mere appendage of the future republic—a speck on the map of the United States—a sort of out-lot with a cotton field at

16*

one end and a manufactory of wooden clocks at the other;
yet they were in sober earnest.

The season of the year was that which poets delight
to describe: when the birds are singing their sweetest notes,
and the trees assuming the beautiful hues of spring. The
snows were melting on the mountains, and the channels of
those little streams which, at a later season, murmured
quietly along their valleys, were now filled to their brinks
with foaming torrents. The Ohio was swollen to a great
flood, filling its deep channel to the brim; and its tide was
crowded with the vessels and passengers who throng the great
avenues of commerce at this propitious season. Among the
boats were many of that description in which families
emigrating to the West usually descended the Ohio, before the
introduction of steamboats into general use. These were
large flat-boats, unfit to stem the current, and so constructed
as to float with the stream. Though slow and unwieldy,
they were large, safe, and roomy, affording space enough for
families, merchandise, and even cattle.

One fine morning, a boat of the kind described was seen
to approach the landing-place at a small town on the Ohio.
The passengers sprung joyously ashore, as if delighted to
escape from their confinement. It was an English family,
just arrived from the old country. Mr. Edgarton, the head
of this little band of adventurers, was a man of about thirty-
five, sprightly, and good-looking, but rather oddly accoutred;
for his dress exhibited a whimsical mixture of fashion and
rudeness. He wore cambric ruffles, a diamond breast-pin, a
dandy waistcoat, and a store of jewelry appended to a gold
watch-chain; but his nether limbs were clad in long spatter-
dashes, reaching to the knee, a farmer's coarse frock covered
his shoulders, and a great fur cap was on his head. He was
equipped, moreover, with a powder-horn, shot-pouch, and bird-
bag, and held in his hand an elegant double-barrelled gun. We
mention these things to show how difficult it is for men

to throw off their accustomed habits, and to assume those which are suitable to a change of country or condition. Mr. Edgarton, when at home, was a modest, and a well-dressed man; but in attemping to assume the guise of a farmer and the equipment of a hunter, had jumbled together a grotesque assortment of costume, which gave him the appearance of a stage-player dressed for exhibition, more than that of a plain man of business, which was his real character. His wife was a genteel, handsome woman; a neat article, and neatly put up; for her dress was as graceful as herself; and the children, some four or five in number, looked as fresh and rosy as the morning. Then there was a maid, a grayhound, a pug-dog, and a parrot, all in good order and well conditioned.

There was another member of the family, whom I have reserved, as in duty bound, for a separate mention. This was Mr. Edgarton's sister, a fair lady whose age, if it be not impolite to specify too particularly on so delicate a point, was somewhere on the *right side* of twenty. A maiden sister is a very creditable and useful appendage in any gentleman's family. If she happens to be young, pretty, sentimental, and affected, nothing can be more amusing; while the opposite of these qualities most generally elevate her into a rational companion. Julia Edgarton was handsome enough to pass for a beauty in any country; she was sentimental enough to admire the beauties of nature, yet not so sentimental as to travel with a pencil in her hand or a book in her reticule; she had just affectation enough to be very agreeable, for a handsome woman should always have a slight tinge of coquetry; she had taste enough to enjoy the writings of Scott, but not so much as to enable her to dream over the rhapsodies of Byron. In short, she was a sensible, clever girl, and that is saying as much as it becomes any grave historian to say of a young lady—especially if there is any chance that his work will ever be reviewed in England.

The goods and chattels of this party were numerous, but
not bulky, nor particularly well assorted.  The *knick-nacks*
considerably outnumbered the useful articles—indeed, there
was no end to those *nondescript* contrivances which brother
Jonathan very aptly denominates *notions*.  Of household furniture there was but little; of farming utensils there was
rather more than a little; the latter consisting chiefly of new
inventions, remarkably neat and useless—horse-rakes, patent
ploughs, straw-cutters, and man-traps.  The heaviest article
of transportation was the wardrobe, which was sufficient to
have furnished a respectable slop-shop.  The stores of linen
and flannel, the dozens upon dozens of night-caps and socks,
the coats, great-coats, frock-coats, coatees, and surtouts, provided to suit every occasion and contingency, were absolutely
miraculous.

Although Mr. Edgarton was going *to farm* in a new country, he had not been a farmer at home.  He was a mercantile clerk in London, who by his assiduity and good management had been able not only to support his family respecta-
bly, but to lay by each year a small portion of his earnings.
He had never been out of London until latterly, when, beginning to feel independent, he was induced on several successive holydays to make excursions into the country, accompanied by his wife; whereby his mind was improved, and his
thirst for travelling increased to such an extent, that he ventured at last to a watering-place on the coast, where he spent
a week.  He became enamoured of the country, and began
to talk of rustic pursuits and sturdy independence, fresh air,
rosy cheeks, and healthy peasants.  His wife threw aside all
her songs, except such as treated of cottages and love, innocence and rural felicity.  He determined to study agriculture,
and immediately purchased "Speed the Plough," "The
Farmer's Boy," "The Cotter's Saturday Night," and "The
Shepherd of Salisbury Plain," all of which he read with such
delight and advantage, that he soon determined to exchange

the smoke of London for the pure air of the country. While in this state of mind he heard golden accounts of the back settlements in America, and was easily persuaded to emigrate to the land of promise. Of his voyage across the Atlantic, and his journey from the sea-board, I shall not speak, as they were like most other voyages and travels, very dull and tiresome. They had been floating for many days down the smooth current of the Ohio, when they found it convenient to halt for a few hours at the rude hamlet to which we alluded above.

After sauntering through the village, the members of our voyaging party were about to re-embark, when a person approached them, and without the ceremony of an introduction, inquired civilly of Mr. Edgarton, if he would accommodate him with a passage in his boat. Surprised at the abruptness of the salutation, the eyes of the whole party were turned towards the stranger. He was a young man apparently not more than twenty-one years of age. His athletic form was clothed in the common dress of the Western hunter. A loose hunting-shirt of blue cotton trimmed with yellow fringe, and confined about the waist with a broad leathern belt, set off his person to the best advantage. From one shoulder was suspended a powder-horn, from the other a huge leathern pouch, in the belt of which rested a long knife. There was nothing remarkable in his appearance, except that his form towered above the ordinary height, and that a rifle which he held carelessly in his hand was double the size of an ordinary weapon, and seemed fit only for the grasp of a giant. His cheek had the flush of youth, his eye was mild, and his countenance open and ingenuous, yet the rifle and the hunting-knife gave him so much the appearance of an assassin in the inexperienced eyes of the Englishman, that the latter was not a little startled at being addressed by such an apparition with:

"Pray, sir, can I get the favour of a passage down the river in your boat?"

The first sensation of a travelling Englishman which is awakened on such an occasion is that of pride ; and Mr. Edgarton, being quite indignant at being asked to *take a passenger*, replied coldly, "Mine is not a passage boat!"

"So I supposed from her looks ; she seems to be rather a crazy kind of concern, but I am not particular about that ; I can put up with any thing."

"We have no wish to increase our company," said the Englishman.

The young man looked surprised, and seemed to think himself rudely treated ; his eye brightened, and the colour deepened upon his cheek, but without making any reply he turned on his heel and walked away.

The boat was again shoved out into the stream, and floated heavily on its course. Nothing worthy of note occurred until the following evening about sunset, when, as they drifted near the shore, our emigrants beheld, on passing a little headland, a deer standing on the margin of the stream from which he was drinking. They came upon him so suddenly, as the boat turned the wooded point behind which he had been concealed from them, that on first discovering him they were near enough to distinguish all the lineaments of his fine form, and even to see the flashing of his dark eye as he gazed for an instant at the boat. It was but an instant, when he turned to fly ; but at the same moment the report of a rifle was heard, and the graceful animal, after a few leaps, fell upon the sand. The hunter, who had been concealed in a tuft of willows that overhung the river, now sprung from his covert and approached his victim. As he advanced, the deer discovered his enemy, and, starting nimbly to his feet, prepared to avenge himself. He swelled with rage, madness flashed from his eyeballs, and all his motions showed that a momentary ferocity had banished the timidity of his nature and overcome the

sense of pain and of weakness. The boatmen, who knew with
what vindictive and desperate courage a wounded deer will
turn upon his assailant, gazed in silent anxiety as they beheld
the hunter standing alone upon the sandy beach, exposed to
the assault of the enraged animal. As the furious beast
rushed upon him with his head down and his sharp antlers
thrown forward, the hunter stepped nimbly aside, and for
that time avoided the deadly thrust, while the spectators
loudly shouted their applause. But the active animal was
not to be thus foiled, and suddenly turning he rushed again
upon his enemy, and in an instant beat him to the ground
with his fore feet; then rising quickly upon his hinder legs
he continued to jump upon the prostrate hunter, striking so
rapidly and violently with his fore hoofs, that the blows were
distinctly heard as they fell in quick succession on the ground.
But the hunter lost none of his presence of mind under these
appalling circumstances, and by dint of rolling and dodging
contrived to avoid his adversary's blows, until, watching a
favourable moment, he suddenly sprang up and threw his
left arm round the animal's neck, while with the right he
plunged his long hunting-knife deep in his side.

Curiosity, as well as concern for the fate of the hunter, now
induced some of the boatmen to jump into the small skiff
which usually accompanies such boats and to row to the shore.
They soon returned, bringing the hunter and his spoil, and our
travellers were not a little surprised to recognise in the former
the same young man who on the day before had solicited a
passage in their boat. The meeting was equally unexpected
to him, and he would have returned immediately to the shore,
had not Mr. Edgarton pressed him to remain with a cordiality
which sufficiently atoned for his former rudeness.

The young stranger, whom we shall call Logan, was a
native of Kentucky, who had been reared in the practice of
all the athletic exercises and sports of his country, while his
intellect had been cultivated by the best instruction which

that region afforded.  His fine form and vigorous understanding corresponded well with each other, and he possessed in a
high degree that hilarity of disposition and ease of manner
which so often distinguish his countrymen.  Having studied
law, he determined to emigrate to a newer State than his own,
and had reached the Ohio river when the accidental loss of
his horse, and the want of means to purchase another, induced
him to proceed on foot.  He accordingly sold his saddle, bridle,
and other equipments, and having purchased a rifle and hunting-shirt, was about to renew his journey, when the boat of
Mr. Edgarton stopped at the village in which he happened to
be.  Disappointed in his attempt to procure a passage, he
manfully threw the small valise containing his wardrobe over
his shoulder, and struck into the woods about the same time
at which the Englishman's boat departed; but as the latter
floated with the current round a circuitous bend of the river,
while Mr. Logan pursued a shorter path which led across the
country, they met again as we have stated.

Where all parties are disposed to be pleased with each
other, cordiality is quickly established.  The family of Edgarton, accustomed to the excitement of a city life, and to the
enjoyment of the various expedients by which the idle hours
of persons in easy circumstances are amused in the British
metropolis, had begun to tire of the silence and monotony of
the forest and the confinement of a boat.  To them, therefore,
the accession of an agreeable member to their party was not an
unimportant event; and no sooner did Mr. Edgarton ascertain
that the person whom he had before treated with so much indifference was a gentleman of easy manners and cultivated mind,
than he felt his curiosity awakened and feelings of kindness
springing up in his bosom towards the stranger.  As for Mr.
Logan, he was infinitely amused at the odd ways of the emigrants, their strange notions about matters and things in Amer
ica, and especially with their cultivation and intelligence in other
respects as contrasted with their total ignorance of this coun

try, and the childlike simplicity with which they wondered at every thing that attracted their attention. Besides, Miss Julia Edgarton, as we said before, was a very pretty young lady, and, as we did *not* say before, sang like a nightingale and talked like a book ; and having been for some time deprived of all society but that of the married pair, the children, pug-dog, and parrot aforesaid, was of course delighted, however unwilling she might have been to confess it, to obtain a more suitable companion, and altogether disposed to exert her powers of pleasing in his behalf.

Thus organized, the party began to realize the pleasures of travelling—those pleasures which ever await such as have sufficient taste and good temper to enjoy them. The Edgartons displayed their books, their engravings, their knick-nacks, and exotic curiosities, and endeavoured to edify the young American with descriptions of the magnificence and the wonders of London, while the latter was equally communicative in relation to his own country, and especially that portion of it through which they were passing. In the mild serene evenings, as the sun sunk behind the western hills, and the long shadows of the forest extended quite across the river, they would sit on the deck gazing at the rich hues of our noble forest trees, and listening to the song of the mocking-bird or the distant notes of the boatman's bugle. Sometimes Edgarton would take his flute or the ladies would sing. Logan derived pleasure from these amusements, but they were not sufficient for his inquisitive mind and active habits. He often took his rifle and wandered along the shore, keeping pace with the boat, and returning loaded with game, and sometimes prevailed on the ladies to accompany him in the skiff, and to visit the cabins of the settlers.

The difference of character between the two gentlemen who were thus thrown together was striking and amusing. Both were amiable and honest men. Edgarton, enervated by a city life and sedentary habits, felt severely all the little pri-

vations and inconveniences of the journey; accustomed to a
certain round of duties and enjoyments, he was keenly sensitive of the slightest encroachment upon his personal comfort,
and selfish in his exactions of attention from all around him;
and, proud of his native country, was offended if others did
not flatter his national vanity. His habits were formed in a
land abounding with artificial luxuries, where all the arts which
promote comfort or facilitate business exist in high perfection,
and where money can purchase every necessary of life, and
every personal attention which the most fastidious require.
He was now in a country where many of these comforts and
luxuries could not be purchased, because they did not exist,
or existed only in the possession of those who would not
barter them for money, and where the stranger could only
procure them from the hospitality of the people. But too
proud to accept that for which money would not be received,
too reserved to cultivate the acquaintance of strangers, he
passed through the country without acquiring any knowledge
of the character of its inhabitants or rubbing off any of his
own prejudices, and suffered many privations which a little
affability on his own part would have taught him how to
relieve.

Logan had all the freshness and originality of character so
common to the youth of our country. Accustomed to regard
habits and modes of life in reference to their usefulness, and
to pay but little deference to mere form, he was prepared to
adapt himself to circumstances, and to take the world as he
found it. Mr. Edgarton, though he could not resist the attraction produced by the intelligence, amiability, and interesting frankness of the manners of the young American, who
seemed as much at home as if in the bosom of his own
family, could not, on the other hand, divest himself of that
suspicious and repulsive feeling which his countrymen are
apt to entertain towards strangers. Logan, unaccustomed to
the refined deceptions which are practised in crowded cities,

considered every man a gentleman whose exterior and conduct entitled him to that appellation, and felt a disposition to
cultivate the acquaintance of any such whom he might meet;
while Edgarton, who buttoned his pocket-flaps and kept a
bright look-out at his trunks whenever a *stranger* approached,
was continually wondering that so genteel a young man
should travel without letters of introduction, and that he himself should be so imprudent as to admit into his family-cir-
cle a person of whom he had no personal knowledge. These
opposite feelings occasioned some amusing interludes in the
first scenes of the intercourse between the parties, who
approximated each other much after the fashion of vessels
floating on an agitated sea, which meet with a jar and instantly recoil, but which still float along together, and come
into harmonious contact at last when the waves subside. So
the gentlemen in question, after some sharp repartees, and
after their respective nationalities had bumped and jostled
awhile, settled down into amicable travelling companions,
and maintained the most friendly relations until their arrival
at the place of debarkation, where the Edgartons, finding that
Mr. Logan's route lay in the direction of their own, insisted
on his continuing to travel with their party.

The place at which the party landed was a small village
on the bank of the river, distant about fifty miles from a settlement in the interior to which they were destined.

"Here we are on dry land once more," said the Englishman as he jumped ashore; "come, Mr. Logan, let us go to
the stage-house and take our seats." Logan smiled, and followed his companion.

"My good friend," said Edgarton, to a tall, sallow man in
a hunting-shirt, who sat on a log by the river with a rifle in
his lap, " can you direct us to the stage-house ?"

" Well, I can't say that I can."

" Perhaps you do not understand what we want," said
Edgarton; " we wish to take seats in a mail-coach for ——."

" Well, stranger, it's my sentimental belief that there isn't a coach, male or female, in the county."

" This fellow is ignorant of our meaning," said Edgarton to Logan.

" What's that you say, stranger? *I spose maybe* you think I never *seed* a coach? Well, it's a free country, and every man has a right to think what he pleases; but I reckon I've saw as many of *them are fixens* as any other man. I was raised in Tennessee. I saw General Jackson once riding in the elegantest carriage that ever mortal man *sot* his eyes on— with glass winders to it like a house, and *sort o'* silk *curtings*. The harness was mounted with silver; it was *drawd* by four blooded nags, and *druv* by a mighty likely *nigger* boy."

The travellers passed on, and soon learned that there was indeed no stage in the country. Teams and carriages of any kind were difficult to be procured; and it was with some difficulty that two stout wagons were at last hired to carry Mr. Edgarton's moveables, and a *dearborn* obtained to convey his family, it being agreed that one of the gentlemen should drive the latter vehicle while the other walked, alternately. Arrangements were accordingly made to set out the next morning.

The settlement in which Mr. Edgarton had judiciously determined to pitch his tent, and enjoy the healthful innocence and rural felicity of the farmer's life, was new; and the country to be traversed to reach it entirely unsettled. There were two or three houses scattered through the wilderness on the road, one of which the party might have reached by setting out early in the morning, and they had determined to do so. But there was so much fixing and preparing to be done, so much stowing of baggage and packing of trunks, such momentous preparations to guard against cold and heat, hunger and thirst, fatigue, accident, robbery, disease, and death, that it was near noon before the cavalcade was prepared to move. Even then they were delayed some minutes longer

to give Mr. Edgarton time to oil the screws and renew the
charges of his double-barrel gun and pocket-pistols. In vain
he was told there were no highwaymen in America. His
way lay chiefly through uninhabited forests; and he considered it a fact in natural history, as indisputable as any other
elementary principle, that every such forest has its robbers.
After all, he entirely neglected to put flints in his bran new
locks instead of the wooden substitutes which the maker had
placed there to protect his work from injury; and thus
"doubly armed," he announced his readiness to start with an
air of truly comic heroism.

When they began their journey, new terrors arose. The
road was sufficiently plain and firm for all rational purposes;
that is to say, it *would do* very well for those who only
wanted to get along, and were content to make the best of it.
It was a mere path beaten by a succession of travellers. No
avenue had been cut for it through the woods; but the first
pioneers had wound their way among the trees, avoiding
obstacles by going round them, as the snake winds through
the grass, and those who followed had trodden in their
footsteps, until they had beaten a smooth road sufficiently
wide to admit the passage of a single wagon. On either side
was the thick forest, sometimes grown up with underbrush to
the margin of the *trace*, and sometimes so open as to allow
the eye to roam off to a considerable distance. Above was a
dense canopy of interwoven branches. The wild and lonesome
appearance, the deep shade, the interminable gloom of the
woods, were frightful to our travellers. The difference
between a wild forest in the simple majesty of nature, and
the woodlands of cultivated countries, is very great. In the
latter the underbrush has been removed by art or destroyed
by domestic animals; the trees as they arrive at their growth
are felled for use, and the remainder, less crowded, assume
the spreading and rounded form of cultivated trees. The
sunbeams reach the soil through the scattered foliage, the

ground is trodden by grazing animals, and a hard sod is formed.  However secluded such a spot may be, it bears the marks of civilization : the lowing of cattle is heard, and many species of songsters that hover round the habitations of men, and are never seen in the wilderness, here warble their notes. In the western forests of America all is grand and savage. The truth flashes instantly upon the mind of the observer, with the force of conviction, that Nature has been carrying on her operations here for ages undisturbed.  The leaf has fallen from year to year; succeeding generations of trees have mouldered, spreading over the surface layer upon layer of decayed fibre, until the soil has acquired an astonishing depth and an unrivalled fertility.  From this rich bed the trees are seen rearing their shafts to an astonishing height.   The tendency of plants towards the light is well understood ; of course, when trees are crowded closely together, instead of spreading, they shoot upwards, each endeavouring, as it were, to overtop his neighbours, and expending the whole force of the vegetative powers in rearing a great trunk to the greatest possible height, and then throwing out a top like an umbrella to the rays of the sun.  The functions of vitality are carried on with vigour at the extremities, while the long stem is bare of leaves or branches; and when the under-growth is removed nothing can exceed the gloomy grandeur of the elevated arches of foliage, supported by pillars of majestic size and venerable appearance.   The great thickness and age of many of the trees is another striking peculiarity. They grow from age to age, attaining a gigantic size, and then fall, with a tremendous force, breaking down all that stands in their downward way, and heaping a great pile of timber on the ground, where it remains untouched until it is converted into soil. Mingled with all our timber are seen aspiring vines, which seem to have commenced their growth with that of the young trees, and risen with them, their tops still flourishing together far above the earth, while their stems are alike bare.

The undergrowth consists of dense thickets, made up of the offspring of the larger trees, mixed with thorns, briers, dwarfish vines, and a great variety of shrubs. The ground is never covered with a firm sward, and seldom bears the grasses, or smaller plants, being covered from year to year with a dense mass of dried and decaying leaves, and shrouded in eternal shade.

Such was the scene that met the eyes of our travellers, and had they been treated to a short excursion to the moon they would scarcely have witnessed any thing more novel. The wide-spread and trackless ocean had scarcely conveyed to their imaginations so vivid an impression of the vast and solitary grandeur of Nature, in her pathless wildernesses. They could hardly realise the expectation of travelling safely through such savage shades. The path, which could be seen only a few yards in advance, seemed continually to have terminated, leaving them no choice but to retrace their steps. Sometimes they came to a place where a tree had fallen across the road, and Edgarton would stop under the supposition that any further attempt to proceed was hopeless—until he saw the American drivers forsaking the track, guiding their teams among the trees, crushing down the young saplings that stood in their way, and thus winding round the obstacle, and back to the road, often through thickets so dense, that to the stranger's eye it seemed as if neither man nor beast could penetrate them. Sometimes on reaching the brink of a ravine or small stream, the bridge of logs, which previous travellers had erected, was found to be broken down, or the ford rendered impassable; and the wagoners with the same imperturbable good nature, and as if such accidents were matters of course, again left the road, and seeking out a new crossing-place, passed over with scarcely the appearance of difficulty.

Once they came to a sheet of water, extending as far as the eye could reach, the tall trees standing in it as thickly as upon the dry gronnd, with tufts of grass and weeds instead of the usual undergrowth.

"Is there a ferry here?" inquired Edgarton.

"Oh no, sir, it's nothing but *a slash*."

"What's that?"

"Why, sir, jist a sort o' swamp."

"What in the world shall we do?"

"We'll jist put right ahead, sir; there's no dif*fick*ulty; it's nice good driving all about here. It's sort o' muddy, but there's good bottom to it all the way."

On they went. To Edgarton it was like going to sea; for no road could be seen; nothing but the trackless surface of the water; because instead of looking down, where his eye could have penetrated to the bottom, he was glancing forward in the vain hope of seeing dry land. Generally the water was but a few inches deep, but sometimes they soused into a hole; then Edgarton groaned and the ladies screamed; and sometimes it got gradually deeper until the hubs of the wheels were immersed, and the Englishman then called to the wagoners to stop.

"Don't be afeard, sir," one of them replied, "it is not bad; why this aint nothing; it's right good going; it aint a-going to swim your horse, no how."

"Anything seems a good road to you where the horse will not have to swim," replied the Englishman surlily.

"Why, bless you," said the backwoodsman, "this aint no part of a priming to places that I've seed afore, no how. I've seed race paths in a worse fix than this. Don't you reckon, stranger, that if my team can drag this here heavy wagon, loaded down with plunder, you can sartainly get along with that *ar* little carry-all, and nothing on the face of the *yeath* to tote, but jist the women and children?"

They had but one such swamp to pass. It was only about half a mile wide, and after travelling that far through the water, the firm soil of the woods, which before seemed gloomy, became cheerful by contrast; and Edgarton found at last, that however unpleasant such travelling may be to those who are not accustomed to it, it has really no dangers but such as are imaginary.

As the cavalcade proceeded slowly, the ladies found it most pleasant to walk wherever the ground was sufficiently dry. Mrs. Edgarton and the children might be seen saunter-ing along, and keeping close to the carriage, for fear of being lost or captured by some nondescript monster of the wild, yet often halting to gather nosegays of wild flowers, or to exam-ine some of the many natural curiosities which surrounded them. Logan and the fair Julia lingered still farther in the rear. They were in that season of life when acquaintances are readily formed, and when cordiality soon ripens into con-fidence. A few days had sufficed to inspire them with an interest in each other, which was growing fast into tender sen-timent.

The spring of the year is supposed to be particularly pro-pitious to the passion of love. When the birds are singing, and Nature assumes her softest and most beautiful attire, the fancy becomes excited, the heart awakens to the influence of gentle affections, and like the flower buds, the germ of love swells and expands in the genial atmosphere. Independently of those attractions of mind and person, in which some indi-viduals greatly excel others, there is a loveliness in youth itself sufficiently alluring to create attachment. The temper is then most apt to be amiable, the affections ardent and generous, the mind cheerful and unsuspecting. The cares of life have not clouded the imagination, nor its disappointments chilled the fountains of kindness; Nature is then arrayed in all the graces of a distant landscape, in which the harsher features are unseen, and the beautiful outline, with its delicate hues and deceptive shadows, alone discovered in the far per-spective; and man is contemplated in the pristine innocence

17

of Eden, while to the worldly eye he is known in the vices of a fallen creature.

The sun was about to set when the wagoners halted at an open spot, covered with a thick carpet of short grass, on the margin of a small stream of clear water. On inquiring the reason, Mr. Edgarton was assured that this was the best *camp-ground* on the route, and as there was no house within many miles, it was advisable to make arrangements for passing the night there.

"Impossible!" exclaimed the European gentleman; "what! lie on the ground like beasts! we shall all catch our death of cold!"

"I should never live through the night," groaned his fair partner.

"We shall be *heaten* up by *vild volves* or *ungry hingins*," whined the maid.

"Don't let us stay here in the dark, papa," cried the children.

Logan expressed the opinion that an encampment might be made quite comfortable, and the sentimental Julia declared that it would be "delightful!" Edgarton imprecated maledictions on the beggarly country which could not afford inns for travellers, and wondered if they expected a gentleman to nestle among the leaves like Robin Hood's foresters.

"I wisht I hadn't never left Lunnun," sobbed the lady's maid, "this comes of *hemigratin* out of *Hingland* to these here back voods. Only to think of gentle volks and vimmen and children having to vaunder in the voods, like Rob Roy in the novel, or Walentine and Horson in the play. Oh! I shall never live to see the morning, so I vont! do Mrs. Hedgarton let us turn back!"

This storm, like other sudden gusts, soon blew over, and the party began in earnest to make the best of a bad business by rendering their situation as comfortable as possible. The wagoners, though highly amused at the fears of their

companions, showed great alacrity and kindness in their endeavours to dissipate the apprehensions and provide for the
comfort of the foreigners; and, assisted by Mr. Logan, soon
prepared a shelter. This was made by planting some large
stakes in the ground, in the form of a square, filling up the
sides and covering the tops with smaller poles, and suspend-
ing blankets over and around it, so as to form a complete enclosure. Mrs. Edgarton had a carpet taken from the wagons
and spread on the ground; on this the beds were unpacked
and laid, trunks were arranged for seats, and the emigrants
surprised at finding themselves in a comfortable apartment,
became as merry as they had been before despondent. A fire
was kindled and the tea-kettle boiled, and there being a large
store of bread and provisions already prepared, an excellent
repast was soon placed before them, and eaten with the relish
produced by severe exercise.

The night had now closed in, but the blaze of a large fire
and the light of several candles threw a brilliant gleam over
the spot and heightened the cheerfulness of the evening meal.
The arrangements for sleeping were very simple. The tent,
which had been divided into two apartments by a curtain
suspended in the middle, accommodated all of Mr. Edgarton's
household: Logan drew on his great-coat, and spreading a
single blanket on the ground, threw himself down with his
feet to the fire; the teamsters crept into their wagons, and
the several parties soon enjoyed that luxury which, if Shaks-
peare may be believed, is often denied to the "head that
wears a crown."

The light of the morning brought with it cheerfulness and
merriment. Refreshed from the fatigues of the preceding day,
inspired with new confidence, and amused by the novelties
that surrounded them, the emigrants were in high spirits.
Breakfast was hastily prepared, and the happy party, seated
in a circle on the grass, enjoyed their meal with a keen relish.

The horses were then harnessed and the cavalcade renewed its march.

The day was far advanced when they began to rise to more elevated ground than that over which they had travelled. The appearance of the woods was sensibly changed. They were now travelling over a high upland tract with a gently-waving surface, and instead of the rank vegetation, the dense foliage and gloomy shades by which they had been surrounded, beheld woodlands composed of smaller trees thinly scattered and intermingled with rich thickets of young timber. The growth though thick was low, so that the rays of the sun penetrated through many openings, and the beaten path which they pursued was entirely exposed to the genial beams. Groves of the wild apple, the plum, and the cherry, now in full bloom, added a rich beauty to the scene and a delightful fragrance to the air.

But the greatest natural curiosity and the most attractive scenic exhibition of our Western hemisphere was still in reserve; and a spontaneous expression of wonder and delight burst from the whole party, as they emerged from the woods and stood on the edge of *a prairie.* They entered a long vista, carpeted with grass, interspersed with numberless flowers, among which the blue violet predominated; while the edges of the forest on either hand were elegantly fringed with low thickets loaded with blossoms—those of the plum and cherry of snowy whiteness, and those of the crab-apple of a delicate pink. Above and beyond these were seen the rich green, the irregular outline, and the variegated light and shade of the forest. As if to produce the most beautiful perspective, and to afford every variety of aspect, the vista increased in width until it opened like the estuary of a great river into the broad prairie, and as our travellers advanced the woodlands receded on either hand, and sometimes indented by smaller avenues opening into the woods, and sometimes throwing out points of timber, so that the boundary of the plain resembled the irregular outline of a shore as traced on a map.

Delighted with the lovely aspect of Nature in these the most tasteful of her retreats, the party lingered along until they reached the margin of the broad prairie, where a noble expanse of scenery of the same character was spread out on a larger scale. They stood on a rising ground, and beheld before them a vast plain, undulating in its surface so as to present to the eye a series of swells and depressions, never broken nor abrupt, but always regular, and marked by curved lines. Here and there was seen a deep ravine or drain, by which the superfluous water was carried off, the sides of which were thickly set with willows. Clumps of elm and oak were scattered about far apart like little islands; a few solitary trees were seen, relieving the eye as it wandered over the ocean-like surface of this native meadow.

It so happened that a variety of accidents and delays impeded the progress of our emigrants, so that the shadows of evening began to fall upon them, while they were yet far from the termination of their journey, and it became necessary again to seek a place of repose for the night. The prospect of encamping again had lost much of its terrors, but they were relieved from the contemplation of this last resource of the houseless, by the agreeable information that they were drawing near the house of a farmer who was in the habit of "accommodating travellers." It was further explained that Mr. Goodman did not not keep a public-house, but that he was "well off," "had houseroom enough, and plenty to eat," and that "*of course*," according to the hospitable customs of the country, he entertained any strangers who sought shelter under his roof. Thither they bent their steps, anticipating from the description of it a homestead much larger and more comfortable than the cheerless-looking log-cabins which had thus far greeted their eyes, and which seemed to compose the only dwellings of the population.

On arriving at the place, they were a little disappointed to
find that the abundance of *houseroom* which had been promised
them was a mere figure of speech, an idiomatic expression by
a native, having a comparative signification. The dwelling
was a log house, differing from others only in being of a larger
size and better construction. The logs were hewed and squared
instead of being put up in their original state, with the bark
on; the apertures were carefully closed, and the openings representing windows, instead of being stopped when urgent
occasion required the exclusion of the atmosphere, by hats,
old baskets, or cast-off garments, were filled with glass, in
imitation of the dwellings of more highly civilized lands.
The wealth of this farmer, consisting chiefly of the *plenty to
eat* which had been boasted, was amply illustrated by the
noisy and numerous crowd of chickens, ducks, turkeys, pigs,
and cattle, that cackled, gobbled, and grunted about the house,
filling the air with social though discordant sounds, and so
obstructing the way as scarcely to leave room for the newly-
arrived party to approach the door.

As the cavalcade halted, the foremost driver made the fact
known by a vociferous salutation.

"Hal-low! Who keeps house?"

A portly dame made her appearance at the door, and was
saluted with,—

"How de do, ma'am—all well, ma'am?"

"All right well, thank you, sir."

"Here's some strangers that wants lodging; can we get
to stay all night with you?"

"Well, I don't know; *he's* not at home, and I harly know
what to say."

"I'll answer for *him*," replied the driver, who understood
distinctly that the pronoun used so emphatically by the good
lady alluded to her inferior moiety; "he wouldn't turn
away strangers at this time of day when the chickens is jist
goin to roost. We've ben a travellin all day, and our crit-

ters is mighty tired and hungry, as well as the rest of us."

"Well," said the woman, very cheerfully, "I reckon you can stay; if you can put up with such fare as we have, you are very welcome. My man will be back soon; he's only jist gone up to town."

The whole party were now received into the dwelling of the backwoodsman by the smiling and voluble hostess, whose assiduous cordiality placed them at once at their ease in spite of the plain and primitive, and to them uncomfortable aspect of the log house. Indeed, nothing could be more uninviting in appearance to those who were accustomed only to the more convenient dwellings of a state of society farther advanced in the arts of social life. It was composed of two large apartments or separate cabins, connected by an area or space which was floored and roofed, but open at the sides, and which served as a convenient receptacle to hang saddles, bridles, and harness, or to stow travellers' baggage, while in fine weather it served as a place in which to eat or sit.

In the room into which our party was shown there was neither plastering nor paper, nor any device of modern ingenuity to conceal the bare logs that formed the sides of the house, neither was there a carpet on the floor, nor any furniture for mere ornament. The absence of all superfluities and of many of the conveniences usually deemed essential in household economy was quite striking. A table, a few chairs, a small looking-glass, some cooking utensils, and a multitudinous array of women's apparel, hung round on wooden pins, as if for show, made up the meagre list, whether for parade or use, with the addition of several bedsteads closely ranged on one side of the room, supporting beds of the most plethoric and dropsical dimensions, covered with clean cotton bedding, and ostentatiously tricked out with gaudy, parti-coloured quilts.

The "man" soon made his appearance, a stout, weather-beaten person, of rough exterior, but not less hospitably dis-

posed than his better half, and the whole household were
now actively astir to furnish forth the evening's repast, nor
was their diligent kindness, nor the inquisitive though respectful cross-examination which accompanied it, at all diminished
when they discovered that their guests were English people.*
Soon the ample fireplace, extending almost across one end of
the house, was piled full of blazing logs; the cries of affrighted
fowls and other significant notes of preparation announced
that active operations were commenced in the culinary de-
partment. An array of pots and kettles, skillets, ovens, and
frying-pans, covered the hearth, and the astonished travellers
discovered that the room they occupied was not only used as
a bedchamber, but "served them for parlour, and kitchen, and
hall."

We shall not attempt to describe the processes of making
bread, cooking meat and vegetables, and preparing the delightful beverage of the evening meal, a portion of which took
place in the presence of the surprised and amused guests,
while other parts were conducted under a shed out of doors.
A large table was soon spread with clean linen, and covered
with a profusion of viands such as probably could not be
found on the board of the mere peasant or labouring farmer
in any other part of the world.† Coffee was there, with sweet

---

* The term *Britishers*, which English writers, and especially their
tourists, persist in attributing to our people, as one in general popular
use, is entirely unknown, in conversation or otherwise, in any part of the
United States. If any foreign traveller ever heard it in this country, he
must have brought it with him, or gathered it from an English book.

† I cannot resist the opportunity of nailing to the counter a wretched
fabrication of some traveller, who represents himself as dismounting at a
Western house of entertainment, and inquiring the price of a dinner. The
answer is, " Well, stranger—with wheat bread and chicken fixens, it would
be fifty cents, but with corn bread and common doins, twenty-five cents."
The slang here used is of the writer's own invention. No one ever heard
in the West of "chicken fixens," or "common doins." On such occasions, the
table is spread with every thing that the house affords, or with whatever

milk and buttermilk in abundance; fried chickens, venison, and ham; cheese, sweetmeats, pickles, dried fruit, and honey; bread of wheat and corn, hot biscuits and cakes, with fresh butter; all well prepared and neat, and all pressed upon the hungry travellers with officious hospitality. Had the entertainment been furnished in regal style at some enchanted castle by invisible hands, the guests could scarcely have been more surprised by the profusion and variety of the backwoods repast, so far did the result produced exceed the apparent means afforded by the desolate-looking and scantily-furnished cabin.

If our worthy travellers were surprised by the novelties of backwoods *inn*-hospitality which thus far had pressed upon them, how much was their wonder increased when the hour for retiring arrived, and the landlady apologized for being obliged to separate the guests from their entertainers.

"Our family is so large," said the woman, "that we have to have two rooms. I shall have to put all of you strangers into a room by yourselves."

The party were accordingly conducted into the other apartment, which was literally filled with arrangements for sleeping, there being several bedsteads, each of which was closely curtained with sheets, blankets, and coverlids hung around it for the occasion, while the whole floor was strewed with pallets. Here Mr. Edgarton and his whole party, including Logan and the teamsters, were expected to sleep. A popular poet, in allusion to this patriarchal custom, impertinently remarks,

> "Some cavillers
> Object to sleep with fellow-travellers."

And on this occasion the objection was uttered vehemently,

---

may be convenient, according to the means and temper of the entertainers. A meal is a meal, and the cost is the same, whether it be plentiful or otherwise.

17*

the ladies declaring with one voice that martyrdom in any
shape would be preferable to lodging thus like a drove of
cattle. Unreasonable as such scruples might have seemed,
they were so pertinaciously adhered to on the one side, and
so obstinately resisted by the exceedingly difficult nature of
the case on the other, that there is no knowing to what extremities matters might have gone, had not a compromise
been effected by which Logan and the wagon-drivers were
transferred into the room occupied by the farmer's family,
while the Edgartons, the sister, the maid, the greyhound,
the pug-dog, and the parrot, remained sole occupants of the
apartment prepared for them.

A few more hours brought them to the place of their destination. Mr. Edgarton had as yet no house, nor any spot
selected for his residence. In choosing a neighbourhood, he
had been directed by the advice of some English friends, but
he had now to exercise his own judgment in purchasing land
and erecting buildings. He found the inhabitants kind and
hospitable, especially in giving him such advice and information as his situation required, and many eligible spots were
pointed out to him on the vacant lands of the government.
An Englishman, however, drop where he may, considers it
his prerogative to know more about the country than its own
inhabitants, and our emigrant wisely concluded that he was
the best judge of his own business. He looked for a picturesque spot. Unacquainted with the nature of soils, or the
business of farming, he imagined that rural occupations could
be carried on as successfully at one place as at another, and
having pleased his eye on the surrounding scenery, was satisfied that he had found all that was necessary to happiness.
His fancy was attracted by a long arm of the prairie reaching
back into the forest to the vicinity of a large rivulet. In the
depth of this recess he placed his house, so that its front commanded a view of the widening vista, while its sides and rear
were embowered in woods. In vain was he told that the

prairie at this point was low and flat, that the soil was a cold sterile clay, and that the surface being concave retained the water. He could drain it; the most dreary morasses had been reclaimed in England. In vain was he told that the rivulet in the rear of his house annually overflowed its banks, leaving standing pools, and creating noxious vapours. He would convert these inundated lands into meadows, and become a benefactor to the country by abating a nuisance. His little cottage was soon reared upon the spot at which he intended, at some future day, to build a splendid mansion, and the delighted man, surrounded by scenes as beautiful as the most romantic fancy could imagine, sat down contented in the solitary wilderness.

What was to be done next? Fields were to be enclosed, grain to be planted, and stock to be purchased, and our farmer's notions of either of these operations were so vague, that he was unable to take the first step without advice. The neighbours, whose admonitions had been already rejected, were applied to, and gave the desired information. Books were also consulted, and at length Mr. Edgarton matured a scheme of operations. A plan of the farm was laid down upon paper. Here was to be a garden, and there a lawn; here an orchard, there meadows, and there corn-fields. The requisite lanes, hedges, fences, and ditches, were dotted off with mathematical accuracy; plans of the mansion, the ice-house, the dairy, the barn, &c., were drawn separately; Miss Julia, who had a pretty taste for drawing, coloured them all very handsomely, and they were shown to visitors with no small degree of exultation. Hope bloomed with promising luxuriance, and the happiness of expectation was fully enjoyed.

The next thing was to put these splendid plans into operation; but Mr. Edgarton now found, to his surprise, that it was almost impossible to procure labourers. The first settlers of a new country are farmers who do their own

work, and but few persons could be found who would work
for hire. With great difficulty a few men were employed at
extravagant prices; the buildings were deferred until another
year, and the enclosing the fields commenced. Planting was
out of the question, because the ground was too wet; drain-
ing was attempted, but for this also the season was unpro-
pitious, and after a fast expenditure of labour and money, Mr.
Edgarton found that he had scarcely advanced a step towards
accomplishing the herculean task before him. We shall not
weary the reader with a detail of all his bad speculations, in
buying horses that turned out to be unsound, cattle that ran
away, and were never again heard of, and sheep that were in-
continently eaten up by the wolves, nor shock the feelings of
the sympathetic by reciting the dismal fate of numerous
broods of innocent chickens and goslings, nurtured by the
tender assiduity of Miss Edgarton, and which fell an easy
prey to the cunning fox and the audacious raccoon. Troubles
thickened on every side; the sturdy peasantry afforded no
society for the polished inmates of the cottage, and the advantages of rural felicity began to be doubted. Often did
Mr. and Mrs. Edgarton wish themselves back again in their
snug back parlour in one of the smokiest streets of London;
and as often did the pretty Julia wish to see Mr. Logan,
who was understood to be figuring at the bar of a neighbouring county.

Summer came, and the little cottage, which served for
parlour, kitchen, and hall, was found to be oppressively confined and hot. Nor was this all: while the salubrious region
around was blessed with genial breezes, the dreadful malaria
hung in baleful clouds over the dwelling of Edgarton. The
rivulet was dried up by the fervent heats of the season, leaving
along its former channel a few stagnant pools, which gave
birth to myriads of musquitoes, who, from their musical propensities and sanguinary dispositions, might be imagined to
sing, as they hovered around this ill-fated family.

" Fee faw fum,
   I smell the blood of an Englishman,
   And dead or alive I will have some."

Where the musquito sings, the malaria is brooding not far
distant.   These dreadful precursors of disease were, as usual,
soon followed by the pestilence itself.   The summer wore
away, and the autumn found the family of Edgarton writhing
under burning fevers.   Mr. Edgarton was first attacked, and
in a few hours was prostrate, helpless, and delirious.   Burning
fever, raging thirst, and intense pain, seemed to threaten a
speedy and excruciating death.   The sallow death-like complexion, the blood-shot eye, the throbbing arteries, and the
distortions of the countenance of the sufferer, filled the minds
of his trembling family with the most agonizing apprehensions.
Now it was that the helplessness of their solitary condition
impressed their hearts with terror.   Their nearest neighbour
resided at a distance of several miles, and they had no domestic.   To the females the idea of losing a husband and
a brother, their dearest relative and only protector, was sufficiently mournful ; but when they reflected that he might ex-
pire for want of assistance which they knew not how to
procure, the thought was full of agony.   But women are not
apt to yield to despair when the objects of their affection are
in danger; and while Mrs. Edgarton assiduously attended
the sufferer, Julia boldly mounted a horse, and rode to the
nearest house for assistance, although the way led through
the forest by a dim path with which she was little acquainted,
and the approach of night rendered the attempt somewhat
dangerous.   She succeeded, however, in procuring a messenger to go in search of a physician.   Before medical
assistance arrived, which was late the next day, Mrs. Edgarton
had taken the fever—then the children, one after another,
until Julia was left alone, the sole nurse of all whose blood
was kindred to her own in the new world.

Week after week rolled heavily away.   The Edgartons,

parents and children, still withered in the grasp of the pestilence.   Julia, pale and worn down with fatigue and watching,
was their devoted nurse.   Giving up her whole heart to this
duty with that intensity of affection and singleness of purpose
of which woman is alone capable, she had become skilful in
the management of her patients.   A physician came as often
as his duty to others would permit; the neighbours were
kind, but they were few, and their own cares often called
them away.   Then came the long, the solitary, the anxious
hours, when poor Julia, left alone with her heavy charge, had
need of all her fortitude to support her.   The invalids under-
went many changes; some grew better and others worse
alternately; hope was excited one day by the favourable
symptoms of one, and on the next the danger of another
created thrilling alarm.   At last there came a trying crisis.
The youngest child, an interesting boy of two years old,
breathed his last in the arms of Julia.   The rest of the family
were lying some insensible, and all unable to rise.   Not
another human being was near, and as Miss Edgarton wept
over the corpse, she was bowed under a sense of hopeless
despondency that seemed to wither all her energies.   All the
fond hopes that had so long cheered the path of duty were
destroyed—the angel of death had entered the dwelling; one
victim had fallen, and the others, all, all seemed to be
hovering on the brink of the grave.   It was evening when
this melancholy event happened.   The sun was setting.   Julia
went often to the door, and looked over the prairie in the
eager hope of seeing some human being; but none appeared.
Night came, and she was alone with the dead and the dying.

    At last her agony became insupportable, and she left the
chamber of disease for the purpose of refreshing herself for a moment in the open air.   As she stepped out of the door a brilliant
light attracted her attention, and she discovered to her surprise
that the southern horizon glowed with a resplendent blaze, which
threw its radiance over the whole landscape, and rendered

every object as distinctly visible as at noonday. The prairie
was on fire! The novelty of the spectacle could be equalled
only by its splendour. The fire itself was not yet visible, in
consequence of the rising ground that intervened, but the spot
where it raged was distinctly indicated by a strong and vivid
glare, which extended along the horizon from east to west.
Above were seen heavy volumes of smoke rolling upwards in
masses of inky blackness, tinged with a fiery redness on those
parts which were exposed to the reflection of the element.
The foreground of the scene was a prairie, covered with dried
and yellow grass, illumined with a fearful and peculiar radiance. Here and there stood a solitary tree, tinged with light
on one side and throwing from the other a shadow of supernatural length across the plain. The forest on either side
was thrown back into a deep shade, which bounded the
prospect, except where here and there a point of timber,
running out into the prairie like a cape into the ocean, became
exposed to the full glare of the fire, and presented its hues
and outlines distinctly to the eye. All was still and silent;
no animated object was seen upon the plain, not a sound was
heard except that occasioned by the conflagration, a low,
incessant roaring resembling the distant but tremendous rush
of waters.

The fire had now reached the most elevated grounds, and
was seen advancing in a long line, fanned by a breeze from
the south. Its march was slow but fearfully regular. Then
the breeze died away and was succeeded by a calm. The
smoke now curled upwards for a short distance, and then
descended in thick volumes upon the plain, discolouring the
atmosphere, and giving a red and ghastly hue to the surrounding objects.

Julia Edgarton gazed at this scene with intense interest.
At first its sublime beauty awakened a lively feeling of admiration; and she watched with timid wonder the progress
of an element always awful when raging uncontrolled in its

splendid and terrific majesty; but when the flame was seen
extending across the whole plain, and advancing towards the
dwelling that contained the helpless objects of her affection,
heart sickness and unconquerable panic filled her bosom.   In
another hour perhaps that dwelling would be surrounded by
the flames, and they must all perish together.   Her first impulse was to fly; but the selfish thought was instantly
banished, and she resolved rather to die than forsake her
charge.   A slight noise drew her attention, and looking round
she beheld several animals that she knew to be wolves,
crouching upon the ground, and glaring upon her with their
fierce eyeballs.   By a sure instinct they had scented the
house of death, and waited for their prey.   Julia rushed dis-
tractedly into the house.

  "Aunt," said one of the little girls, " is the sun rising? oh
how cheerful the light is!"

  "Oh! the dreadful flame!" groaned Mr. Edgarton, whose
senses were quickened to an exquisite acuteness, "I see it!  I
hear the dreadful roaring!  The fiends are preparing their tortures! oh my God, why did I not seek thee before it was too
late!"

  Julia was stricken to the heart by these words.   Like
most rational and well-disposed persons, she had always entertained a respect for religion, but it had formed no part of
her education, and had seldom occupied her thoughts.   Now,
abandoned by all the world, and surrounded by the dreadful
ministers of death, she was convinced of the solemn truth,
that no hand less powerful than that of an Almighty God could
bring relief.   In vain had she exerted her tenderness, her
ability, her heroism—in vain had she relied on herself.   The
words of her brother sunk into her heart, "Why did I not
seek *thee* before it was too late!"   She dropped upon her
knees, and for the first time in her life prayed with earnestness and sincerity.   A calm resignation followed the performance of this act of duty, and although no supernatural hand

was seen stretched out to snatch herself and those who were dear to her from the jaws of death, she felt that courage was given her to abide the event. As she rose, her hand was grasped with a gentle pressure, a tender voice pronounced her name, she turned and sunk weeping with joy and gratitude upon the shoulder of Logan.

He bore the afflicted girl into the open air, and having assured her that the danger from the fire was much less than she apprehended, she had courage to contemplate again the terrific scene. The line of flame was advancing slowly toward the house, extending entirely across the plain in front, and into the woods on either side. As it rolled on, the flames were seen darting upward, like agitated waves, and the spectator could scarcely resist the idea that a sea of flaming liquid was spreading its boiling and foaming billows over the land. The heat was now intense ; the roaring and crackling sounds of the conflagration, as deafening as the din of a tempest. On it swept until it reached the beaten ground in the vicinity of the house, which afforded no fuel, and there the flame separated into two divisions, and passing along on either hand, swept away the fences, the stacks and other combustibles, leaving nothing but the solitary cottage and its wretched inmates upon that widespread and smoking plain.

Julia acknowledged her gratitude to God, and felt that, although in a land of strangers, and surrounded by dangers, she had now one Friend whose hand is mighty to save those who put their trust in Him.

On the following morning Mr. Logan made arrangements to procure assistance for this afflicted family. The deceased infant was decently buried, and the rest of the family carefully removed to the houses of the neighbours, where skilful attention and pure air soon restored them to health. Mr. Logan remained with them, and having convinced his friend of the futility of his agricultural schemes, easily induced him to remove to the village where he was settled himself, and to invest the remains of his fortune in merchandise. The change was a happy one. Mr. Edgarton, embarked in business for which his education and talents fitted him, succeeded to the utmost extent of his hopes. Health and cheerfulness smiled again at his fireside. The interesting Julia became *Mrs. Logan ;* both families are now in easy circumstances ; and the members of the happy circle, in reciting their adventures, never fail to ascribe praise to that Providence, which conducted them in safety through the perils of the ocean, the wilderness, and the pestilence, and gave them a pleasant home in a land of strangers.

# BARRACK-MASTER'S DAUGHTER.

## A LEGEND OF FORT CUMBERLAND.

———◆◆◆———

EVERY person of taste who has enjoyed the luxury of travelling over that splendid monument of national munificence, the *Cumberland road*, must have been struck with the romantic beauty of the village from which it takes its name. It is situated on a small plain in the bosom of a deep valley, surrounded by tall mountains, whose abrupt cliffs seem to be inaccessible, unless to the soaring eagle or the adventurous hunter. A small tributary of the Potomac flows in a clear and beautiful stream through the vale, winding its serpentine course round the bold promontories and sharp angles of the mountain, until it reaches the plain, where it forms a graceful curve round the site of the village. The sides of the mountains are rocky, and their summits covered with pines; but the valleys are rich, and thickly wooded, luxuriant in vegetation, and lovely to the eye.

Here stood Fort Cumberland, a frontier fortress, in the colonial wars between the French and English. At the period at which we commence this narrative, in the year

1758, the fort was garrisoned by a numerous and gallant host, engaged in active preparations for a distant enterprise. Colonel Grant, a Scottish officer, at the head of eight hundred Highlanders, was about to lead an expedition against Fort Du Quesne, on the Ohio, and every young officer who panted for fame was anxious to volunteer in this arduous service.

"What think you, Major Gordon," said the colonel to his second in command, as they strolled one evening along the banks of Will's creek, at some distance from the fort, "will the French be able to stand against our brave Highlanders?"

"Of the French, could we meet them fairly in the field, I have little fear," replied the other; "but I must confess that I think our troops but poorly calculated to contend in the mountains against their Indian allies."

"Pshaw! Major Gordon, I'm ashamed of you. It is a reflection upon the honour of His Majesty's troops, to mention them in the same breath with a horde of naked savages! Sir, with my regiment, I can burn all the wigwams in North America; and punish the mutinous sachems for their contumacy, at a drum-head court-martial, if they should dare to object."

"You may, perhaps, live to change that opinion. At all events, be advised, in so important an enterprise as the one before us, to employ the necessary caution to ensure success."

"What *cautious* measure would the chivalrous descendant of the noble line of Gordon suggest?" inquired the colonel, in a tone which *almost* conveyed a sneer.

"The one I have so often pointed out," replied his friend calmly, "the employment of a small body of men from the frontiers of Virginia, whose knowledge of the country, and of the habits of the enemy, might serve as a safeguard against stratagems, to which our ignorance would expose us."

"A safeguard!" retorted the proud Scot, drawing up his fine form, and darting a glance of unmingled scorn from his fierce eye, "truly, it would be an edifying sight to behold the Grant and his followers marching to victory under the protection of a guard! a guard, too, of paltry peasants! a squad of militia led by a negro driver or a village attorney! If such notions are the result of your long residence in America, Major Gordon——"

At that instant Gordon suddenly halted, and directed the eye of his companion to some object before them. They had just passed a solitary cabin surrounded by a few acres of cultivated land, where an adventurous backwoodsman ventured to reside, beyond the reach of the guns of the fort. Beyond this clearing their path led through a slip of marshy ground covered with high grass and bushes. The attention of the officers was drawn to two boys, the children of the backwoodsman whose hut they had just passed, one of whom was about eight, and the other ten years of age, who were stealing through the woods with cautious steps, bearing a couple of muskets, the *butts* of which were borne by the larger boy, while the muzzles rested on the shoulders of the smaller. They stopped by a large log at the edge of the swamp, and peeped eagerly over it, and the officers then beheld, a few paces from the log, a large bear, apparently asleep, imbedded in the mud. The boys, having ascertained that the animal remained where they had discovered him a few minutes before, placed one of the guns over the log, and the oldest lad, after taking a deliberate aim, fired. The bear, mortally wounded, sprung up in his bed, and uttered a howl of agony. The youngest boy ran towards the house, while the other climbed nimbly up a small tree. Here he sat in security, watching with delight the expiring struggles of his victim, until the latter sunk exhausted in the mire, when he screamed after his brother, "Bill, come back, I've *saved* him!" Again they took their post by the log, and gazed at their grim adversary, who by an occasional twitching of the muscles showed that life was not entirely gone.

"I guess he's *sort o' 'live* yet," said one of the boys.

"Let's give him another pill," rejoined the other.

Accordingly, the other gun was pointed over the log, and discharged. The larger boy then advanced with a long stick, with which he felt his adversary at a distance; and having thus satisfied himself, he at last approached the body, and seated himself on it in triumph. He then shouted for his brother, "Come here, Bill! where are you? why *you're no account,* to be afraid of a dead bear. I've *used him up,* the right way. He's *cold as a wagon-tire.*"

The officers now came forward to speak to the heroic children, and learned that they had discovered the bear while at play, and ran to the house; but finding that both their parents were absent, and knowing that their father's guns were always loaded, they had determined to attempt the exploit themselves.*

When the officers turned to retrace their steps, Colonel Grant expressed his admiration of this singular adventure in strong language; and Major Gordon took the opportunity to remark that it afforded an apt illustration of the subject on which they had been conversing. "It is thus," said he, "that the people of the frontier rear their children. Their very sports lead them into danger, and they learn the artifices of the chase so early, that the knowledge is almost an instinct. The moment a lad can carry a gun, he becomes a hunter, as the young falcon as soon as he can prune his wing darts upon his prey."

"What inference do you draw from that fact?"

"Simply, that these backwoodsmen are better fitted for a campaign in their own forests than our European soldiers."

Perhaps the colonel was convinced. It is no small evi-

---

* Founded on fact.

dence in favour of such a supposition, that he dropped the subject and remained silent for some time. He then gaily asked his young friend, " when he had last seen the barrack-master's daughter ?"

" This morning," replied the other with some hesitation. .

" And will not the gallant Major Gordon who has met His Majesty's enemies on so many fields, acknowledge that his stock of prudence has been very suddenly and marvellously increased by his tenderness for the safety of a fair lady ?"

" Whenever my commanding officer can show his right to act the part of the father-confessor, I will answer the question."

" Pardon me, Gordon; I pry not into your secrets. Here we are at the gate. Go to the fair Alice, if such be your intention. At two we meet in council at the mess-room."

Perhaps the most important character, at this time, in Fort Cumberland, was the barrack-master. Ensign Hagerty had entered the service some thirty years before, a spruce, Irish lad, with no other ambition than that of living like a gentleman and dying like a soldier. The first he had always done, and the last he had never avoided. But although he used to boast that he had been in more battles than he had hairs on his head, he had somehow never been able to advance beyond the grade of ensign. Yet he had all those good qualities that used to be so highly regarded in the mess-room. His good-humour was infinite, he sung an excellent song, told a story well, loved good eating, and could starve, on proper occasions, with the patience of a camel. He had married, for love, a beautiful but penniless woman, and become the happy father of five girls, who were now grown— the youngest just turned of fifteen, and the eldest in the full bloom of her beauty. What would have become of these girls after the death of their mother, it is hard to tell, had not a relative in Philadelphia taken them and reared them. The decease of their kind friend which had recently taken place threw them once more on the hands of the ensign, or, as he expressed it, obliged him to take command of his own company.

It is necessary to state in this place, that the worthy ensign was not only above the ordinary stature, but had been annually increasing in circumference, until he had grown so unwieldy as to be wholly unfit for actual service. Putting all these things together, he conceived himself a fit subject for the special favour of His Majesty's government, and accordingly waited on the commander of the forces to solicit some employment which would impose less duty and yield more profit, assigning for reasons that he had a larger amount of clay to nourish than ordinary men, and more daughters than became an ensign. The consequence was that he received the appointment of barrack-master at Fort Cumberland, where there were no barracks to superintend, with several other sinecures, the aggregate emoluments of which placed him in easy circumstances. What was still better, he was promised, on the reduction of Fort du Quesne, the office of town major, with the addition of a lucrative post in the commissariat. After all, his five daughters constituted his greatest wealth. They were tall, beautiful women, very showy, and quite accomplished. A remarkable circumstance was the strong likeness which they all bore to each other in form and feature; the two youngest particularly could scarcely be distinguished by their acquaintances. It may be well supposed that, with such a family, the barrack-master was a prosperous candidate for all sorts of honours. The title of major fell to him by courtesy. His house became the rendezvous of all the officers, as it certainly afforded the most attractive society in the garrison. Whenever there was a profitable job to be executed, or a fat contract to be given, he was sure to get it; and after spending the prime of his life in hardship, neglect, and poverty, he had reached that enviable period in the career of an old soldier, when he might lawfully sit by his own fireside,

smoke his pipe, sing merry songs, and tell over his campaigns
to the young officers.

The preparations for the march were now going rapidly
forward. The troops had been for some time engaged in
cutting a road across the mountains, and had advanced as far
as the Laurel Ridge. The fort was surrounded by the Indian
allies of the British, who had been engaged to join in the expedition, and whose slight lodges were scattered irregularly
through the valley. The warriors, fancifully painted, and pro-
fusely decked with feathers and other ornaments, were seen
strolling about or engaged in councils, war dances, or athletic
exercises.

While things were in this situation, the young Alice—to
wit, Miss Hagerty Number 4—went one day to visit the sick
wife of a soldier, who resided in a hut outside of the fort, and
having paid her the attention which her situation required,
attempted to return by a path that seemed to be nearer than
the usually travelled road, which was somewhat crowded
with soldiers and Indian warriors. Another motive might
have induced her to wander from the beaten track. Alice
had given her young heart and plighted her faith to Major
Gordon; and as it is a generally received opinion that
ladies thus situated are much given to solitary contemplation,
it is possible that she might have chosen this secluded way
in the hope of enjoying in its picturesque shades a few moments of delightful abstraction. If that was the case, the
young lady displayed more good taste than prudence, for it
was a romantic path, leading by a serpentine course to the
little rivulet that waters this noble valley; and she lingered
along the bank of the stream, delighted with miniature cas-
cades and eddies, and the various attractions of the scenery,
still keeping the narrow pathway, which was closely hemmed
in with bushes. At last she began to fear that she had lost
her way. But she was a high-spirited girl, and felt little
alarm. Although the fort was not visible, she could occasion-

18

ally, through the openings of the woods, see its proud flag, waving gaily in the breeze, and she felt no apprehension of an enemy while in sight of that emblem of her country's power. It would be easy, too, to retrace her steps, and she was about to do so, when a bird of beautiful plumage attracted her attention.  Young ladies in love are fond of birds too— for the tender passion softens the heart and renders it sensitive to all that is lovely in nature, and the plumed songster, so melodious in the expression of his attachments, so tender, faithful, and assiduous, is an especial object of sympathy. She followed it with her eye as it alighted on the bough of a large tree, and was attentively watching its graceful movements, when the figure of an Indian sitting among the branches arrested her attention.  He was painted with colours so nearly resembling those of the bark of the tree, that it was difficult to distinguish his form among the branches; and Alice would not have discovered him, had not her glance been intensely fixed upon the very spot where he sat, but a few yards above her head.  She started back in terror, and the spy, for such he was, hastily discharged an arrow that whistled by her ear and buried itself in the ground.  Uttering a piercing shriek, she turned to fly, while the Indian, dropping from his place of concealment, pursued, caught her flowing dress, and was raising his tomahawk to strike, when a young man of athletic frame thrust himself between them.  With one hand he pushed back the assailant, and with the other brandished his knife.  The Indian waited not for the attack, but darting backward, fled at full speed.  The forester shouted a signal cry, and in a moment a number of the friendly Indians appeared, who, being informed of the cause of the alarm, dashed off in pursuit of the fugitive.  The warcry was re-echoed by a hundred voices : the whole of the surrounding woods seemed instantly to be alive ; the terrific yell sounded on every side ; the tread of feet upon the dry leaves and the tramp of horses announced that the whole Indian host was awakened. Then all was silent. The alarm given and the cause understood, the warriors were tracking the fugitive spy with noiseless steps. Again, another shout arose; they had secured their victim.

In the mean while, the stranger who had so providently rescued the barrack-master's daughter from the tomahawk, offered her his arm and reconducted her to the fort. He was a young man, who might have been considered surpassingly ugly, if it had not been that his features, though coarse and irregular, wore an expression of courage and honesty. He was a lieutenant in a company of volunteers recently arrived from the frontiers of Virginia, and had already served several campaigns against the enemy. Though of a good family, he was rugged and unpolished; for the country, in its then unsettled state, afforded none of the means of education, and while other gentlemen were sent to distant schools, the youthful Dangerly engaged as a private soldier in all the military enterprises of the frontier. Naturally modest and sensible of his ungraceful appearance, he soon became bashful, and was famous among his comrades for his aversion to female society; and while he never shrunk from the face of an enemy, the approach of a lady never failed to put him to instant flight. In the field he was in his element, daring, active, and fertile of expedient; in camp he was the best of all good fellows— always happy, ready for duty, and true to his friend, enjoyed an excellent appetite, and slept as soundly on the ground as in a feather-bed.

Mr. Dangerly was not a woman-hater—he had too much good feeling for that, but a woman-fearer; and on this occasion the distress of the beautiful girl, who stood trembling and almost fainting, called all his better qualities into action. He was surprised into the politeness of a true cavalier, and gave her his arm with the kindness of a brother and the ease of a gentleman. He assured her of the absence of all danger, and soothed her inquietude in tones which, though habitually

rough, were bland and sympathetic. Had he been patting
his favourite horse on the neck, he could not have used more
coaxing language; and his brother officers were struck with
astonishment when they beheld the worthy lieutenant advancing towards the fort arm in arm with the barrack-master's
daughter, and pouring soft expressions in her ear with the
eagerness of a devoted lover.

Mr. Dangerly was not aware of the warmth of his expressions or the tenderness of his manner, for they sprang warm
from as kind a heart as ever throbbed, and thinking only of the
fears of his companion, he gave full vent to the utterance of
his native benevolence. He was placed, too, for the first
time, in contact with a young and lovely woman, who, besides
being habitually polite, was under the excitement of a deep
sense of gratitude towards her protector, and replied to his
remarks with an ease and spirit, softened by the circumstances
of the moment into that confidence which so easily steals
into youthful hearts. The gracefulness of her beautiful form,
as it hung for support on his manly arm, her low, tremulous
voice, and the rich melody of her tones, all went directly to
the heart of the gallant Virginian ; and he wondered how it
happened that, among the numberless enjoyments of life, he
had never before learned to estimate the most exquisite of
them all, the love of woman. It was therefore with some surprise that, on accidentally looking round, he found himself an
object of general attention, and saw that he was detected in
the fact of gallanting a lady. But there was no room for
retreat; the lady was under his escort, and although the main
entrance of the fort was thronged with spectators, drawn
thither by the alarm, and whose glances were more formidable to him than the guns of that fortress would have been in
an engagement, yet, having satisfied himself, by a hasty
glance, that he must run the gauntlet, he boldly prepared " to
pass defile in front," and push on. The evolution was happily accomplished ; and the British officers being all engaged

in a council of war, he conducted his fair charge to her father's door without interruption, and then, having exhausted his stock of courage, hastily bowed and retired, covered with confusion, to his own tent. We pass over the rough jokes that were levelled at our worthy officer by his relentless companions. He bore them with his wonted composure, but inwardly vowed that while he would cherish through life the delightful vision that was impressed upon his fancy, he would never again venture his heart within the fascination of a woman's eye, nor subject himself to the shame and ridicule which had followed his first adventure under the banners of Cupid.

The event just related induced Colonel Grant to hasten his preparations. A part of the troops had already been sent forward, and were employed in cutting a road across the mountains. Washington, then a young officer, had urged Colonel Bouquet, who commanded on this frontier, to advance the troops by the route which had been travelled by General Braddock three years before, which followed the trace usually pursued by the Indians, and being now somewhat beaten, was better than any new road could be made with the small force and limited means at the disposal of that officer. But "those whom the gods doom to destruction they first deprive of understanding;" the same power which decreed the downfal of British power on this continent, seems to have almost invariably used her own officers as the instrument of defeat; and the contempt of the latter for the advice and aid of their colonial friends produced always the same disastrous consequences. Month after month had been consumed in the herculean task of opening a military road over the Alpine cliffs and gloomy abysses of the Alleghany range. The work had now proceeded as far as the Loyalhanna, a mountain stream, where a post was established, at which the troops were about to be concentrated.

Arrived at the latter place, Colonel Grant's detachment,

consisting of the Highlanders and a small body of Virginians from the regiment of Colonel Washington, attached to it much against the will of Grant, was organized, and set forward on their march towards Fort Du Quesne. The alacrity of this leader, and his gallant bearing, were now as conspicuous as his total ignorance of the country and of the habits of his enemy. He had no idea of the rapidity and secrecy of movement which form the most striking feature of border warfare; where every soldier carries his own ammunition and provisions, sleeps in his blanket under a tree, and is ready for a march or for battle at a moment's warning. But under every disadvantage the brave Highlanders moved forward with a noble spirit. The newly cut road by which they passed, embracing all the ridges of the Alleghany mountains, was already blocked up in some places by fallen trees, or rendered almost impracticable by deep ravines washed by the heavy rains that poured in torrents down the sides of these precipitous heights. Sometimes the path wound over a series of hideous precipices, which seemed inaccessible; and sometimes an impetuous river, rushing and foaming over the sharp fragments of rock which formed its bed, seemed to render any further advance impracticable. But this inhospitable region was at length left behind them, and they entered that great Western valley which was destined to become the home of millions.

Major Hagerty, the barrack-master, accompanied the expedition, for the purpose of being on the spot to enter on the new duties which would devolve on him at the capture of Fort Du Quesne. Notwithstanding his unwieldy ponderance of body, he made his arrangements with the alacrity of an old campaigner. Though not elated like his junior companions with the hope of laurels to be gathered on the field of battle, he entered with spirit into their cheerfulness, and seemed to share their bright anticipations of success. There was, it is true, some difficulty in procuring him a suitable conveyance; some of the officers proposed to stow him in an extra baggage-wagon; others suggested that a fatigue party should be detailed to carry him on a litter, while a better opinion seemed to be that he might be advantageously mounted in a horizontal position on a gun-carriage and drawn by four horses. The worthy man, however, was seated at last on a strong charger, and set out in high glee; and if on any occasion his unwieldy bulk and difficulty of locomotion rendered him burthensome to his companions, he fully compensated for the inconvenience by the life and merriment with which he inspired the whole party.

After many toils they descended into the vale of the Monongahela, and never did the traveller's eye trace the course of a more lovely stream. Winding through bold hills with a gentle current, the river itself is as placid as the surrounding scenery is wild and picturesque. At some places the steep promontories that hemmed it in seemed barely to afford room for its passage, and at others it was margined by fertile valleys and rich table lands. The most remarkable feature of the scenery was the gigantic growth of the forest trees and the exquisite luxuriance of the foliage. The boughs were weighed down with their load of leaves; there was also a depth and richness of colouring which the face of Nature displays only in the most favoured climates and luxuriant spots. In the many varieties of green exhibited in the forest, there was always a brilliancy of hue which conveyed to the mind an impression of vigour and freshness; the flowers and wild fruits assumed every shade of the gorgeous and the delicate in colour; while the whole was illumed with the intense brilliancy of a September sun, which had slightly tinged the most prominent points of the uplands with autumnal tints, without destroying the verdure of summer.

An excursion through such a region in so delightful a season might, under different circumstances, have afforded high enjoyment to a romantic mind. But here were dangers to be

surmounted and toils to be endured.  Sometimes the thunder-
cloud, rolling along the mountain side, poured down torrents
of rain, the vivid lightning shattered the tall trees, and the
heavy explosions, reverberated from a thousand caverns,
struck the stoutest heart with awe.   Sometimes a whole day's
march was performed without rest or food.   A lurking Indian
was occasionally seen prowling around the camp, and darting
away when discovered with the fleetness of the antelope,
yelling defiance or laughing in derision.   The straggler who
imprudently wandered from his companions, perished of hunger among these savage fastnesses or fell under the tomahawk; while the nightly howl of the wolf admonished the
weary soldiers that the beast of prey was patiently pursuing
their footsteps and eagerly thirsting for their blood.

After a long and arduous march, they at length reached
the vicinity of Fort Du Quesne.  It was late in the night
when they descended towards the fortress and encamped on
the brow of a small eminence which overlooked it.   The
enemy slept in security, unconscious of their approach.   The
French were doubtless aware that such an expedition was in
progress, but the attempts of the English to penetrate the
wilderness in this direction had hitherto been uniformly disastrous, and but little danger was now apprehended from the
troops of that nation.   Perverse in their opinions, rash and
headstrong in their plans, they had neither conciliated the
Indian tribes, availed themselves of the aid of the native
American troops, nor gathered wisdom from the lessons of
experience.   The French, therefore, prepared and awaiting
their enemy in the confidence of success, supposed him to be
still at the distance of several days' march.

The British soldiers slept that night with their accoutrements on and their arms at their sides, ready for action upon
the first alarm.

An hour before the dawn of day, Colonel Grant was
awakened by a slight touch of a friendly hand.   He sprung

from his mattress with the alacrity of a well-trained soldier.

"Ah, Major Gordon! What is the matter? It is not day!"

"No, but it soon will be; and if we are to fight the French this morning, it is time to be stirring."

"You are right. It will be a glorious day for us, I trust. And yet if I was a believer in some of the superstitions of our country, I should feel discouraged by the dreams that have haunted my pillow during the night. Do you believe in such things, Gordon?"

"It is hard to believe that which is contrary to reason; yet it is difficult to deny what so many of our ancestors have asserted, and what many of our countrymen still hold to be true."

"You are a believer, then; I might have known that. Where is the true Scot who will give up one jot of the faith of his fathers? But come, let us see if all's well."

So saying, the two officers stepped out of the tent and walked through the encampment. The morning was clear and calm. The air had that chilliness which precedes the dawn of day. The soldiers slept; not a sound was heard in the camp or in the surrounding forest. The dim form of the sentinel as he walked his post was the only object that moved. The officers passed round the chain of sentries, giving the word in a low tone, and then returned towards the colonel's tent.

"It is strange," resumed Colonel Grant, "that the firmness of a man can be shaken by a mere phantasy. I am not superstitious. Yet, last night, lying, as I supposed, wide awake, I distinctly saw our soldiers passing one by one through my tent, so slowly that I could recognise every individual. They were all bloody and mutilated. I have seen men stretched on the field of battle, but never did I behold such dreadful gashes, such marks of wanton butchery. They

18*

seemed to bid me farewell. I arose, looked round, but saw
no one. The sentry in front of my tent assured me that no
one had entered. I threw myself down, but again, and again,
and again the same apparitions appeared. This incident has
affected me. But come, let us shake off these unbecoming
fancies; they are unworthy of British soldiers, especially of
us, who have really no danger to encounter, and are sent
to crush a nest of half-civilized French and ignorant savages."

"You despise our foe too much," replied Major Gordon;
"however deficient they may be in discipline, they are brave
and cunning; and their fortress is capable of affording a stout
resistance to a force like ours, unprovided with a train of
artillery."

"Mere fudge!" exclaimed the colonel, "they know better
than to resist us. At the first sight of his majesty's flag they
will sue for peace."

"Believe it not; with their advantage of numbers, of
position, of ample supplies, and of a familiar knowledge of
the country, success on our part will be gained only by hard
fighting and artful management."

"What artifice would Major Gordon propose?"

"No other than an early attack, by which the enemy shall
be surprised before he is aware of our presence."

"No, by Jupiter! I'll fight the rascals *here*, and by daylight. I hate ambuscades, midnight attacks, and scaling walls
like a thief in the night. They will be sufficiently *surprised*,
I take it, at not being allowed time to run away. No, sir, we
will fight them at our leisure. Let the reveillé be sounded.
We will try the metal of these Monsieurs. If they are brave,
let them come out and fight us on the plain; if not, let them
surrender."

"Perhaps they may not choose to do either."

"Then by St. Andrew we shall scale their ramparts in
broad day. A band of brave Scots, with a Grant and a Gor-

don at their head, need fear no odds. Let the music sound, if you please, major."

With a reluctant step, and a melancholy foreboding of the disastrous consequences of so imprudent a measure, the second in command obeyed the orders of his superior. In a few minutes the cheerful tones of the bugle were heard echoing from hill to hill, the ruffle of the drum and the shrill notes of the fife succeeded, and then the martial melody of the full band burst upon the repose of the valley. The troops paraded at the sound and stood by their arms, slowly and gradually filling up the long line, as a number of the beautiful airs of their native glens were played in succession and the music floated over the hills. The darkness of the night was around them, but a number of lights held by the serjeants who called the rolls, shed a faint light along the ranks, and showed a line of stern faces and athletic figures, clad, as was allowable, in all the varieties of military undress. Some were in regimentals, some in great coats, some wore the Highland bonnet, and others night-caps; but all these gallant soldiers, as they leaned on their muskets, showed the stern indifference or careless courage of men who, having imbibed the opinions of their leader, felt no sense of danger to themselves or of respect for their foe. The officers strolled along the lines, yawning from their slumbers, or collected in groups, some looking suspiciously towards the surrounding thickets, and others conversing in low accents on the anticipated events of the ensuing day.

"These are new tactics," said the old serjeant-major to the barrack-master, as they sat together on the end of a log.

"Quite novel," replied the latter; "the Frenchman ought to be much obliged to us for giving him timely notice of our approach. If Monsieur would only stretch his courtesy so far as to invite us all to breakfast, I should take it as a kindness. This bush-fighting, O'Doherty, makes sad inroads upon the regular habits of old campaigners like you and I. Nothing but cold meat and forced marches. If we were snug in yonder fort I should like it, if it were only for the honour of the regiment and the credit of sitting once more at a decent table."

"Young men will have their own way," croaked the serjeant-major, whose appetite just then was not the keenest.

"Aye," rejoined his friend, "and old soldiers who look for promotion should have quiet tongues—bushes have ears as well as walls."

The day now began to dawn, and Colonel Grant, advancing towards a circle of officers, began to give orders.

"Major Lewis," said he to a brave Virginian, who commanded the small corps from the regiment of Colonel Washington, "you will take charge of the baggage, and retire with it two miles to the rear."

The major bowed assent, remarking that it would have been gratifying to him and to his men to participate in the action.

"It will be a mere skirmish," replied the commanding officer, "these fellows will not fight, depend upon it; and if they should, your militia, major, would only be in the way."

"Captain Brinton," continued he, "you will take an escort and reconnoitre the enemy's works. We have no time to spare, sir; ride up to the esplanade and take a rough plan. If there are any buildings in the vicinity that would interrupt our approach, burn them. Let us dress for parade, gentlemen, and after that, if the Frenchman should not be polite enough to give us the first call, we will pay him a morning visit."

The troops dispersed, and were soon engaged in active preparations for breakfast, for the morning parade, and for battle. Fires were kindled round the encampment, and the business of cooking commenced. Men were seen brushing their clothes, burnishing their guns, placing new flints in their locks, and preparing in various ways for the active business

of the day. The sun now rose in unclouded splendour over
the eastern hills, lighting up a landscape of unrivalled beauty.
The camp was situated on a small hill, overlooking the woods
on either side. On the left was seen the Monongahela, a
placid, serpentine river, meandering through a broken, picturesque region and margined with forests of matchless luxuriance. Beyond this stream was a range of tall hills, covered
with timber, and whose western exposure, not yet lighted by
the morning sun, was clothed in the deepest and richest shades.
On the right was the Alleghany, a bold, rapid current, rushing
over broken rocks and covered with foam, which sparkled
with sunbeams, while the hills beyond were glowing with
brilliant hues. In front, these rivers were beheld mingling
their waters, and forming by their junction the beautiful and
majestic Ohio, which swept off to the west in a broad, smooth,
and rapid stream. On the point of land formed by the
" meeting of the waters," stood Fort Du Quesne, whose
massy parapets were embosomed in forests, and whose gaudy
flag was sporting its gay colours over a wilderness of green.
Not a sound was heard from that solitary fortress, not a living
creature was seen, to give evidence that it was the abode of
man or the seat of military power. Between that and the
British camp was a plain, thickly wooded, with the exception
of a strip occupied by a cluster of straggling huts and a few
small newly-cleared fields. Such was the scene displayed to
the eyes of the military strangers; and if its silence and
solitude conveyed to their minds an idea of the timidity of
the foe, who seemed to shrink from observation and retire
from conflict, there was also a sense of awe induced by the
vastness of the amphitheatre and the noiseless repose of its
secluded valleys. The excitement produced by the sight of a
proudly marshalled enemy, by the clangor of arms, the rapid
transit of neighing steeds, the flourish of trumpets, and the
bustle of military evolutions was absent from this exhibition,
and the soldiers gazed around them in doubt and silence.

Suddenly a thick column of smoke was seen ascending into the air, and in another moment the cabins near the fort were wrapped in flames. Still not an enemy was seen. The engineer who had been charged with the duty of reconnoitring the fort, and who had fired the village, marched leisurely and carelessly back to camp, with the security of one who having taunted the foe by approaching to the muzzles of his guns, was convinced of his cowardice or weakness.

"What news?" inquired the colonel, as his emissary advanced to report the execution of his orders; "I hope you had a pleasant visit, captain, and found Monsieur in good health and spirits."

"Monsieur was *not at home*," replied the officer; "I found the gate locked, and not even a porter to answer my call. Having no opportunity, therefore, of even leaving my card, I kindled a bonfire, as the only feasible mode of announcing to him that I had paid my respects."

"A very good idea, captain; now, gentlemen, let us to breakfast, and after that, if this unsocial Frenchman should continue to keep his gates barred, we will try the virtue of an escalade."

The officers retired to their tents, the soldiers sat in little groups in the open air with their smoking messes before them, and all were engaged in doing justice to the coarse fare of a camp with the keen appetites of veteran campaigners, when the report of a musket was heard and a bullet whistled over their heads. The soldiers started to their feet and the officers rushed from their tents.

"Who fired that gun?" demanded the officer of the day.

No one replied, and the soldiers looked round at each other, for even yet none suspected that a foeman was near.

"The enemy! the enemy!" shouted several of the sentinels, and the same moment a shower of balls poured in upon the British, accompanied by the signal calls of numerous bugles and the loud yell of the savage.

"To arms !" exclaimed the colonel.

"Fall in ! fall in !" cried the company officers.

"Form your companies, gentlemen !" roared the colonel, "the day is our own, my brave Highlanders ! Music there ! beat all the drums and drown that cursed yelling ! Let the guard be called in ! Major Gordon, take a company and dislodge the enemy from the thickets on our right !"

Before these several orders could be executed, the battle thickened around the devoted party, and the bullets poured in upon them from every side. The Indians, hideously painted and decked in their savage finery, advanced audaciously so near that their dark forms could be plainly distinguished as they glided from tree to tree. The sharp shrill sound of the war-whoop, uttered in tones resembling the barking of a small dog, acquired a terrific volume and frightful energy from the number of voices engaged in the horrible concert. The sentinels, disdaining to fly, were slain at their posts before they could be relieved, and their bodies wantonly butchered in full view of their comrades by the fiends who tore them in pieces with hellish exultation.

Colonel Grant displayed all the coolness and gallantry of an accomplished soldier, exposing a solid front to the enemy, and bravely attempting, by desperate charges, to dislodge them from the surrounding coverts. But he now learned how unavailing is courage when it is not guided by prudent counsels and accurate information, and how inefficient are the tactics of regular warfare in a contest with barbarian hordes in their native forests. The French and Indians, dispersing themselves through the woods, occupied every thicket which afforded concealment, and lurked behind every object which afforded the protection of a natural rampart. Some were placed in the ravines and hollows, stretched at full length on the ground ; some kneeled behind the great trunks of fallen trees, while the boldest warriors advanced singly, each selecting a standing tree as a cover, and firing from behind it with but little exposure of his own person. If they pressed forward, it was by darting rapidly from one tree to another; if they retreated, the same operation was practised in an inverted order; and thus while the European troops stood together in compact ranks, affording a broad and stationary mark to an army of sharp-shooters, their own bullets whistled harmlessly through the forest.

The lines of the brave Highlanders were rapidly thinned, and their leader, stung to desperation, determined at last to rush into closer conflict, be the consequence what it might. Placing himself at the head of the whole detachment, he dashed forward into the thickest body of the enemy. The Indians, smeared with blood and excited to fury, closed around them. The bayonet and the cutlass came into contact with war-club and tomahawk, and the shouts of the maddened soldiers were mingled with the yell of the savage. For a moment the stout Scots felt the stern joy of gratified revenge as their foes fell around them; but their success was but momentary; outnumbered, hemmed in, and entangled in the brushwood, they were rapidly dwindling in force, while the places of their slain foes were continually supplied by new reinforcements.

At this crisis a heavy volley was heard in the rear, mingled with loud and reiterated cheers, and Major Lewis, with that band of Virginians who had been ordered away, that they might not impede the motions of the regulars, was seen advancing. Adopting, to some extent, the Indian mode of warfare, his men came forward in a long, irregular line, firing from behind the trees, and each individual aiming at a particular foe, and discharging his rifle at his own discretion with deadly effect. Rapidly but cautiously they moved on, sweeping the enemy before them, and reached the battle-ground just as Colonel Grant had been struck down and was about to be dragged away by the Indians. Major Lewis rushed to the rescue, but these officers were soon separated from their

troops and both taken captive. The patriotic Virginians stood
their ground, undismayed by the loss of their commander
and undaunted by the fierceness of the battle, while the enemy
fell back under the destructive energy of the American rifle,
and collected their forces for a more desperate effort. Two
hundred of the Highlanders had now fallen, and the remainder,
panic-struck and thrown into confusion, stood crowded together
in stupid dismay, while their brave defenders faced the enemy
with cool disciplined courage. The battle still raged with
great fury, for the Virginians, adding experience to ardour,
and magnanimously devoting themselves to the protection of
those who had so lately spurned their assistance, fought like
men resolved to conquer or to die. The enemy was soon
forced to act on the defensive, and at length, after a great
loss, retired sullenly from the contest. Major Gordon rallied
the Highlanders, and a retreat was effected in good order to
the place where Major Lewis had left the baggage under a
small guard. The conduct of the handful of Americans who
so gallantly turned the fortune of the day, may be estimated
not only by their brilliant success, but by their loss. Out of
eight officers, five were killed, a sixth wounded, and a seventh
taken prisoner; and of one hundred and sixty-six privates,
sixty-two were killed.

But what became of the barrack-master? Having no
command, and being too honourable to fly, Major Hagerty
stationed himself as near the centre of the troops as he could,
from a prudent conviction that an unnecessary exposure of
his person would neither benefit his country nor himself.
Here he stood for a long while, pushed forward when the
troops advanced, pushed backward when they recoiled, and
dreadfully pushed all the while, in his fat sides, by the soldiers' elbows and the butts of their muskets. At last wearied
with this exercise, he very deliberately seated himself on a
log, and watched the conflict with a wary eye, until finding
that the prospect of becoming town major was every moment

growing more faint, his military ardour began to kindle, and
seizing the sword of an officer who had fallen, he stepped into
his place. Here he performed good service until the retreat
was ordered, an evolution which was performed in good order,
but with such rapidity that he was soon left puffing and blow-
ing in the rear. The Indians in full pursuit were yelling
behind him like a pack of hungry wolves, while the Virginian
rangers were fiercely beating them back and covering the
retreat. On he waddled nearly exhausted; at last the Highlanders were almost out of sight, and the covering party came
sweeping by, led by an officer mounted on horseback, and
covered with blood and dust.

" Run, Falstaff !" shouted the officer.

" Run yourself !" replied the exhausted veteran, "my race
is over."

" Hurra, boys !" shouted the officer ; " beat back the blood-
hounds ! Old Virginia for ever ! Run, old gentleman !"

The barrack-master stopped, folded his arms, staggered
against a tree, and stood in sullen desperation awaiting his
fate ; " I can go no further," said he, faintly ; " I can die—
my poor children !"

In a moment the officer, who was Mr. Dangerly, was at
his side, and dismounted ; " Take my horse," said he.

Hagerty was brave, but exhausted with heat and unwonted
exertion, daunted by the near approach of a cruel death, and
overcome by the recollection of his helpless family, a desperate
apathy was creeping over him. He gazed at his preserver
wildly. A mingled expression of stupidity and fierceness
marked his features, mental agony and bodily exhaustion
combined to unsettle his faculties. " Let them come !" he
exclaimed ; "I can die but once. Tell my poor girls that I
acted like a soldier, and run as long as I could."

Dangerly, assisted by his men, placed him on the horse ;
the change of position brought him to his senses, he looked
round for a moment like one awakened from a dream, then

pressing his heels into the charger's sides, was borne in a few minutes to his companions.

"There goes the last of them!" shouted Dangerly; "now for another charge! Hurra, my brave fellows! Virginia for ever!"

The Indians, once more driven back, pursued no further, and the covering party, dripping with sweat and blood, soon joined the main body.

This was a proud triumph for the Virginia troops. At the commencement of the expedition their services had been pressed upon Colonel Grant against his wishes, and he had on the morning of this eventful day ordered them away from the field of battle in the most ungracious manner. Forgetting these indignities, they came to the rescue of the king's troops with a magnanimity as creditable to them as the skill and gallantry displayed in the conflict. They had decisively beaten the same enemy which had first defeated a vastly superior number of the regular forces; and while the latter were well content to escape captivity or death, the brave Virginians were entitled to all the laurels of this hard-fought field. Mr. Dangerly especially looked back upon the events of this day with emotions of pride and pleasure. Although a very young officer, the death or capture of all his superiors had placed him in command, and to him chiefly redounded the glory of retrieving the battle. But, above all, he felt a secret joy in the service which he had rendered to the barrack-master. The beautiful vision of Alice Hagerty had not faded from his memory. The adventure at Fort Cumberland, the only one of his life in which a fair lady was a party, had been cherished and brooded over until it had made a permanent impression upon his imagination. Ardent and romantic in his temperament, he suffered his fancy to dwell upon this agreeable incident, until that which was at first viewed as a mere possibility, began to assume the form of truth, and he not only became fully persuaded that he was in love himself, but even ventured to fancy that the young lady might in time be proved to possess a heart as susceptible as his own.  As for the barrack-master, he was not ungrateful, as will be seen in the sequel of this veracious legend.

We shall now leave these perilous wars, of which the reader has perhaps had a surfeit, and change the scene to Fort Cumberland.  The troops had returned, and Major Hagerty sat by his own fireside, surrounded by all his social comforts, and tall daughters.  He was repeating the story of the battle —the twentieth edition with copious notes—and was dwelling especially on his own miraculous *hair*-breadth escape from the *barber*-ous surgical operation of scalping, wherein he spake eloquently of the magnanimous conduct of Mr. Dangerly, in giving up his horse at a time when this heroic young man was so exhausted from fatigue and loss of blood as to render the act one of generous self-sacrifice.

" What a noble deed !" exclaimed Alice.

" Considering that he was never out of America, it was quite remarkable," said Miss Hagerty Number 1.

" A very clever action, I declare," echoed Number 2.

" We are under infinite obligations to him," simpered Number 3.

The barrack-master puffed the tobacco smoke in large volumes from his mouth, and after musing for some minutes, said, with a significant glance,

" I fear, Alice, my dear, that he has lost his heart."

The young lady blushed deeply, for the impression made by her beauty upon the heart of the American officer had been the subject of so much conversation and merriment, that the allusion could not be misunderstood.

" Gordon need hardly fear such a rival," remarked Number 1, ironically—for Number 1, with reverence be it spoken, had passed the mature age of five-and-twenty, and sometimes spoke tartly in relation to young men.

The father seemed hurt, and warmly replied, " You might

be proud, either of you, of such a lover. Would to Heaven
he had placed his affections on either of my daughters, except
Alice, whose heart is not her own."

" I hope, papa," said Number 2, bridling her pretty head,
" you do not intend to *offer* us to this singularly uncouth
young man ?"

"—A person of no family—" continued Number 3.

"—And a mere colonist—" added Number 1.

" Don't be at all alarmed, girls," exclaimed Number 5, a
blooming maiden of sixteen, with an arch eye, a round blushing cheek, and a forehead of snowy whiteness, " be quite easy
—I intend to have Mr. Dangerly myself."

" Eleanor !" said Miss Hagerty.

" Nay, do not lecture me, sister. If my seniors choose to
waive their birthrights, I shall put in my claim. I set my
cap for the lieutenant—shall I not, pa ?" cried the laughing
girl. And there the conference ended.

Eleanor was quite in earnest. She was a girl of high
spirit, with a warm heart, and a quick wit. Dangerly's chivalrous conduct on two occasions, in both of which her family
had become so largely his debtor, had interested her greatly in
his favour. She was very young, and her feelings were easily
excited. Having never seen Mr. Dangerly, her curiosity became
strongly awakened, and her impatience to behold one whose
name was now frequently mentioned in connection with his
brilliant exploits, contributed to kindle in her bosom certain
tender sensations, which she called admiration, but to which the
experienced reader will be able to affix a much more appropriate
appellation. Besides, she had been brought up in Philadelphia,
and though too young while there to go into company, her
taste was formed, and certain associations impressed upon her
mind. These were by no means favourable to His Majesty's
officers, who were now her only male companions. She liked
neither their red coats nor their red faces. Accustomed to
the neatness, order, intellectuality, and strict morals of a re-

spectable Philadelphia circle, she found little to please her in
the overbearing manners, the coarse wit, and dissipated habits
of the British officers; while the young American was always
spoken of as one whose good sense and virtue equalled his
courage.   It will therefore not be wondered at, that the fair
Eleanor should have formed the determination expressed
above, nor that while she thus spoke in jest, she should in
sober earnest have resolved to "set her cap for the lieutenant."

One more scene, and we shall have ended.  Lieutenant
Dangerly, in spite of his bashfulness, had resolved to pay a
visit to the fair Alice.  Perhaps he never would have plucked
up courage for such an enterprise, had not his comrades
teased him until he became desperate, while the report of her
engagement to Major Gordon awakened his jealousy.  "If it
be true," thought he, "that her heart is plighted to Gordon,
I shall not complain.  He is a fine fellow, and deserves her.
But I shall feel better satisfied when I know from her own
lips that there is no hope for me."

Behold him now seated in the barrack-master's parlour,
twirling his hat in his hands and watching the door with a
palpitating heart.  At length a light step is heard, and the
fairy form of Eleanor glided in.  The lieutenant rose, scraped
his best bow, dropped his hat, picked it up, and was about to
hand a chair, when he perceived that the young lady was
already seated.  He glanced wistfully at the door and meditated a retreat; "If I could only avoid a close action by
passing defile in the rear," thought he—but it was too late.

Eleanor was too polite, and entertained too sincere a regard for her visitor, to notice these things.  She led the way
in conversation—talked of the recent campaigns, of guns,
horses, and parades, with the fluency of one well versed in
such subjects ; and her visitor, forgetting his embarrassment,
unconsciously fell into an animated dialogue.  Dangerly's
heart was now irrevocably gone.  If the young lady's beauty

had fascinated his senses, her wit, her spirit, above all, her respectful politeness, and the evident interest with which she listened to him, completed the conquest of his affections. An hour rolled away, when, unable to remain longer in suspense, he said,

"May I, without giving offence, ask you one question?"

"Oh, yes; I love to answer questions."

"Are you—is Major Gordon—pardon me for seeming so inquisitive—are you *absolutely* engaged to Major Gordon?"

"I am not engaged to Major Gordon!"

"Not engaged! Do you say that positively?"

"I never was more in earnest," replied the blushing girl.

"Strange! Why, the whole garrison believed you to be on the eve of marriage with Major Gordon!"

"Major Gordon is engaged to my sister," replied Eleanor, quite composedly.

Dangerly rose and paced the room; his heart was in his throat, and his limbs trembled with emotion. Eleanor walked to a window, and began to feel a little choked too.

"One more question," said he, approaching her.

"I only promised to answer one."

Dangerly involuntarily laid his hand on hers. She did not withdraw it. Their eyes met, and a language which cannot be mistaken, revealed to each the treasured secret of the other's heart.

At this moment Alice entered the room leaning on Major Gordon's arm. "Mr. Dangerly," said the latter, "I have never until now felt authorized to thank you for the brave service which you rendered to this lady, for I was not before at liberty to mention her name in connection with my own; but the happy day being now appointed, I am privileged to indulge my feelings of gratitude."

"*That* lady! You mistake sir; *this* is the lady to whom I was so fortunate as to render a slight service."

"It is you that mistake," replied Alice.

Dangerly gazed at the two sisters alternately. "If such is the fact," said he, "Pythagoras was right in his doctrine. To that lady I gave a heart which had never before been touched by the exquisite sensation of love, and it is equally certain that it has transferred itself to the person of this her lovely sister. I am very sure that I love *this lady;* there is no mistake about that."

A month after this time the two sisters stood together before the hymeneal altar, dressed exactly alike.

"Gordon," said Dangerly, "be good enough to stand a little further off, for fear we change partners. You took the first pick, but I love my Eleanor too well to have the slightest inclination to *swap.* Be pleased, Mr. Clergyman, to dress the ranks before you begin, and take care not to get the parties mixed."

# ISLE OF THE YELLOW SANDS.

THE legends of the northern Indians speak of an island in Lake Superior, which is called the "Isle of the Yellow Sands," and was said to be protected by spirits. The sands were thought to be of gold; and whenever a mortal approached the shore, the vultures, and other animals of prey, as they seemed to human eyes, but which, in fact, were malignant spirits in those shapes, raised such a dreadful outcry, as to terrify the traveller who wandered unwarily to those shores. It is said that no one who persisted in landing on the fatal beach ever escaped. The following lines describe the fate of an Indian maid who voluntarily sought the island, induced either by that curiosity which our first mother is supposed to have bequeathed to her fair descendants, or by that love of the "Yellow Sands" which is inherent in the whole race of Adam.

> She has gone to the isle of the golden sands,
> In the prow of her light canoe she stands,
> And the south wind howls, and the billows roar
> As they bear the maid to the magic shore.

But her spirit is high and her heart is proud,
She dreads not the wave nor the lowering cloud,
For her soul is undaunted, and swift is her way,
As she guides her canoe through the foaming spray

She has left a brave lover—ah! feeble and cold
Is a young maid's affection when tempted by gold!
She has left the lone wigwam, too lowly for her
Who could follow the chase, or could mingle in war.

" Ah pause, heedless maid! ere to pause be too late,
For see, all around thee, the omens of fate ;
And the shore of that terrible isle is nigh,
Where the spirits dwell, and the death birds fly."

A voice through the tempest thus kindly essay'd
To arrest the wild course of the Indian maid,
But a sunbeam fell bright on the yellow sand—
And she urges her skiff on the fatal strand.

" Then onward! speed onward! thy story is told,
Thou hast barter'd thy innocence, maiden, for gold!
The spirits have warn'd thee, the elements speak,
Then onward! fly onward! thy destiny seek!"

In vain the monition—" Ga, su( ا.es the maid,
"See the gold how it glitters, let fools be afraid,
Though my mother may weep, and my lover may swear,
Be mine the bright treasure that dries ev'ry tear."

She has reach'd the bright isle of the golden sand,
And she gazes in fear o'er that lone wild land,
For the clouds are low, and the night birds shriek,
And her frail canoe is a shapeless wreck.

" Yet turn thee, dear maiden, while life is thine,
Nor gaze at the gems that deceitfully shine,
For before thee is tempest, and death and the tomb,
And behind thee is peace, and affection and home."

She turn'd—'twas her lover, came o'er the wave,
Through tempest, through danger, that dear one to save,
She paus'd—and the bold hunter stood by her side:
" I claim thee, I claim thee, Moina, my bride !"

Ah feeble of purpose! what woman can hear
Unmov'd the fond name to her bosom so dear,
Or could balance the wealth of a golden isle,
With a bridal kiss and a lover's smile?

Her dream is past o'er, and her fault confess'd,
She has hidden her face in her warrior's breast,
And she vows if each sand were a golden isle,
She would barter them all for that one lov'd smile;

THE END

www.ingramcontent.com/pod-product-compliance
Lightning Source LLC
Chambersburg PA
CBHW030952110726
47900CB00004B/1237